MAP OF THIEVES

PRAISE FOR MAP OF THIEVES

A great mystery with an ingenious plot, MAP OF THIEVES reminds me of Dan Brown and Steve Berry thrillers. This is the latest novel I've read by Karpovage, and his best to date. The book is a real page-turner, packed with action and suspense. At the same time, it does an amazing job of weaving in mysterious artifacts, historical information about the Civil War, and Native American lore. I particularly liked Jake Tununda and the sexy Rae Hart. I hope they'll be back for another book.

—*Lee Gimenez, bestselling author of eight novels, including* Blacksnow Zero, *Atlanta, GA*

Karpovage's new book has all of the ingredients for success. Betrayal, suspense, and historical fact, brilliantly mixed with present day fiction, make MAP OF THIEVES an intriguing read that is extremely hard to put down. The flow of writing propels you into the story as if you are part of the events and not just a bystander. And when you do have to go back to reality, you'll find yourself still absorbed and wanting nothing more than to immerse yourself once again in the fiction world of a treasure hunt.

—*Paula Howard, reviewer, Indianapolis, IN*

MAP OF THIEVES weaves history, mystery, murder, a master thief, a crooked politician, and a hidden Cherokee treasure into a spell-binding fabric that's fast-paced and filled with surprises. A stand-alone sequel to CROWN OF SERPENTS, this is Michael Karpovage's second, must-read mystery thriller that combines historical fact and fiction in a page-turning adventure. MAP OF THIEVES also continues to follow Jake Tununda and his partner Rae Hart, but this time in Georgia against the backdrop of true Civil War history. As with Karpovage's previous book, I couldn't put this one down. His works have played in my mind like a movie as I'm reading them.

—*Gene Conrad, reviewer, Berkshire, NY*

Karpovage's thrilling new novel is yet another exciting adventure that makes the hidden past come alive. With Native American legends, Masonic traditions of honor, and a roller coaster ride of emotions, you'll enjoy your sleepless nights as much as I did!

—*Brother Timothy S. Yarbrough, reviewer, Northwest Lodge No. 1434, Spring, TX*

MAP OF THIEVES is another great, action-packed adventure by Karpovage. The story takes Lieutenant Colonel Jake Tununda and Rae Hart on a harrowing quest in search of stolen, priceless WWII artifacts once owned by Hitler and Göering. They are unexpectedly exposed to a secret code hidden in a Civil War general's hat that reveals clues to a vast hidden treasure from the once proud Cherokee nation. The characters are confronted by an unscrupulous and ruthless U.S. congressman who will stop at nothing, including murder, to secure the treasure for himself. MAP OF THIEVES is a must-read for those who like jarring suspense and fast-paced adventure.

—*Alex Walker, author of* Toltec *and* Cuzco, *action/adventure novels, Atlanta, GA*

MICHAEL KARPOVAGE

www.MapofThieves.com

/MapofThieves

THE TUNUNDA MYSTERIES:
Crown of Serpents (2009)

MILITARY THRILLER:
Flashpoint Quebec (2003)

KarpovageCreative.com

This is a work of fiction. Names, characters, places, and incidents either are the product of the author's imagination or are used fictitiously, and any resemblance to actual persons, living or dead, business establishments, events, or locales is entirely coincidental.

Published by
Karpovage Creative, Inc.
5055 Magnolia Walk
Roswell, Georgia 30075
www.karpovagecreative.com

ISBN: 978-0-9856532-1-7

Printed in the United States of America
First Edition

Cover / interior book design, maps and illustrations created by
Karpovage Creative, Inc.
designer • map illustrator • publisher
www.karpovagecreative.com

To my father, for bringing out the explorer in me.

AUTHOR'S NOTE

Although *Map of Thieves* is a work of fiction based on pure speculative narrative, and all present day characters are creations of my imagination, some of the historical figures in this book are real people. They existed and left records of themselves, some more abundant than others. I tried to be faithful to their actions and encounters as best I could determine from historical sources.

The great thing about handing down history, though, whether oral or written, is it generates legends. And legends—such as the Cherokee Tunnel treasure cache or even the *Map of Thieves*—typically start with a grain of truth, then become immortal. Generation after generation then stretch that truth through embellishment, thus keeping the story alive and partially believable, or better yet, attainable. Countless men and women have been sucked into obtaining that dream, sacrificing untold days, years, finances, and careers to make it a reality. It's a vicious cycle of hope and disappointment—even craziness. The results may end in broken relationships, betrayal, theft, or even worse; murder. In the end, the legend will still live, for it's that irresistible draw of sheer adventure that keeps it alive.

So what if you had one last shot at proving the legend real? That the dream does exist, that finding treasure *can* come true. That all the time, effort, and burned bridges along the way could finally be vindicated? Would you pass up that chance?

I bet you wouldn't.

Jake Tununda sure doesn't.

For a breakdown of the historical facts versus the embellished legends used as the backstory within this novel, be sure to read the end notes of this book. And then visit **MapofThieves.com** for pictures and more.

— *Michael Karpovage*

GEORGIA STATE MAP

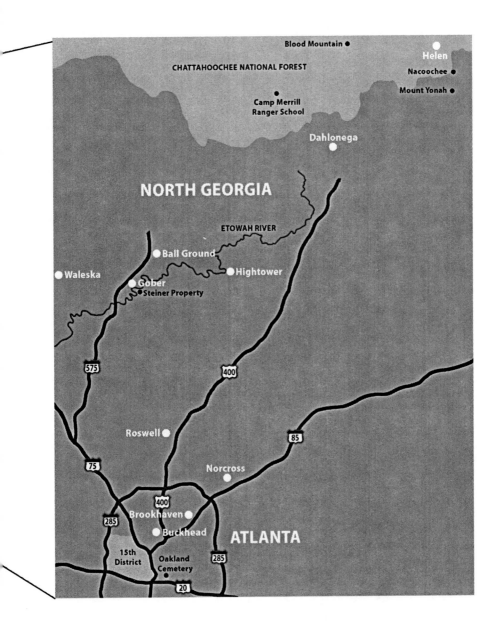

NORTH GEORGIA MAP

MAP OF THIEVES

PROLOGUE

THROUGH THE TELESCOPIC SIGHT OF HIS COVETED Whitworth sniper rifle, Confederate Corporal Thomas Black Watie Jr. immediately recognized the galloping target coming down the little wagon road through the thick woods. His heart pounded. He blinked several times and tried to clear the sweat that had dripped into his eyes. It's actually him, the twenty year-old Cherokee rebel thought. Union Major General James Birdseye McPherson was finally within his deadly grasp.

Trigger finger twitching, young Watie aimed for McPherson's handsome, black-bearded face. But then his long sought-after prey suddenly checked his horse so sharply it slid on its haunches. Watie panned his scope and noticed a Confederate officer had jumped from the shrubbery alongside the road and had raised his sword demanding surrender of the general. We've got him prisoner, Watie thought, easing his finger off the trigger.

From behind the officer, a group of gray-clad infantry skirmishers also emerged from the underbrush. Even from his far away, elevated tree position, Watie could hear their distinct shouts of "Halt! Stop there! Halt!" echo through the dense woods east of Atlanta, Georgia.

The rebel officer stepped forward and continued to point his sword at the general. Watie adjusted his aim behind the general where two of his staff aides also came to a stop, one of them raising his hands in surrender. McPherson then did the unexpected. He lifted his hat to the Confederate officer, as gentlemanly as if he were saluting a graceful lady, and unexpectedly wheeled his horse's head directly to the right and galloped off at full sprint back up the narrow forest road.

Watie panicked. His hands shook trying to regain his target. McPherson's two staffers followed the general's lead and drove their steeds as fast as they could in retreat, too.

The Corporal would now have to shoot the general in the back. *So be it.* This was the best opportunity he had been waiting for—killed for—since McPherson confiscated his coveted waybill and deposited it inside his hat almost two months prior.

As sweat streamed from his brow, Watie exhaled and focused his aim on the moving target. It would be a mere 40-yard shot, made easier from his roost in a loblolly pine tree. *Damn him for making me do this.* McPherson bent over his horse's neck as he sprinted off the road into a thicket for cover.

Watie pulled the trigger.

With a deep, bellowing boom and heavy recoil, a deadly, hex-shaped bullet sliced its way through the air. The infantry opened up with their own volley not a second later.

Through his scope Watie watched McPherson spring upright, hit in the back. His hat became entangled in the overhead branches as his horse passed between two pine saplings. He then rolled from his horse and bounced off the ground, knees and face first, yet still clutching the reins. His two escorts also went down; both horses shot out from under them. The last Watie saw, before gray smoke obscured his scope's field of vision, was McPherson's black horse standing over his body.

Time to get his hat. And my waybill.

As the thunderous sounds of battle escalated further up ahead through the woods, Watie slung his Whitworth across his back and extracted himself from his sniper's perch. On his way down he heard the skirmishers give their distinctive, high-pitched rebel yell in delight of what they undoubtedly thought was their kill. It didn't matter to him. He had killed so many Yankees in the last two months of fighting he didn't care who claimed the shot that brought down the well-liked general.

Lowering himself onto the last branch, he jumped to the soft pine needle covered ground and removed his gray slouch hat. With a forearm he wiped away sweat on his well-tanned, copper-colored face. On top of his hat he made sure the black raven feather plume was firmly secure inside the head band. Placing the hat back on his head, he adjusted the turned-down brim over his brown eyes.

Relief overtook him. He sighed loudly. He could now finally fix his mistake of getting intercepted by McPherson's cavalry two months ago at Barnsley's Woodlands mansion in Adairsville, Georgia. Now he could continue on with his secret mission for which he had been dispatched from Indian Territory. It was time to live up to what he had lived his entire life in preparation to fulfill.

He hoped the spirit of his father, Thomas Black Watie, was proudly watching him now. He hoped all of the executed kinfolk of the Western Cherokee were watching from beyond their graves. Payback for their political assassinations, carried out by Principal Chief John Ross's henchmen as far back as 1839, would bring harmony and balance back into their spirits so violently taken. Once that revenge was exacted—including his father's heinous murder in 1845—only then would their drifting souls be released to enter the darkening land.

Thomas's secret mission had been conceived by his well-known uncle back in Indian Territory: Cherokee Chief Stand Watie. Stand had risen to become an important political rival and Ross's lifelong nemesis in the tumultuous early years of the new Cherokee Nation in the West. Marked by brutal internal feuds, peace among the Cherokee people meant carrying a pistol or a knife, and always watching your back. Stand did just that in thwarting two assassination attempts on his own life by Ross's men.

When the War Between the States broke out in 1861, real peace between the Watie and Ross camps was finally realized: they stood united under the Confederate cause. Stand had created the Cherokee Mounted Rifles and had been fighting a successful hit-and-run guerilla campaign against Union forces in the West. His young nephew, Thomas Jr., had enlisted, as well, and soon became one of the unit's most lethal sharpshooters.

But when Ross, the elected leader of the Cherokee Nation, became a Federal turncoat in 1862, as predicted he would, Stand made a shrewd opening move of renewed revenge. Before Ross and his band of followers could flee Cherokee Territory with the nation's treasury under guard of the Union Army, Stand ensured the traitor's two most important personal possessions went missing.

Stolen by a Watie spy, a Cherokee staffer inside Rose Cottage—the home of Ross and the council house at the capital Tahlequah—the two inseparable items couldn't function without the other. One was a waybill, the other a Bowie knife. The knife's blade, engraved with Cherokee runes, acted as the key to decipher the symbols on the waybill.

The waybill pinpointed the location of the legendary Cherokee Tunnel; a huge, 200-foot-long gold depository hidden back in north Georgia near the small village of Ball Ground on the Etowah River. This secretly carved tunnel held John Ross's personal gold inventory as well as those of many of his most trusted followers and the elite families of the nation.

Unable to transport any of their gold possessions during the infamous 1838-39 Trail of Tears when the last of the Cherokees were forcibly removed from the state of Georgia, the depositors had made a pact to secretly carve a tunnel from a steep cliff face to stash their gold and valuables in until they could come back and retrieve them at some future date. But most of the depositors perished along the 2,200-mile journey to Indian Territory, including John Ross's wife. Over 4,000 ended up dying in total. More depositors died over the subsequent years during resettlement in the West. Several clandestine attempts were made by remaining heirs; but none could ever get close enough to the location due to trigger-happy white Georgians who had since possessed their former lands. In the end, the secret treasure had remained untouched in the heavily concealed tunnel for over twenty-five years: not one depositor having ever breached the entrance.

Confined to Indian Territory and waging some of his most incredible victories to date, Stand could personally do nothing with the stolen waybill and knife. As the new leader of the Cherokee Nation, he was actively engaged with fighting the Union and providing for his people. To Stand, the cache location was supposedly still safe inside Confederate territory. Any pursuits would have to wait until after the war ended.

All that changed in May of 1864. As a newly promoted brigadier general in the Confederate Army, Stand had learned of the massive Union offensive penetrating Georgia from Chattanooga, Tennessee. He needed to act immediately before the enemy compromised the tunnel cache, or worse, Ross being given access to search for it from the Federals whom he now aligned himself with. And so, Stand called on his twenty year-old nephew to race to Georgia before the Union Army overran the state.

Thomas Black Watie Jr. remembered his uncle's words clearly: "The blood of our kinfolk and the father you never knew—my younger brother—needs to be washed away with the blood of John Ross. Your time to act is upon us."

Thomas's north Georgia mission was threefold.

First, after finding the Cherokee Tunnel from the waybill clues, locate the most valuable of all the treasure hidden inside and steal it. Many years ago Ross was overheard bragging about one of the last deposits made before the tunnel was sealed up. Called the Golden Horse, it was a highly-prized trophy depicting a magnificent Spanish Andalusian. Made of solid, 24-carat gold by an ancient Cherokee goldsmith, it marked the ousting of Spanish explorer Hernando de Soto's expedition during the 1540s. Stand said to Thomas that whoever possessed that trophy could shoe every horse in the Cherokee Nation with solid gold, alluding to a secret within.

Second, inventory the rest of the tunnel's contents, take what he needed for expenses, but conceal the entrance once again upon exiting. He was then to go directly to General Joseph E. Johnston himself, who was fighting Union General Sherman, to request a party of troops to transport what was inside so they could use it in the treasury of the Confederacy.

And the third, most important part of Thomas's mission?

Assassinate John Ross.

Eye-for-an-eye vengeance—a basic human instinct the world over—was necessary for a family's or a tribe's strength and survival. To let a murderous act or an insult go unavenged would only bring further suffering and humiliation. Doing nothing was a sign of weakness and thus encouraged further attacks. Thomas was told that after he found the tunnel he should then pursue Ross at all costs using any means necessary.

Ross had to be assassinated, not only for personal family revenge, but for Cherokee Nation redemption. He was the head of the snake who now openly cavorted with the enemy. Rightfully so, he was a murderous conspirator, a devious traitor, a conniving hypocrite, and a power-hungry dictator.

Squinting through the smoke-filled woods in the direction where he had shot McPherson, Thomas Black Watie Jr. encountered a wall of dense underbrush. Further complicating matters were stray minnie balls slicing through the trees from the main assault up the hill. He found a trail of trampled underbrush the infantry had made during their initial advance and headed out.

That advance had met early success despite bad execution. Confederate General John Bell Hood had ordered an exhausting 12-mile night march from Atlanta to what was supposed to be a morning surprise attack on Union General Sherman's left flank east of the city. Watie had advanced into the woods with his 1st/15th Arkansas Infantry Regiment and captured the entire Union 16th Iowa Infantry Regiment and eight artillery pieces. But now it was past two o'clock and their mid-day attack was marred by rugged terrain and the overpowering heat of a Georgia July.

During the chaotic ebb and flow of battle, Watie had taken in with a severely depleted unit of Memphis Irishmen from the 5th Tennessee. They also picked up some stragglers from the dismounted 24th Texas Cavalry. Soon they stumbled upon a wagon road deep in the woods. Being the best sniper in the brigade, Watie was ordered to provide cover from his tree position at the rear of the skirmishers as they paused to reload, regroup, and make another push forward. Plus, they could ill-afford a Whitworth getting into the hands of the enemy.

Now stepping through the brush, Watie unholstered his ivory-handled Colt Navy .36 caliber revolver as close-in protection. It was given to him by his 1st Arkansas Regiment colonel during last month's brutal Union assault on their lines at Cheatham Hill south of Kennesaw Mountain. The Yankees lost 1,000 men in less than an hour with no penetration of the defenses. It had been his most horrific combat experience of the war. On that day of June 28th, he had lost track of how many men he personally killed in front of their entrenchments near the infamous Dead Angle. Scores more were trapped in the burning woods, screaming and dying in front of them. But it was Watie's role in the humanitarian cease-fire rescue of those same enemy wounded being burned, that earned him his Colt pistol.

In his other hand he slid out the stolen Ross blade from its leather sheath. He called it his Arkansas "toothpick." The beautifully custom-crafted Bowie knife was the only weapon General McPherson had unwittingly allowed him to part with upon his release in Adairsville. This same blade—serving as the legend key to his lost waybill and ultimately to the tunnel—now guided him to his victim as he hacked away at foliage among the thickets and trees.

As the smoke from the skirmishers' volley drifted away, he could see the wagon road ahead through the dense brush. A busted wagon wheel stood leaning against a tree. Broken ammo crates, discarded clothing, and other sundry items of battle debris lay scattered about from the Union retreat. He watched as the gray line of rugged, veteran Confederate soldiers disappeared into the woods across the road to make their final ascent on the enemy breastworks. Cannonading commenced and rifle fire cracked as their attack was met. Soon Watie heard their frightening rebel yell blend with the ungodly sounds of a ferocious assault.

Movement to the left caught Watie's eye. Union blue in the brush. A tall, older man with a salt and pepper, handlebar mustache emerged as Watie centered his Colt on the man's chest. He was unarmed, head bowed in defeat, eyes covered by his dark blue, Kepi-style hat. An insignia on top of a gold infantry bugle marked him as an officer.

A gaunt looking Union soldier, face drained white, limped behind the officer. Behind them a Confederate soldier prodded the prisoners with his bayoneted rifle. Watie gave a short owl's hoot and raised his revolver to the sky in a non-aggressive manner so his fellow soldier wouldn't drill him.

The rebel soldier immediately recognized him. In an Irish accent he asked, "You're the sharpshooter, right? They call you the Raven?"

Watie nodded. He picked up the nickname when he joined the Army of Tennessee back in May asking to serve with a unit from Arkansas. Proving himself an expert marksman, he shot a flying raven from an incredible distance while two important fellow Arkansians watched—brigade commander Colonel Daniel Govan and division commander Major General Patrick Cleburne. They rewarded Watie with one of their rare, smuggled British Whitworth rifles after the previous owner was shot through the head. Watie wore the slain raven's feather in his hat ever since.

The overly excited, fast-talking, rebel infantry skirmisher gestured with a thumb over his shoulder. "We bushwhacked the Yankee general, McPherson, back there up on the road. Corporal Coleman shot him."

"In the back, right?" Watie asked flatly.

"Yup. Coleman's headed back to our lines with the general's horse. I'm taking these here prisoners back, too. They're part of his staff. Lucky bastards both got their horses shot out. This here is a colonel," he said, pointing his thumb at the prisoner. "Scott is his name, I do believe. Not even a scratch on him. The young one says he's McPherson's orderly. Named Thompson. Escaped with a knock on his head."

Lowering his revolver to his side, Watie walked up to the prisoners.

The orderly cried openly, his shoulders shaking. A trickle of blood seeped from somewhere on the top of his sweat- and dirt-matted hair. He looked up slowly. His red glassy eyes grew wide as he and Watie recognized each other from Adairsville.

"You?" the Yankee soldier asked in a concussive daze. "Thomas Watie?"

"Yup," Watie snipped. The orderly was A. J. Thompson, the general's personal assistant, who had been especially harsh on him the night he was detained. Watie angrily pointed his Bowie knife at the man. "I warned the general there'd be consequences if he took my property. Didn't I?"

Thompson merely stared back with lost eyes.

"Didn't I?" Watie barked, his Bowie knife inches from the man's face. This time the orderly nodded and Watie lowered his blade.

"When your cavalry took me prisoner I wasn't fighting this goddamn war," Watie lamented, changing his tone. "I told the general the truth. I was a civilian then. My business was Cherokee business only. I told you both that. But you took my waybill anyway! I had no other choice but to rejoin and hunt him down to get it back." He raised his blade to the man's neck. "Now you tell me this, is it still inside his hat?"

"As far as I know it is," Thompson said, eyes wide.

Getting the answer he was hoping for, Watie sighed with relief and immediately turned to leave.

"You have killed the best man in our army," the orderly mumbled.

Watie pretended he didn't hear those last words. Instead, he scampered off toward the road and reached it in less than a minute. To his right were two freshly killed, bullet-riddled horses. To the left of the saddled, bloody rumps were two unarmed Union soldiers under a tree. They were squatting on the ground over a long, lifeless body clad in a dark blue Union coat. Lighter blue pantaloons were tucked inside black, mud-spattered boots. He couldn't quite see the face but did notice a black beard. Was it McPherson? If so, where was his two-star, gold shoulder boards of a major general and the gold breast buttons of his uniform coat?

The two Yankees seemed in a heated argument when Watie quietly snuck up on them. A hatless soldier, his bloody left arm shattered at the elbow, cradled the victim's head in his lap while yelling at the other Union soldier to, "Put it back."

The other Union straggler held a pocketbook and a handful of Federal bills, stuffing them in his coat. "We'll split it then."

"No, I won't split it with you," the injured soldier said. "We need to protect all of his items and return it to his staff. I won't go along with your robbery. Put it back, I say."

They were fighting over the dead Union man's pay.

Watie pressed his revolver against the thief's head. "Listen to him."

The Union robber didn't even look up. He raised his trembling hands and dropped the pocketbook on the ground.

Watie placed his long blade under the soldier's chin and ordered him to stand up. "Get the fuck out of here or I'll cut your bowels out." A wet stain formed at the Union thief's crotch. Watie let the man go and kicked him in the ass for good riddance.

The soldier plunged aimlessly into the woods.

Watie looked down to the other Union soldier, a private, and briefly locked eyes. He then glanced at the dead man he was cradling in his lap and recognized the man's face.

It *was* McPherson.

There was a ripped exit wound on the right breast of the general's buttonless coat. Blood freely ran out. Suddenly, he moved an arm and clutched at his chest with a yellow, leather riding gauntlet. His eyes blinked open, then closed. He groaned. Bright red blood dribbled from his mouth and spread throughout his dust-encrusted black beard.

He's still alive!

Watie stared down at the figure, transfixed with his victim, realizing he must have shot him through the lungs. It was a mortal wound. He'd be dead within minutes.

The private looked up to Watie. "I was protecting this dying man," he explained in a quivering voice. "That wretch stole his money."

How ironic, thought Watie. "This man is your own General McPherson. You know that, don't ya?" The private nodded back.

"Where's his shoulder boards? His coat buttons?" asked Watie.

"I cut them away to conceal his identity," stated the grimacing man.

Not wanting to linger, Watie turned away from his dying foe and holstered his revolver. Regret overtook him. He didn't want this memory embedded in his mind. This was too personal. A general shot in cold blood. In the back. Unarmed.

He looked above him up in the pine sapling, searching for the general's distinct Hardee-style, high crowned, black hat with a rolled brim. He had remembered it suspended in the branches after the general went down. But it was nowhere in sight. He looked all around. And then he spotted the gilded, braided hat cord that would normally be around the base of the crown. It lay a few feet away, deliberately discarded. He snatched it up. Next to it was a dirty, gray Kepi cap, it being nothing but a ripped rag with a black brim. But no general's field hat was anywhere to be seen.

Frantically, he searched the ground again, then the trees, and brush. "Where's his hat? Where's the general's hat?" Watie demanded of the wounded soldier. He held the hat cord up and shook it, the gilded acorn terminals swinging back and forth. "Did you take this bullion cord off?"

"No. I didn't touch his hat."

"It's supposed to be here. Up in these branches." He pointed with his knife. "Where did it go?"

"Your own men took it," the wounded man shrugged. "They thought the general deceased."

"Goddamn!" Watie wailed.

The Union man spoke up. "I got hit after our rifle pits were overrun and was making my way back when I saw what happened and played dead in the thicket. One of your Johnnies traded out his old hat for the general's hat. Said it was his trophy."

Watie picked up the gray Kepi at his feet and looked inside for a name of the previous owner. Nothing. He slammed the hat back to the ground then angrily shoved the general's bullion cord in his pocket.

"They took his field glasses and his sword-belt," the private continued. "Got his watch and some papers, too. And some corporal took the general's horse back toward your lines. Then they all double-quicked it up through that pine thicket to engage our army. That's when I cut his buttons and boards or else he'd be stripped naked if found again. I sat here with him and I couldn't believe it but he came to. It's my sacred duty to protect him."

McPherson moaned. Both Watie and the wounded soldier looked down at him. His lips moved and his eyes fluttered open looking at the wounded man. He spoke in a whisper. "What's your name?"

"Private George Reynolds, Company D, Fifteenth Iowa Infantry, sir."

"You're a good man," McPherson's dry, weak voice cracked. "Water? I need water." His mouth bubbled with more blood, his breathing strained.

A faint Reynolds, himself reeling from loss of blood, tried to unstrap his canteen with his good arm but only fumbled in pain. Watie sheathed his knife. He lifted the strap and canteen over the private's head and popped the cap. Bending down, he cradled the general behind his neck, and gently lifted his head to wet his lips.

Turning to Reynolds, he pleaded with him to go back to his lines. To get to a field hospital. That he wasn't his prisoner.

"I won't leave him! He's the ablest and purest general in our army."

"His wound is mortal," Watie said. "He's done. Now leave or I *will* make you my prisoner."

The private stood up and started away, but he stopped and looked back at his general.

Watie ignored him. He peered back into the general's blanched face as he gave the dying man more water. "I'm sorry it came to this, but you must tell me something. Is my waybill still stashed inside your hat?"

McPherson opened and locked his deep blue eyes with Watie's. His thick black eyebrows raised in sudden recognition. After a moment, he responded in a whisper. "It is, Watie." He then coughed up more blood, accidentally spraying the cheek of the young man who stole his life. His voice wavered. "G-g-get my hat. I-I'll return it." The general turned his head slowly, searching for his hat.

Watie shook his head. "It ain't here."

Staring back up at Watie, the general's eyebrows creased in confusion. "Where is it?" His eyelids fluttered as he strained for words. "Where is—" another gurgling inhale. His last warm breath exhaled on Watie's face. "My. . . Haaaat?" His eyes stopped moving. They remained frozen, staring straight up, the light of life fading to emptiness.

Watie blinked several times. A tear trickled out of his eye and dripped onto McPherson's lifeless face. "I don't know," he answered back. He lay the general's head on the ground and whispered. "Damn this war to hell."

He heard sobbing a few feet away. Private Reynolds. He, too, had watched the general expire. Watie screamed at him to leave and this time the wounded man trotted off back up the road. He then took off his own hat. From under his sweat-stained shirt he extracted a thin leather necklace and pulled it over his head. On the end of it dangled a small, translucent, rock, quartz crystal. He bunched it up in a fist and placed it in the inner pocket of McPherson's coat, directly over his heart. An ancient Cherokee token, the protector crystal would ward off any blackbird witches who preyed on a fresh heart.

Hat back on his head, Watie rose to his feet and unslung his Whitworth to reload as he double-stepped into the woods toward the sounds of battle. Catching up to his infantry was all that mattered now.

And finding out which one of them took McPherson's hat.

1

Present day. Friday. July. 6:57 p.m.
Cherokee Rose Manor
Savannah, Georgia

OLD MAN TOMMY BLACK WATIE IV LAY BLANKETED in his antique, king-sized, four-post bed, head propped up by pillows. He stared at a car insurance commercial on his 60 inch wall-mounted, flat-screen, high-definition television. The sound was muted, the way he liked it when these repeat commercials came on. Behind an oxygen mask, his loud breathing was steady but labored. His ninety year-old heart started to race though as he fumbled with the buttons on the TV's remote control.

"Too many tiny buttons on this dadgum thang," he mumbled in a muffled Southern drawl. He scratched at his scalp covered in long, stringy white and silver hair, bangs swept back over his forehead, and squinted at the remote. While doing so, the cord of his fingertip-attached pulse oxymeter, which measured his pulse rate and blood oxygen level, pulled tight and almost knocked over the portable bedside stand.

"Now where's that mute button? My show's gonna start any minute."

Sitting in a corner nook of the second floor master bedroom in Watie's historic Italianate manor, reading a showbiz magazine, and nibbling on Girl Scout Thin Mints, was Becky Holden, his personal PDN or private duty nurse. The reliable, thirty-something, robust black woman knew the routine all too well. She had been assigned to Tommy for about three years now dealing with his various ailments. His latest, a bad bout of pneumonia, was just about over.

She was at his house almost every day of the week, at all hours, on-call 24/7. She not only acted as his nurse, cook, and personal assistant—and paid quite handsomely for her duties—but she had become a close companion for the lonely, elderly man who had no one left in his waning years.

Placing the magazine on an end table and brushing off the cookie crumbs from her white blouse and matching pants, she uncrossed her legs with a sigh of redundancy and stood up to relieve her client of his remote control dysfunction.

"What's that you say, Mister Tommy?" she asked loudly, compensating for his hearing loss. Waddling on over to his bed, she noticed his heart rate monitor displayed about seventy-five beats-per-minute, a slight increase from normal.

Tommy pulled his oxygen mask away from his mouth to be heard. "The dadgum mute button. Can't find it." He held the remote in front of his light-brown face, aimed it at the TV and pressed a button. The channel switched to some apparent celebrities engaged in ballroom dancing. "Ah, son-of-a-bitch," he cussed, snapping his mask back over his mouth and nose.

Holden calmly extracted the remote from his hand as she had done countless times already. "You hit the recall button by mistake again. That takes you back to the previous channel." She switched back to the channel he was on and replaced the remote back in his hand, guiding his finger over the proper button. "Right there. That's the mute button. Press *that* one."

Tommy pressed it and the volume turned on—quite loud. He smiled back. "Thanks, Sweetie."

"Can you hear it okay? Want me to turn it up?" Holden straightened out his oxygen mask and ran her eyes down the long thin tube attached to the tank sitting beside his bed to make sure the line wasn't tangled.

"Shush now, show's starting," he admonished her. Holden playfully nodded with a flash of large white teeth while reading the gauge on the oxygen tank to see how much remained. Another hour and she'd have to change it out. All was well. She resumed reading on the cushy corner chair while grabbing another Thin Mint.

Tommy's favorite new show on the Military Channel was called *Battlefield Investigators,* a mix of military history and mystery investigation. Still in its first season the show had already aired six, highly-watched episodes featuring experts on military engagements and rare battlefield artifacts. Each hour-long episode featured a guest host who took the viewers on an adventurous ride as they investigated a military mystery from battles past. Tonight's new episode would be bringing back the popular duo of a rough and tumble military historian, Lieutenant Colonel Jake Tununda and his beautiful co-host, Investigator Rae Hart.

During episode three, several months ago, Tununda and Hart had retraced the tragic mission of a Revolutionary War scout, his torture death at the hands of enemy British Freemasons and savage Iroquois, and the stunning discovery of lost British gold in a sunken cannon deep within an Upstate New York lake.

What aging World War II veteran Tommy Watie liked the best about their episode was that they weren't just reciting a boring narration like some of the other guest hosts did. Instead, they passionately took viewers to the real-life scenes where history unfolded, getting down and dirty along the way. From a hallowed battlefield to a quiet hall of a research library, to the depths of a deep blue lake, Tununda and Hart had kept Tommy mesmerized as they re-enacted their successful hunt for lost gold. Tommy was hooked from the get-go, along with millions of other viewers who loved seeing artifacts dug up from the past. Plus, it didn't hurt that the fellow decorated combat vet Tununda obviously had some Native American blood in him like himself. Or that the young woman was one helluva fine looker, too, he thought.

Tonight's episode of *Battlefield Investigators* was especially enticing to Tommy because it was based on the Civil War, or as he put it all his life: the War of Northern Aggression. This episode would talk about the Battle of Atlanta in the summer of 1864.

From the trailer that had run the last few weeks, they had hyped up Tununda and Hart's investigation of a mystery item surrounding a well-known Union general killed during that battle. The previews had flashed the general's portrait without mentioning his name. However, Tommy knew the picture by heart. It was Major General James B. McPherson, the highest ranking Union officer to be killed in combat during the war.

By Tommy's namesake granddaddy.

Old man Tommy's heart rate increased even more. For it was a coveted secret held by the Watie family that twenty year-old Arkansas Confederate Corporal Thomas Black Watie Jr. had assassinated McPherson. He had shot him square in the back. Other soldiers were given credit over the years, but the Thomas Black Watie namesakes over the next generations knew he was the real triggerman.

And the real reason why he had to take the general's life.

The show's slick opening war graphics and contemporary, fast-paced hard rock music started playing. Tununda and Hart appeared in action scenes from their last hosted episode. The theme then dramatically changed to the Civil War era with the playing of a slow ominous flute. Tununda appeared in a full Class "A" Army Blue Service Uniform, arms crossed over a wide chest filled with medals and ribbons, black beret cocked confidently.

He stood outside on a sunny day in front of the McPherson monument; a single, huge, iron cannon, embedded breech-down in a granite block, muzzle pointed straight up into the clear blue sky. The spot was now surrounded by a dense residential Atlanta neighborhood. A screen caption below the host read: *Lieutenant Colonel Robert "Jake" Tununda, Military Historian, U.S. Army Military History Institute.*

The camera zoomed in on his tan, handsomely square, beardless face with high cheekbones. The light brown of his eyes sparkled in the sunlight. Crow's feet and graying temples on his short-cropped, black hair marked him somewhere around forty.

"I'm Colonel Jake Tununda and you're watching Battlefield Investigators.*"* Jake placed his hands on his hips and with a stern voice started the introduction. *"In tonight's episode we're taking you back to the Civil War and the Battle of Atlanta. We'll focus on the death of Major General James Birdseye McPherson whose life was snuffed out right where I'm standing."* He made a gesture toward the monument.

A stunning woman, slightly shorter and several years younger, stepped into the scene and stood close to him almost touching shoulders. The screen caption below her read: *Rae Hart, former New York State Police Investigator.* She wore a black leather jacket over a deliberately revealing white button down blouse. Her long reddish-brown hair, curled at the ends, sat on her well-endowed upper chest. Tommy perked up from his bed and whistled behind his mask. Nurse Holden glanced up, too, caught Hart's image and couldn't help but notice her natural beauty. She looked to be a combination of Latino and Asian with mesmerizing, narrow green eyes, a petit nose, luscious red lips, and a perfectly rounded face. Yet she carried with her the air of determination of someone who doesn't get taken lightly.

Hooking a thumb in the front pocket of her size-4, tight-fitting blue jeans she took up the show's introduction where Tununda had left off.

"On July twenty-second, eighteen sixty four, the Battle of Atlanta raged deep in the woods just to the east of this rebel city stronghold. By the end of the day the bloody battle would claim the life of Union General Sherman's most cherished young commander. Some historians even believe McPherson would have eventually become president of the United States." The picture changed to a black and white photograph portrait of a hatless McPherson. *"He was a revered general on both sides of the war. His kind treatment of Confederate prisoners after the capture of Vicksburg earned him his enemy's admiration. But after McPherson was shot and killed here in Atlanta is where our mystery begins."*

Tommy's breathing became fast and heavy and it wasn't because of the young woman's looks. He propped himself further up on his pillows; eyes glued to the television screen.

Holden took a peek at Tommy's pulse monitor. Not good at all, she thought while chomping on yet another cookie. Her patient was getting himself all worked up. She paused from reading and edged forward on her seat, watching the television to see what was getting him so bent out of shape. Something about some Civil War soldier getting killed. Ho-hum.

The screen changed to a famous period lithograph by war artist Alfred R. Waud, which portrayed McPherson at the moment of being shot. Head tossed back, body falling off his horse, his field hat suspended in the air.

DEATH OF GEN. J. B. McPHERSON.
In Battle of Atlanta, July 22, 1864.

Death of Gen. J. B. McPherson by Alfred R. Waud.

His mounted signal officer, Colonel Scott, watching in the background. The camera then zoomed in on the hat and held the shot. Tommy's eyes widened. He froze in anticipation.

Tununda's voice chimed in. *"After he was shot, McPherson's body was rifled of his personal possessions by Confederate soldiers. His binoculars, sword belt, his gold watch, a dispatch from his commander Sherman, and his hat were all stolen as he lay fighting for his life."*

Hart's voice took the narration. *"But soon after, all of these items were recovered after the Confederate soldiers were surrounded and captured. With the lone exception of McPherson's field hat. It became* lost *to history.* She paused for dramatic effect. *"Until today. "*

Tommy gasped. Memories flooded his mind as if a filing cabinet had spilled its contents. He was overwhelmed, couldn't catch his breath. His heartbeat shot through the roof, his head felt dizzy. The room suddenly became cold like a draft had blown in. He heard the distinctive cackle of a raven outside his window and his heart beat palpitated with terror. A loud thump hit the side of the house. A shadow seemed to pass by.

It was his nurse hovering at his side.

The screen switched back to the co-hosts in front of the monument. Tommy stared as the narration switched back to the Colonel.

"McPherson's lost hat has been discovered!" Video appeared of the duo flanking a three-foot high pedestal on which sat a tall, worn, black Hardee-style hat with a rolled brim. The clip changed to a close-up of Tununda's right hand slowly reaching for the hat. For a split second you could see a shiny gold ring on his third finger. On the ring's flat, ruby face was a raised gold and silver emblem; the square and compasses of the ancient fraternity of the Freemasons. His hand lifted the hat off the pedestal and turned it over while the camera zoomed inside until it reached the interior peak of the crown. The picture stopped on a small white tag attached to the silk liner. The tag held McPherson's signature.

"Yes, the very same hat he lost in death," continued Tununda. *"In tonight's episode we'll take you on the long, strange chain of possession this hat has taken; how it was stolen as a trophy of war; how it sat lost for over a century, forgotten in a box; how it ended up at the Military History Institute and ultimately on loan at the West Point Museum, where it now sits on display with the rest of the general's uniform."*

"Stay tuned as we begin our journey into the past," Hart finished as the show switched to a commercial.

Tommy sat upright and pointed to the television with a shaky finger. Through wheezy muffled breaths, he ordered his nurse to, "Call West Point now!" He tore his oxygen mask off and saliva streamed onto his white stubble chin. "I want Tununda! Granddaddy's waybill is in that hat!"

Then, with a loud moan, his eyes rolled back into his head.

Holden caught him before he crashed back to his pillow. He lurched upward as if something had pulled on him. The nurse held tight as he went stiff as a board. His heart rate stopped altogether on the monitor, followed by his breathing.

"Oh, no you don't, Mister Tommy!" Holden shouted as she fished her phone from a pocket and dialed 9-1-1. She then mashed the power button on the remote control to turn off the high volume. Putting her phone on speaker, she started cardiopulmonary resuscitation while waiting for the dispatcher.

"Nine-one-one. What's your emergency?" a female voice asked.

"Heart attack," Holden responded calmly and clearly. "Ninety year-old male. CPR in progress. Send ambulance to twenty-one West Gordon Street. And make it snappy, girl."

2

"YES, THIS IS HE," REPLIED AN OVERLY IRRITATED Lieutenant Colonel Jake Tununda to the weak voice over his iPhone. The caller had even butchered the pronunciation of his name. "How can I help you?"

The question was blunt and didn't disguise Jake's annoyance. Hell, it was the sixth call this morning from the same 912 area code his phone displayed. The calls had started around 8 a.m. and continued every ten minutes or so. But he hadn't known because he was deep underground making some electrical repairs on his secretly-owned, igloo-style Army ammunition storage bunker. And of course there was no reception nor Internet access inside. It wasn't until he had come back up to the surface and opened one of the two, heavy, steel entrance blast doors to step outside that his phone reconnected and the calls were listed on screen.

He figured it must be some automated recording or some asshole telemarketing representative who had penetrated his Do Not Call authorization. But no voice message was left behind. And then the seventh call came in. Jake debated on whether to take it or not because his rendezvous *guest* would be arriving shortly for their early morning motorcycle ride. He decided to take the call.

Standing in the sunlight of a clear, mid-July morning in the Finger

Lakes of Upstate New York, wearing a vintage WWII-era, brown leather, zip-up riding jacket over blue jeans, Jake waited for the caller's response.

"It's 'bout McPherson's hat," said what sounded like an old man in a slow, deep Southern accent. He neglected to introduce himself and got right to the point.

Jake figured he was a fan of *Battlefield Investigators*. He remembered all of the calls they had gotten after his and his girlfriend, Rae's, debut episode many months ago. Well, *she* had gotten most of the calls. A slew of marriage proposals to be exact. Jake asked to whom was he speaking.

The old man cleared his throat and spoke louder this time. "This here is Tommy Black Watie the Fourth. You can call me Tommy."

The man pronounced Watie as "Waaaaa-Teeee" in two long syllables of a thick Southern drawl. "Okay, Tommy," Jake replied as he shed his riding jacket and slung it on the handle of the blast door. Underneath, he wore a tight olive green t-shirt with the words "Army Ranger" stenciled in white capital letters across his wedge-shaped chest. "I take it you saw the show a couple of nights ago?"

Jake was in prime physical shape for a man his age, who didn't run ten miles a day. With large biceps and Popeye-like forearms, he preferred doing reps of push-ups, crunches, and stretches as opposed to the sweat and exertion of a daily weight lifting regimen. Although his five-foot-ten inch frame was still firm-muscled and flexible, he just didn't have that same level of stamina and endurance as he did in combat some twenty years ago.

As a former U.S. Army infantry officer with the 10th Mountain Division he was in the "shit" with constant deployments throughout his many years of frontline combat duty. From the Balkans to Afghanistan to Iraq, he had participated in the ravages of all-out war. He was a highly intelligent, fearless leader respected by his men. Being one of the most lethal warriors in the 10th, he had earned a Silver Star and a Purple Heart with an Oak Leaf Cluster for two wounds sustained in combat. His battlefield exploits were the stories of legend—especially the hand-to-hand fight at the 2001 Mazar-i-Sharif prison takeover in Northern Afghanistan.

During that encounter, Jake had confronted three armed enemy Taliban in a blown-out basement. The first he knocked unconscious. The second he shot dead. The third he plunged a knife in his heart. Both dead men then had their scalps ripped off with a blood-curdling Indian war whoop. Thus the legend of Jake Tununda, Seneca warrior, was born.

The last few years, though, saw him leave the infantry behind for his new field historian position at the U.S. Army's Military History Institute based out of Carlisle, Pennsylvania. Thinking he'd have a quiet end to his military career pursuing his lifelong passion of military history, he couldn't have miscalculated more.

It had started out on as an adventurous hunt for an ancient Iroquois crown which ultimately led to a keg of buried British gold coins. But death still followed him like a shadow. The only blessing in that whole affair was that he met the love of his life, who was now on her way to meet him.

"Well, Colonel," Watie said, pausing, smacking his lips. "I caught the first part on Friday night and you literally gave me a heart attack when I saw that there general's hat."

This time Jake laughed out loud, playing along. "Really now?" He caught the old man using his officer's title. It was a respectful gesture and Jake assumed he must have served in the military.

"I'm ninety years-old and I ain't never had one dadgum heart attack in all my life, son. Thank God for my bedside nurse. She done saved this old geezer's life. Her and those paramedics with their ayy-eee-dee-thing-a-ma-jig, they jolted me right back to life."

"Good God, I'm, uh, sorry to hear that," Jake said, genuinely feeling like an ass at wanting to berate the caller at first and then not believing about his heart attack. He started pacing on the cracked pavement outside his bunker and noticed out of the corner of his eye as several brown deer ran down the secluded lane of storage igloos on the abandoned Seneca Army Depot base. One of the base's famous white deer followed closely behind the brown herd.

"I'm glad you made it, Tommy. I think you're referring to what they call an automated external defibrillator. Are you doing alright now?" Jake asked, not quite sure how to handle this stranger's brush with death over the phone. He ran a hand through his short hair. "Are you sure you should be making a phone call so soon? You want to call me back later, sir?"

"Naw. I'm okay now," Watie said with a laugh. "I was out for only a little bit they said. Technically, I'm a dead man walkin', guess you might say. But I need to talk to you now, Colonel. Been trying all morning. Do you mind?"

"Sure. Sure. Go ahead. I don't mind."

"It's that dadgum hat," started Watie. "I watched the rest of your show last night when it re-ran. My doctor wouldn't let me at first—didn't want me all riled up again. But when he left my house I convinced my nurse to put it back on. Had her track down your number after."

The old man was rambling loudly in his ear. Jake put him on speaker phone and continued pacing back and forth.

"Colonel, I'm just gonna cut to the chase because it wasn't mentioned in your show and it gives me a ray of hope. I need to know something about that hat that's been doggin' my family for three generations. I need to know when you looked inside of it if you found anything. Like a paper?"

Jake paused, then frowned. "Umm. Not quite sure what you mean, Tommy. We did find McPherson's signature on a sewn-in tag, if that's what you're getting at. And like we said in the show, we had a forensic handwriting expert verify that the signature was in fact his, thus authenticating the hat and the story behind the captain from Mississippi who picked it up as a war trophy."

"Naw. Naw. Naw," Watie barked. "I mean *inside* of his hat. Underneath the fabric and inner lining and such. Did y'all look in there?"

Jake twitched his cheek, somewhat confused. He scratched his temple with an index finger. "Well, I can't say we looked *inside* the inside. I mean we handled the hat quite a bit. Lots of people—experts—inspected it in both my and Rae's presence. None of us saw anything out of the ordinary. I do recall all of the stitching was pretty well secure given the age of the hat and wear and tear it had gone through. We didn't lift out any of the material inside the sweatband if . . ."

"So, you didn't find anything hidden, right?" interrupted Watie. "Like a paper with any symbols on it? Something that looks like a map?"

"Noooooo. Nothing like that," Jake replied, stopping in his tracks. "Was there something *supposed* to be hidden in there?"

This time it was the old man's wheels that were turning. The silence lasted too long. Jake asked if he was still there.

"Yeah, yeah, I'm here." But he didn't answer the question.

"Tommy, what's your full name again?" Jake asked, his radar now turned on.

"Thomas Black Watie," the elderly man replied. And then quickly added, "the Fourth."

"Watie, you say?"

"Yep, four generations of us. Well, five if you count my dirty rotten son. But he only goes by Tom Black. Oh, 'scuse me, United States *Congressman* Tom Black. He officially killed the Watie name back when we had our great fallin' out years and years ago. That son-of-a-bitch was my son no more after that."

Jake shook his head. This was out of hand. Who is this guy? Bitching about an estranged son of his?

"Tom Black? As in that new firebrand congressman from Atlanta, Georgia?" asked Jake.

"That's him all right," Watie ripped with complete disgust. "Lying, thieving, no-good, greedy con artist."

"Okay then." Jake was flabbergasted. He certainly knew of Congressman Black. Newly elected in Atlanta, he was the latest piece of demagogue, garbage politician to be voted into office by an ignorant, uneducated, emotion-laden general public. But no sense in giving his caller another heart attack again by prying further—wasn't any of Jake's business. In the distance, the distinct rumble of a motorcycle approaching caught his ear.

"Despite my own son, the Watie's are a proud Cherokee family, Colonel. A proud American military family. Great Granddaddy was the brother of Cherokee General Stand Watie who fought out in the Indian Territories during the War of Northern Aggression. Granddaddy fought in the Atlanta campaign of sixty-four against that devil Sherman. Daddy fought alongside Teddy Roosevelt as a Rough Rider and I done fought with Patton in Europe. My lazy son, the *Congressman*, and his drugged out, liberal, hippie moron friends protested against our Vietnam vets returning home from the war. That's been his contribution to our military."

There's that animosity again, Jake thought. But the Watie name finally rang a bell. "You're directly related to Stand Watie?" he asked, a bit too excitedly. But he also had the presence of mind to turn on a handy iPhone app he had been using for research purposes. Called Recorder, it allowed him to record phone conversations. With a tap of his finger the recording was on.

"Proud of it," Watie answered.

"Tommy, I'm honored to speak with you," Jake said, sincerely, "as a fellow combat vet." At the same time, the motorcycle sound became louder, closer. The motorcycle was just around the corner now, the familiar old rumble echoing off the row of grass-covered concrete bunkers down his deserted lane. Within seconds, it rounded the bend and Jake caught a glimpse of a white, five-pointed star painted on an olive drab fuel tank. The older model WWII bike headed for Jake. A female rider in a matching olive drab helmet and jacket gave him a wave. He waved back but had to turn his phone off speaker and placed it to his ear to hear better.

"Thank you, Colonel. I do appreciate that. My great granddaddy— brother to Stand—was *murdered* when my granddaddy Thomas Junior was just a baby. Stand was a big influence on Junior's life growing up. After he fought in the Cherokee Mounted Rifles, Stand sent him to Georgia when he was twenty. It was pertaining to Cherokee business during the summer of 1864, but he done got caught by mistake in Adairsville by General McPherson's cavalry. He was let go though—talked his way out of it—sort of like me—I talk too much."

Jake was completely mesmerized by this story. "No. No. Go on, please continue." He pressed the phone harder to his ear as a 1944 U.S. Army Indian Scout motorcycle, in pristine condition, complete with brown leather saddle bags, cruised slowly toward him. His own matching motorcycle sat waiting for him back inside the bunker.

The woman rider gleamed with a big happy smile. Jake ran his hand across his throat in a quick motion, giving the universal sign for her to cut the engine. She frowned as she turned the engine off and let the bike glide in neutral gear toward him. He pointed to his phone and intentionally widened his eyes letting her know it was an important conversation. The woman lowered both knee-high, brown leather riding boots to steady her bike, and Jake walked up and planted a nice kiss on her lips. He then raised an index finger to his own lips for her to keep quiet and placed the call back on speaker so she could hear the conversation, too.

"McPherson's men, who caught my granddaddy, thought he was a spy because they found a waybill on him with Cherokee symbols on it. It's like a map."

"Ahhhh," Jake said, the puzzle pieces starting to fit. "What was it a map *to* if I might ask?"

"None of your business," Watie shot back.

"Duly noted, sir." That door quickly slammed shut, Jake surmised.

Rae Hart, Jake's co-host in *Battlefield Investigators* or, as he dubbed her, his "co-host in crime," mouthed the word "Wow." They were in fact a very serious couple, as she liked to express it. They've been going strong for well over a year now after a death-filled investigation they both had survived. She took off her olive drab, dual visor, Outlaw half helmet, adorned with a pattern of ghosted skull symbols and hung it on the handlebars. Jake had his eyes glued on her, scanning her lean curvaceous body with probing desire. She reached back and undid her pony tail band, fluffed up her long auburn hair, and flung it over her shoulders while tilting her head toward the phone to listen better. Her sizzling green eyes, framed with long eyelashes and bronze eye shadow, met his. She winked and Jake's heart skipped a beat.

"But he wasn't no spy!" shouted Watie, causing Jake to blink back to the call. "And McPherson had no evidence to prove it. Couldn't very well keep him prisoner. He and his staff couldn't even read the dadgum waybill. But the general confiscated it. To be *cautionary*, he said. And, in front of my granddaddy and another witness he hid that waybill inside his field hat. The same hat that is now sitting at that museum in West Point. Is that where you're at now, Colonel?"

"No. No. I'm not at West Point. I'm about four hours away in the central part of New York State. Where are *you* calling from?"

"Savannah, Georgia."

"Beautiful city. Been there a couple times. Many moons ago. Sooo,"

Jake said, getting back on subject and summarizing for Rae's benefit. "You're claiming your grandfather, Thomas Black Watie Junior, had his Cherokee waybill confiscated by General McPherson and supposedly it's still inside his hat?"

Watie paused. Rae's mouth fell open.

"Well now, yes indeed, that's what I'm claimin'," the old man said. "His hat went missing after Granddaddy shot the general in the back. He knew one of his comrades took it but could never find out which one as lots of 'em ended up being captured by the Yankees during the battle. He thought it was lost for good."

Jake tried to get a word in but Watie kept talking.

"It wasn't until some forty years after the war, in an issue of the Confederate Veteran, that Granddaddy found out it was that captain from Mississippi, Captain William A. Brown, who took the hat. He tracked Captain Brown down all right. Found his grave marker. Already had died in eighteen eighty-nine though, and the hat was long gone. Sold off. Granddaddy searched the rest of his life for that dadgum hat. He sent inquiries out, placed newspaper ads, but never got any replies about it. Even visited Clyde, Ohio once. McPherson's home. And that hat never showed up like the rest of his possessions did. Was obsessed with it. And he passed the story down to us as family legend. My Daddy and I caught the bug, too, and searched and searched most of our lives whenever we had free time. About cost me my marriage. After my dear wife Margaret passed, I about put that hat out of my mind. Until your show last night."

"Wait, could you go back a little?" Jake asked, a bit louder than normal in order to dominate the conversation. "You said your grandfather shot McPherson? I have to take friendly issue with that. Evidence shows that a Corporal Robert Coleman of the 5th Tennessee Infantry Regiment actually made the fatal shot. This is according to eyewitness statements Captain Richard Beard made. He was the Tennessee officer who ordered McPherson to surrender at sword point."

"Colonel, all of us in our family read what Beard claimed. Heck, if you'd have done your homework young man, you'd realize others gave the credit to Robert Compton of the 24th Texans. Compton or Coleman?

Doesn't matter. We know it was Thomas Junior who shot him."

"But—," Jake muttered.

Watie spoke louder. "Thomas was known as the *Raven* to his fellow soldiers. He was a sniper armed with the famous Whitworth rifle. And he shot McPherson seconds before any of the other skirmishers got their volley off. All they shot was the horses! I've got the letter my granddaddy wrote to his uncle Stand to prove it. But listen to me, I'm not interested in trying to prove you wrong on this account. Not my beef. Thomas Junior even said others would take credit. He didn't care about that. Matter of fact, he regretted killing the general. Spoke to him before he died, too. McPherson told him the waybill was still inside his hat. Only problem was Captain Brown already took it by the time Junior got to the general. I'm only interested in getting our family property back from inside that hat."

"You're claiming that waybill belongs to *you?*" Jake fired back, clearly miffed after having been schooled in history. "Even if it is still hidden in there after all these years?" Rae placed a hand on his arm to calm him.

"Abso-dadgum-lutely, I'm claiming it as our family property." The old man said excitedly. "On. My. Life."

Jake's eyes darted back and forth. He felt his face flush with rising tension. He had been down this road before—an important family member, another Indian no less—claiming hereditary rights to a newly discovered artifact. Last time this happened a trail of dead bodies ended up all across New York State—even on the ground he was standing on. Correction, *under* the ground he was standing on. He needed to take those lessons learned and approach this right. Looking at Rae, he remembered all too well the horror they went through just over a year ago. She raised a cautionary eyebrow as if reading his mind.

Jake acquiesced, deliberately adjusting his tone to one of friendliness. "Tommy, I'd like to work with you on this. You've been through enough already. I can't have on my conscience anything more happening to your health over this matter. Let's do this together; as partners. If we can find that waybill you speak of, hidden inside the hat, then we can figure out who gets rightful ownership. Does that sound good?"

"*Sound good!?*" Watie angrily shouted through the phone. "Sound *good*? How about soundin' like I can *prove* that waybill belongs to me?"

"How so?"

"By the written receipt that McPherson signed when Granddaddy was being held prisoner in Adairsville. He said he could claim that waybill back when the war was over. The general signed it, Granddaddy signed it, and McPherson's orderly signed it, too, as a witness. The war is over and the hat is *back*. I have the receipt. And I *want* what's inside of it."

Jake was stunned. He stammered with a reply. "Okay, sir. I can't beat that. If the waybill is there, and your receipt is authentic, then we have a deal. You have my word. Let me place a call to the West Point Curator of Arms at the museum and we'll get this taken care of right away. They open at ten thirty. I'm not even sure if he's there on Sunday, but I've got your phone number. I'll give you an update as soon as I find anything out and we'll go from there. Okay?"

Uncomfortable silence again. Finally, the old voice replied, "I'll wait for your call." Followed by a click of dead air.

Jake promptly turned off the iPhone app recording the conversation. He looked up and he and Rae stared at each other with mirrored serious expressions. They knew all too well that once a secret of the past was revealed, unexpected consequences soon followed, some good, some deadly but definitely a hidden mystery waiting to be solved.

3

DROWNING OUT THE INCESSANT RINGING OF THE West Point Museum curator's office phone was the overbearing, ear-piercing, rhythmic whooping of the building's fire alarm. Coupled with the severe audio warning, was the visual alarm of bright, flashing strobe lights at nearly every corner inside the smoke-filled four levels of one of the nation's premiere military history museums.

Security guards were already scrambling about trying to evacuate the public in practically invisible conditions as thick white smoke billowed from unknown sources. The smoke had started in the sub-basement gallery where large weapons were on display such as a WWI tank, a cannon, even an atomic bomb of the type that was dropped on Nagasaki. The dense smoke rose up and filled the balcony gallery in the basement level, sending most of the security staff down to investigate the source. Their portable radios, rendered useless against the extreme audio conditions, further hampered their abilities to lead panicked patrons to proper exits. Within minutes, the main first floor gallery filled with the same white smoke. It wasn't long before evacuating visitors on the second floor slammed into people on the first floor causing a rush for the exits. Several women screamed in fear thinking their lives were at risk.

In the midst of the mounting chaos, a lone, hunched-over, elderly,

World War II veteran stood calmly leaning on his wooden cane. Wearing a dark gray overcoat over a shabby suit, topped with an old black fedora hat, he was tucked away in the far corner of the first floor gallery. He kept a calculating gaze in front of a wide, seven-foot tall, glass display case that exhibited famous graduates of the West Point Military Academy; among them Civil War generals Robert E. Lee, Ulysses S. Grant, and James B. McPherson. Soon, he too, became invisible as thick smoke wafted around him. With a darting glance around, he sensed the timing was right.

Reaching inside a coat pocket, he pulled out the last of his smoke grenades and pulled the pin. The grenade was actually a consumer fireworks product made in China of which he had purchased several cases a few years back. It was all plastic, even the pull pin, making it easy to bypass metal detectors. The five-inch tall grenade practically mirrored the same size, shape, grip, and dark green coloring of a WWII U.S. Army issued grenade. What made this smoke screen device especially useful was it did not require ignition with matches or a lighter like a typical fused smoke ball would. The pin the old vet pulled was attached to a short piece of string that created ignition inside a tiny tube at the top of the grenade.

A tongue of flame shot out the top and sizzled for two seconds until making connection with the active ingredient inside. Balls of thick white smoke spewed out, adding to the already smoke-choked first floor. A typical consumer smoke grenade would only burn for a minute. But with some homemade tinkering the vet had inserted special chemicals to have his grenades burn four times longer.

The old vet tossed the grenade in the center of the room and then nonchalantly took his coat off and hung it over his arm. With a lance-like, forceful thrust of his wooden cane he pierced the single-pane glass display case in front of him. Large chunks of glass shattered to the carpeted floor. It was just a split second of crunching, masked perfectly by the fire alarm.

No one heard, saw, nor cared. The surveillance cameras were rendered useless from the smoke. There was no direct video evidence of him actually igniting the last grenade nor shattering the display case.

Placing the curved handle of his cane on the wrist of the arm his coat was draped over—just as he had practiced in his inn room the night before—he reached into the display case and snatched an old black hat off the uniformed mannequin portraying General McPherson. The wool felt hat was immediately hidden under his coat and held firmly against his body. He replaced the missing hat on the mannequin with his own fedora, revealing a half-bald, age-spotted scalp of stringy, gray hair.

The general's field hat was the sole item he was hired to obtain in this high-risk, hastily planned endeavor he had agreed to just yesterday. His New York City-based art and antique broker had contacted him with the initial offer in the early hours of Saturday morning. She had been negotiating with an individual who represented the client, a wealthy Civil War collector from Atlanta. After a counter offer, a large, final price was agreed on, amicable to all parties. The hat was apparently priceless in the client's eyes, given the substantial sum of money to be wired into his Cayman Island account upon completion of the job.

Transportation to the job had been quick and easy. An hour cab drive north from the city deposited him at an inn at Highland Falls, home of the West Point Military Academy. He had checked into a first floor room at the West Point Inn & Suites under one of his dozen false identities and paid cash in advance for a two night stay. Saturday afternoon he spent as a visitor and cased the museum.

He snapped pictures with his cell phone, developed a plan, and even implemented part of it before leaving by setting off the fire alarm without being noticed by the many security cameras. Afterward, he learned of the intense auditory stimulation, evacuation procedures, and time accrued for fire response—all key factors to be used to his advantage.

After purchasing a fedora, cane, and overcoat at a hospital thrift shop located in the next little town over, and rounding out other supplies not already in his burglary kit, he waited all night for approval to execute. It was his prerogative when to make the actual theft, whether to pull off one of his signature daylight attacks or whether to try for an after-hours insertion. But he had been told that the deed needed to be done and the hat delivered by Monday night as a gift for the client's birthday party in Atlanta. A hefty cash bonus would await him should he arrive before midnight Monday.

During scouting, he also had observed nighttime motion detectors throughout the museum. Being on such a tight schedule he opted against an evening insertion. It was best to stick with a plan at which he excelled and was least expected: a theft right under the noses of the public, conducted through a literal smoke screen of deception, disguise, and con artistry.

This Sunday morning's entrance through security was also his first test with a new disguise he recently purchased. It worked like an absolute charm. Especially convincing was the incredibly realistic, silicone, full-head mask that turned him into a crotchety-looking old fart. To conceal his eyes he wore oversized tinted glasses. No one gave him any long looks—well maybe at his somewhat shabby appearance—but nothing was given away on his face.

With today's technology in make-up and special effects materials readily available to the public, almost anyone could be fooled with a disguise. His mask was so life-like that it behaved like real flesh and muscle when he spoke. He first got the idea from reading about a white man who used a black man head mask and pulled off six robberies in Ohio back in 2010. Cops arrested a black man whose face looked exactly like the mask and the suspect's mother even thought it was him on television. The robber would have gotten away with it had he not left the mask lying about in his hotel room where his girlfriend found it along with dyed bank money and turned his ass in.

The old looking thief even made sure his heavily-veined, exposed hands were aged correctly with some foundation blotting. Toss in an American flag and an Army lapel pin and he looked like every other aging WWII veteran that visited the museum—someone who security would least expect.

It also had been a breeze limping through the lobby metal detector with plastic smoke grenades hidden on his body—nothing metal—nothing to set it off. It was his wooden cane, however, that gave him the biggest scare just as he stepped out from under the metal detector.

An overzealous, young security guard confiscated his cane and offered, as an alternative, a specially-provided, disabled person's sit-down scooter to explore the museum with. The thief's superb acting skills then kicked in. Sticking with his disguise personality, he angrily demanded his cane back as the only way he could move about the museum.

Refusing to budge one inch, he stood behind the metal detector and held up the visitor line for emphasis. Heads turned as he had raised his gravelly, old voice saying he wanted to walk, not ride in some "damned scooter!" After the security guard put up a weak argument about some national security bullshit about his cane being used as a potential weapon, several people queued up in line behind him, laughed aloud, and urged the guard to give him back his cane. The old vet tried to trump the stubborn guard by citing his rights under the Americans with Disabilities Act. It didn't work.

Finally, the thief used his patriotic ace-in-the-hole to elicit sympathy. He told the security guard he was a very old WWII Army veteran and Purple Heart recipient who had been surrounded by the Germans at Bastogne, during the Battle of the Bulge, and this was his first and probably last time visiting the museum. The guard questioned what Army unit he was with. After a pause, the old man mumbled the 82nd Airborne. The naive security guard nodded his belief, thanked him for his service and sacrifice, and handed his cane back. The vet gave him a tip of his fedora amid the applause of the other patrons.

With the stolen Civil War hat now in hand, the elderly thief walked quickly—without the limp—to his last two target items. The non-toxic smoke bombs were still holding up well, giving him the time and cover to conceal his movements in the camera-monitored museum. He counted the strides along the way, having memorized the number and path he needed to take from his recon the day before. These next items were purely personal, beyond the scope of the contract, targets of opportunity he had observed during his visit and something he simply needed to take. It was pure obsessive excitement and desire, his addictive high of which he could never get enough of.

On the way into the next room he bumped into a coughing mother and teenage son wandering blindly toward a partially lit exit sign. He yelled for them to keep moving and gave them a little shove in the right direction before continuing his pre-planned steps to the next display case. Just before reaching the corner, he lashed out with his cane and smashed open two more cases merely to sow confusion.

Even though the West Point Museum housed the oldest and largest public collection of military artifacts in the Western Hemisphere, it was still like most museums across the world with lax or inadequate protection for those priceless items. Budgets were tight, resulting in fewer security cameras for each room. Reduced security staff meant fewer eyes probing visitors' actions and whereabouts. Investing in after-hours motion detection technology was great, but overlooking inferior materials for display cases meant easy pickings for bold professional thieves like himself. All the reasons why he took the risk of a few more minutes to get what he wanted. He knew the game, the rewards, the consequences. Why not go for broke?

Racking up over $8 billion a year in stolen losses, art theft was a highly lucrative field that offered one of the best risk versus reward ratios for criminal enterprises. For a career choice it beat the hell out of armed robbery, drug dealing, arms trafficking, or money laundering considering hardly any art thieves lost their lives or garnered lengthy prison sentences. And, with the right connections, the payoffs were huge.

The only thing in the back of this thief's mind was this was the first time he ever stole something on U.S. Army property. He didn't know what kind of additional heat that would bring. All the better to get more than just a lousy Civil War hat if he was risking his own neck in the process, because these items would also serve as his "get-out-of-jail-free card." If he was captured down the road after already hiding the prized items, he could negotiate with authorities and say, "Cut me a lesser sentence and I'll reveal where the trophies are."

His payoff was sitting in a waist-high, double-pane glass cabinet now before him. The trophies of WWII from Nazi Germany reflected back at him through the smoke. Among the many items in the case were his two prizes: the famous Lilliput golden pistol of Adolf Hitler and an ivory baton of Hitler's second in command, Reichsmarschall Hermann Göering.

He attacked the glass cabinet with a swift wallop of his cane. This time the double-pane glass proved stronger and his cane bounced back. Double-fisting the shaft he slammed the cane down again and broke through the first layer of glass. The cane cracked. A loud burglar alarm instantly blended in with the already blaring fire alarm. Two more heavy blows and the cabinet top shattered, along with half the cane. He tossed the other half, its usefulness elapsed.

During yesterday's scouting, when he found out the museum cases were all housed in either single-pane or double-pane glass, it felt like he had hit the jackpot. He had thought with hundreds of billions of dollars in the annual military budget, the Pentagon could at least allocate for shatterproof armored glass as a viable replacement for their treasured items.

Sorry bureaucrats. Your loss.

Hitler's gold plated Lilliput Model I, .32 caliber, semi-automatic pistol was the first item he grabbed. The small wooden box it was housed in made it even easier to take as a whole. It held the palm-sized gold pistol, a gold plated magazine for six bullets, and a gold cleaning brush all nestled in a molded black, velvet-lined interior. The box wasn't even wired down. He simply shut the top and snatched it. The box, no bigger than a thick hardback book, was stuffed inside McPherson's hat, both being concealed by the coat over his arm.

Next was Göering's baton. What a morbid beauty, he thought for a split second. After clutching the foot-long ceremonial baton, he was surprised at how heavy it weighed. It felt about five pounds. The shaft was made of white elephant-ivory embossed with twenty gold eagle insignias and twenty platinum German Iron Crosses. The solid-gold cap ends held bands engraved in platinum and were encrusted with 640 diamonds making this Nazi artifact just as priceless as the pistol. The thief shoved the baton down the front of his pants securing it to a cloth loop he had stitched on the inside of his waistband. The length of the baton stretched down the inside of his pant leg with a bulge making him rival the grotesquely-hung 1970s porn star, John Holmes.

His heart pounding in the thrill of the moment, it was time to leave, but not through the main lobby. It would be too crowded with too many watchful eyes and too many well-wishers wanting to help out an old man. Instead, sticking with his plan, he made for a rear emergency exit he had found during his recon mission. The smoke had dissipated upon reaching the exit. Perfect timing, he thought, as he opened the emergency door and stepped outside.

Down a walled-in stairwell, he made it to ground level and immediately skirted a trash dumpster. Next, he headed toward some shadowy trees bordering the property's fence line. Lady Luck stuck with him as no one was around on that far side. He quickly made it to the bus parking lot where he squeezed between several charter buses for a breather and observation.

Two fire trucks, a police car, and ambulance were parked outside the concrete car bomb barriers lining the front entrance, their lights flashing. Throngs of visitors were still pouring out the front doors of both the museum and the adjacent visitor's center. Several security guards helped coughing patrons as a team of fully-equipped firefighters with air packs, axes, and a hose line hustled into the museum. Onlookers from the village, like moths drawn to light, also gravitated onto the fenced-in museum property from one of two parking lot entrances on Main Street. Rubbernecker drivers had already clogged the street as a police officer waved at them to keep moving.

While attention focused on the chaos at the entrance, no one noticed an old vet, walking with a different sort of limp, off Army property. He soon disappeared across the road and into his room at the inn.

Three minutes later the true man emerged. Thirty-five year-old Nathan Kull stepped out with a tightly packed backpack of stolen items. Standing at five foot, nine inches with a firm body weighing in at one hundred seventy-five pounds and facial features rivaling any GQ model, he wore black wrap-around sunglasses and a black ball cap, brim angled low. A gray hooded sweatshirt over khaki cargo pants rounded out his casual attire. He hustled over to the small parking lot where his Alamo rental car was parked. Having already rented the nondescript blue four-door sedan yesterday morning after his museum recon, he was all set for a quick getaway. With his travel duffel bag and burglary kit previously placed in the trunk, he wasted no time in getting out of town.

Heading west out of the village, he passed a fast-moving U.S. Army Military Police sports utility vehicle surely headed to the scene of his crime.

Within ten minutes, he hit Interstate 87 and headed south.

To Atlanta.

4

Sunday. 11:45 a.m.
Ruloff's Restaurant and Bar
Ithaca, New York

AFTER LEAVING A VOICE MESSAGE WITH JIM RYAN, the unreachable curator of arms at West Point Museum, Jake placed a return phone call to Tommy Watie. He, too, was unavailable. Jake left a voice message informing Watie he would let him know of any new information once he spoke with his contact at the museum. In the mean time, he and Rae rode off on their Indians taking advantage of the balmy weather and dry roads. Their cell phones were powered off for no distractions.

Their picturesque motorcycle ride south from the Depot took them on Route 89 along the western shoreline of Cayuga Lake, the longest Finger Lake in the wine-making region. With a stop and a short hike at Taughannock Falls State Park, they headed into the city of Ithaca. After meandering about on a tour through Jake's alma mater, Cornell University, their plans were to make the entire loop of the 38-mile long lake with a return trip up the eastern coast line. But lunch came first at the famous Ruloff's Restaurant on College Avenue.

While Rae munched gingerly on a Cape Cod salad, Jake had already inhaled half of his Ruloff's Burger. On the table was a brochure explaining the story behind the restaurant's name: how Edward H. Ruloff had murdered his wife and daughter in 1845 and hid them in a chest, which was, according to legend, sunk in Cayuga Lake. The bodies were never recovered. Jokingly, Rae suggested another lake dive to find out if the story was true. As he powered on his cell phone to check messages, Jake responded with a hearty laugh that he'd rather stick with old artifacts than finding old murder victims. But something glimmered in his eyes.

Rae caught it. "Actually honey," she said, intertwining her hands and looking into his eyes. "I think this whole waybill-in-a-hat affair with McPherson would give us an excellent follow-up episode on *Battlefield Investigators*. Our show ratings on Friday night were through the freakin' roof. The Civil War is a hot topic. If Tommy Watie is right, then I think we may have a little-bitty adventure brewing, don't you?

Jake nodded. "How long have we been together? Over a year now? You've got me pegged already, Babe. I haven't been able to get my mind off Tommy's phone call this morning."

The intoxicating aroma of adventure permeated the air around him. For a restless man who thrives on the next adventure, it was an addicting scent. One that compared with the pure sexual arousal that Rae often emitted in his presence. He couldn't resist it—the excitement of the hunt, the journey into the unknown, the danger, and the drive for success. It's what living was all about. His phone dinged with the alert of several text messages. He blinked. Scanning the texts, his smile soon faded.

"Uh oh. Not good."

"What's up?" Rae asked, dabbing her mouth with a napkin.

"A bunch of texts from Jim Ryan. Ah, something happened at the museum." Jake kept scrolling and reading. "Been trying to contact you. Call ASAP."

Rae rolled her eyes. "Well, your phone *was* off."

Jake continued through the texts with a tap and drag of his index finger upon the touch screen. "There's been a burglary."

"Oh shit."

"I gotta call him back. Going outside."

"If you're done, I'll pay the bill?"

"Yeah, I'm all set. Thanks, Hon." Jake took a swig of ice water and grabbed his coat before stepping outside to place the call.

He had the curator on the phone within seconds.

"Sorry for the delay, Jim," Jake said, cutting out any pleasantries. "My phone was off. What happened?"

Ryan grunted. "Two of the U.S. Army's most prized trophies of war were just stolen—like an hour ago. Adolf Hitler's gold-plated pistol and Hermann Göering's diamond baton."

"Holy crap!"

"Tell me about it," Ryan replied in a defeated voice. "This is like losing the crown jewels under your watch. Hitler's pistol was estimated at $70 million alone. Unless I can find out who did this and recover those objects, I'll be fucking crucified. And you're the only lead I got right now to help me solve this thing."

"Me? What? How?"

"McPherson's hat, goddammit," Ryan said, frantically. "The voice message you left this morning before I got in!"

"Huh?"

"They stole McPherson's hat, too."

"Is this a fucking joke?" Jake angrily asked aloud, causing several people to glance his way as they strolled by. "Some kind of prank?"

Ryan sighed. "No! They replaced it with some old fedora style hat. We didn't notice it at first when we did an inventory sweep after the fire was put out."

"Fire?"

"Yep," Ryan continued, talking faster. "Whoever pulled this off were some brazen sons-of-bitches. Broad daylight. Museum packed with people. They set off like three or four smoke grenades on different floors. Caught the carpet on fire."

"Anyone hurt?"

"No. Everyone was evacuated. But once firefighters extinguished the blaze and ventilated the smoke they realized some display cases were smashed open. We went back in and that's when we saw the two Nazi trophies gone. Nothing else was stolen. Or so I thought."

"What do you mean?" Jake asked, still struggling to follow.

"McPherson's case was smashed, too, but I totally overlooked the hat.

Looked like nothing was missing. Then the MPs arrived and took the museum over as a possible terrorist crime scene because of the grenades. Started detaining patrons. Interviewing them. Searching them. We've got the whole place on lock down. It's a damn mess here."

"Jesus," Jake said, brushing a hand through his short hair.

Ryan went on. "But that's when I went back to my office and noticed a message on my phone. It was you calling about McPherson's hat. Wanting me to check something inside it. So I go back to the case and BAM! That's when I realized the original was stolen and was replaced on the mannequin with the fake. Jake, listen man, you've got to tell me everything you know."

Jake started pacing the sidewalk in front of his and Rae's parked motorcycles. "Sure thing, Jim. Umm, early this morning I got a call . . ."

Ryan interrupted. "Jake, I'm putting you on speaker. I have the head of the MPs here with me and he needs to speak with you, too."

A new deeper voice came over the phone. "Lieutenant Colonel Tununda, this is Lieutenant Colonel Cliff Paxton, I'm the Provost Marshal here at the academy. We met a year or so ago when you did your talk here on that British gold you found."

"Yes, I remember you Colonel. All six foot eight inches of you," Jake said, lightheartedly. "I heard what happened. I'll help in any way I can."

The equally ranked officer chuckled back, heading off any tension. "Yeah, anything you've got in this early phase will give us a jump start. But I've got to record this conversation for my own notes. Is that gonna be alright with you?"

"Absolutely, I understand. And I appreciate you asking first," Jake replied, just as Rae stepped outside to join him.

"So, Jim told me he got a call from you about this McPherson hat, right?" Paxton asked.

"Correct. I received a strange call early this morning from a man named Tommy Watie. He's related to Cherokee General Stand Watie—"

"Of the Civil War, right?" Ryan chirped in, for the sake of Paxton's recording.

"Correct," Jake acknowledged while staring at Rae in disbelief. "This Tommy, who's like ninety years-old, saw our show on McPherson's hat the other night, Friday night. Apparently, not only did it jog his memory but it also literally gave him a heart attack. He said he was brought back to life with an AED."

"You're shitting me?" Paxton asked.

"Can't make this stuff up. He also claims his grandfather was the soldier who shot and killed General McPherson and the only reason he did so was to recover a *waybill* that was stashed inside McPherson's hat."

"What?" Ryan blurted. "A waybill?"

"Really?" Paxton added. "That's like a map."

"Yeah, I know," Jake said. "He refused to tell me what it was a map *of.* He said McPherson gave his grandfather a receipt to claim the waybill back after the war, but ended up shooting and killing him first. Never got the waybill, though. It disappeared. The Waties have been looking for it for generations. And then it reappears like six months ago, out of nowhere. Colonel, are you familiar with that part of the story? The provenance? The chain of possession and how the hat ultimately ended up in our hands at the Military History Institute?"

Rae stood close to Jake, listening as best she could.

"Yes, I actually caught your show the other night, too. I'm a fan," Paxton admitted. "A rebel captain took it off the dead general as a war trophy, but was then taken prisoner. Ended up wearing that hat all through his time as a prisoner of war and then back to his home after the war. But he sold it, right? And it disappeared from there."

Jake nodded. "That's right. It was Captain William A. Brown who took it. He sold it to a traveling antique dealer after the war. That dealer, who was from Chicago, we found out from our research, in turn sold it to a customer from Indiana. Then the hat basically sat in a circular hat box untouched for over a century until recently when a woman bought it at an estate sale for $1 and her son recognized the general's name on the tag inside the hat." Jake started pacing. "Plus, they had documentation from the dealer also inside the hat box. Those papers showed it was originally purchased from Captain Brown, thus proving the provenance. That's when I got a call at MHI from the woman offering the hat as a donation. We kept it totally secret, researched and produced the story, loaned the hat to

West Point for public relations purposes, and then we aired the episode."

Rae grabbed Jake lightly on the arm and corralled his pacing. She then made an open and closing gesture with her hand that he was jabbering a bit too much.

He got the hint he was probably confusing Paxton and needed to get back to the essentials. "To make a long story short, this Tommy Watie got a hold of me this morning and I, in turn, tried to call Jim to check out what's inside the hat. I needed to find out if this waybill story was true or bullshit. It was before hours so I left a message and then Rae and I took off for a motorcycle ride."

"A map inside of a Civil War general's hat?" Ryan yelled over speaker phone. "What in the *hell* has that got to do with Hitler's pistol and Göering's baton?"

"I don't know, Jim!" Jake fired back, irritated.

"I'm sorry, Jake," Ryan backed down. "I'm under a ton of stress. I've had shatterproof glass for all of our display cases on order for nine months now so something like this would NOT happen! And the pencil pusher pricks keep delaying it. A tornado of shit is whipping up from top Army brass and I'm the one on the firing line. I need all the help I can get. I need answers . . ." His voice faded off. "My God, Jake, the pistol and baton are priceless. Why steal an old hat, too?"

Hearing this for the first time, Rae whispered to Jake. "They *stole* McPherson's hat?" Jake's eyebrow arched. He pursed his lips.

Ryan sounded overwhelmed. Jake went easy on him, truly trying to help his friend and professional colleague. "My guess is it has to be related to that waybill inside of it. Shit like this is no coincidence, believe me."

"Or a distraction from what they really wanted," Paxton countered.

"But they replaced the hat with a fedora," Jake replied. "Why go through the trouble to disguise the theft? Did they do the same with the pistol and baton?"

Rae nodded silently onto his line of thinking. Her investigative mind was already turning with the one-sided conversation she could barely hear.

"No," Ryan flatly answered.

"I've got to get a hold of the old man that called you," Paxton said.

"You have his number?"

Jake tapped his phone's screen and pulled up the recent number from this morning and read it aloud. He told the Colonel to tread lightly with the old man because of his heart attack. "He's physically fragile. He's an old World War II vet."

"But you don't know that for a fact, Jake," Rae interrupted. "It needs to be confirmed."

Jake knew she was right. "On second thought, Colonel . . . I'm going to let you speak with Rae Hart. As you know she's a former New York State Police investigator and has her own private firm now. She just made an excellent point." He handed the phone to Rae.

Rae didn't waste time. "Colonel, this man's story is just that. A story from a phone call. We don't know for a fact that he even exists, let alone had a heart attack. He might be sending us on a wild goose chase. Before you call him and tip your hand, you need to find out who he is, where he lives, if there was an ambulance sent to his house on Friday night like he claims. You know what I'm saying?"

The Colonel agreed.

Rae continued. "He told Jake specifically the paramedics used an AED to revive him. Paramedics had to be dispatched. There are 9-1-1 records of all of this . . . if it's true. So, the first step is to verify this event."

"Absolutely, Miss Hart," Paxton said. "Where did this take place?"

"Down in Savannah, Georgia," Rae said, nodding to Jake. "He told Jake he suffered the heart attack while watching our show on Friday night, so that would be shortly after seven p.m."

"I'll get one of my investigators to make a call to Savannah dispatch and find everything out." Off conversation, the Colonel asked Ryan to summon one of his investigators.

"One more thing," said Rae.

"Yes?"

"With all due respect, sir, because you might have already done this, but a lot of art thefts are inside jobs," she explained. "You're gonna want to interview each and every employee, security guard, volunteer, administrator, whatever. Even if they weren't working today during the theft. No one is off limits."

"Miss Hart, I'll act on your advice as soon as we end this call," Paxton said. "I've got to tell you, nothing like this has ever happened here at West Point. All we pretty much deal with are traffic offenses and misdemeanors so your investigative angle is much appreciated."

"Thank you. Here's Jake again." Rae winked at Jake as she handed him the phone back.

"Colonel?" Jake started, "I just remembered there's one other thing this Tommy Watie told me that will help identify him."

"What's that?"

"He said his son is that billionaire Congressman Tom Black from Atlanta, Georgia."

Silence on the line.

"Colonel?"

There was a deep sigh from Paxton. "You gotta be shitting me? All we need is Black the Bullshitter on the periphery. Ah, Christ!"

"Yeah, my sentiments exactly," Jake agreed. "Plus, the prick loathes the military, too. We'll have to handle him with kid gloves."

A click on the line. "I took you off speaker," Paxton said. "And I just stopped recording this conversation, too . . . for my own sake . . . so no one has this on record. But Congressman Black," he continued, with slow oozing disgust, "reeks of a ripe New York subway men's room after a homeless convention."

Rae guffawed.

Jake emitted a cringing laugh and sarcastically told Paxton he fully concurred with his situation report.

"Colonel Tununda? Listen, umm, I need to ask something from both of you."

"Go ahead."

"You and Miss Hart have stellar reputations and experience . . ." Paxton said, applying the butter. "My investigations office, shall we say, doesn't quite have that depth of experience—especially in dealing with thefts of this magnitude *and* the political artillery barrage that's sure to hit. I need to be proactive. What I'm getting at is, I'd like to officially bring you two onboard as consultants, given the fact that McPherson's hat is among the items stolen and you're the experts on its history. Plus, you've had contact with our best lead at this point—the Watie man. The commandant of West Point already gave me authorization to recruit anyone I need. Is there any way you both can join our team here at West Point?"

"Colonel, it's my duty to assist you. And I can speak for Rae that it would be our pleasure." Rae nodded to Jake with assurance. "The director of MHI will wholeheartedly concur, too, once he hears the situation. But, we're in Ithaca right now, on motorcycles. Totally unprepared. We'd have to go back to my field office at the Seneca Army Depot which is about an hour away, get all of our overnight gear, and then we'd have to turn around and make a four-hour drive down to West Point." Jake paused for a moment. "Instead, let me offer you this. We take that same amount of time, fly down to Savannah, and pay Mr. Tommy Watie a face-to-face surprise visit."

Rae nodded her head vigorously.

"Yes, I like it," Paxton said. "Plan on that. While you're headed back to the Depot we'll verify his identity. Don't anyone call him, though. Let him find out about the theft through the news. If he calls you again, don't answer. Let him sweat it out and then he'll get a knock on his door from you guys in due time. He'll be off guard and nervous. That's the best time to confront him. I'll arrange an investigator from CID to meet you in Savannah. He'll take the lead on the case down there. Expect to meet that person at the airport."

"Ten-four," Jake replied. "This time I'll keep my phone *on* in case you need us again."

MICHAEL KARPOVAGE

5

NOT WANTING TO TAKE ANY CHANCES ON HEADING further south using the same Alamo rental car he had fled West Point in, Nathan Kull had reached Philadelphia and rented a new sedan from Enterprise-Rent-A-Car. This one was under yet another false ID but with legitimate paperwork leading back to a credit card. He had chosen the Philadelphia International Airport rental location to give the impression he may have taken a flight. And if any investigator happened to make it this far in tracking his movements he made sure there was one other piece of bread crumb evidence to throw them off kilter.

Deliberately placed between the front seat and middle storage compartment of the Alamo rental car was a folded piece of paper that looked like it may have accidentally slipped out of the driver's pocket. It was hidden enough from view that any car rental employee would either overlook it upon cleaning for the next customer or simply not be able to reach his hand in between the small space. The note was meant to be found only by investigators who were on to him and his rental. Otherwise, it was a harmless scribbled piece of trash from a careless traveler.

Better to assume the law was always on your trail and take precautions rather than be a sure-fire know-it-all. It's this attitude that had enabled Kull to have never been busted once in his entire twenty-year career as a master thief. Or as he titled himself, a *wealth redistribution expert.*

The small handwritten notepaper, taken from his room at the West Point Inn & Suites, would clearly connect the car to the crime and give investigators further gum to chew on once they deciphered the message, thus tying up their resources on a false lead.

The notation referred to a business in Berlin, Germany along with the owner's name, address, phone number, and website link. Poor guy was chosen randomly from a Google search in Berlin of gold and antique dealers the day before. The dealer's website even showed several WWII-era German weapons, jewelry, and assorted antiques. Who else would be interested in a couple of prized Nazi items for a return trip back to the *Vaterland*? What a perfect black market suspect.

Once investigators pieced together the rather easy cryptic characters at the top of the note, they would realize their suspect was on a 5 p.m. flight from Philadelphia, to London, Heathrow, and on to Berlin. Any dumb investigator would surely know once in Berlin the suspect would be paying a Mr. Sebastian von Blücher a visit.

Oh, was he in for a nightmare, thought Kull. They'd have to bring in the FBI, State Department, Interpol, and a multitude of German law enforcement. The man would be interrogated for days, his place of business searched, property seized. His personal relationships and reputation would be ruined. Unfortunately, it was this type of cruel, heartless, collateral damage that allowed Kull to survive in his line of business. He grinned widely and shrugged to no one as he embraced his own cleverness at hurting others while protecting himself.

Now leaving the airport in his new silver Lexus sedan rental, Kull sat back with a stiff arm on the steering wheel. With a full tank of gas and a belly full of fast-food from Wendy's, chased with a Red Bull from a 7-11—all paid in cash—he made sure to keep his speed as common as possible with the flow of traffic. Not being overly careful or cautious, but driving normal was the key. Blending in with everyone else. And never making a traffic violation. Always using his blinkers. No tailgating. He had to be invisible to any highway police patrols.

He breathed a loud sigh of relief. Finally, he could relax, the getaway was intact. Now all he had to do was dodge moronic drivers on the interstate while fighting off fatigue from lack of sleep. Motoring south, this time on I-95, he was in for a 13-hour trip to Atlanta for delivery of the hat. His grin grew to a wide, glimmering smile and he finally allowed himself to enjoy the moment. He had just pulled off one of his most daring heists ever and the rush was like a drug addict's fix. A shiver of utter success pulsed throughout his body.

Raised in a wealthy, gated subdivision in the Hamptons on Long Island, Nathan Kull was a tantrum-filled, scrawny, spoiled, only-child whose single, advertising executive mother doted on him to the extreme. Whatever his demanding, cute-little heart desired, he got. And on the rare occasion his mother said no, then he'd simply persist until she gave in.

Or he'd just steal.

He distinctly remembered his first theft of a bag of Gummy Bears at the local grocery store. He was seven and the bag nearly dropped out of his loose pants. More candy, toys, and sports equipment followed. At age ten the neighborhood kids fell prey to his sticky fingers. After ripping off his friend's baseball cards he'd gotten a black eye and a bloody nose, but that didn't stop him from stealing the same kid's entire take of fundraising money from chocolate bar sales several months later.

That persistent attitude of getting whatever he set his eyes on morphed into a strong-willed, mean personality to persevere at anything he set his mind to. His self-confidence soared as a young teenager. An honor student at one of the best high schools on Long Island, he was attracted to engineering and what made things tick. He learned the inner workings of machinery, hand tools, and locks from his industrial arts teacher. Soon, he was picking his own school's locks, entering late at night, and screwing with the janitorial staff until they were convinced a ghost was haunting the building.

Laughing at that fun memory, Kull accelerated the Lexus and reset the cruise control. He remembered taking the janitor's master key for all the hall lockers, duplicating it, and then returning it the next night. With access to over three hundred of his fellow student's lockers he had a field day, every day. Popping in an out of their lockers both during and after school, he stole money, drugs, cigarettes, chewing tobacco, clothing, sneakers, music players, you name it. Some of the most coveted pickings he would sell back to other kids, thus generating a nice profit.

His game stepped up a notch with his first employer. Landing a part-time job as a prep cook and dishwasher at a local country club, bottles of booze and cases of beer soon disappeared from inventory counts. He would resell the items to his fellow classmates. As their demand for alcohol increased, his resale cost increased. Since they were all rich and underage drinkers he gouged his prices accordingly. By the time he graduated high school he had so much cash and stolen goods he was hiding it in bags under the insulation of his attic.

High school for him had been a different education. He had honed his skills in elusiveness, observation, negotiation, and acting. Most importantly he bragged only to himself, telling no one of his exploits. He learned if you kept your mouth shut, then no one had anything on you.

Kull had attended college at the New York Institute of Technology in Old Westbury, Long Island. Between ripping off the school's computer equipment and pick pocketing fellow students' possessions, he supplemented his college education with classes at local acting studios. That is where he became the perfect con man of many disguises and personalities. No one suspected the upright honor student with so much charm and confidence, to be a thief within their midst. Graduating with dual bachelor's degrees in electrical engineering and computer science, Kull's college education allowed him to bypass the latest security systems within minutes. The decade following, he put that knowledge to good use with art and jewelry heists all across the nation.

Checking himself out in the rearview mirror, he brushed away a loose blonde hair on his forehead. He wore a short, cropped-style haircut left longer on top so strands of blond bangs could be gelled to stick up stylishly. He winked at himself, flashing blue eyes. Kull was an exceptionally handsome, metrosexual man with an incredible career as one of the elite thieves of the world. He was living proof that crime could pay.

"In huge, fucking dividends," he shouted to no one.

A particularly famous score on his career stat sheet, as well as law enforcement's, was when he infiltrated a highly secure, walled estate of a famous Miami Dolphins NFL wide receiver. The place was like a French chateau, but with bodyguards and Rottweilers on patrol. Showing up at a rap party with a harem of purchased strippers for the night, he conned his way in as the pimp. As the only white man at the all-black party, he ended up being one of the most popular guests, partying and dancing with an entourage of black thugs, music artists, and athletes. When most of the guests and bodyguards were either too drugged up or engaged in sexual activities, he stole the arrogant wide receiver's rare Andy Warhol painting right off the wall and walked out.

Boy, what a con that was, he thought with a smirk.

Shrewdness, not ruthlessness, made him successful. He never carried a gun going into a job even though he owned several for personal protection. Violence wasn't part of his modus operandi. Thinking like a criminal investigator was. Up on the latest techniques, he excelled at outwitting those who would place him in jail.

By the time he was twenty-nine, he had made his first million. Law enforcement dubbed him the *Phoenix*, simply because he vanished into thin air and reappeared Phoenix-like, as someone else, his true identity unknown.

With another long exhale of air and an ear-to-ear, teeth-filled, shit-eating grin pasted on his face, Kull pounded the steering wheel in self-congratulations. "Goddamn, I can't believe I did it!" He looked in the mirror. *Well, of course I did.* "You, Nathan Kull, are living proof that you *can* get away with it." And then he winked at himself.

Kull had earned the right to spike the football with head-expanding, self-aggrandizing flare, but he still new the game was far from over. He had to deliver the hat to his broker's client—a middleman who represented the real client in Atlanta. That would ultimately finish the job. But first he needed to stash *his* Nazi trophies in a storage locker he'd have to rent in the city, getting them out of his immediate possession. He knew he couldn't move those two items for a long while. Probably would have to sit on them for at least five years to let the storm of investigation blow over while making highly discreet inquiries for potential buyers in the private collector's black market. Or he might even hold them for ransom against the museum's insurance company and get an even better payoff. Who knew what they'd bring in cash.

Time to check in. He pulled his iPhone from his belt holder and texted his broker while driving. Using a substitution cipher for the hat that they had previously agreed upon, he typed: *General Tso's chicken in the wok.*

Within minutes he received a confirmation text reply back: *I bet it tastes oh so good. Delivery time?*

Kull texted back: *12 hours. Where to?*

Details to come, was the reply.

Fifteen minutes later Kull received a phone call from his broker's cell. He placed the call on speaker while driving. "Got that address?" he asked, getting straight to the point, wanting to keep the conversation short.

A familiar sultry female voice answered back. The working name she had given him and that they had used for years was Mona. She explained only once it was from her favorite painting—da Vinci's *Mona Lisa.* He had worked with Mona on many fine jobs but they never met in person and preferred to keep their distance for business life expectancy purposes. But he always fantasized of what face and body accompanied the sexiness of her voice. "Change of plans," she said. "Top of the food chain sent word down through my *caterer* that you, umm, need to check inside the chicken for a hidden paper."

Kull cocked his head. "What the fuck is this, a fortune cookie?"

"Easy Phoenix," she replied, using the name he was given from law enforcement. "If there's something in there, message me a photo of it so I can pass it back up." She hung up.

Kull's brows furrowed. This was an unexpected twist to the job. He didn't like the meddling from his broker, nor her client, nor this Civil War collector, birthday-boy customer whom her client represented. He needed to think through the implications on this request.

Forty miles later, just inside the state border of Maryland, he would find out. He pulled off at a rest stop and parked well away from the main facilities. The car continued idling and faced out in his parking slot for an easy exit. Reaching in the back seat, Kull grabbed the backpack holding the stolen items. Placing it on the front passenger seat he unzipped it to reveal the hat stuffed inside. Underneath it were the Nazi items hidden in dirty clothing. With a quick glance outside to make sure no one was watching, he pulled the wool felt hat out.

Now, let's see what's inside that's so important to birthday boy.

Flipping it over, he saw a white silk liner, sweat-stained with patches of yellow and brown. A little tag was sewn onto the liner at the very peak of the interior. It held a faded black signature in flowing script. James B. McPherson. A two and a half inch leather sweatband overlapped the liner at the base of the interior crown. Looking closer at the sweatband overlap, Kull traced the circumference with his finger. He pulled the flap down to inspect the liner stitching hidden underneath. It looked normal at first glance, intact all around.

"There's nothing here," he mumbled to himself, shaking his head and returning the sweatband flap to its proper position. He was about to place the hat back in the backpack, but instead he figured he'd better be more thorough before sending word back to Mona.

He popped the trunk with a little button on the Lexus' dashboard. Exiting the rental, he headed to the rear and opened his burglary kit.

Reshuffling some tools, he grabbed a small LED flashlight and sat back in the driver's seat. A glance to his left and right and all looked well. The only thing in his immediate vicinity of the parking lot was a parked RV about fifty yards away. A lanky man of retirement age emerged from a side door. In front of him, pulling on a leash, was a tiny toy poodle with fluffy white hair. The man wore a flat, black and red plaid, taxi driver-style cap.

It was time to take his little doggy for a dump, thought Kull.

Holding McPherson's hat upside down again, he unfolded the sweatband as before and then illuminated the liner stitching with a swath of white-blue light. The stitches looked consistent and tight all the way around until he reached the part of the sweatband that met the back of the wearer's head. Here he noticed the stitching, although still looking normal, had in fact been keenly cut, exposing a subtle gap of three inches between the liner and the wool felt.

Kull's eyes narrowed. He placed the hat on his lap and hunched over as close as possible, shining the light in the gap while probing it with a finger. He hooked the tip of his index finger inside and stretched it further.

"Well, well, well," he smiled, touching something. Stuffed inside he could see the corner of paper folded several times. It was snug under the liner. "There *does* seem to be a fortune inside this cookie."

What a clever little hiding place, thought Kull. Obviously it was created with great care in order to conceal a hidden document. Not knowing in the slightest who this Civil War guy McPherson was, how he died, nor the history of the hat, he had no idea what the paper might reveal. But he knew this was the key to the puzzle of why a seemingly worthless hat held such high value in the collector's eyes.

Slipping the tip of his finger deeper inside the gap, he was able to move the corner of the folded paper down slightly. This allowed him to pinch it with his thumb and slowly pull it out. He couldn't afford to cause any damage to the document.

Suddenly, three sharp wraps on his driver's side window caused him to flinch right out of his seat. He looked over, his heart in his throat. It was the man in the plaid cap from the RV.

"Jesus Christ!" Kull gasped.

RV Man held up his hand to apologize. "Oh, I'm sorry!" he shouted through the window, stepping back a few feet to show he meant no harm.

Kull leaned his head back on the head rest and caught his breath. At the same time, he slowly lowered the hat below the steering wheel to hide it down around his feet. Then he powered down the window and smiled reassuringly at the man.

"Sorry about that, son," said the man. "Didn't mean to scare you. Just wanted to let you know you left your trunk open is all. Didn't want you driving away like that."

Kull exhaled. "Oh, okay. Thanks so much. I do appreciate it, sir." He laughed nervously at being caught so off guard.

"No problem. I'll shut it for you. You stay right there."

"No. No, I can do it." But before Kull could unlatch his door the man was already at the rear of the car with his hand on the top of the trunk.

Right before slamming it shut, RV Man couldn't help but notice the couple pieces of luggage inside. One was an open duffel bag with some exposed items. In the split second before the trunk fell, his mind had registered a small crow bar, a short bolt cutter, and what appeared to be a Halloween mask of a decrepit old man.

Once Kull felt the trunk slam shut he accelerated out of the parking slot and gave two short beeps of his horn.

RV Man waved back in his rear view mirror. His dog gave two little yelps as if to say, "You're welcome."

▼

Ten minutes later

After a paranoid, obscenity-laced tirade that saw him reach speeds into the nineties, Kull had finally pulled his rental sedan onto the shoulder of the road. He needed to calm down and think clearly on whether RV Man had indeed seen anything incriminating in his trunk. And he needed to pull the paper out of the hat.

First things first. Cover his tracks. He popped his trunk and stepped to the rear of the car.

"Fuck!"

Zipping up his exposed burglary kit, he slammed the trunk shut with extra force. He sat back down in the driver's seat and pulled his door shut equally as hard. Yes, Kull thought, RV Man did probably see the most damning of all of his tools—the mask. And probably got a good description of himself while he was at it. *If so, now what?*

"Think. Think," he urged himself. "Slow down. Relax." And then it occurred to him maybe news of the theft hadn't even gone public yet and his fears were pointless. He turned the radio on and scanned the AM news channels for several minutes. Nothing. He did the same on the FM stations. Same results.

He breathed easier. There was no way that guy could make the connection. Even if somehow the news story already broke on another form of media, like a smartphone or portable computer, and the guy had wind of it, there would have to be a clear image of the old vet disguise as the main suspect. RV Man only saw a folded portion of the mask for maybe a second. Not the full frontal view and certainly not wearing his glasses. Kull felt better. But he still erred on the cautious side. He used his iPhone news apps to see if anything had broken over the internet. From AP to CNN to FOX News, the usual networks with scoops didn't have jack. He checked the Drudge Report to be extra sure. Nothing.

He breathed easier. "Close call." He pulled out another caffeine pill from the pack he had bought at the convenience store in Philly and swallowed it. "Now, where's that goddamn hat?"

He remembered grabbing it from his feet and tossing it when he took off. He found it on the passenger side floor, the backpack having rolled on top of it. Scooping it up, he pulled it to his face again and jammed his fingers in the lining gap. This time he wasn't so ginger.

Out came a paper folded into a long rectangle approximately two inches by nine inches. Kull unfolded it three times to reveal the contents.

"What the—?"

6

ONGRESSMAN TOM BLACK OF ATLANTA'S NEWLY
drawn 15th U.S. Congressional District waddled back and forth
in a heavy, slow tread across the ceramic tiled floor of his posh Roswell
mansion's cigar room. It was probably the most exercise the obese man
would get all day long. Turning his head left and right, following Black's
every step, was his bored chief of staff Jaconious Johnson who calmly
sat sucking on a cigarette. To Johnson it was like watching a turtle play
tennis with himself. But he was secretly reveling in his boss's rare display
of nervousness. Then again, this wasn't their typical, business-as-usual,
political crime they had pulled off. This was the most daring of the Black's
lifelong illegal activities.

It was pure, unadulterated, personal revenge against his elderly father.
The man had come full circle.

Having already gotten word back forty-five minutes ago from their
fixer that the museum job was in fact an utter success, the sixty-five year-
old, billionaire, Democrat Congressman's signature hot-headed impatience
still got the better of him. He had since demanded to know if there was
some type of paper or waybill or what appeared to be a wayfinding map
hidden inside the hat the contract thief had just stolen. And the only one
who could tell him was Johnson, who had hired the fixer. But the fixer was

waiting on the broker, who waited to hear back from the thief.

And so Black paced, lost in thoughts of vengeance.

After hearing of his father's heart attack early Friday night and what specifically brought it on, Black had nonchalantly kicked back with a cigar in the very same room and watched the late repeat episode of *Battlefield Investigators*. He was stunned frozen when he, too, saw the discovery of General McPherson's hat. It was his father's lifelong dream to find that one highly prized item that his grandfather, Thomas Black Watie Jr., had lost during the Civil War. The Watie family worshipped their famed ancestor like a god. But he knew the family secret, too, behind his father's obsession with the hat. There was a legendary Cherokee waybill supposedly hidden inside of it.

In Black's twisted mind, the hat revelation spawned a plan to get his dear old Daddy back after almost thirty years of being his tossed away, piece of trash son. What the heart attack couldn't do, he would finish by stealing his father's dream. He would wave that fucking McPherson hat in front of his face and declare victory—and then burn it before his eyes. The hat that three generations of Watie men had obsessed over would come to an ash-filled end once and for all.

His father could take that last image to his grave.

That same Friday night, Black had summoned Johnson to his mansion in the wealthy north, metro-Atlanta suburb of Roswell, where he outlined what he wanted done at the West Point Museum. He totally conceded it was a hasty plan, but he insisted the job be accomplished before his father recovered from his heart attack and possibly sought the hat out himself. Plus, he wanted it for his birthday bash come Monday night. It would make a fine addition to his costume. He offered up an obscene amount of "fuck-you" play money for his operation and told Johnson to make things happen.

Jaconious Johnson, a handsome, dark-skinned, black man in his late thirties, sporting the trendy, short 360 waves haircut and a thin, artistically shaved mustache and goatee, had accepted his orders in stride. Although Black was the hand that grasped the backstabbing blade, Johnson was the one tasked with putting the blade in motion. He knew how the game was played, knew his role and was very well compensated for it. More than that, he simply loved being one of the power-playing, political elite. Screwing with and screwing over the "stupid people" was something he reveled in as much as his boss.

After the meeting, Johnson had contacted his fixer, a trusted go-between who quietly made illegal connections. The Atlanta-based fixer, in turn, contacted a female art and antique broker from New York City, named Mona. Although she ran a legitimate dealership, she also happened to specialize in the illicit trade of those same items. She, in turn, called on one of her many independent, professional contractors who would best fulfill the actual theft of the target item. Thus, a multi-tiered cushion of deniability was established so Congressman Black could claim ignorance, deny all culpability, and even pass a lie detector test if questioned. It was a shadowy system based on referral, large sums of money, and deadly payback if compromised. It was the way smart politicians and heads of organized crime families retained power. It's how they eluded a prison term. It's how Tom Black made his career as a parasite on American society.

With the hat due to arrive in Atlanta early tomorrow morning, Black couldn't wait to find out if the waybill his father and grandfather had told him about was truly hidden inside. It was a story from a long time ago when he was a smart ass, rebellious, pot-smoking, entitled, young teenager. He had scoffed at their Cherokee story, calling both men "dickheads" at the time for coming up with such a far-fetched fantasy. He had made it plainly clear he wanted no part in their so-called Indian adventure—his friends would laugh at him and he'd be embarrassed. All he cared about at the time was partying and girls, and money to pay for both pursuits. He couldn't give a shit about his family's heritage. He always resented how they cherished their military history and the pressure they put on him to carry on their good name through accomplishments.

Black thought if the waybill was really inside, then the gamble to steal the hat in the first place would be that much sweeter when he would taunt his old father with it. Now if they could only get an answer back, the weekend's little project would truly have a cherry on top. Willing a quicker response from the fixer to call back, he huffed and puffed out loud.

Like the uber, filthy-rich pig that he was.

Tom Black had spent a lifetime transforming himself into an embarrassing specimen of a man. He had given up on his body in his mid-thirties, primarily due to physical laziness. Some thirty years later he looked as if someone had crammed a three hundred pound watermelon down his throat that stopped at his hips.

Although a handsome man in his early years, he was now possessed of a half-bald, pear-shaped head of wiry gray hair and oversized ears. A bulbous, drinking-man's nose centered his copper-colored face, rounded out by drooping jowls and a double chin. His mouth was thin-lipped and full of bright white dentures with a slight underbite. Always frowning, his dark-brown eyes sagged with double bags. One of his political opponents had brilliantly pegged him as the love child of Democrats Henry Waxman and Sheila Jackson Lee.

Black's early demise came at age thirty-five, after he was busted for stealing from the Watie family's Civil War collection and reselling the items for personal profit. He'd made almost a half million dollars then. But when he was discovered, his wealthy father, Tommy Black Watie of Savannah, swiftly disowned him in return. After the excommunication, his father still wasn't finished.

At his father's urging, the FBI had charged Black with multiple counts of theft, embezzlement, fraud, obstruction of justice, tampering with a witness, and destruction of evidence. You name it, they piled on the charges hoping at least one would stick. However, Black's lawyer exposed a technicality when the government agents had filed search warrants early on in the investigation. Exploiting an apparent illegality, the lawyer blew the entire case wide open and all charges were dropped. It was an embarrassing loss for the FBI that cost an agent his job.

Black never faced prosecution. He had spent considerable time in jail before trial, though, and his personal and professional reputation was ruined. He lost all of his friends and a woman he had loved deeply. The whole episode was treated as a huge scandalous affair in Savannah. To make matters even worse he was then forced to make it on his own for the first time in a life where everything had been handed to him.

But he succeeded beyond his wildest expectations.

By cheating.

Taking the new name of Tom Black and with hundreds of thousands of dollars in seed money gained from his thefts, secured in off-shore, untraceable banking accounts, he immediately re-engaged in his nefarious ways. He moved to Atlanta and hit the financial management industry.

A loner and contrarian, Black's ambitions were too big for him to settle for a desk job in an established financial institution. Taking orders from no one and always gambling big, his early rip-offs ranged from Pyramid and Ponzi schemes to mortgage fraud to a low of embezzling funds from a fraudulent military veterans charity he established supposedly to help wounded warriors.

His persuasive salesmanship coupled with the art of delegation—having others under him doing the real dirty work—substantially grew his coffers over the years. Soon he created a private equity investment company managing other peoples' portfolios. And manage he did, gambling their life long savings in a wide range of stocks while betting against or hedging their market risks by longing or shorting the value. At the same time, he engaged in insider stock trading while skimming off the top of his clients' investments with so-called performance fees.

Between his legal investments and his ill-gotten gains, by the time he was fifty he had accumulated a one billion dollar nest egg. And a severe case of narcissistic personality disorder. He was King. Early retirement was his reward. Before he was caught stealing.

Again.

Black purchased a six bedroom, six bath, gaudy abode of some 10,000 square feet on tony Stroup Road in Roswell. He renamed it Black House. After five years of golfing, fishing, hunting, traveling the world, and having anything he so desired, he was simply bored beyond belief. Missing the "game," he re-entered the workforce in the "good ol' boy" network of Georgia state politics.

Black took advantage of a retired state seat representing the north metro Atlanta areas of Roswell and Alpharetta. With deep pockets and a network of buddies, he ran as a conservative Republican, touting his business success in the financial market. He was easily elected. He fit in perfectly as a politician, cashing in on every opportunity to scratch a fellow man's back while getting his own equally massaged. His back door wheeling and dealing, bribery, and corruption elevated him to more authority. He was instantly addicted to the power that public office could wield over the masses. Politics was where he excelled. It was his true life's calling. He had then set a bullseye on obtaining a U.S. congressional seat. Not out of duty to serve the country, but instead to become a member of America's elite political royalty. It's where the real power and celebrity was.

Adding extra weight to a pompous personality he consistently struck out with sophisticated, educated women over the years. Simply put, they found him utterly distasteful. No decent woman ever lasted with him. His longest relationship was just six months and that ended with a triple slap across his face when he was caught cheating on her with a trailer-trash prostitute.

His failure to lead a meaningful, mature, loving relationship with women had led him to seek lower forms of satisfaction. Besides routinely sexually harassing his female staff, he had also developed a crude fetish for under-aged Asian prostitutes.

Under the guise of titles like massage therapist, escort, or companion, Black *donated* exceptionally well for their sexual favors. Girls would either come to his house or a hotel room to service his aching extremities. He was well known in their circles as a "hobbyist," a man who made it a hobby of seeing as many girls as he could. Viagra with alcohol was his usual combination for hours of sexually deviant illegal engagement. And with a never-ending supply of illegal massage parlors throughout Atlanta to choose from—some even engaged in human trafficking—Black was always happy to use and abuse the young prostitutes.

As he paced across the room, his oversized, white dress shirt was stretched tight at the belly. Buttons strained to pop. Droopy man-breasts flopped underneath. A black tie hung loose around an unseen neck. With suspenders holding up the fifty-inch waistline of his black dress pants, top button undone, zipper half down, belt drooped low, he looked every part the white-trash, welfare king. At first glance no one would have pegged him as a billionaire. A pedophile, though, for sure.

Movement and intense color on his high-definition television set caught his eye. He moped in front of the screen while Johnson turned up the volume from a remote. It was a breaking FOX News report. He hated the network, just as much as his inner city district constituents did, but privately he knew they were the best in the business and one he often used to make appearances to garner full media exposure.

A distinctive church bell toll accompanied a screen-filling, yellow rectangle with red capital letters that screamed NEWS ALERT. A flashing red siren completed the sensationalized graphics. An attractive blonde daytime anchorwoman appeared on screen at her desk in the network's New York-based studios. Black had gone toe-to-toe many times with the spunky, conservative bitch. He passionately derided her on air, but secretly desired her in bed. *Oh, my hypocrisy never ceases to amuse me.* A photo of the front façade of the West Point Museum bordered in yellow and black crime scene tape floated over the woman's shoulder. Black took a breath.

"FOX News Alert now. Breaking news. This morning the prestigious West Point Museum was attacked with smoke grenades. The incendiary devices caused a fire and immediate evacuation. During the grenade attack we understand that three highly valued items in the museum's collection were allegedly stolen. We're not sure if the attack and theft were part of a coordinated effort by professional thieves or an isolated incident. No reports of any deaths, but three people were treated for smoke inhalation. Joining us now is our expert on art theft cases . . ."

Before the guest expert could rehash the events and speculate on the obvious as so often the talking heads did, the Congressman turned off the TV and spun around to his chief of staff.

"*Three* items were stolen? Three?" Black asked incredulously. "Jaconious, you stupid, incompetent motherfucker. I said the hat and that's it. Get your fixer on the phone, now! I'll deal with him direct."

Johnson stood up, blowing cigarette smoke from his nose. He was lean and muscular at well over six feet and stood straight as a plumb line. Being called a *stupid, incompetent motherfucker* was what Black called everyone.

He had since learned to ignore the label many years ago. Johnson pointed his cigarette at Black and spoke in a rich, deep bass voice.

"No. You know the rules. No talking to my man. No direct contact. No names. No recognition. We don't ask how the job gets done, only that he delivers."

"Fine, fine. Yeah, yeah," muttered Black, his way of admitting he was wrong. He plopped his jiggly body down in his favorite leather recliner. The chair groaned back as a long hiss of air emitted from flattened cushions. Black leaned back, his feet rose, and he lay horizontal, a profile in competition with Stone Mountain. With a heavy sigh, he kicked off his black dress shoes and wiggled his black-stockinged toes to settle in.

And then snapped his fingers.

"Gimme a gin and tonic on the rocks. Twist of lime."

Typical Tom Black, lazy fat cat, thought Johnson as he sauntered over to the cigar room's wet bar. "Why yessir, Massa' Tom, I be gettin' right on dat, sir," was his reply in the best Southern slave accent he could muster. Black snickered back.

Jaconious Johnson was the only person in Black's lonely, miserable life who could get away with talking back to him. As an idealistic, young political science major fresh out of Clark Atlanta University in the early nineties, he had landed an affirmative action, diversity program internship in the office of the wealthy and famous Georgia State Representative Tom Black, a so-called die-hard Republican and conservative at the time. He soon realized Black's fame came from having one of the highest staff turnover rates in the Georgia General Assembly. He was a complete and utter hypocrite when it came to his conservative principles.

Most of Black's staffers had averaged one year of employment under his cruel, abrasive, often sexist behavior. Others cracked after several months. Johnson's success was that he went chest-to-chest with Black early on. He got in his face, with spittle. He called the Congressman's bluff and proved that a young black kid wouldn't be intimidated. Those confrontations had earned him Black's respect.

A political opportunist, Johnson was not one to be crossed. Thereafter, he rose rapidly up the staff ladder. From events coordinator, to legislative director, to public relations director, he had absorbed Black's abuse and harassment every step of the way while delivering excellent political solutions. He was the lone survivor. Soon he morphed into a combination of confidant, personal assistant, bodyguard, and chief of staff, reaping the financial benefits that came with each new role.

Johnson ended up serving the legislator for the next fifteen years in the Georgia General Assembly. By keeping him out of jail mostly, as Black was driven by a frighteningly self-serving ambition coupled with a breathtaking sense of entitlement. Whether it was the numerous ethics or sexual harassment charges filed against him, being pulled over multiple times for drunken driving, illegal firearms possession, or the sleazy hookers he frequented, Johnson had greased the wheels of justice with Black's "contributions" and had gotten him off about every time with a slap on the wrist. He was Black's loyal "sin eater" who shielded the Congressman from responsibility for his actions and then spun the news stories to keep their constituents happy. In return, Black helped Johnson when he too went afoul of the law.

Ever since raping the girl in college, and getting away with it, Johnson had been arrested nine times for various crimes such as battery, obstructing an officer, burglary, driving with a revoked license, and probation violation. He spent a minimum time in jail and never once lost his job with Black.

Their mutually destructive, crime-ridden relationship was all about using the other for political gain while watching each other's back. It was a marriage of realpolitik and ruthlessness that had finally paid off a year ago when Black threw his finger up in the wind, saw politics blowing in a different direction, and had shockingly switched political parties to become a once-hated Democrat.

Purchasing a condo in the newly drawn 15th U.S. Congressional District and manipulating it as his primary residence, along with gaining key endorsements through bribery, he qualified for a seat on the Democrat Party ticket to represent Atlanta's most densely populated, predominantly black sections of the city.

Because of Atlanta's continual booming population the new 15th district was cut like a tiny slice of pizza from the 5th District in the northwestern downtown area. The new boundaries stretched from the Chattahoochee River and Fulton County Airport/Brown Field on the far west side to State Route 41 on its east. I-20 made up the south border while the massively sprawling Norfolk Southern railroad yard closed it in on the north.

Successful industrial complexes dotted the new district's western boundary mostly along Fulton Industrial Boulevard. The Atlanta University Center of historically black colleges and universities made up the southeast section of the district. However, on the far eastern boundary some of Atlanta's largest and wealthiest employers—Coca-Cola, the Georgia Dome, the Philips Arena, the World Congress Center, the Georgia Aquarium, and the Georgia Tech campus—that should have been included in the district were notably left out of the newly drawn lines. A strong and wealthy middle class did prosper in certain exclusive areas, but what was left in the heart of the 15th district was another world altogether; a war zone that most Atlantans had shunned or had simply forgotten.

And what Black represented.

Known as "The Bluff," the combined downtown residential neighborhoods of English Avenue and Vine City held the highest crime and poverty rates in the city while routinely being in the top five in national FBI crime statistics. Marred by high unemployment and low education, the residents of the neighborhoods suffered generation after generation of murder, gang warfare, drugs, and prostitution. And a cycle of broken promises from an array of Democratic political leaders, preachers, and community organizers supposedly looking out for their best interests.

95% black in its racial ethnic profile, The Bluff was an experiment in forced government gentrification gone wrong. After its heyday in the 1950s and 1960s, as a stout, middle-class black neighborhood, race riots and suburbanization started to drain the area of all economic vitality. The next thirty years saw public housing and economic revitalization programs fail time and again from waste, corruption, and bureaucratic incompetence until it reached its peak under the Great Recession started in 2008 precipitated by the financial meltdown of the real estate market. While the newly elected president bickered back and forth with his equally dysfunctional opponents in Congress for yet another failed economic stimulus plan, the chaotic result in Black's district was rampant unemployment at 25%. No work and no mortgage payments resulted in foreclosed homes.

The core of the once-thriving district had simply rotted out. Third- and fourth-generation, entitlement-addicted families depended on monthly welfare, disability, housing assistance, unemployment checks, food stamps, and a thriving underground of black market trade. Able-bodied but lazy to the bone, most in this lower class simply despised getting a job and earning their fair share. Most young men had dropped out or had been kicked out of high school and joined gangs, their lives shortened either through incarceration or the continued plague of black-on-black killings. Overall, those in The Bluff were the desperate throw-aways of wrenching inner-city poverty. It's no wonder Bluff meant: *"Better Leave U Fucking Fool."*

Tom Black took full advantage of their despair. Because that's where the majority of voters were.

During the 15th District election campaign he and Johnson had used fear, race, and class warfare in a hate-filled, misogynistic strategy against a popular, conservative Republican, white female CEO of a Fortune 500 company. The best she could do was call him a carpetbagger and a flip-flopper. However, then-candidate Black deftly positioned himself as the alternative racial minority because of his mixed Cherokee blood. He became another progressive Democratic savior of the economically downtrodden district, promising everything the core constituency wanted to hear to continue their status quo of government hand-outs. He was perceived as the billionaire sugar-daddy for a paternalistic entitlement society after copying the successful 2012 reelection campaign of President Barack Obama over his Republican rival Mitt Romney.

Black's exceptional political talent was delivering a convincing speech with phony charm, riling up the crowd, and making the ignorant masses believe anything he promised even though he was the epitome of everything they despised. Appearances, rhetoric, and pandering emotions are what gets politicians elected. Real world solutions do not, and Black knew this.

He was an expert snake oil salesman peddling his finest utopian remedies from a bottomless war chest.

In Johnson's estimation, what put the election over the top was the dumb, yet catchy and ambiguous campaign slogan he had personally come up with: "Backin' Black." Coupled with the rock band AC/DC's classic 1980 hit *Back in Black*, the slogan appeared everywhere. With virtually unlimited funds, they saturated the district with hip-hop celebrity concert appearances, and alcohol-filled, barbecue block parties combined with television commercials, billboards, yard signs, posters, and banners. They used social media, robo-calls, direct mailers, and outright lies to skewer their opponent in one of the nation's dirtiest, racist elections ever. Black had even resorted to handing out cold hard cash and bricks of marijuana to bribe certain constituencies with promises they would turn out the vote in return. With a tad bit of absentee-ballot voter fraud squeezed in for good measure, Black cruised to an overwhelming victory that made national headlines in the liberal controlled media as a rare example of a true Native-American serving a black constituency. He was painted as yet another Democratic hero to the poor and middle-class, this time offering them real hope and change they truly could believe in. His constituents loved him as much as Santa Claus.

Since the election win, the duo had entered the big leagues of the D.C. elite. And that's all both men really wanted. Johnson was already knee-deep in establishing a network of back-room relationships with the real power-brokers on both sides of the political aisle who ran the nation. Why Black wanted to risk his and Johnson's progress climbing the ladder on some weekend escapade of revenge against his elderly father was beyond all logical comprehension. Johnson knew Black and his father had parted ways a long time ago over embezzlement allegations and hadn't spoken since.

Couldn't he just let the old man die without twisting the blade one more time? Regardless, thought Johnson, the whole charade would soon be over once the thief arrived in Atlanta with the hat. He handed Black his gin and tonic cocktail. A "thank you" was not reciprocated, as was par for the course.

A phone in Johnson's pocket rang. It was his temporary, untraceable throw away cell phone just for this weekend's job.

"Who is it?" Black demanded.

Fed up with his boss's impatience, this time Johnson cut him an icy stare and let the phone ring a couple more times.

"Well, aren't you going to answer it?"

Johnson ignored him. Four more rings later he pressed the answer button on the old cell phone. "Go ahead," he told the caller. It was his fixer.

The fixer said the word "drop," then hung up. After pocketing the cell phone, Johnson deliberately took his time in walking back across the cigar room to his shoulder satchel containing his iPad. With a cigarette dangling out of his mouth, he turned the tablet computer on and finally looked over to his boss. "My guy. Wanna know what he said?"

"Want a hot poker shoved up your black ass?" Black bantered back, gulping half his cocktail down. He couldn't tolerate the suspense.

Johnson smirked and stubbed his cigarette out in one of the room's many ash trays. "Touché. Clever one, Tom. We've got a message awaiting. I'm accessing it now." He heard Black loudly clear his throat. Johnson simply held up an index finger for him to wait while he tapped the tablet's ultra high resolution display screen. Gmail opened and he logged in under an anonymous name to a temporary email set up only for this job. This particular email account was accessible by both Jaconious and his fixer since they both shared the same account log-in information. When one logged-out, the other could log-in. It was their way of exchanging crucial information and messages without being traced by law enforcement.

There was no message in the inbox. There never was. Instead, Johnson opened the Drafts folder—their "drop"—and found a single, unsent draft email message awaiting. By not actually sending an email from one person's account to another over the Internet and instead placing it in the Drafts folder, each party, upon logging into and out of the account, could still read the message. This simple procedure eradicated each party's electronic trail and unique IP address or internet protocol address. A string of numbers unique to a particular electronic devices such as a phone, tablet or computer accessing the internet is what makes up an IP address. It's an electronic fingerprint triggered when an email is sent. Obtaining an IP address allows authorities to track the identity of the person who sent the e-mail or even when they visited a website.

The draft email message dropped in the folder contained no subject line, nor text. There was only an attachment of a JPEG file. The National Security Agency, therefore, had no key words to illegally search under. With a tap of his finger, the attachment opened into a full screen view. Johnson's brows furrowed. He had never seen anything quite like it. He glanced up at Black.

"Well, looks like there *was* a drawing inside your hat."

"And?"

"Wanna see a picture of it?" Johnson teased.

His mouth agape, Black's underbite protruded even more. He wore an expression that said, "How dare you ask me such a stupid question." Johnson walked over and handed his boss the iPad before he exploded.

With drink in one hand, Black rested the tablet upright on his stomach and stared at the screen.

Seemingly random black markings and symbols, as if a child had drawn them, were scribbled on what appeared to be browned or aged paper. A puzzled look appeared on Black's face.

"Hell's bells! Looks like a pisspot kid drew this little map." He followed with a condescending unimpressed spitting sound then finished off his drink in three gulps. Still, he could not accept that the waybill existed.

"That's a map?" asked Johnson.

Black's upper lip curled in disappointing rage. Childhood memories of his father's treasure map stories flooded his head. "The old geezer wasn't full of shit after all," he sputtered to himself. "I'll be damned."

"*This* is the real reason you arranged to get the hat, isn't it?"

"No. I just wanted the hat, period," mumbled Black, staring at the screen. "Seriously. The hat's a symbol to me. A trophy in fact. Like a hunter mounts a head on a wall. This waybill or map or whatever it is, however," he said, tapping the screen, "was a lost memory I never believed in. It was an Indian legend. To me it was crap and caused a lot of animosity you could say, between me, my father and even his father. It's the moment I lost respect in their eyes. Guess you could say it's karma, me possessing it now. It's sort of like a bonus." Black chuckled for a moment. "With my fuck-you money."

Upon closer examination of the waybill he realized it was a smaller, cropped portion of a larger image. "There's more here we're not seeing. Tell your man I want the thief to send the *whole* waybill. All of it."

Black placed the tablet computer on an exquisite end table/cabinet cigar humidor. It was ergonomically positioned next to his recliner so he could simply pull the top drawer out without sitting up. Out of the five hundred plus cigars stored in the humidor he picked the absolute best for his little coup: a Dunhill Estupendos from Cuba. Rolled in 1983 this cigar was one of the finest cigars ever made, having been rated a perfect 100 by *Cigar Aficionado* magazine. He had purchased eight of them at auction for a staggering $2,000 each.

Johnson used his older temporary cell phone again to call the fixer back with the immediate request for the full waybill to be sent. After hanging up, he stated, "Now we wait, again, and hope the contractor complies."

Black sighed with impatience and proceeded to trim the cap off the luxury cigar with gold-plated clippers. A piece of tobacco fell on the tiled floor, left for the cleaning staff. He placed the cigar in his mouth and lit the end with a gold Butane lighter he had produced from the humidor. Rolling the cigar while he puffed it, the end flamed with every breath until it was uniformly burning with a bright orange glow. He blew out several thick aromatic smoke rings, smacked his lips at the taste, placed the lighter on the table, grabbed his empty cocktail glass, and jiggled it so the ice clinked obnoxiously loud.

"Get me another drink."

Johnson complied.

While waiting, Black picked up Johnson's iPad once more and inspected the waybill image again. Smoke drifted from his mouth as memories became clearer. His eyes narrowed, then glazed over, lost in the past, back to his teens when he and his father started having their personality clashes. "You know, I think we're going to fly down to Savannah this afternoon," he announced abruptly.

"Now?" Johnson gasped from behind the wet bar. "I thought you wanted to wait until the hat arrives tomorrow morning and then we make arrangements to visit your old man. Wasn't that the plan?"

"It was. But things have changed since the waybill really exists." With a grunt Black leaned forward to the upright position in his recliner. "I just now remembered the old man telling me about a particular item that goes hand-in-hand with reading these waybill symbols. It's an old Bowie knife that acts as the key to deciphering them. I'm going to personally emancipate it with my own hands."

"What, you?" Johnson questioned with a fake unbelievable look on his face. "Stealing from your own father? Say it ain't so."

"I know exactly where the shithead keeps it," Black explained as he took several more puffs then carefully rubbed out his barely smoked cigar, saving it for later. "He's got this sacred ancestor room in his house with a bunch of war artifacts as a shrine dedicated to the Watie men. He never let anything leave that room. Loved it more than he loved his own son." He paused in anger. "I fucking hated that room. It's like their family Hall of Fame. I was never good enough." He went silent again.

"I'm going to waltz in there on an unexpected visit to check on his *well-being*." Black used air quotes to emphasize his hypocrisy. "The timing is perfectly legit given the fact he's almost dead. If I run into anyone, I simply say I've come to make amends. The long lost son, now a successful, celebrity congressman coming to pay his last respects." He laughed at his sarcasm. "I have every right to be inside that house. Besides, don't worry.

He'll be in the hospital. Old man with a heart attack. Shit. He'll be in there all week. But I'm gonna get me that fucking knife of his, that much is for damn sure."

Wasting no time Black slipped his dress shoes back on and stood up to adjust his pants and tie. Spiffed up as best he could, he indicated he wanted to leave immediately.

"You really want to do this now?" Johnson asked in all seriousness.

Black was already dialing on his cell phone. Without looking up he replied, "I've done it before to him. It's a breeze. Trust me."

His phone up to his ear, Black spoke to the pilot of his private airplane. "Adam? Prep the Piper Meridian. Immediate departure." He paused, listening to a question. "Yes, today. No, not Washington. We're going down to Savannah. As soon as you can arrange it." Black frowned, listening again. "I don't give a fuck if it's your wife's birthday! You're paid to be on call." He paused again, smiling. "Apology accepted." He listened to another question. "No, this ain't a public show. We'll keep it on the downlow. Give Myers Airpark a shout. It's a private strip we can land at. I'm golfing buddies with the owner. He owes me. It's just a few miles from the city. Have him arrange a car for me, too." The pilot had one more question. "Me and Jaconious," Black answered. "We're on our way now."

Still standing behind the wet bar, Black's gin and tonic refill in hand, Johnson stood transfixed, jaw dropped.

Black pocketed his cell phone and grabbed his suit coat. "Forty-five minute flight down. In and out from the ancestor room. Forty-five minute flight back. And then once the hat and waybill arrive here in Atlanta, we're going to plan a treasure hunt in the north Georgia mountains, my friend."

"Huh?"

"There's gold in them thar hills, Jaconious," said Black waddling off into his house. He had mimicked the famous line associated with America's first gold rush in Dahlonega, Georgia starting in 1828. That discovery of gold by the white man—although already long known by the Cherokee—would be the demise of the Cherokee Nation. Within a decade their lands would be confiscated and their people forced west on the Trail of Tears to their new home in the Indian Territory. A brutal internal civil war would follow pitting Black's ancestors in the Watie clan with the John Ross clan. "I'll tell you all about it on our way to DeKalb-Peachtree Airport. We'll go in style. Pull my Camaro around front," Black ordered, his back turned.

"Tom, this is bullshit! There's too much risk involved for you personally. We need to delegate this. Let me hire someone local in Savannah to go in and lift the Bowie knife instead of you."

Black spun around and plodded back to Johnson at the wet bar. His copper face had turned burgundy red, contorted in an ugly, evil grimace. He pointed an index finger right in Johnson's face.

"Revenge is more satisfying when the long-feared Raven Mocker unexpectedly arrives at the door of his victim. You know who told me that?" he asked, retracting his finger. "My own father!" Black took a breath. "It's how I'm going to pay him back for murdering the good-looking, happy young man I used to be. I've never forgotten." He produced a sinister laugh. "Oh, the cruel irony of it all. I'm going to be my father's Raven Mocker."

Black turned and left the room.

Drink still in hand, Johnson stood dumbfounded, not knowing what the hell a Raven Mocker was. But worse: his boss was talking patricide for some past dysfunction. He was talking murder.

He shrugged. *Well, wouldn't be the first time.* "So be it," he said out loud, and tipped the cocktail glass, draining it all down his throat.

Several minutes later he pulled Black's $400,000, 1,500-horsepower, customized, late model, Camaro SS convertible around to the front circle. The top was down and he relished the rare opportunity to sit behind the wheel. The heavily waxed, black, luxury sports car was a limited edition model with only one hundred made. Black had purchased the third car off the assembly line, had the workers apply his vanity plate that read "BLACK," and then drove it home.

As the Congressman approached from the house, he flipped a thumb over his shoulder for Johnson to get out from behind the wheel. Johnson cursed under his breath, slipped out of the idling muscle car, kept the driver's door open, and stepped aside as his boss entered his prized possession.

7

THE TWO HOUR FLIGHT DOWN FROM ROCHESTER, New York to Savannah, Georgia was on time and uneventful as Jake and Rae's commercial airliner made its final descent into Georgia's oldest city. As expected, Jake had gotten the green travel light from the director of the Military History Institute after he briefed him on their role in the investigation. Also, before boarding Jake had received a call from Paxton at West Point confirming the Savannah 9-1-1 report on Friday night that Tommy Black Watie IV was, in fact, a legit person. His story checked out, along with his address. Additionally, they found out he'd been released early from the hospital so he was expected to be at home.

Jake and Rae spent the bulk of their first-class flight time trying to dig up as much as they could on the Watie family history. Jake was particularly interested in the claims Tommy had made about his grandfather Thomas Black Watie Jr., and how the waybill ended up in McPherson's hat. Headphones on and taking copious notes, he and Rae listened over and over again to the original phone conversation that was recorded. With electronic device restrictions recently lifted for airline flights, Jake also directed his crack team of MHI staff researchers to delve into their institute's Civil War archives for any corroborating materials.

As they approached the Savannah/Hilton Head International Airport, their minds were armed with valuable background information for the upcoming surprise visit with Watie. A smooth touch down of their airplane, a short taxi to the main terminal, and they were soon walking the corridor to baggage claim.

A quick text message from Paxton informed them a High Mobility Multipurpose Wheeled Vehicle (HMMWV), also known as the Humvee, the military's modern version of a workhorse, would be curbside outside of baggage claim awaiting their arrival. An Army Criminal Investigation Division (CID) special agent, assigned to the pair, would be on the look out for them.

Travel bags in hand after a short wait in baggage claim, the pair now headed outside. Jake immediately placed his black beret on his head and donned his sunglasses before strolling through the automatic sliding doorway exits. He was dressed in his impressively crisp, blue Class "A" Army Service Uniform, which was required for most workday situations and informal public functions. A four-in-hand black necktie with white dress shirt underneath, a dark blue, almost black coat, dark blue trousers with a gold stripe up the sides, and highly polished black dress shoes rounded out his attire.

This new "Army Blue" uniform had officially replaced the green uniform just a few years back. Dating back to the Revolutionary War and George Washington's Continental Army, blue uniforms helped identify the rebels on the battlefield from their British Army enemy in red coats. Blue also recalled the Union Army's uniforms during the Civil War. All over Jake's dark blue coat were pinned the required ribbons, badges, insignia, tabs, tags, and medals showing military campaigns in which he had participated, specialized skills obtained, and service awards for exceptional bravery.

The main medals included a Silver Star, and a Purple Heart with an Oak Leaf Cluster for two wounds sustained in combat. Under those awards was a Ranger pin denoting advanced intelligence and warfare training. On his coat's right front was his current unit insignia of the Military History Institute. On top of each shoulder was his rank insignia of Lieutenant Colonel: two silver oak leafs per shoulder strap.

But on Jake's right hand ring finger was the one "unofficial" piece of personal jewelry that he wore with pride wherever he went: a gold ring with a distinctive badge of its own. He used to wear the symbol as a tiny lapel pin on his official uniform as a deliberate rebellious act against Pentagon authority and its absurd bureaucracy, but after a friendly reprimand by his director, it was deemed way too politically incorrect and he could face official punishment. Instead, Rae gave him his new gold ring as a birthday gift, as a way of circumventing the strict rules against individuality in the ranks and a way to communicate with others who he was.

It was a badge once worn in combat, most notably during the Civil War, to identify the wearer that he was part of a special brotherhood that even his enemy would recognize. This ancient fraternity transcended state loyalties and if a brother happened to fall into the hands of his enemy, who was also part of the secret organization, he could expect respite and preferred treatment if his character was deemed trustworthy. Many of the signers of the Declaration of Independence, many U.S. Presidents, and many WWII Army generals were all part of this fraternity. Some of the most notable names being: Mark Clark, James Doolittle, Omar Bradley, Douglas MacArthur, George Marshall, and George Patton. Jake's ring bore a raised letter G with three tiny diamonds. Surrounding the letter, which meant God or Geometry, depending on the wearer, were the symbols of a builder's square and measuring compasses.

It was the mark of a Freemason.

And many older combat veterans Jake had spoken to instantly recognized the ring and the Mason's mark when they shook hands. This was the key introduction, for if another man was a Freemason he would then shake hands with Jake in a secret manner with a subtle relocation of a certain finger that denoted he, too, was part of the brotherhood. It served both parties to instantly become comfortable with each other as sharing a bond that each understood, a way of breaking the ice with a stranger or reconnecting with a friend.

Sunny, late afternoon humid weather greeted the pair. The temperature was eighty-two, but with the high humidity it felt like someone had turned the oven on. A slight breeze from the salt marshes, just miles from the airport along the Savannah River, offered slight comfort. With sunset soon approaching, the sky had changed to a light lavender backdrop. Rae fluffed up her hair as it caught in the breeze. She had on an open neck, light blue dress shirt, black dress slacks, and matching shoes.

Not fifty feet away to their left, parked curbside, was a newer model hardback Humvee painted in a forest camouflage scheme of dark green, brown, and black. An oversized protective bumper donned the front of the world-recognizable, wide grill that distinguished this rugged truck from its predecessor, the Jeep. Mounted on top was a thin bar of red and blue law enforcement lights. A soldier dressed in an Army Combat Uniform of the tan, gray, and green blended Universal Camouflage Pattern leaned against the side of the vehicle and faced the airport. A simple Velcro patch with the legend "CID" worn on his left arm above his division's shoulder sleeve insignia—along with his holstered SIG Sauer 9mm firearm—identified him from a distance as Military Police. He, too, wore a black beret and sunglasses. His young, white face showed a sharp, muscular jaw line and a distinctly Italian-looking nose. With arms across his chest, he scanned the crowd looking for his guest arrivals.

The CID agent finally glanced far to his left and caught the pair approaching. He stood at attention and saluted Jake as he walked up. Jake saluted back and the agent lowered his arm, placing his hands to his side, chest puffed out. Jake noticed no rank insignia on the agent's uniform. A mere "U.S." patch centered his chest where a rank would have been displayed. Both men stared each other down behind sunglasses, faces expressionless.

The agent finally broke the ice. "Colonel, I'm Sergeant First Class Marco D'Arata, Special Agent with the Criminal Investigations Division out of Hunter Army Airfield. I've been reassigned to be your direct liaison to Lieutenant Colonel Cliff Paxton up at West Point. It's my pleasure to be working with you on this case, sir."

Unflinching, Jake continued to stare at the soldier. Rae shifted nervously behind him wondering what the pissing contest was all about.

The two men then smiled simultaneously with wide, shit-eating grins. They shook hands heartily, a finger on each of their hands relocated in a split second denoting membership in their shared brotherhood.

Jake grasped the sergeant's shoulder. "Great to see you, Marco!"

"You too, Colonel," the sergeant said with relief. "Christ, you had me there for a second, you dick. When I was notified you were coming down here I pulled out the stops to be assigned to you."

"Am I relieved," Jake agreed. "I was wondering if we were going to get some green gomer. I had no friggin' idea you were stationed here." Jake turned to introduce Rae.

"Marco, my lovely sweetie peaches pie, Rae Hart," he said with an affectionate snort. An embarrassed Rae gave the sergeant a firm handshake.

"Pleasure to meet you." She turned to Jake with lips parted. "Lovely sweetie peaches pie? What the hell's that?" She cracked him hard on the arm and raised an index finger. "I'm going to get you back, Mister." Rae turned to D'Arata and shook her head. "We've been one-upping each other with cheesy nicknames and the big jerk here just took the lead. I take it you guys served together?"

The sergeant reached for her bag while answering her. "Yes, ma'am. Tenth Mountain Division. We deployed together in Afghanistan." He stowed her luggage in the rear hatch. "That big jerk there was my company commander at the time. Then we were sent to Iraq and when he joined the task force to hunt Saddam Hussein, he took me on his intelligence staff. Started my career in investigations. And it's all his fault."

"And now, you're returning the favor," Jake said to the sergeant as he opened the back door for Rae to step up and in.

With luggage stowed, Jake in the front passenger seat and Rae in back, D'Arata was already pulling the Humvee out of the airport pick-up lane.

"Sorry I'm not dressed better, sir. Everything came down the pipe today on short notice. Normally, I'd be in a nice suit."

"No problem."

"What's the command group your with out of Hunter?" asked Rae.

"3rd Military Police Group Headquarters," D'Arata explained. "We conduct criminal investigations of felony level, serious, sensitive or special interest matters in the eastern half of the United States."

"This case fits that bill," Jake said.

"That's a huge area of operations," Rae commented.

"Sure is, ma'am," D'Arata said, glancing at her in the rear view mirror.

"First order of business then," D'Arata said. "You both carrying?"

"Roger that," Jake replied.

"Ten-four," Rae chimed in.

Both had already rearmed themselves with their concealed firearms. Jake carried an Army-issued Beretta M-9 pistol under his coat in a hip holster. Rae had a New York State registered Ruger LC9 in a waistband holster concealed at the small of her back under her shirt.

"TSA give you any problems, ma'am? Especially coming from New York State? Their reciprocity laws are among the worst in the nation."

"No problem. New York finally added Georgia to their list," Rae said. "And if you call me *ma'am* one more time I'm going to rudely acquaint you with my Ruger."

D'Arata laughed hard. "I think we'll get along just fine, *Rae*." He then gunned the Humvee's engine and headed toward State Route 21 to downtown Savannah, not ten miles away.

▼

Cherokee Rose Manor
Savannah Historic District

After touching down at Myers Airpark, a private airstrip fifteen miles southwest of Savannah, Tom Black and Jaconious Johnson immediately hopped into a Lincoln Towncar courtesy of the strip's owner. Black's plane would remain on standby ready to take them back to Atlanta as soon as they returned.

Before setting out, the fixer finally called. It wasn't good news. The fixer said the thief was playing hardball and refused to send the entire waybill image. They would have to wait until he delivered the hat and waybill in whole to Atlanta in person. Black was in no position to argue and relented in his demands.

In less than twenty minutes, the duo had already entered the Historic

Landmark District of Savannah from the southside where Black ordered Johnson to head north up Drayton Street. Forsyth Park was on their left. Just past the park they took a sharp left onto West Gordon Lane, a narrow brick-paved service alleyway behind the tightly packed backsides and garages of the houses fronting West Gordon and West Gaston Streets. Two blocks west, down the dumpster filled alley, lined with off-kilter utility poles, the Lincoln stopped at the second to last house on the right in front of a closed, one-bay garage.

With dark hat and sunglasses concealing his face, Black stepped out and immediately walked over to a five foot high, brick wall enclosing the back of the house, the wall spilling over with three more feet of overgrown ivy. A magnolia tree with large, creamy white flowers and oily-looking, dark, green leaves towered over the nicely hidden backyard. He then disappeared behind a shadowy nook in the wall, out of direct view of any watchful neighbors' rear windows. Johnson took off with the Lincoln and made a left on Whitaker where he'd wait for his boss behind the Georgia Historical Society, their predetermined rendezvous spot, not a block south.

Black now stood at the backyard entrance to his father's home: Cherokee Rose Manor. This was hardly a lavish home as the name implied. When his Civil War ancestor, Thomas Black Watie Jr. had it constructed in 1873 upon settling in Savannah, he considered it an appropriate name at the time. In reality, it was a very typical, narrow and long, two-story city home with a Georgian side hall floor plan and an Italianate brick façade. At a mere 24 foot in width and length of only 73 foot, the rectangular house was sandwiched tight between two, much taller, three-story homes which were definitely considered the stately manors Savannah was famous for. The only area where one could walk on the outside of the house was the small backyard which led to the lane and garage. It was right where the wayward son was now standing.

A rarely used iron gate was barely visible among the overgrown ivy on the wall. It was locked. Black had to work fast. He pulled aside the ivy and scanned the wall for a brick with lettering on it. There were many. But after a nervous thirty seconds of searching he finally found the right one. Engraved on the red brick was "C.C. Stratton & Co Brick," the faded name of the Macon, Georgia-based brick company that supplied many of the bricks for Savannah's buildings and homes. This particular brick however, was cracked in half and crumbling at the corners, the mortar having long since been separated.

It had been deliberately broken and hidden in plain sight by Black many years ago as a means to gain access to his father's house without his parents knowing.

Grabbing a finger hole on the bottom edge of half a brick, he shimmied it back and forth until it slipped out of the wall. On the reverse side of the brick was a carved notch holding a hidden key.

Right where I've always kept it. And where the cops could never find it.

Unlocking the gate, Black replaced the half brick and concealed it again behind the ivy. But he kept the key. He entered the small backyard at the rear of his father's house and slowly closed the gate.

He was back in Cherokee Rose Manor.

Sweat from his forehead began to roll.

Quickly advancing on a paved path, lined on both sides with tall shrubs of fragrant blossoms made of pure white petals and gold centers, anyone could see why the name of the house was appropriate. Cherokee roses were dotted everywhere, almost as if snow had fallen upon their bright, glossy green and glabrous leaflets. The State of Georgia flower, it was also tied to the infamous Trail of Tears march when the Cherokee were forced to relocate out West in 1838. Legend said when the women shed tears along the dangerous and deadly route that white petals would appear representing the women's grief and hardship. The flower's gold center also symbolized the gold stolen from the Cherokee and the real reason why the government confiscated their native homelands.

Greed.

He made his way to the main house, brushing up against many densely packed flowers and getting yellow pollen dust on his black sport coat. Slowly he stepped up a narrow rear staircase under a covered back porch to a windowed back door that gave entrance to the kitchen. He hid to one side, out of view, breathing hard. Memories swirled in his head. It all seemed so weird to him, like a déjà vu in crime.

It had been over thirty years since he had last stepped foot on this rear porch and had broken in. That was his last time stealing artifacts from his father's war collection and selling them on the black market. He was finally caught trying to deal the stolen goods and his life took a scandalous downward spiral soon after.

The bottom came when his father disowned him.

Calmly stowing his sunglasses inside a coat pocket, he tipped his hat up and peered inside the window to look for movement in the kitchen.

He saw no one.

Next he looked for signs, stickers, a keypad, or cameras indicating the place was protected by an electronic home security system. Johnson had warned him to be on the lookout for that. Remarkably, all indications were that his father had nothing of the sort.

He tried the door.

Locked.

▼

Entering Savannah's Historic District from the northwest, CID Special Agent D'Arata drove his Humvee due east on Bay Street, paralleling the Savannah River and the famous cobblestone River Street on their left.

"Oh my God, that is something!" Rae said, as she caught sight of a massive cargo ship out her side window. Making its way up river toward them was a Maersk Line Triple E container vessel coming into port. This was the largest class shipping vessel in the world. Packed tightly and stacked eight containers high with hundreds of multi-colored intermodal containers able to fit on a railroad car or tractor trailer, the freighter and its bridge superstructure towered over the old stone warehouses and brick buildings that lined the original colonial waterfront area of Savannah. "Seems so close you could reach out and touch it."

Jake looked over and his eyes widened. "Looks like a skyscraper that fell on its side. That is just massive!"

His last word was drowned out by a deafening, low-pitched, prolonged blast of the ship's horn as it gave notice it was entering port and soon would be passing under Savannah's Talmadge Memorial cable-stayed bridge.

"You ever been to Savannah before, Rae?" asked D'Arata as the horn died down.

"No, my first time here."

"Hon, it's simply a beautiful city, the Historic District that is. Tons of architectural treasures," Jake said. "Georgia's oldest city, too. Over there, check out the live oak trees and Spanish moss."

"Just gorgeous," Rae replied as she placed a hand on Jake's shoulder. "I hear Savannah is America's number one romance destination, too. How come you never booked us a trip down here, Big Boy?"

"Ahhh, well," Jake stammered, looking for an answer. "Maybe because I'm afraid of ghosts? It's America's most haunted city, too, ya know?"

"Yeah, you afraid of ghosts," Rae bantered back. "Sure." She lightly flicked his ear lobe.

"This section on our left here is the waterfront district," D'Arata chimed in. "Pretty much full of tourists all day and all night. River Street gets clogged tight like one big party. You can even walk around with a drink in your hand."

"It's like one of only three cities in the U.S. where you can do that, right?" Jake said.

"Yep. Las Vegas and New Orleans are the other two."

"Maybe we should come on down here later tonight, huh Jake?" Rae asked. "Grab a drink or two or three?"

Jake nodded. "Or four. Already planned out. I booked us a room at the Olde Harbour Inn right on River Street overlooking the river."

"Hotshot!" D'Arata chuckled.

"See, I can be romantic."

Rae snickered. "I'll be the judge of that, Casanova."

"A few more blocks and we'll head south on Whitaker to Watie's place," announced D'Arata.

Rae tapped D'Arata on the right shoulder. "What's his address?"

"21 West Gordon Street. His place is called Cherokee Rose Manor. The address puts him up near the Mercer-Williams House."

"No idea where that is," Jake stated while Rae typed the address in her iPhone Google Maps app.

D'Arata pointed to the map compartment on the dash. "Look in there. There's an illustrated map of the historic district on top."

Jake opened the compartment and grabbed a folded map brochure with an Americana-style logo design on the front cover with the title *Savannah Historic District Illustrated Map*. He unfolded it to poster size revealing a colorful, birds-eye-view illustration of the district. The map was also chock full of history factoids, images, and statues of popular attractions. "Awesome map. Ah, let's see, so, we're on Bay Street, right?"

"Yes," D'Arata said, glancing over and pointing. "We're running parallel to River Street. And then we'll head all the way south down Whitaker Street toward Forsyth Park. Watie lives near Monterey Square."

"Oh, I see it," Jake nodded, his nose deep into the map.

"I've got it, too," Rae said, showing Jake her phone. "On my phone."

"Sorry. This map rocks. Print will never die."

Just then D'Arata got a call on his cell phone. "Sergeant D'Arata here. Yes sir, Colonel Paxton. They're both with me. Uh, huh. ETA to Watie's in approximately five minutes. Okay." D'Arata placed the call on speaker and set it down in the space between the front seats. "You're on, sir."

Lieutenant Colonel Cliff Paxton's voice filled the inside of the Humvee. "We've got a person-of-interest I wanted to bounce off you. Someone we haven't been able to find when we detained all of the visitors. Can you hear me okay?"

"Go ahead, Colonel. You're good," Jake said.

"After reviewing security video at the museum we noticed there was a bit of a commotion when the early crowd entered this morning and were going through the metal detector."

D'Arata made a right onto Whitaker Street and headed south while Jake and Rae nodded toward the cell phone, anticipating more.

Paxton continued. "An older vet walked through the detector fine, nothing was set off. But he really took exception when one of the security guards tried taking his wooden cane away. Jim Ryan said they do this for safety and liability reasons after a visitor with a cane fell down the stairs a year ago. So they offer a scooter for the older visitors and those with disabilities. But this guy made a big fuss of it and wouldn't give up his cane. Had an argument with the guard, got the other visitors on his side. The guard relented and ultimately the vet limped away with his cane. Make a long story short, we interviewed the guard and he said almost everyone takes the scooter option. But if a guest balks then they usually give in. Sort of an unenforced policy if guests put up a stink. Especially if they're vets."

Rae pounced first. "How did you know he was a vet, Colonel?"

"The guard said he noticed an Army lapel pin. And the man said he had a Purple Heart from World War II. I'm going by my interview notes here. Umm," Paxton paused. "He bragged that he was, um, surrounded by Germans during the Battle of the Bulge. At Bastogne, in fact. Guard asked him what unit. Vet replied 82nd Airborne. And then went on that it would probably be his first and last time visiting the museum. Guard gave him back his cane."

"Boy, this guy really laid it on thick to keep that cane," replied D'Arata.

"My thoughts exactly, Sergeant," Paxton agreed. "A little too much information, maybe? And the fact that he's nowhere to be found sort of raised my hair a bit."

"Wait a second!" Jake said, excitedly. "What unit did he say he was with in Bastogne?"

Paxton reiterated it was the 82nd Airborne Division.

"Bull. Shit!" Jake shouted, shaking his head. "That's bullshit. It was the 101st Airborne surrounded at Bastogne. The 82nd was well to the north on the left flank of the bulge."

"Crap!" Paxton gasped. "How could I miss that?"

"Look at it this way, you're the one who had a funny feeling on this guy," Jake said, trying to comfort the provost marshal for making such an embarrassing error. "You just may have blown this case wide open."

"Precisely why I asked you guys on board. To catch stuff like this I wouldn't know," Paxton mumbled, still pissed at himself for not catching such a well-known Army historical fact in a legendary battle. "I studied law and public administration, not history."

"Colonel, what was this old vet wearing upon entry," Rae asked.

"Umm, just a minute," Paxton replied. "I've got the video here in front of me. Just need to back it up a little. Umm, okay." There was a pause and a nasty obscenity shouted. "He was wearing a black fedora," the Colonel admitted in a low voice.

"Same one found on McPherson's mannequin, I'll wager," Jake said.

Another self-directed obscenity from Paxton was heard.

"Track that vet in all of your security video, sir," Rae instructed, as she leaned forward to speak. "Two things to look for. His fedora is the obvious. If you can see when it comes off, or doesn't, will determine if it's *his* hat or *not* on the mannequin. The other subtle clue is the limp."

Both Jake and D'Arata nodded their heads in an "a-ha" moment.

"It's a tell-tale sign if he really depended on that cane throughout his entire visit," Rae continued. "Or used it for something else. Like smashing display cases? You not finding him during your roundup also tells me he must have exited early once the alarms went off. Take into account his age. He may have been confused with the chaos all around him. Panicked even. So be sure to check all exterior video feeds to confirm he actually did make it out. For all we know he may have gotten so scared from all the smoke and fire he simply freaked out and went home, or back to his hotel, or even out for a cup of coffee."

"Got it," Paxton said. "Good stuff, guys. Real good stuff."

"Sir, what's his physical description?" D'Arata asked.

"White male. Early nineties. Blotchy skin. Tinted glasses. We have a pretty good close up image on his face."

Jake nodded. "Could you send that image to us? Like right away?"

"I'll take a picture of the video with my cell phone right now. Wait, you don't think—?"

"Well, it's a big maybe," Jake said. "Your old vet may in fact be *our* old man down here."

D'Arata turned with a perplexed look on his face just as he stopped at a red light. "Huh, how's that?"

"Yeah, how so?" Rae repeated. "There's no way a frail old man with a confirmed heart attack Friday night here in Savannah could pull this off."

"All I know is I get a call early this morning before the museum opens from an old man who is persistent in finding out about a waybill in McPherson's hat. Sure, it was a 912 Savannah area code in his phone number, and I remember asking him where he was calling from and he did say Savannah, but that doesn't mean he really *was* in Savannah. He could have been right there at West Point. If he found out we *did* find a waybill in the hat then maybe he calls off his theft knowing the waybill would most likely be in an archive drawer or something, you know? Out of reach. But I told him we found *nothing* and then not two hours later the museum is robbed. Maybe he felt like if we didn't find anything in the hat then it could still be inside it. I did tell him we did not look in the liner of the hat. That's why I called on Ryan to check it out. But he was too late."

"Whoa!" D'Arata said and stepped on the gas with a green light. "And it's doable him catching a plane from New York City back down here to Savannah this afternoon. If he's even here!"

"Hmm, I dunno, Jake," Rae said, pursing her lips.

"Worth probing Mr. Watie about," Paxton said in a static-filled voice over the cell phone. "See if he has a legit alibi for yesterday and today."

"Listen," Jake agreed. "I know it's wild speculation. Once we get his face shot we can compare images. We'll see if he walks with a limp and even has a cane, too. And I'll ask about the Army unit he served with in Europe. Said he was with Patton I recall. If it's not him, it's not him."

"And if it's not him we'll see if he recognizes the man in the West Point camera as someone he does know," D'Arata offered.

"My thoughts exactly," Paxton said in a broken voice. "I just messaged the face shot to your phone, Sergeant."

D'Arata leaned over to talk in the phone. "Roger that. Good timing. We're almost at Watie's."

"Colonel, one last thing cause you're breaking up," Rae said. "Tommy Watie has a real deep Southern accent. Ask that security guard if he detected that on his old vet."

"Okay, I'll get back to you with my findings. Good luck with your interview. Out." With that, Paxton ended the call.

All three were silent, their respective investigative minds spinning.

"I tell you what," Jake said, breaking the silence. "Sounds like Paxton has our man pegged. Lying about Bastogne. Won't give up the cane.

Wearing a fedora."

The Humvee motored past the Mercer-Williams House and made a left onto West Gordon Street. "We're here," announced D'Arata, abruptly wheeling into a parking spot in front of a narrow, two-story, brick Italianate style townhouse wedged between two much larger, grander homes.

Jake unstrapped his seat belt and looked at D'Arata in all seriousness. "An old Seneca clanmother once told me, 'too many coincidences is not a coincidence. Something is begging to be revealed.'"

Rae nodded, knowing full well who that clanmother was.

D'Arata's phone chimed with an alert of a new message. He looked down at his phone and saw a picture on screen of an old veteran's smirking face. He wore a black fedora and glasses. D'Arata held up the phone for the other two to see. "We'll soon find out," he remarked.

▼

Let's hope that old piece of shit didn't change the lock over the years.

Black held his breath and inserted the key. A twist and the dead bolt unlocked. "Bingo," he whispered. *Just like old times.* Pocketing the key with a shaking hand, he turned the doorknob slowly and pushed the door inward to enter the dark kitchen.

As he stepped inside, a long creak on the floor welcomed the estranged son back to his childhood home. He softly clicked the door shut behind him and stood silent on the tiled floor, listening for anyone moving about the house. The kitchen was sparkling clean. No dishes in the sink. Not even fruit on the table.

Straight ahead was an open door that led to a heavily shadowed main hallway which ran the length of the house all the way to the front entrance. Early evening light spilled in from the front stained-glass door at the end.

He crept his way slowly into the hallway, a long stair case to the upper bedrooms on his left. He noticed a chair lift had been installed, obviously to help his elderly father get up and down. He paused, glancing upward and listened again.

Nothing. It was eerily quiet. So much so he could even hear a truck pass by outside at the front of the house.

To his immediate right was a closed wooden door. He tried the locking mechanism, a warded lock containing a large keyhole, the original from when the house was built. It, too, was locked, but this one was expected.

Black bent down on one knee, pushed his hat back on his head, and pressed his eye against the keyhole to peer in. A faded Confederate battle flag standing next to a large, oak antique desk in front of a set of shuttered windows with barely visible light filtering through confirmed the ancestor room was still intact. It beckoned him to enter once again.

A deep familiar voice suddenly crooned from an upstairs bedroom. It filled the balcony space overlooking the hallway where he stood below.

And now, the end is near;
And so I face the final curtain.
My friend, I'll say it clear,
I'll state my case, of which I'm certain.
I've lived a life that's full.

I've traveled each and ev'ry highway;
But more, much more than this,
I did it . . . my way.

It was Frank Sinatra's classic 1969 song "My Way." Black froze, for he knew his father was now home. *Yeah, you did it your way alright. Your way or the highway.* He utterly loathed his father's favorite song as typical self-justification for being the stubborn, difficult, drunken old buzzard that he was. Then he realized how close the apple had actually landed from the tree and it made him even more pissed off. This heart-pounding anger, combined with an adrenaline kick of the thrill associated with stealing once again, caused him to sweat even more. His shirt and pants stuck to his body. He could even smell his own ripe body odor rising.

Must act fast.

This was the final curtain alright. Get in and get out of the ancestor room before the old man came down and wandered about the house.

Black dug into a pocket and produced a skeleton key he'd brought with him from his own house. He made the key himself, back in the days of stealing from his parent's secret money stash contained within the room, which then led him to later pilfer his father's historical war artifacts. His key was another hard piece of evidence neither investigators nor his father had ever discovered. In fact, they never did figure out how he had entered the locked ancestor room for he was never caught red-handed, but instead his bust came while cutting a deal in Charleston with a well-known antique arms collector.

The key worked, as always. And with a twist of the bolt he was in. He clenched his teeth as the door creaked loudly. *Jesus!* Then he eased it shut behind him with a click. Sinatra's song faded.

Quickly looking about in the darkened room, chock full of war memorabilia, he couldn't believe he was in there again. Wasting no time, he went for his prize. Over to the fireplace on his right, up on the mantle he looked. The knife would be in a glass and wood display box.

The door bell suddenly rang.

Sinatra stopped. Black spun around and reopened the door to listen. *Shit. Shit. Shit.*

▼

Sergeant D'Arata stood behind Jake and Rae on the raised, covered front porch of the beautifully decorative home of Tommy Watie. He leaned on a highly ornate, wrought iron railing designed with floral patterns reminiscent of a Cherokee rose. As Jake buzzed the door bell again, D'Arata stole a peek inside one of the tall, three-bay windows that fronted the house.

"Don't see anyone about."

"He's old," said Rae. "Give him a minute."

Jake had his hands cupped over the front door's stained glass window peering through a small clear section. "Someone's coming down the stairs." He stepped back and straightened his uniform and beret.

The door opened about a foot and a large-boned, black woman, dressed in a nursing uniform of a matching white shirt and pants, appeared with raised eyebrows. She seemed taken aback. "Yes? Can I help y'all?"

Jake spoke, introducing himself as being with the Military History Institute and asking if this was the residence of Tommy Watie. The woman nodded. He then asked if Mr. Watie was at home and inquired if they could speak with him.

"What's this in regards to? Mr. Tommy's a very sick man and I'm under strict doctor's orders not to disturb him."

"Ma'am, Mr. Watie telephoned me this morning inquiring about a Civil War hat that appeared on a television show we co-hosted this last Friday night." Jake turned toward Rae as he spoke. The nurse followed his gaze in the same direction and Rae gave a slight nod to the nurse. The nurse's eyes widened. "We just flew in from New York to follow up with him in person. I promise we'll only be a few minutes. If we could just . . ."

The nurse whipped open the door and pointed a finger at Jake. "I knew I recognized y'all!" She said loudly. "You're that couple from *Battlefield Investigators*. Done gave him a heart attack!"

Jake looked at Rae and cringed.

The nurse placed her hands on her hips and blocked the entrance. She seemed to now berate him. "My Lord, he made me watch your show again and again after that. Something about some ol' general's hat got him all going. And then he made me track down your phone number." She then relented and her voice sweetened like brown sugar as she stepped aside. "Y'all come in now. He just woke up from a very long day of napping. He's gonna be just thrilled you're here in person. He loves your show to no end. Uh, huh."

The trio spilled into the front foyer of a long wainscoted hallway stained in a rich, dark hue. Stairs on their right led to the second floor and a balcony overlooking the hall. The two military men took off their head cover and held them under their left arms.

"I'm his private nurse, Becky Holden," the black woman said, introducing herself as she closed the front door. She held out her hand. "I basically live here. Do everything for him."

All three gave their names and shook hands with Holden. She urged them to go have a seat in the parlor then excused herself and stomped upstairs to go fetch her patient. The house became deathly quiet, the only noise coming from the nurse's heavy footsteps above them in the master bedroom.

They entered the luxurious front parlor, decorated in genuine 19th century antique furnishings, except for a small, modern television on an old table against the wall. Two oversized antique parlor chairs, arranged side-by-side, sat opposite a lounge couch with a blanket and throw pillows on it. An antique chess table stood between the furniture set atop a thick oriental rug. A beautiful chess set of painted Civil War figurines sat on top of the table. Blue and gray soldiers were neatly arranged on opposite sides of the black and white chess board, anticipating a new battle.

Rae whispered to Jake and the CID agent. "Sounds like we've got an alibi for today. He's been sleeping."

Jake grunted as he observed the chess set.

D'Arata stood at the fireplace, one of three on the first floor, looking at a dozen or so family photographs hanging on the wall above it. With phone in hand—the old vet's facial image from West Point on screen—he looked up and down from photograph to phone.

"And," he quietly added, "no match with any of these pictures."

Jake walked over next to him and compared the wall photos and phone picture as well. "Yep, you're right. Not even close." He viewed a few more photos and his eyes lit up. "I'll be damned. That's General Stand Watie. He was a legend in the Cherokee Nation and the Confederate States of America during the Civil War."

A door clicked shut from another room further down the hallway. Rae heard it and turned. So did D'Arata. They both walked over to the hallway expecting someone to appear. They popped their heads back into the hallway looking toward the back of the house. Nothing moved.

"That was weird," Rae said.

At the same moment a loud grinding sound at the top of the stairs drew their attention up and away. A very old, scruffy, white-haired man with large ears had started slowly descending the stairs while seated in the chair lift, followed by Nurse Holden walking next to him.

▼

Tom Black shut the door to the ancestor room louder than he had wanted. He had just finished eavesdropping on the visitors at the front entrance. Paranoia kicked in.

"Son-of-a-bitch," he spat quietly, backing into the room. *That couple from the TV show! They're on to me. Did they already catch the thief? Do they know I arranged West Point? Did they follow me here? Is my house tapped, my phone bugged? Did Jaconious sell me out?*

Too many questions were clouding his head and his judgement, but he knew the item he had in mind would certainly give him an edge against this couple. It would give him the answers he so desired. No time to waste now. It was make or break time.

He went for it.

Looking about he found a cup on his father's desk holding several pens and pencils. Reaching into his inner coat pocket he slipped out a sharp looking, gold, fully functional ballpoint pen and pressed the clip on it. He then dropped it into the cup with the other writing tools.

The pen was actually a crystal controlled UHF radio voice transmitter, a disguised surveillance bug he had used many times in the past to illegally record conversations. Most recently he had Johnson plant one in the office of his rival during the heated 15th U.S. Congressional District election. The $800 pen was battery operated with 100 hours of life and held a tiny antenna that allowed burst transmissions of audio pick up when activated by a cell phone ping.

With the spy bug in place, he turned to what he risked everything for.

Centered on the fireplace mantle he indeed found the antique Bowie knife housed in a wide oak box. It was framed in a pattern of clear and stained glass panels. Flanked on each side of the knife display were two more glass display boxes. One housed an Ivory-handled pistol with a small note and an illustration of a battle. The other case held a gilded, braided hat cord accompanied by a piece of paper yielding a message. Above the mantle on which the knife box sat, mounted on the wood paneled wall, was a Whitworth sniper rifle with a side-mounted brass telescope. All of these items dated back to his direct descendant, Corporal Thomas Black Watie Jr., and his service in the Confederate Army during the Civil War. That much Black knew. Ignoring the other valuable artifacts, he focused on the knife case.

Inside that display box, the knife itself was propped up on its side while a leather sheath with inlaid Rattlesnake skin lay in front of it, flat. Gripping the box with both hands he carefully pulled it down off the mantle and set it on the desk. The box hinged opened from the top, but it was locked as he tried to raise it. Clearly, it was a major oversight. Black had completely forgotten about it needing a key.

"Fuck me," he mumbled.

Standing still in complete silence, except for his own heavy breathing, a sense of panic spun through his mind. And then he heard a loud machine-like droning coming from the hallway. His father was coming down the chair lift to meet his guests.

Shit.

Heart racing, sweat dripping from his face, Black grabbed the closest thing he could find off the desk: a cold-cast bronze sculpture of Confederate General Robert E. Lee atop his trusted steed, Traveller. Lee's arm was raised with sword in hand. Standing at ten and one-half inches high the impressive sculpture weighed at over three pounds, surprising Black as he wielded it above the box. He lightly tapped the top glass panel with the bottom of the sculpture, but it didn't break. He smacked it much harder and the glass shattered inward, the sculpture slipping from his sweaty palm upon impact. In what seemed like slow motion, Lee bounced off the desk with a knock and then thumped hard on a thick rug over the wooden floor. Incredibly, the Rock of the South remained intact.

"Jesus Christ," whispered Black, now in total panic knowing there were three people in the front parlor who surely heard the ruckus he had just caused. He reached in to grab the knife and promptly sliced the outside of his right thumb from a shard of glass still embedded in the panel.

"Aaargh," he quietly moaned. Still, he got a hold of the knife and wrenched it out. He sucked in a breath, held it, and listened intently for anyone coming. All that he heard was the continual hum of the chair lift.

Black exhaled quietly. Holding the knife up for the first time in his life was an absolute rush. The blade itself was 9 inches long and 2 inches wide. Etched on one side were barely visible Cherokee symbols, several of which he recognized from the image of the waybill from McPherson's hat he had viewed earlier. The other side of the blade contained a long etched sentence in the Cherokee language. Adding in the silver blade guard, coffin-shaped antler bone handle—edge wrapped in silver—the knife was 15 inches in overall length. His father had never deemed him worthy enough to touch it, let alone handle it.

Triumphant he grasped the untouchable Watie family heirloom in his shaky hand, blood dripping from his cut, down his wrist, and onto the desk and rug. Sweat fell from his face as he took slow, quiet, deep breaths. He had violated the ancestor room to its core—right under his father's nose—and damn, it felt so fucking good.

The thrill was short-lived however, as he knew escape was the next order of business. *Screw the sheath.* He shoved the knife under his belt against his hip, the blade guard tight against a massive overlap of stomach bulging his dress shirt out. The knife would never slip out. He pulled his coat over the blade, wiped his face with a sleeve and readjusted his hat. At the door he listened again.

Loud voices emerged down the hall, one of which he hadn't heard in half his lifetime: his father's distinct Southern drawl. He was greeting his guests in the parlor. They all started chattering with introductions. Now or never, he told himself as he cracked the door open.

No one in his end of the hallway was visible. He opened the door further. It creaked again and he paused. Popping his head out, looking straight down the hallway, he noticed a heavyset black woman dressed in white at the foyer. She was walking behind his father who shuffled slowly into the parlor. This was the same woman he had heard earlier answering the door. Her voice clicked with familiarity. It was his father's nurse.

Once she passed into the parlor, Black stepped out into the hallway, snicked the door shut behind him, and made a quick left back into the kitchen. To the rear door he went, twisted the knob open, and exited. He didn't bother shutting the door all the way as he was already scurrying down the rear porch steps. Double-bounding it down the rose path, he was through the iron gate and in the alleyway in less than thirty seconds after leaving the ancestor room.

As he made his way onto Whitaker Street, he laughed with an exhausted impish chuckle as the fear-induced adrenaline high came crashing down. Knowing he had pulled off a victory of a lifetime, Black strutted up to Forsyth Park a half block and crossed over Whitaker to the Georgia Historical Society. There, in the back service alley behind the immense mansion, he happily rendezvoused with his chief of staff, Johnson.

Tom Black was a big, bloody, smelly, smiling mess of a man with a long knife on his large hip, but he loved every minute of being back in the game.

Collapsing in the passenger seat of the car, he punched a few numbers into his cell phone and held the device up to his ear. Now it was time to listen in when his father found out what he had done.

And maybe Daddy'll finally drop dead.

MICHAEL KARPOVAGE

8

AT LEAST JAKE KNEW TOMMY WATIE WASN'T THE thief from West Point. *No limp. Barely able to walk. Face doesn't match the surveillance camera suspect. Been sleeping all day.* Now all he had to do was be the bearer of bad news.

"Mr. Watie?" Jake started.

"Please. Call me Tommy, son," Watie cackled in his deep Southern accent. "How many times I got to tell you?" Nurse Holden assisted him as he eased into one of two parlor chairs. Tommy groaned from an achy back. "Y'all sit down now, too." He motioned to the other chair and couch across from him.

Jake smiled nervously, taking a sofa seat opposite Tommy. Rae sat next to him, their thighs touching. D'Arata sat to the right of the old man. "Tommy, we appreciate you seeing us. I've got some bad news though. It's the reason we flew down from New York."

"Go ahead."

Jake peered at the utterly exhausted-looking elderly man across the chess table. "Have you watched any news today or listened to the radio?"

"Nope. Been sleeping. Get to the point."

"Sir, shortly after we spoke this morning, the McPherson hat was *stolen* from the West Point Museum. It's *gone*."

"You some kinda joker?"

"No, sir," said Rae, leaning forward on the couch. "We know what this hat means to you and your family. The history behind it. It was stolen. The display case was smashed and someone *took* it. It's all over the news."

"This is some kinda reality show you're pulling with me, right? You two being on TV and all." Tommy shifted nervously in his chair. No one said a word back. His breathing quickened as he pointed to a small television on a corner table. "Becky, would ya turn on that set and see if they're telling the truth?"

The nurse turned it on and channelled over to CNN. There was a live feed from West Point. Within minutes of digesting the news, Tommy was convinced. The commander in charge of the investigation, a Lieutenant Colonel Cliff Paxton, had even appeared during a press conference, giving the media some details about the stolen items. He clearly mentioned McPherson's hat and the two Nazi trophies. Tommy sagged in his chair, deflated, saddened.

"Sir?" Sergeant D'Arata then asked. "Would you happen to know of *anyone* who could have done this?"

Tommy shook his head slowly, staring down at the floor.

"I'll be right back, Mr. Tommy," Holden said, patting his shoulder. "Gonna run upstairs to grab your oxygen tank, okay?"

Tommy mumbled, still staring at the floor. He scratched his head, strands of silvery white hair falling over his face. The life seemed to be draining from him.

Rae slipped out of her seat and followed Holden into the hallway. She quietly asked the nurse if she could answer of few questions in private. Holden agreed as soon as she retrieved the oxygen tank and some medical equipment to monitor Tommy's vitals.

D'Arata persisted. "Do you know *why* anyone would steal that hat?" He knew the truth, but still wanted to get Watie's reaction.

Tommy looked up, blinking wildly. "Well, sure. It's probably because of what's inside of it. The missing waybill, that's why."

Jake cut in. "Tommy, why is that waybill so important? Why would someone go to such great lengths to steal that hat when they probably weren't even sure there really was a waybill inside of it? I mean, I didn't know there was anything in there. All the people who handled the hat and inspected it during research never found anything. What is so important about that waybill?"

Tommy placed both hands over his face and rubbed his forehead. "I can't tell you. It's a family secret." He stuttered a bit and was hesitant.

"Tommy, *you* called me this morning. I tried helping *you* out. Please help *us* out. National treasures were just stolen in an incredibly brazen theft from West Point. Please give me something. Some sort of reason why."

"It's such a long story," Tommy started and then stopped.

"Go on, sir," Jake urged.

Tommy relented. "Aww, hells bells. So much was riding on that waybill from the day Granddaddy done lost it during the Battle of Atlanta in eighteen sixty-four. I mean he never got it back after McPherson stashed it in his hat. Point being is he failed part of the mission he was sent to Georgia for in the first place. It tore him up, Colonel. Tore him up for many years after the war."

His nurse had just returned with the tank and tried slipping a breathing mask over Tommy's head. He flat out refused, waving her away. She acquiesced but did take his pulse by grasping his wrist and determined he was doing okay. She then slipped back out in to the hallway to speak with Rae.

Watie spoke some more. "That failure on his part was something that his son—my daddy—wanted to help him fix. And myself, in turn. In Granddaddy's later years, us three were real close. That was in the thirties and forties. We always wanted to right that wrong for the family's sake. For the sake of history. And reputation. And accomplishment."

"I understand," Jake said.

"Sort of a lost cause, though," Tommy continued, scratching his scalp again. "Until I saw that hat on your TV show Friday night. It brought me some hope."

"It brought you a heart attack, too," Jake said, looking directly into Tommy's sad eyes.

At the same time, Rae was quietly inquiring with Holden about Tommy's whereabouts from Friday night's heart attack on up to this afternoon. It was confirmed that Tommy was hospitalized all Friday night, all through Saturday night, and then returned home under Holden's care early this morning. He had been released a couple days ahead of the norm. Rae thanked her and they both reentered the parlor to hear Tommy speaking.

"That it did, Colonel," Tommy agreed. "That heart attack was a close call for sure."

Holden chuckled lightly as she moved to his side. "But we got through it alright now, didn't we, Mr. Tommy?"

"I suppose so," Tommy replied. "But you might have been better off letting me go, though, now that the hat is stolen. At least I would have left this world with the taste of hope still on the tip of my tongue."

"Mr. Tommy, don't-cha go on talking like that," Holden scolded him.

"I'm sorry, young lady," Tommy laughed. "Y'all did real good there with your zapping machine bringing me back. I do thank you for it. I didn't mean what I said."

While Tommy was talking, Rae quietly informed Jake that Holden confirmed his presence in Savannah all weekend. Jake gave a nod to D'Arata and then down to his cell phone. D'Arata leaned in and held his phone in front of Tommy's face and asked him politely if he recognized this older WWII veteran. He explained he may be a suspect in the museum theft.

Tommy took the phone and held it closer to his eyes. "Naw, sure haven't seen him around before. And I've met a lot of veterans. This something to do with those Nazi items that were taken, right?"

Nurse Holden, standing next to Watie, also looked at the cell phone image. She frowned. "Can I see that?" D'Arata let her have the phone and she inspected the face rather intently.

"Possibly, sir," D'Arata replied. "This man claimed he was with the 82nd Airborne at Bastogne when they were surrounded by the Germans during the Battle of the Bulge." D'Arata winked at Jake.

Tommy frowned instantly. "Well, that's a load of crap. Everyone knows it wasn't the 82nd boys there. It was the Screaming Eagles of the 101st. I was with Patton's Third Army when we rode in and rescued 'em." Now he was more animated. "I was nineteen years-old then but still remember that battle clear as day. I was with the 4th Armored Division's 37th Tank Battalion spearheaded by Creighton Abrams. We raced over 100 miles of icy roads and attacked Manteuffel's southern flank and rescued them boys in Bastogne. Did it in 48 hours."

"You are sharp as a tack, Mr. Watie," nodded D'Arata. "That's what Colonel Tununda caught, too. This man was a liar and is now our main suspect."

Jake smiled. "But, Tommy, the 101st Airborne will tell you they weren't rescued at all by you and Patton. They've always said they just needed to be *reinforced*."

Tommy smiled back. "Heard *that* before."

Holden was murmuring to herself while zooming in on the museum suspect's image with a pinch of her fingers on the touch display. "I've seen this face before."

The trio of investigators stole glances at each other.

"It's a mask though. I'm pretty sure of it. You can get 'em online."

"What?" Rae asked, bewildered.

"Oh yeah, sure," explained Holden, handing the phone back to the CID agent. "This face is a standard old man look. One of my male friends—a black man—decided he was gonna be an old white man at a Halloween costume party last year. He said he saw the mask on some crime show that people were using for robberies. So he just decided to buy one as a joke."

D'Arata's mouth fell open. "You're kidding me?"

"Nuh, uh. I got the website bookmarked. Here I'll show y'all." She pulled her own cell phone from a pocket and started tapping in a web browser. In seconds, she had the mask product page up. "See? Told ya so."

D'Arata and Rae compared the old vet's camera capture to the costume mask and were stunned at the match. Jake merely shook his head.

"Unbelievable," the agent said, "I'll text Colonel Paxton right now."

Jake needed to turn the conversation back to the subject of the waybill and Tommy's story of a failed mission on his grandfather's part. "Tommy, you mentioned a receipt on our phone call this morning," he inquired, leaning forward on the sofa, elbows on his knees. "You said General McPherson wrote it out, and that there was a witness. You also said the receipt specifically stated the waybill would have been returned to your ancestor after the war was over."

"Yes, that's right."

Jake elaborated. "I'm thinking this might have something to do with the theft. It might be a lead we can build on since this waybill *was* known to others besides your granddaddy. McPherson and this other witness at the very least. Would it be too much to ask if I could see that receipt and take a photograph of it?"

"Yes, yes. I see what you're getting at, Colonel," Tommy said, perking up and nodding vigorously. "You think one of their descendants may want to get their hands on the waybill, too!"

"You are spot on," Jake said, pointing at Tommy.

Tommy stood up with the help of his nurse and motioned them out into the hallway. "Follow me, y'all." He took the lead and started doing his shuffle walk. "You're gonna get a rare visit inside our Watie family ancestor room. The receipt's in there."

Slowly making his way down the hallway in tepid steps, Tommy passed by the dining room entrance on the left. His nurse followed behind him as precaution from falling. The trio of investigators took up the rear of the slow moving freight train.

"Ooh wee," Holden exclaimed. "What in the Lord is that *smell?* Mr. Tommy, did you . . . ?"

"Girl, when I fart, y'all be the second to know," Tommy joked. They all got a big kick out of that. It was nice to see he was in good spirits considering the news of the hat theft.

Tommy shuffled up next to the ancestor room door and pulled an old key from his pocket. He was just about to insert it into the keyhole when something in his peripheral vision caught his attention in the kitchen. The back door was wide open, a slight breeze blowing in.

"You leave that door open?" he asked his nurse. "Maybe that garbage smell is coming from the back alley."

"Nope," Holden replied. "Wasn't me. I've had this house locked tighter than a drum." She walked into the kitchen to close it but noticed wet spots on the white tiled floor, like someone had spilled water. And several tiny red splatters, too. She grasped the door knob but pulled her hand back as it came in contact with something slick. Looking at her palm, she noticed it was smeared with blood.

"Y'all get in here! There's blood on this door. On the floor there, too!"

Rae and D'Arata hustled into the kitchen as Holden pointed to the floor showing them blood drippings. Rae stepped outside on the rear porch noticing more blood droplets. D'Arata retraced the trail back through the kitchen into the hallway right where Tommy stood at the closed ancestor room door. Tommy looked at him, then placed his hand on the door knob. He turned it, expecting the door to be locked. Instead, to his dismay, he pushed it wide open.

Jake had already drawn his pistol and stepped in front of Tommy to enter the room. D'Arata was a step behind, his sidearm out as well, scanning for intruders. They entered the study. It was packed with war memorabilia like a museum. There wasn't much room to even walk around except on a large oriental rug in front of a huge, wooden antique desk.

"Clear on the left," Jake yelled.

"Clear on the right," D'Arata replied.

"I'm going out back," Rae shouted from the kitchen. "Blood trail leads outside."

Creeping into the ancestor room, Tommy saw his sculpture of Robert E. Lee on the floor at the foot of his desk. As he moved closer, he noticed the knife box sitting on the desktop, the glass lid shattered, his prized Bowie knife gone. With a gasp his knees became weak, his arms folded and he collapsed over the desktop, knocking over several desk accessories including a cup full of pens and pencils. Luckily, D'Arata was right behind him to break his fall.

They placed him in his oversized, leather desk chair and he sat moaning and holding his head in his hands from despair. Jake ordered D'Arata to clear the upstairs and he would clear the rest of the main floor.

It was about three minutes before Tommy had come back to his senses. His vitals were fine, Nurse Holden advised after checking him out. She had already affixed the oxygen mask over his mouth with clean air flowing from the tank she had wheeled in from the parlor.

"You fainted, Mr. Tommy," Holden said, holding his hand. "You're gonna be alright. These good folks are checking everything out."

Tommy acknowledged her by nodding his head, but stared at the knife box, his mind trying to comprehend the magnitude of theft.

Jake and D'Arata had already swept the entire house to see if anyone was hidden inside. They had just regrouped back inside the ancestor room when Rae called Jake on her cell phone telling him the backyard and alley were clear, but that she was headed down Whitaker Street toward Forsyth Park still following the blood trail. Jake told her to be careful.

"How's he doing?" Jake whispered to the nurse.

"I'm iffy about calling an ambulance."

Tommy snapped out of it. He stood up from his chair with a grunt, tore off the oxygen mask, and pointed a finger at his nurse. "No ambulance! I ain't going back to that hospital, you hear?"

Holden held up her hands. "Okay, Mr. Tommy. Okay. I hear ya, loud and clear. No ambulance."

Jake holstered his firearm and asked Tommy point blank what was stolen in the box.

"It was Granddaddy's Arkansas toothpick." Tommy said, leaning on the desk, looking inside the shattered box. He carefully extracted the knife sheath and held it up for all to see. "A big ol' Bowie knife given to him by Uncle Stand. It was up there on the mantle with Granddaddy's other possessions from the War. All locked up. The bastard who did this didn't have the key to get in so he broke the glass."

Jake was already on his cell phone tapping the speedial for Rae while he ordered D'Arata to hold the fort. Then he darted out the study door. "Going to back up Rae," he shouted.

With Jake already out the back door, D'Arata turned back to Tommy. "Whoever did this cut himself in the process," he said, pointing to a shard of glass sticking from the hinged lid frame. "We found a trail of blood from this desk, across the rug, through the kitchen, and down your back path. Rae's still following it on Whitaker Street."

Tommy touched a fingertip to the piece of glass that had blood on it, then rubbed the blood between his fingers. "It's fresh." He shuffled around the desk and slowly walked over to the fireplace where he inspected the other display items in their boxes.

"They must have broken in when he was sleeping," Holden said, shaking her head and plopping down on a guest chair in front of the desk. She looked shocked, exasperated. "But surely I would have heard something."

"Not likely as there's no signs of forced entry into the house," D'Arata remarked. "I checked the rear door. If someone were breaking in they would have either broken the glass on the door to get to the dead bolt or kicked their way in. The door jambs would have been splintered."

"Trust me, this house was locked up tight," emphasized Holden, rather angrily. "I always make sure of it. Front and back doors. Even the alley gate. Mr. Tommy gave me the only extra key to this house and it stays with me at all times in my pocket here." She patted her thigh.

Tommy turned around to back up her statement. "And I double check those doors even after she locks 'em. I did it right before lunch and my afternoon nap. I'm damn sure of it."

Holden nodded. "He's paranoid like that. It gives him exercise though, which he likes. Besides, no one dares come in this room without Mr. Tommy. He's got the only key to get in here. And that thing is one of a kind. Isn't that right?"

Tommy took it out of his pocket and showed the agent. It was a vintage, 19th century, heavy brass key.

"So someone must have had an extra key to get in?" D'Arata asked, directing his question to Tommy.

Tommy stared at him, not answering. He looked angry. Then said, "There ain't no other key."

"Rae and I both heard a door shut up the hall when we were waiting in the parlor," the army investigator said. "I thought there was someone else in the house. Maybe another family member. I didn't think much of it and then you and Nurse Holden came down the stairs and that lift was so loud we forgot all about it."

Tommy looked at D'Arata, fury in his eyes. D'Arata didn't know what he had said wrong. He veered away from the old man's intensity.

"Sir, where was this sculpture located?" D'Arata asked, pointing to the Lee statuette still on the floor.

Tommy pointed. "Right there on the desk. Put it back."

D'Arata ignored his request. "Sorry, we need to leave everything as is, sir. This is now a crime scene. I'll need to photograph it." He then looked from the knife box to the fireplace mantle, thinking out loud. "So, whoever did this took the box down from the mantle, placed it here on the desk, couldn't get in. So they grabbed the closest object they could find to smash it. This shows *desperation* and *impatience* and a *ticking clock* for them to get that knife."

"Sergeant, shouldn't we call the Savannah po-lice?" Holden asked, shrugging her shoulders.

"Ma'am, with all due respect, I am the *police*. The Army Criminal Investigation Division also has jurisdiction over civilian personnel *if* there's probable cause with a nexus to the U.S. Army. I'm not sure if there is a connection yet. If there *isn't* then this would be a local police matter."

"No!" Tommy barked. "Don't you dare call those dumb cops. I don't need nobody else in my house and I don't want all of Savannah knowing about this. Everyone knows everyone here and I won't be the talk of gossip. I *know* who did this."

"What?" D'Arata asked. "Who?"

"I smelled him," Tommy said, shaking. "It wasn't garbage I smelled earlier. It was *his* smell. I know it. I'm sure of it."

"Who?" the sergeant pressed, raising his voice. "Someone you know? Someone in your family?"

"I ain't got no family! I ain't got no one left."

"What about your son, the Congressman?" Holden asked, innocently. "He's family. I had to call him Friday night at his home in Atlanta after you went in the hospital."

Tommy spun around and faced her, almost losing his balance. He braced himself on the fireplace mantle. His upper lip twitched with rage. "You did *what*?"

Holden spread her arms out, palms up in a pleading gesture. "What'd I do wrong? I had to notify next of kin per caregiver regulations. He was the only one listed on your official documentation from several years back."

"He ain't my son!" Tommy screamed, pointing a finger at Holden. "And you had no right calling him. I disowned him some thirty years ago."

Tears welled up in Holden's eyes. "But I didn't know. I didn't know. You had a heart attack. There was no one else to call." Her chest heaved.

"I know it was him. I know it. *Smelled* it," Tommy hissed. "He's done this before. Right outta this very room. He stole money from my wife and me. He stole from the Watie war collection. Sellin' them items off. Until we caught him. But those dumb Savannah cops. Those dumb FBI agents. Dumb as rocks. They messed it all up and he walked away scott-free."

"I didn't know, Mr. Tommy," Holden said, openly weeping. D'Arata placed a hand on her shoulder to comfort her. "I had no idea. It's all my fault, isn't it? It's all my fault," she continued.

"What'd you say to him?" Tommy demanded. "What'd you tell that dadgum boy?"

Holden looked up with red eyes, tears running down her cheeks. "I just told him you were watching your favorite TV show *Battlefield Investigators*, about some Civil War hat that caused your heart attack. I told him the truth is all."

Tommy's shoulders sagged. "Oh Lord Jesus, I need to sit down." D'Arata immediately guided him back in his chair behind the desk.

Holden bawled openly. "He even said he would come visit, but not to tell you we spoke. I'm so sorry." She caught her breath. "I didn't know he'd come back and do *this* to you."

In a slow crescendo of deep disgust, Tommy howled about his son. "That devious, no-good, rotten son-of-a-bitch. He preys on good people. All his life. He's like a Raven Mocker coming to tear my heart out. And I ain't gonna give it to him. I ain't. No-sir-ee."

Holden cried harder while Tommy shook with rage. D'Arata just stood there, taking it all in, utterly perplexed as to what was meant by a Raven Mocker tearing his heart out.

Tommy finally sighed loudly. "Becky, Becky, I'm sorry I yelled at you. It ain't your fault, Sweetie. It ain't your fault. You've been good to me. You saved my *life*. You had no idea my son and me hadn't spoken or seen each other in over thirty years."

"Don't be mad at me, Mr. Tommy." Holden said, sniffling. She looked up at him. "Please?"

"You're okay, Sweetie. I ain't mad at you." Now it was Tommy's turn to get weepy-eyed. His voice trembled. "You've been by my side for three years straight now. You're all I got."

Nurse Holden rose from her chair and walked around the desk and hugged Tommy. He put his arms around her and hugged her back. She whispered a thank you and then kissed him on the forehead.

D'Arata bowed his head, somewhat embarrassed, somewhat dismayed at the rollercoaster ride of such intense emotions. Holden had made an innocent phone call to Tommy's estranged son, thinking she had done the right and gracious thing. But those good intentions backfired wildly with terrible consequences.

"I'll clean this mess up for you," Holden said, sniffing again while making her way out of the room. " I gotta get a broom and a sponge."

"Miss Holden, why don't you hold off on cleaning anything up for now," D'Arata stated firmly. "We have an active crime scene here and I need to process the evidence first."

"You go on and clean yourself up now, girl, ya hear?" Tommy said. "And bring me back some of those Thinny-Mint cookies you're so fond of. Them Girly Scout ones." He winked at her, obviously trying to make up for his outburst.

Holden smiled, even laughed. "Thin-Mints, Mr. Tommy. From the Girl Scouts. Not Girly Scouts. How many times I got to tell you?" She excused herself from the room and headed into the kitchen.

"Tommy," D'Arata said loudly. "We've got to act fast on this. You've got to be straight with me. You're not telling us everything. Why would your own son steal your granddaddy's Bowie knife? Was it part of the failed mission of your granddaddy? What's the connection?"

Tommy went silent. He looked up at D'Arata. His bright eyes, deep within hollow sockets, changed from anger to fear and back to anger again. He peered down and squirmed nervously in his chair, shaking his head in deep thought. Seemingly ready to speak, his lips trembled, but he turned away and clammed up again.

D'Arata was getting frustrated at Tommy's lack of response. It was obvious the old man was holding back. He pressed him some more. "Do you want us to nail Tom Black or let him get away with this? We're here trying to help you. Jake and Rae are down the street somewhere I'm sure hot on his trail. So level with me, will ya?"

After a stare down from D'Arata, Tommy gave in with a slow sigh. "It's a map key."

"A map *key*?" the sergeant repeated. "What is? The knife?"

Tommy nodded. "Granddaddy told us the waybill in McPherson's hat is a map drawing of Cherokee symbols that had to be decoded with a *key*. The key is etched on the blade of the Bowie knife. And there's only one other person living to this day besides me who knows that."

"Tom Black," D'Arata answered for him.

"Yep."

"Hold on, sir," D'Arata ordered. "I need to call Colonel Tununda."

"No need to," Jake huffed, breathing heavily. Rae was standing right behind him at the ancestor room entrance. She, too, was catching her breath after they both had run back to Cherokee Rose Manor. "We lost the blood trail at the corner of Forsyth Park. Right there at Whitaker and Gaston. What's up, Sergeant?"

"Mr. Watie thinks he knows who stole his knife. Tell him, sir."

"Tom Black," spat Tommy, with disgust. "Positive of it."

Jake nodded, not at all surprised.

Sergeant D'Arata brought Jake and Rae up to speed on how the Bowie knife acts as a legend to the waybill in McPherson's hat. He also briefed them on Nurse Holden's innocent, next-of-kin call to Tom Black. The puzzle pieces started coming together to form a picture of motivation.

"You think Black stole the hat at West Point, too?" Jake asked Tommy. "Or maybe *arranged* for it to be stolen?"

"For sure. Becky said she told him about your TV show. That the hat caused my heart attack, right? I betcha once he found out whose hat it was he probably shit his big, ol' britches. He knew how much that hat meant to me. And now he's got the knife, too. It's like he wants to take all my most prized possessions. It's like he's tormenting me on purpose. Hell, we don't even know if there's a waybill *inside* that hat!"

Jake placed his hands on the desk, leaned forward, and looked into Tommy's fiery eyes. "Now tell me the *this*." He tapped his finger on the desktop when he spoke next. "What does that waybill lead *to*?"

"I want you to get him," Tommy said. "I really do, but I can't tell you about our family secrets." He bowed his head.

"Listen," Jake said, his pulse racing. "Adolf Hitler's gold pistol and Hermann Göering's diamond baton, two of the most prized trophies of World War II, were also stolen. It's not just *your* prized possessions and *your* family secrets. You're not the only one who has been violated."

Tommy glanced up at Jake, listening, waiting to see where he was going with this new tactic.

Jake paced in front of the desk, his voiced raised with passion. "*You*, of all people, a World War II combat veteran, should know what those war trophies mean." He stopped and faced Tommy again. "They are *priceless*. And I don't mean dollar value. It's what they symbolize to so many millions of people who suffered and died because of those fucking Nazi bastards. I've spoken with hundreds of veterans like you who've told me confidential battlefield stories. Heart-to-heart conversations. And they still take pride, after all these years, at beating the piss out of those Nazis."

Jake had Tommy mesmerized. The older man nodded involuntarily in agreement, fully comprehending the magnitude of what the much younger man said.

"Those trophies belong to *all* of us. It's *our* American victory over evil. Tom Black stole more than just a Watie family secret," Jake stressed, eyes boring into Tommy. "He stole the history of a generation of warriors. And I personally want to get those trophies back and make him pay. Now I ask again, what does that waybill lead to?"

Tommy stood up slowly, his own eyes blazing, never leaving Jake's. Face-to-face he spat out his answer.

"Lost Cherokee gold!"

9

TOMMY BLACK WATIE IV INSISTED JAKE AND RAE STAY at his manor that night. They readily complied, fearing for Mr. Watie's safety and sensing he still had a lot more to reveal to further their investigation, especially about lost Cherokee gold. They cancelled their bed and breakfast lodgings on River Street and unloaded their bags, taking an upstairs guest bedroom. For the next hour they showered, changed into more comfortable clothing, relaxed, and compared notes while jotting down information in their smart phones. They were expected to be in the dining room to join Tommy by 8:00 p.m. Nurse Holden had promised them some fine Southern homestyle cooking.

Special Agent D'Arata also went off-duty and headed home after reporting the information about Congressman Tom Black being a prime suspect amid the connection of the waybill and stolen knife. Probable cause was established, linking the Savannah civilian theft of the knife with the theft of the hat on U.S. Army property at West Point, thus the Army CID was still designated as the lead investigative authority.

D'Arata's CID commander, Colonel David M. Perkins at Hunter Army Airfield, and Lieutenant Colonel Paxton up at West Point had already engaged in several highly energized conference calls about the implications of a sitting U.S. congressman involved in criminal activity.

Cleared by his superiors to proceed with the crime scene analysis, D'Arata explained to Tommy how he would do the evidence collection to prove his son was the culprit. It would be similar to paternal testing, he said to the older man. With crime scene equipment readily available in his MP Humvee, and trained in forensic evidence collection procedures, D'Arata took little time in photographing the scene and processing the evidence. The collected blood evidence was en route to Fort Gillem in Atlanta to the Army Forensics Lab for secret priority overnight analysis. Accompanying that sample was a saliva swab from Tommy Watie's cheek. Since there would be no difference between DNA from cheek cells when compared to DNA from blood, the results would prove beyond a reasonable doubt that Watie's only son was indeed in the house and had stolen the knife from his biological father. Now all they had to do was wait for an answer, which they were told would be by early morning.

Everything hinged on a DNA match before anyone could act. A match would mean assets would be deployed to reign in Tom Black. The CID would conduct surveillance at his home in Roswell, his Congressional field office in The Bluff, and his Washington, D.C. office. No one knew where he was, but they would hunt him down. Search warrants would be issued in preparation of confronting him and finding the stolen items. Jake and Rae felt they had done than their part and others would take the ball from here.

Promptly at eight, Jake and Rae, dressed in casual jeans and button down shirts, met Tommy and his nurse in the dining room. It was beautifully furnished with floor to ceiling antique cabinets, rich paintings, and another finely designed wood trimmed fireplace façade. The eight-seat antique dinner table was crowded with a center spread of sweet-smelling food worthy of a court of knights. There was a platter of fried chicken and cornbread dressing and another of sweet potato souffle. Around the platters were brimming bowls of buttery mashed potatoes, black-eyed peas, okra gumbo, corn muffins, and biscuits. Lastly, a heaping mound of banana pudding was waiting for dessert, if they could fit it in.

No one wasted any time in filling up their plates, passing bowls of hot food, and digging into the scrumptious Southern fare. Amazed at how much food there was and how incredible it tasted Jake and Rae complimented Holden on her culinary skills. Tommy and she reacted with boisterous laughter until they finally revealed their little secret: she didn't make any of it. The hot food had been delivered special order from the famous Savannah restaurant, Mrs. Wilkes' Dining Room, not three blocks away on West Jones Street. All Holden did was lay out the table.

Holden explained that Tommy rarely gets any home cooked meals since he became homebound. Among the many restaurants throughout Savannah, he was quite well known, not only as a food connoisseur, but as a prolific talker. At Mrs. Wilkes' he had become one of their VIP customers over the many years since his wife had passed. He had always tipped handsomely and had even given generous Christmas gifts to their hardworking staff year after year. As a result, he was given special treatment for personal delivery of meals, even on a Sunday night when they were usually closed.

While enjoying their dinner, the group had light conversation of Tommy's experiences in World War II and of Jake's own deployments in various parts of the world. Rae and Holden bantered about the TV show her and Jake were on and how they had met in Upstate New York at a crime scene. Soon Holden was clearing the table along with Rae's help. In the kitchen, they had even cracked open a bottle of wine for themselves.

Tommy invited Jake into the ancestor room to speak further. They rose from dinner and Tommy shuffled in with Jake in tow. He whispered something to his nurse before entering the room. Inside, he turned on a desk lamp to give the room a faint warm glow and took the seat behind his grand mahogany desk. The busted glass case that housed the stolen Bowie knife still sat on top, the empty knife sheath still inside. Tommy told Jake to be seated as he cleaned up some pens and pencils that had been knocked over from a cup. Eyes squinting at a particular gold ballpoint pen, the old man shrugged his shoulders not remembering where it had come from, then placed it back in the cup holder.

A minute later Holden entered with a large tray bearing two short cocktail glasses, each filled with ice and a twist of lemon. Next to the glasses were two MoonPie snacks on a plate and a bucket of ice. Rae was behind her holding several cans of the soft drink Tab and a few cans of

Coke. The ladies placed the items on the desk and walked out. Rae told them to have fun, winked, then shut the door behind her.

Tommy opened a desk drawer and pulled out a bottle of 100 proof Southern Comfort, a flavored spirit with fruit, spices and whiskey from New Orleans. Jake's eyebrows arched and he smirked, never shying from a good nightcap. Tommy wasted no time in pouring both glasses half full. He grabbed a Tab and Jake a Coke and they mixed their drinks with a butter knife on the tray.

Tommy raised his glass. "To the grand ol' drink of the South!" he toasted and touched glasses with Jake's.

"Cheers!" Jake nodded and took a long refreshing sip of the whiskey and soda drink. "Aah, that hits the spot. Thank you, sir."

"My pleasure, son," Tommy said after sipping off some of his own drink. "I figured after all the bullshit we've gone through today we both need a little pull. No matter how old I am." He grabbed a MoonPie and dipped it into his drink and chomped down on the marshmallow, graham cookie and chocolate snack. He made a satisfactory groan.

"Got that right." Jake gave a big sigh of relaxation.

"Try one of these," Tommy mumbled, his mouth full. A few crumbs spilled out onto his chest.

As Jake dipped his MoonPie into his drink and enjoyed the Southern snack, Tommy reached down into a drawer, fiddled with something on the interior and produced a small wooden box. He placed it on the desktop and opened it. Inside was a thick, gold, diamond and black onyx ring with tiny hints of red glimmering off of it. Old man Watie slipped the large ring onto a thin finger, held his hand out and showed Jake.

"I didn't notice it right away, but you're a fellow Traveling Man. I saw your ring. What do you think of this one?"

Jake leaned forward and took Tommy's rough wrinkly hand into his own and studied the ring. Turning it on his finger from side to side he commented at how incredible and luxurious the craftsmanship was. Against a top face field of black onyx was a oversized, raised gold letter G filled with small diamonds. A small square and compasses graced the inside of the G and a multi-faceted, dark red ruby centered the main crest.

Raised gold symbols of various Masonic tools swept down each side of the black enameled and gold band, each tool having a small ruby or a diamond incorporated into them.

"Brother Tommy, I've got to tell you," Jake said, still chewing his MoonPie. "That's one of the best Masonic rings I've ever seen. I can tell it's an antique too. Where's your home lodge?"

"Right here in Savannah. Solomon's Lodge No. 1, oldest continuously operating Masonic lodge in the Western Hemisphere. Since 1734," Tommy said proudly, dipping the MoonPie into his drink again. "How 'bout you?"

"I was made a Mason in Iraq during deployment," Jake said. "A traveling military lodge dispensed from New York: the Land, Sea, and Air Lodge No. 1. It dates back to 1917 and World War I." Referring back to Tommy's ring, Jake asked, "But where'd you get this beauty is what I'd like to know?"

Tommy sat back, pleased with Jake's compliment. "I'm gonna tell you a bit of story how it came to be, son. It's all connected with what's going on with the hat and knife. And it's all the dadgum, honest-to-God truth."

Jake sat back in his chair. "*Oh*-kay." He crossed his legs and balanced his drink on the armrest, dipping and eating his chocolate snack. He knew when a respected elder wanted to talk and said it was a "bit of a story" that he had better listen well and relax for the long haul. The more Tommy spoke, and for that matter, drank, the more Jake would glean information for his investigation.

Tommy cleared his throat and spoke slowly in his deep drawl. "Stand Watie mined this ring's 24-carat gold himself way up in north Georgia, near Rome, up along the Oostanaula River. It was on his uncle's property, Major Ridge. This was sometime around 1820 when the Cherokee owned the lands of north Georgia, Alabama, Tennessee, and North Carolina. It was our homeland. We were a wealthy, civilized, educated nation.

"Major Ridge now, he was a full blood Cherokee, descended straight from a family of warriors. He and his brother, David Watie, were of the wealthiest plantation owners and the political elite. Ya see, many Cherokee mined their own gold and silver and gemstones. We were some of the dang richest folks in the entire *U*-nited States. And so when Stand was raised a

Freemason he took some of that gold he found and had this ring crafted just for himself."

Jake nodded politely, drinking, following along. Little did he know how dark the story would turn.

"But things went sour when the white man announced *they* discovered gold up near Dahlonega in 1828. Shit, Jake, it was our gold the white man discovered. We'd been mining it since before the Spaniards came in the 1540s!" Tommy laughed out loud. "Well, Dahlonega was the nation's first gold rush and the Feds and the politicians of Georgia set out to craft discriminatory laws to confiscate our lands and seize our gold after that." Tommy took a sip of his drink, all primed up, eyes darting side to side.

Jake knew that tiny north Georgia mountain city of Dahlonega quite well. He had frequented it many times when he was nearby at Camp Merrill while training during the mountain phase of Army Ranger School earlier in his military career.

"Major Ridge, his own son John Ridge, his nephew Stand Watie and brother Buck Watie—who actually changed his name to Elias Boudinot— well they and a bunch of other Cherokee leaders all signed a treaty to cut a deal with the Feds in exchange for new lands out West. But their younger brother Thomas Black Watie, my great granddaddy, did *not* sign it. Even so, he was still part of their group. They were all called the Ridge-Watie faction.

"But another up-and-coming politician and wealthy plantation owner himself, named John Ross, was against this treaty, Hell, he wasn't even hardly a Cherokee. One eighth Cherokee is all. Anyway, this dictator had most of the people behind him and they waited it out and fought all the way up to the Supreme Court. Ross stalled and stalled and stalled. The government offered us five million for the lands, but Ross—the greedy pig—he wanted *twenty* million. In the mean time, the Ridge-Watie kinfolk and thousands more Cherokee already moved out West and resettled. Our Cherokee nation was split because of these two factions. It was the start of our own civil war."

"Wasn't the Ridge-Watie faction called the Treaty Party? And the other Ross side was called the National Party?"

"Yes, you got it, son," Tommy said in a dry voice, nodding his head vigorously. He took another sip of his drink to quench his thirst. After pouring more whiskey into his glass, along with a few more cubes of ice from the bucket, and a dash of Tab, he continued.

"Our side saw the writing on the wall that the U.S. government *always* wins out in the end. And they wasn't gonna pay no twenty million dollars to us. Removal was inevitable. Long story short, the Feds took the Ross faction's remaining lands by gunpoint, seized people's homes and their possessions inside. They rounded up our people in stockades like the Nazis did the Jews. Then forced them out West on the Trail of Tears with whatever they could carry on their backs. Killed thousands of our people."

"I've read almost four thousand died."

"Or more! And what did John Ross and his henchmen do when they reunited with they Old Settlers out West?" Tommy pursed his thin lips in anger. His long, silvery white hair dropped in front of his eyes.

Jake shook his head, waiting for Tommy's response.

Tommy brushed away his hair and his deep-set eyes met Jake's. He slowly and quietly emphasized his words. "On the night of June 22, 1839, John Ross *unilaterally* charged our family and others with treason, punishable by *death*. He sent out execution squads to enact the Indian 'blood law' for those responsible in ceding our ancient Georgia homelands to the U.S. government by signing the treaty.

"That was the official reason so his men could escape prosecution. That's been the dadgum official reason handed down through history. Makes Ross look good in the text books. But *unofficially*, the real reason he targeted only those leaders was because they were obstructing his power grab. The Waties had been putting up road blocks to thwart Ross at every chance and so they had to die, but others who signed the treaty were untouched. The blood law was bullshit. He targeted the most powerful men who stood in his way of taking complete control of the Cherokee Nation."

"So, what happened with your kin?" asked Jake.

"I'm getting there. I'm getting there," Tommy grunted, rubbing his stubbled chin. "Ross's henchmen were armed with *hatchets, knives, and guns.* They slaughtered Major Ridge, his son John Ridge, and Elias Boudinot. Carved up their faces in front of family members. Stand Watie was forewarned and escaped. All told, five others were targeted for death, but survived the night. Stand's younger brother, my great granddaddy Thomas, was attacked sometime later and survived, his hand nearly cut off by a hatchet. He never even signed the treaty, but was still sought out for extermination—just because he was associated with stopping Ross."

"Good God," Jake said, shifting in his chair.

"Yes-sir-ee. And Ross became the chief of the Cherokee Nation and took control of everything. He even refused to enforce the laws to prosecute those killers who murdered our kinfolk. Done let 'em all off. But a few years later in 1842, Stand came across someone who was recognized as one of his uncle Major Ridge's killers. That man attacked Stand and Stand shot his ass dead. He was tried for murder, but acquitted on self-defense. Now, in retaliation for *that* killing, Ross's men went after Thomas Black Watie again in 1845, in Arkansas, and this time they murdered him outright. It was right before that he got married to a woman named Char-wah-you-kah. *She* was pregnant with my granddaddy."

Jake let out a long exhale, dropped more ice in his glass then topped it off with Coke and some more whiskey, still listening as the tale continued.

"You see, Thomas and his wife were staying at a friend's farm. Name was Bear Paw. That night a mob of men entered the guest house they were in while they was sleeping and said he was under arrest. Well, Thomas complied with their orders and said, 'Let me put on my clothes,' and when he started getting out of bed they slammed him in the head with a tomahawk and then shot him twice. His wife escaped, but when she came back later she found him dead on the ground, stabbed some eight times. How do you like that?"

Jake had nothing to say. The Watie ancestors lived lives surrounded by murder and payback, just as every society across the earth has, as far back as history went, he thought. *It's just how we humans are. We live in a cycle of violence. And the man with the biggest weapon and the largest army, rules. Utopia doesn't exist. Never did. Never will. It's kill or be killed.*

Tommy piped up again, truly on a roll. White saliva had formed at the corners of his mouth. "The young sons of all those men killed were ushered out of the territories in fear they, too, would be murdered by Ross's thugs. All in all, over 34 people were murdered during the faction fighting.

My granddaddy—a young man at the time—came back to Arkansas in 1861 at the start of the big war because John Ross and Stand Watie had finally buried the hatchet by then and were allied to fight the Union under the Confederate flag. Thomas Junior became a Master Mason himself at Cherokee Lodge No. 21 in the capital of Tahlequah. They say even John Ross was in attendance during his raising. You see, Ross had already become a Mason back in Georgia in the late 1820s when he and Stand were amicable to each other. Anyhow, Stand started the Cherokee Mounted Rifles and Thomas Junior enlisted."

"Ahh," Jake said. "The Waties and Ross finally put their political fighting to rest. Masonic brothers were finally united and now comrades in arms to fight the Union." Jake thought maybe this would be the end of Tommy's story, a warm ending for Indian Freemasons who had been killing each other all their lives. He was oh-so-wrong.

"Not for long!" Tommy fired back. "Ross and his men became Yankee stooges not a year later. They done switched sides. Ross, and the Cherokee treasury he was in charge of, was escorted under Union guard from the Cherokee capital. How do you like that? How do you like *that*?" Tommy spat with disgust.

"A traitor," Jake stated.

Tommy nodded. "Ross now pledged loyalty to the same Federal government he had fought against in stealing the Cherokee homelands! The same government who stole all Cherokee possessions and our resources and caused so many thousands of deaths on the Trail of Tears. How's *that* for hypocrisy of principle?" Tommy was truly enraged. He smacked his lips, eyes wild. And then he raised an index finger.

"But Stand had one more hand of poker to play. He was not going to let Ross get away with treason so easily. Stand had one of his spies on Ross's staff steal a waybill and a Bowie knife from his home at Rose Cottage. The knife was the key."

"You've gotta be shittin' me?" Jake said, rising out of his chair. "So, that's how it all started? Stand hired a *thief* himself and stole the waybill right from under Ross's nose?"

Tommy bounced his head up and down. "Yes-sir-ee, brother. And don't you think for one minute I don't plainly see the *irony* in that now!"

"This whole thing has come full circle," Jake remarked as he paced across the room, thinking. He was taken aback at the criminality associated with this waybill and that the famous General Stand Watie had set this whole game in motion. Even though Tommy was a Freemason like himself, there still was a matter of testing his trust. So far Tommy had spilled his guts, but Jake had a slight nagging feeling that he should watch his back just in case. These Watie men were a ruthless bunch, no matter how many years had passed.

"Indeed, it has, young brother. But lemme tell you about that little waybill now. I know you been waiting patiently all night to hear about it."

"Yes, please do. But first, fill me up again, will ya?"

Tommy happily poured whiskey into Jake's glass and continued. "Now, here's the juice of the lemon. This is what Granddaddy told me straight from his mouth. It's what General Watie told him: the waybill leads to the secret Cherokee Tunnel. It's the gold depository of *John Ross* and his top henchmen and also some important clan chiefs. It was dug out years before they were forced from their lands.

"You see, they knew they couldn't take any of their valuable possessions with them, let alone gold, because the Federals would steal it all. And removal was all but inevitable. So, they dug the tunnel in secret, deposited their wealth in individual vaults, and hid the entrance. The cache is in north Georgia, south of Ball Ground on the Etowah River. Then they carved an elaborate system of symbols on rocks and beech trees that showed them how to locate the tunnel entrance when they would return. But the only way to decipher the symbols was through a *key*. That *key* was etched onto a specially commissioned knife manufactured by none other than Arkansas blacksmith James Black, the creator of Jim Bowie's famous blade."

Jake's eyelids flickered. He could not believe what he was hearing.

"It was the last Bowie style knife that he ever made. A set of Cherokee runes was concocted for the key and James Black forged the blade in the art of Damascus steel. He then acid-etched the runes on the blade and designed the special coffin handle. He also crafted the sheath, too." Tommy pointed to the busted box on the desk in front of him that still contained the leather knife sheath, inlaid with Rattlesnake hide.

"So, this knife was commissioned by Ross while they were digging the tunnel and carving the wayfinding symbols?"

"Yep. It's a one of a kind. No duplicates. As Principal Chief and keeper of the treasury, Ross insisted on being the keeper of the tunnel, too. He felt it was like a bank for the wealthiest of his Cherokee followers. And he was the bank owner. Strange thing happened though, because soon after James Black delivered the knife, he had his faced clubbed in by his enraged father-in-law who didn't like him sleeping with his daughter. His own dog actually saved his life. Black's eyes were damaged beyond repair and he lost the art of blacksmithing for the rest of his life."

"Damn," Jake said. "Was it deliberate? By Ross?"

"Perhaps," Tommy shrugged. "Ross covering his tracks? Making sure no one knew how to decipher the knife key but him? If so, he would be in sole control of the knife and waybill and the tunnel until he'd have a chance to reclaim his treasures at a later date."

"But later never came," Jake said, finishing Tommy's thought.

"Lots of those original depositors were killed on the Trail of Tears," Tommy said. "Ross's own wife, too. The pool of people knowing about that cache had dwindled down to a handful as time went by. Knowing Ross's character, the fewer people who knew about it, the better for him. A few of the original depositors, who knew firsthand where the entrance to the tunnel was, tried to go back only to say white Georgians who occupied the lands shot at them for trespassing. One man never even made it back. He disappeared. Twenty years then passed and the dadgum secret stash remained hidden and untouched, known only to a small circle of his family and loyalists. Hell, Ross was too busy murdering his own Cherokee brethren to be bothered with it!"

Jake chimed in. "Until the Civil War."

"You mean the War of Northern Aggression, right, son?"

"If that's what you want to call it," Jake countered, not giving into

Tommy's Confederate sympathies. Jake thought of his own Civil War Seneca ancestor from New York, Lieutenant Colonel Ely Parker, who served as Union General Ulysses S. Grant's personal secretary. Over 620,000 soldiers died during that horrific war and he wasn't about to take sides and open that Pandora's box with the old man.

"Stand had the waybill and key, but couldn't get to the treasure because he was fighting the Yankees out West. Was doing so good they made him a brigadier general. So, that's when he sent Thomas Junior out on his mission to Georgia in 1864. He gave him the waybill and the knife to guide him to the Cherokee Tunnel."

"Okay," Jake said, pacing across the room, drink in hand. "I've got this timeline down now. In 1864, the Union Army under Sherman was sweeping south through north Georgia and if they took the land where the stash was hidden he could give access to Ross to finally take all his Cherokee gold back."

"Yes, you got it, brother!" Tommy gushed. He grabbed the bottle, adding a dash of booze to his own glass.

"And so Thomas Junior heads out from Arkansas . . ."

"But not as a Confederate soldier," Tommy interjected, raising a finger to note. "He mustered out of the Rifles. He headed out on this personal family business. As a *civilian*. Make no mistake about it, this was eye-for-an-eye revenge for what Ross did to his own daddy back in 1845. It was for Boudinot, for the Ridges, and for stealing the Cherokee treasury. And turning coat on the nation."

"He made it to Georgia alright, but then the Union Army captured him before he could find the secret tunnel, right?" asked Jake.

"Yep, at Barnsley's Woodlands mansion in Adairsville," Tommy said. "Chance encounter. Yankee cavalry on patrol had a skirmish there and Thomas Junior was caught traveling nearby. He was taken prisoner, his waybill and knife confiscated. They accused him of being a spy and threatened to hang him, but he had an audience with General James B. McPherson that same night."

Jake picked up the story, remembering from Tommy's recorded phone conversation earlier that morning. "And talked his way out of it. Retained his knife. But as a precaution, that's when McPherson kept the waybill and put it in his hat and wrote him the receipt."

"Right on," Tommy laughed. "You got the story. And that there receipt is in the box on the fireplace mantle there behind you," Tommy pointed. "The one with the gold braid. That braid came from McPherson's hat."

"This is crazy," Jake said, walking over to the fireplace. He stared inside the glass display box showing the gilded, braided hat cord with acorn terminals. Next to it was an old faded piece of paper yielding a handwritten promissory note signed by none other than General James B. McPherson. Another signature was by McPherson's orderly, A. J. Thompson, as a witness. The last person to sign was the one to receive the waybill after hostilities had ceased: Thomas Black Watie Jr.

Jake pulled out his smartphone from his pocket. "May I take a picture?"

Already having the key in his hand, Tommy tossed it to Jake who unlatched the hinged glass top. With his phone's built-in, high-resolution camera, Jake snapped several photos of the hat cord and receipt.

While Jake photographed the items, Tommy chirped up again. "After Thomas Junior left Adairsville he had no choice but to rejoin the Confederate Army. It was his best chance to hunt McPherson down and get close enough to retake his waybill. He was going back to war, but for different motives now. He joined up with the Army of Tennessee asking to serve with the 1st/15th Arkansas Infantry Regiment under brigade commander Colonel Daniel Govan and division commander Major General Patrick Cleburne."

Jake was truly impressed with Tommy's memory as he rattled off the names of commanders. He relocked the glass top to the case and tossed the key back to Tommy. "How do you remember all this?"

"Lived it all my life," Tommy replied, wasting no time in continuing with the story. "He was an expert marksman and they outfitted him with a Whitworth rifle. Wore a raven's feather in his hat. They called him the *Raven* after that. Killed many a Yankee. Look up there." Tommy pointed high above the fireplace to the display case containing the rifle he spoke of.

"The one he shot McPherson in the back with?"

"Shit, yeah it is," Tommy said in a higher pitched voice.

Jake raised his camera and shot a slew of close-up photos of the rifle, its cracked wooden stock, and long brass telescope. "That rifle alone could fetch a half million at auction. You see it's the story behind these objects that give them their true worth. These pieces speak to the men who wielded them. I know how much these all mean to you."

Jake's eyes wandered over to the other case on the mantle: the Navy Colt pistol. "And what about this Colt revolver in this case here?" Inside was a long revolver, vine and scroll engraved with ivory grips. There was a paper illustration depicting a battle along with a small note paper inside, too. "That pistol have any meaning to what's happening with the waybill and knife? Any connection?"

"Nope. None at all," said Tommy. "That pistol is an ivory-handled, 1861 Colt Navy, .36 caliber revolver. Granddaddy's 1st Arkansas Infantry commander, Lieutenant Colonel William H. Martin, gave it to him. You see, right after Adairsville Granddaddy waded into battle the likes of which he said he never seen before. It had a profound effect on him. It was different than riding horses in the Cherokee Mounted Rifles. He was now an infantryman on the front lines. But luckily he was kept back just a little because he was the most important sniper in the division. They valued him, didn't want him picked off. So before he knew it he was at Kennesaw Mountain in Marietta, Georgia, and Sherman was making a direct assault on their lines a bit south at Cheatham Hill."

"Yes, I know of this battle," added Jake. "It was a brutal, ugly assault by the Union on the toughest Confederate veterans in General Johnson's Army. It was Sherman's only direct frontal assault against set defenses during his entire Atlanta campaign. He'd never make that mistake again. He lost 3,000 men in less than an hour with no penetration of the CSA defenses. I believe it was at a location called the Dead Angle, am I right?"

"Very good, son. You've done your homework," an impressed Tommy said. "Granddaddy told me it was horrifying. Was sheer *butchery*. The Yankees charged uphill against firm entrenchments and we waited until the last moment and let loose with hidden cannon fire raking their lines. It created a wall of dead bodies all across the Dead Angle. There were dead Union boys from Illinois, Indiana, Kentucky, New York, and Ohio.

Scores more were wounded and trapped when the dry woods across from Granddaddy's unit caught in a blaze from the cannon fire. He said they were crying, screaming, and burning to death in front of them. Some of them poor, burning bastards he shot just to put 'em out of their misery."

"Jesus Christ," mumbled Jake. "I can't imagine."

"But then Junior saw something in the scope of his Whitworth. He saw a Yankee waving his arms up and down in that fire." Tommy gave Jake the secret arm signals of a Mason brother in distress. Jake's eyes widened. "He was giving the sacred sign of a Freemason. He was appealing for his enemy to save his life. Some on our side simply laughed at the Yankee flailing about like a bird, but Granddaddy recognized what it was and immediately told Colonel Martin. That's when the colonel dangerously stood up on top of the parapet and attached a white handkerchief to the end of a soldier's ramrod and shouted the famous cease fire.

"When the shooting stopped, he yelled out to the Yankees: 'Your wounded are being burnt... Some are members of the Masonic Order. Come and get 'em... We'll not fire a shot until they are removed.' That illustration there in the case, it was drawn based on exactly what happened."

The Famed Truce on Cheatham Hill by Alfred R. Waud, 1864.

"My God, Tommy," Jake said, spinning around to view the drawing again. "I've read many stories of enemy Masons helping each other out during the Civil War, but nothing like this one. This is the most incredible example of brother helping a brother I've ever come across. This took place in the *thick* of battle." Jake's mind was keyed up.

"A lot isn't written down, it comes down through word of mouth."

Jake knew how true that was. He had done extensive research on a similar Mason-on-Mason battlefield incident from the Revolutionary War that ended in betrayal and a torture death. His paper was published in a national Masonic publication out of the Scottish Rite Research Society in D.C. He couldn't help but think of a new research article meshing military and Masons once again, this time based on the Dead Angle, Colonel Martin, and the real hero, Thomas Black Watie Jr.

"Tell me more," Jake insisted.

"Sure thing," Tommy said, proudly. "I know this story by heart. A Major Luther M. Sabin of the 44th Illinois Infantry accepted the cease fire. Now get this: our own men scaled the head logs and were soon mixed with Yankees, stomping out the fire and carrying out dead and wounded Feds to their side of the fence."

Jake stood frozen, listening in astonishment.

"And, then," Tommy exclaimed, "when this humanitarian act was finished, a Federal colonel of 31st Indiana Regiment, named John Thomas Smith, so dang impressed was he, that he wrote a short note and then pulled from his belt a brace of fine, ivory-handled revolvers. He presented both of them to Colonel Martin with a little speech from his note in front of men from both sides of the fighting."

"What did he say?" pressed Jake.

"I'm getting there," Tommy smiled. "Follow along, son. It's the same note in the case there." Jake spun around again and read to himself as Tommy closed his eyes and joined in. "He said this: 'Accept these pistols with my appreciation of the nobility of this deed. It deserves to be perpetuated to the deathless honor of every one of you concerned in it; and should you fight a thousand other battles, and win a thousand other victories, you will never win another so noble as this.' "

Jake smiled. It was the truest act of valor he had ever known. At the bottom of the note Tommy had just read out loud, a hand-drawn Masonic symbol of the square and compasses surrounding a G was penned in, and signed with a flourish by Colonel Smith.

"And what did Colonel Martin do?" Tommy asked, continuing with the story. "He immediately called Thomas Junior over and gifted one of them revolvers to him for recognizing the Masonic sign. He gave him that note from Colonel Smith, too. Wanted him to share in the credit."

"Anything else happen?" Jake asked, still hoping for more.

"Within minutes they restarted the battle and the killing started up once again. Granddaddy told me when the Yankees fell back and the firing stopped, he never saw so many broken down men in his entire life. He said he was drenched with blood and sweat and sick as a horse. Most of the men were vomiting from sunstroke and exhaustion. He said their tongues were cracked for water and their faces blackened with powder and smoke, and their dead and wounded comrades piled up inside the trenches."

"Jesus," Jake said softly.

Both men went silent, deep in their own thoughts. They sipped their respective drinks. They could faintly hear Becky and Rae out in the kitchen laughing it up, obviously getting along great.

Tommy finally broke the ice. He wanted to fast forward to McPherson's death. "He found that hat braid next to McPherson's body after he shot him, ya know?" He pointed back at the case with the hat braid in it. "The Yankee private who was protecting McPherson's body told Junior that a Johnny Reb took the braid off and stole the general's hat as a trophy. That's how Granddaddy lost it. Never could locate it during or after the war."

"And that's how he failed his mission," Jake concluded. "He could never recover that hat and the waybill inside and get Ross's gold as the ultimate act of revenge."

"Yes, that part he did fail."

"Huh?" Jake asked as he sat back down in his chair. "That part?"

"Why yes. The mission was threefold," said Tommy, raising three thin fingers. "He failed the first two parts—related to finding the Cherokee Tunnel and a Spanish trophy inside that pointed to even more gold locations throughout Georgia, but he sure as shit accomplished the most important part of all."

Jake shook his head, frustratingly confused. *Spanish trophy? More gold across Georgia.* Did he hear Tommy right or was the booze just getting to him? "And what was that most important part?"

"Why, he assassinated John Ross."

"W-what?" Jake asked, perplexed.

"Poisoned him in late 1865 when Ross returned to Arkansas claiming he was head of Cherokee Nation again, trying to negotiate a treaty with Washington. My, the audacity of that power-hungry fool. General Watie and Granddaddy conspired to finish him off, though. An old witch supplied the poison and the curse and Granddaddy did the honors of slipping it into Ross's shot of whiskey at a tavern. Over the next ten months, his insides slowly ate away. It was a horrendous, yet justified, way to go. He died in Washington, D.C., a befitting place for that fraud of a man."

"Jesus Christ, I guess so," Jake said. *If only we can do that to some of the same wretches that live there today.*

"And that's when General Watie gave him this here Masonic ring as a reward," said Tommy. "Granddaddy handed the ring down to my daddy, Thomas the Third, who was a Mason, too. And I became a Mason and wore it after he passed. And of course, my pathetic, irresponsible, no-good lying son, Tom Black, wanted nothing to do with the Craft. Hell, he would have pawned this ring off if he ever got a hold of it. And so this ring has remained locked away with no heir." Tommy paused.

Silence followed. The entire house was still, it seemed.

Jake turned to Tommy and in somewhat of an accusatory tone said, "Let me get this straight. Your granddaddy saves enemy Freemasons in the heat of battle. Complete strangers. And then he goes and murders John Ross, a fellow Mason, in cold blood *after* the war is over? Not only were they brothers of the fraternity, but Cherokee brothers as well."

"Ross was an out and out power hungry, murdering dictator. His men killed my great granddaddy. His men killed my kinfolk!" Tommy said, raising his voice and standing up in defiance. A finger waggled at Jake. "He wasn't hardly no Cherokee. He was a conniving politician and he finally got a taste of his own medicine. I'm proud of what Granddaddy did. Revenge is ever *sooooo* sweet," he hissed. "And it's ri-damn-diculous for anyone to claim it isn't."

"It is, Tommy." Jake protested, raising his hand to calm the older man down. He knew he had crossed the line by judging Tommy's ancestors' deeds and immediately regretted it. After all, his own past actions were anything shy of tiptoeing through the tulips.

"I've tasted that revenge, too, Tommy," Jake said. "And it *does* taste good. Believe me. I was just stating that family always comes first over Masonic obligations. If one Mason cannot trust another in deed and in character, then he has no obligation, no responsibility and no regrets for whatever happens."

Tommy immediately nodded, the fire in his eyes subsided.

Turning away, Jake scratched his chin and rubbed his temple in thought. Something bugged him still. "Listen, brother. Go back a little, will you? You mentioned a Spanish trophy and even *more* gold? It was when you spoke about the first two parts of the mission that Thomas Junior failed?"

"One, he had to find the tunnel," Tommy reiterated, much more relaxed, sitting back in his chair, hands crossed, fingers intertwined, with the exception of one index finger raised. "That was the first part. And then he was supposed to take an inventory of the deposits because he certainly couldn't carry much out of there. The second part was moving everything out of there with Confederate troops to put it all in our treasury. But then . . . ," his voice trailed off and he took a deep breath.

"He had to confirm that one of the items in the inventory even *existed*," Tommy continued. "It was the most highly-prized trophy in all of the Cherokee Nation. It was supposedly placed there in a vault owned by an elder Cherokee chief by the name of Red Fox. After Granddaddy killed Ross, then General Watie told him the true story of this trophy and why his mission was so critical at the time."

Jake impatiently moved to the edge of his chair, hunched over, head swimming, eyes glued on Tommy. He knew General Watie had ulterior motives.

"This trophy is called the Golden Horse. It's a solid gold statue made by an ancient Cherokee goldsmith."

Jake's mouth dropped open. Just when things couldn't get any more complicated now he was hearing about a gold trophy horse. "You're kidding me, right?"

"I shit you not. It's legendary." Tommy threw his hands in the air to illustrate. "A big, beautiful Spanish Andalusian. It was crafted to celebrate the defeat of Hernando de Soto's expedition back in the 1540s when the Spaniards were mining and stealing our gold and making slaves of our people and raping our women. General Watie said that anyone who possessed this horse was said to have untold wealth, because inside the base block of the horse trophy somehow was a drawer containing a hand-drawn, highly detailed *map manuscript* of the land throughout north Georgia. Apparently, this all-encompassing map showed the location of every gold, silver, gemstone, and rare earth mine ever known. Every metal there was that came out of the ground was supposed to be on that there map in detailed locations."

Jake's mouth was still open, drawing on every word Tommy spoke.

"They say it was illustrated by de Soto's own cartographic engineer. But our people rose up and they stole that map from the Spanish. Killed a bunch of Spanish soldiers and enslaved the cartographer and forced him to teach them his art of mapmaking over the years. Without that map the invaders had no power."

Jake interrupted. "For he who controls the map, controls the lands."

"Right," said Tommy. "Later on, after the Spanish left, the Cherokee nation flourished and they mined their own gold for the next couple hundred years. The map was added on to by Cherokee cartographers and prospectors committed to protecting it in an ancient secret society. It soon became an atlas—a book of many Cherokee maps."

"Astounding!" Jake shouted. "What was this secret society called?"

"Their Cherokee name was Ani-Alisdelisgi-Dalonega."

Jake's eyebrows rose at hearing the last word, again. Tommy had told him earlier they had the nation's first gold rush in 1828. The city also had one of the nation's first Federal gold mints there, too, now a museum. He knew the Cherokee word "Dalonega" meant gold. "I'm not even going to try and repeat that name."

"Translated in English it means: The Guardians of Gold."

"Intriguing. Very intriguing." Jake watched as Tommy sat back drawing a breath, ready to elaborate further. He could tell the old man was rather enjoying himself telling all of these old time stories to an attentive young listener who shared his passion for history.

"In the early 1800s the guardians secretly bequeathed this map to a man named James Vann, a Cherokee plantation owner. He was the wealthiest Cherokee man to have ever lived and was someone they felt could be trusted. Vann was allied with Major Ridge and Charles Hicks. They ruled the Cherokee at the time. Were called the Triumvirate. Based on that gold map, Vann developed many gold and silver mines all across the Georgia mountains. He owned something like 100 slaves who worked those mines. And he owned farms, ferries, and stores, too. At the time, Cherokee James Vann was the second richest man in the United States behind John Jacob Astor. Bet no one ever told you that before?"

"No, they sure have not. I've never heard of James Vann."

"But sure as shit, Vann became a murdering drunkard who abused his gift of the map. He was a real monster when on the juice. Someone eventually murdered him in 1809 in Hightower, Georgia. Shot him dead. His body disappeared. And his killer was never caught. However, some years later the Guardians made it known that the map was back in their hands and safely secured again inside the Golden Horse."

Tommy smacked his lips. "The way the story goes is the Golden Horse didn't appear again until 1838 when Chief Red Fox presented it at the secret tunnel to be deposited. Was the night before the entrance would be sealed up for good. He announced he was one of the Guardians. You see, Red Fox couldn't take it with him during the Indian Removal and he didn't want the map falling into the U.S. government hands, so Ross's tunnel was the safest and most secretive vault there was to hide it in. Especially since Ross's number one enemy was the United States of America."

"And did Red Fox go on the Trail of Tears, too?"

"Yes. And he froze to death that winter, like so many others."

"So, wait a second. Let me get this straight," Jake said, his mind blurred from the overload of information on top of several glasses of whiskey. "One." Jake held up a finger. "The waybill in McPherson's hat leads to the Cherokee Tunnel cache of gold." Tommy nodded. "Two." Another finger up. "Inside that tunnel is a gold trophy horse which apparently holds an ancient mining map of north Georgia. And it shows where gold, silver and gemstones are that date back to the mid-1500s and the Spanish?"

Tommy nodded again. "I guess that map even has locations of veins of even more exotic metals that haven't even been touched. Stuff that predates the Spanish. But that's what I've learned over a lifetime of doing my own research into the legend. I've spoken to many historians, researchers, mining experts, anyone. Even traveled to Spain and dug into the Spanish government archives, too."

Jake held up a third finger. "And, three. Tom Black knows about this legend? About all the research you did into it."

"We told him when he was much younger, but he never did believe it. Matter of fact, he laughed at us and told me and my daddy to, quote-unquote, '*fuck off with your little Cherokee treasure hunt.*'"

"And all the years you spent looking for it? I would imagine you were pretty obsessed by it, too. I know I'd be."

"Obsession is an understatement. My wife Margaret supported me and respected it, but it was a bone of contention between me and my son. Apparently in his world of entitlement, I didn't show him enough attention. Said I loved the Cherokee more than I loved him. He was a big, fucking pacifist pussy. Led to our falling out eventually. And get this: he publicly lied about who made our family business successful. It was in a University of Georgia newspaper article about how incredibly intelligent he was and how he was the brains behind the expansion of our lumber business. He took all the credit for what me, Daddy, and Granddaddy had busted our asses over a lifetime to get generating the kind of wealth that company had; and here comes the Fortunate Son claiming it was because of his genius. The piece of shit was merely a forklift driver at the time! Well, I was *appalled*. Appalled and embarrassed at how my own son was inflating his ego and conning his fellow students at the expense of his own family."

"What a bastard."

"I wish he was a bastard!" Tommy yelled. "That way I couldn't claim him as my own blood. He was nothing but a spoiled, miserable, demanding, useless child. Never satisfied with anything. I set the table for him and he stole the food, you could say. And then some years later he started stealing from our family ancestor collection, too. Damn him! Okay, I've said enough. That's all history now. We know where we stand."

"Well, apparently his memory has been refreshed," Jake said, shaking his head back and forth. "This totally gives motivation for acting so brazenly in pulling off these thefts. It's all about this Spanish mining map that's been stolen over and over again by thieves. Whoever possesses it has untold wealth and power. Who *wouldn't*, with a treasure map like that? Especially a conniving politician with a big head and deep pockets."

"Yes, Jake. The map is really what it's all about."

"It's literally a map of damned thieves is what it really is," Jake stated. "A *map* of *thieves*."

"That it is," Tommy sadly agreed.

"It's one hell of a story I have to admit," Jake said with a wry smile knowing he was already hooked. It's what he craved: to seek and to find, to revel in the joy of discovery. It was an obsession he himself couldn't resist.

Tommy mumbled and then took a deep breath. His words came out slurred from the alcohol. "Listen, I got something more to say."

"Go on."

After a long pause, Tommy spoke. "Jake, I heard the cackle of the raven coming to get me before I had my heart attack. I cheated death, son. And I'm not ready to have that witch steal the years I have left. It ain't gonna steal my dreams."

Jake's brows creased. "A raven?"

"The most evil creature there is. We call it a Raven Mocker or a Kaw-lo-nah Aye-lisk in the ancient tongue. It's also been called the Night Goer, the Imitator, and the Angel of Death. You're not even supposed to say that dadgum name too loud or too many times. Dang thing will hear you." Tommy took a long sip of whiskey. "My son is acting like one now. Coming to visit me with ill will, in my own house. He's tormenting me. He wants to steal my last years before it's time."

"I see."

"What tribe are you affiliated with, Jake?" Tommy had trouble pronouncing the word "affiliated" because of the booze.

"Iroquois heritage. Seneca ancestry. I know of some of the black forces of which you speak. I, too, have experienced the supernatural. Believe me, Tommy." Jake took a long gulp of his drink.

Tommy's eyes grew large. "Iroquois speak of black witches shape shifting into screech owls. It's the same with the Cherokee Raven Mocker. The witch, when looking human, resembles a very old man. Older than me. This creature has lived for hundreds of years, preying on sickly victims. He's like an immortal. He comes to you at night when you're sick. At first he's invisible, but then turns into a raven with big ol' black wings and flies to your home." Tommy waved his hands above his head.

"You hear his cackle. He imitates the sound of a diving raven when he arrives. Shrieking. Wailing. Laughing at you." Tommy pounded a fist on his desk. "He beats on the roof, pounds on the side of your house." He stood up. "Lifts you right out of bed, and slams you on the floor." He slammed his fist again. "He wants death! To torture you and shake you silly. Choke the air out of you. He wants you to die faster and not use up any of the years you have left so he can add them to his own and stay immortal."

"God, I've never heard of this," Jake said, head throbbing, trying to picture this witch tormenting his victim. "What the hell?"

"It's all fact. They exist for real."

Jake tipped his glass to Tommy. Things were getting so complicated. "Top me off, will ya?" Tommy readily complied, pouring more whiskey in Jake's glass. Jake added some more ice. "How does this witch creature actually steal your years?"

"When it finally kills you he carves out your heart without leaving a single trace. He then roasts it over a fire. And eats it."

"W-what? That's crazy!"

"It's true. Roasted hearts have been found in homes of Raven Mockers posing as the old man."

"Well how in the hell do you kill one?"

"Only a 'Witch Killer' can do it, a medicine man. Only he can see one in its human form with a special potion. Raven Mockers aren't invisible to him. He lures it in and sets a trap at the victim's house. He shoots a sharpened silver spear through its head and then in seven days it will die. Any Cherokee person who dies within those seven days? Well, we know it was the witch."

"There's powerful forces out there beyond the living world," Jake blabbered, his eyes fixated on a spot over Tommy's shoulder. "I saw them. Felt them. Was almost killed by them. I know what you mean."

"Did you kill it?"

Jake looked up and met Tommy's eyes. "I did. Rae and I did. She's still traumatized over it, I think."

Tommy nodded. "We've gotta lot in common, brother."

"Indeed we do, sir. We don't piss on our ancestors' graves."

Tommy picked up on that. "A man's achievements as a warrior are a sign of his spiritual leadership and power. My son is not a warrior, my son is not a leader, my son is not even a feared Raven Mocker," he summed up. "He's just a piece of shit *parasite*. And one I want to flush down the toilet for good."

"Hmmm," hummed Jake in agreement, a swig of whiskey more.

"But *you* are a true warrior, Jake. I've read up on your military background after your very first show on *Battlefield Investigators*. You're not some by-the-book kinda soldier. I admire that. You're a man of action, not some wishy-washy, namby pamby who needs a committee to make a decision. You get shit done, son."

"It's why the director of MHI keeps me in the field," laughed Jake. "Because I rub administrators the wrong way. I can't tolerate the bullshit politics. I'd rather get things done than pontificate on the process of how things get done, if you catch my drift."

"And that's why I want you to work for me personally. Off the books. *Not* as a lieutenant colonel in the U.S. Army. Not as a Fed. But as a man worthy and well-qualified."

"Excuse me?"

Tommy raised his glass. "It's why I asked you and your lady to stay here tonight. I wanted to talk with *you* in private. And to tell you the story of what's really going on."

"I knew you had another motive," Jake chuckled.

"That knife was stolen for one reason and one reason only. It means that waybill in the hat *does* exist."

"Right. I figured as much."

"You see, Jake," Tommy said quietly. "Sometimes you spend your whole life pursuing a dream or a legend and it just doesn't pan out no matter how much you wanted it to. My whole life I've been obsessed with our family history and the thrill of the hunt. And proud of it."

Jake agreed. "No shame in that."

"But the dadgum obsession was all for naught. Sucks the life right out of you in disappointment. But, what if, Jake? What if you had one last shot at it? To prove that your dream does exist, that it *can* come true. That all the time, effort, and broken relationships along the way could now be justified . . . could be redeemed? Would you pass up that chance? Hell, NO, you wouldn't!"

"Nope. Sure wouldn't."

"Your discovery of McPherson's hat, the heart attack I had, and me coming back from death, well . . . it was my sign. I acted on it, didn't I? I called you. I didn't give up on my dream. And since my knife was stolen on the same day as the hat, it means the waybill *does* exist. It changes the game. It means my boy is stealing my dream. And there's no way in hell I'll ever let that happen."

Jake caught himself nodding.

"I'm physically gone, brother, but mentally I'm still here." Tommy tapped his temple for emphasis. "You may see an old man on the outside, but behind the wrinkles I am the same nineteen year-old riding in Patton's army itching for a fucking fight."

"Sure are, brother."

"And I want to bring back those Nazi relics, too. You're right. They mean too much to too many folks. I would finish this mission if I could, but I *can't*. I'm homebound. Can't hardly even walk. I'm on my way to that house not made with hands," he said, looking up at the ceiling, referring to the Masonic phrase describing heaven. "And I don't know how long I got left." He stared at Jake.

"So, I'm asking *you* to go back out there and finish the Watie mission for me. Get that hat and waybill, get my knife back. You find that dadgum Cherokee Tunnel for me and let's see if that *Map of Thieves*, as you call it, is really in there. I know you love the thrill of the hunt, too; so now's your big chance."

Jake ran his fingers through his hair and sighed heavily. He didn't give a verbal response, though. He knew he wanted the adventure, the danger, the discovery, but he also knew he'd potentially be going after a U.S. congressman if it turned out Black truly was the culprit. Jake would have to be a thief to steal from a thief. And Black was one of the most dangerous ones around, at that. Black was a creature who could change your friends into your enemies with a simple phone call.

What are the risks? The consequences?

On the flip side, he thought, a quest like this was so far removed from the mundane existence of everyday living. Hunting for lost historical artifacts and treasure is one of the most exciting addictions in the entire world. Deep down he knew he was an addict after the last hunt he had gone on; so to turn down this incredible chance was simply absurd. His inner voice was calling.

Tommy seemed to think Jake's silence meant he was wavering. "I will fund this mission. Any equipment you need. Any transportation. Bring your girl, Rae. Bring anyone on board you need to. I have people in mind that can help you, too. If you accept this mission you will need that help, trust me. Is it money you seek? Money ain't no issue, I've got tons of it."

Jake shook his head and exhaled loudly, still in shock at what the old man was throwing at him.

Tommy was pleading now. He slapped his hand on the desk to get Jake's attention. "Listen to me! As a finder's fee, I will let you have the very first deposit ever made inside that tunnel."

"What would that be?"

"Legend has it there's a stash of seven gold bars weighing fifty pounds each. This bullion was bound for the newly opened Dahlonega Mint and was meant for striking the first gold coins as the exchange to miners for their gold dust and nuggets. But the stagecoach carrying the gold bars got ambushed by Cherokee on the Federal Road in defiance of the year they would be removed from their lands. That was January of 1838. They immediately hid the gold in the tunnel as the very first deposit."

"You're going to give *that* to me if I discover the tunnel?"

"You have my Word as a man and a Mason."

Jake remained quiet, then asked what if the gold bars weren't in there.

"Dadgummit boy," an animated Tommy shouted. "There's gonna be enough treasure to go around. Them tunnel depositors were all part of John Ross's party and they conspired to kill my kin folk. So I'll be divvying up their loot as redemption against their crimes. With one exception, though."

"What's that?"

"I want Ross's personal vault. I decide what to do with whatever's in there. How's that sound to you? That's a square deal for the risks involved I'd think?"

Jake nodded to his offer. "That's more than fair, Tommy. I can live with those terms. But what about the *Map of Thieves*? What will you do with that map if we find it? To possess that kind of knowledge will bring great power. And great corruption, for sure."

Tommy rose up out of his chair and wavered a bit. He steadied himself with two hands on the desk and stared Jake in the eyes. "I have my plans for the map, Jake. Don't think I haven't spent many a sleepless night thinking what to do with it—how best to use it."

"Want to share those plans?" Jake asked. "If I'm going to risk my life in finding it I have a right to know what genie I'm letting out of the bottle."

"Indeed you do," Tommy said, bowing his head. "To be honest, Jake, everyone already knows there's still gold up in North Georgia. So what the hell am I personally going to do with that map? Can't take it with me. My desire though, my requirement is, it cannot fall into the hands of the Federal government."

He paused, stood fully upright, then boomed: "It belongs to the citizens of this country. If the Feds get a hold of it they will rape our lands even worse than what happened when we were removed as a people. Feds cannot be trusted. Period." He crossed his arms over his chest.

Jake tapped his own chest. "But, I'm a Fed."

"You're an upright man, first and foremost. I trust your judgement as a man. You serve the country based on your oath. I'm talking about those career manipulators, the oligarchy of the political elite. Those who would corrupt the knowledge that map contains. Politicians."

Tommy bent over and leaned into the broken knife case on the desktop. He carefully reached in and pulled out the empty knife sheath and pointed it at Jake as he spoke. "I'm for giving the *Map of Thieves* a second chance in the right man's hands. The Guardians thought it could be a force of good. And so do I. I'll leave it wide open like that."

Jake replied that Tommy's proposal sounded completely reasonable.

"But for me personally," Tommy added. "I only want to walk into that Cherokee Tunnel and see all them vaults. Then walk in Ross's vault for our family's final redemption. To lay my hands on the Golden Horse and hold that map in my hands would be the cherry on the sundae. I just want all that work and sacrifice me, and Daddy, and Granddaddy did over so many years to be worth a goddamn. I just want it to end with me knowing it all really exists. That's all this old man wants, to finish chasing that dream."

Jake sympathized with Tommy. The old man had certainly iced the cake. A once-in-a-lifetime treasure hunt at the request of a fellow brother Freemason, Army vet, and Native American from a renowned family? Completely funded. Not answering to any D.C. bureaucrat? And working on a parallel ulterior mission to his current investigation on recovering the stolen West Point Museum items. A mission in which the prize would be bars of gold? The thought was intoxicating, and it wasn't due to the whiskey.

Tommy was 100% correct about the Feds. If Tom Black or the power hungry, governing elite, Democrat and Republican political factions got a hold of the mining map, they would set up front corporations with cronies and mine every inch of that territory. They would subvert the laws and claim eminent domain on every single property a private citizen owned that contained a potential gold or silver mine. They would do it for "national security" purposes and would reap billions in new found wealth for themselves to squander even further. Jake had to bust that cycle of power and history repeating itself. He could never let the map fall into the hands of someone corrupt like Tom Black.

He decided right there to take on Watie's unfinished mission.

Jake stood up and held out his hand. "I'll do it, Tommy."

"You're a good man, Jake Tununda." Tommy smiled and accepted Jake's hand with a firm grip, his thumb moving to a certain knuckle on Jake's. He pulled him close so the two men were chest to chest. Tommy finished the embrace with several more secret Masonic points of contact before whispering in Jake's ear. "You have my Word." He then handed Jake the empty knife sheath. "Find it all for me."

Jake nodded. "So mote it be."

10

N ATHAN KULL WAS SPENT. HE HAD BEEN DRIVING straight through most of the last twelve hours except for a few hour-long naps at rest stops along Interstate 85 South. Garbage from a Krystal fast food restaurant and vending machine snacks littered the interior of his Lexus rental. The nighttime driving had taken its toll. His back hurt, his neck was stiff, his left leg was numb; he could hardly keep his drooping eye lids open, let alone maintain his lane without looking like he was driving while intoxicated. On top of that, he had to piss.

Pushing himself further with caffeine pills that made his hands shake and face twitch, he had finally made it to metro Atlanta where the interstate was lit up from high-powered light poles across the seven lanes on his southbound side. Traffic, this early on a Monday morning, was virtually nonexistent, making it all the easier to get closer into Atlanta. He could then grab several hours of sleep and awake later in the morning fresh for his final delivery of the birthday boy's hat. That location was still yet to be determined by his broker.

First priority was unloading his prizes. Back around Baltimore, after informing Mona that he refused to send the rest of the map digitally, he explored on his smartphone for a storage facility in Atlanta off the I-85. He lucked out when he noticed a Public Storage company and a chain hotel, which offered extended stay studio kitchenettes right next door to each other. Calling Public Storage before they closed for the night, he had reserved the smallest storage compartment available, a 5 foot by 5 foot locker within the confines of the secure main storage building. About the size of small, walk-in closet, the locker was way more than he needed for the hat and two Nazi pieces he had stuffed in his backpack. But he also planned on stashing his burglary kit duffle bag, too. He needed to get everything incriminating off his person until he knew when and where the hat delivery would take place.

The best part about the locker was he would have access to it 24 hours a day, seven days a week, with a special security code to enter the building any time he wanted. For thieves, these storage facilities—ranging from lockers to garages—were essentially mini safe houses. For a nominal fee you could rent and store anything you wanted no questions asked. Stolen goods, vehicles, even bodies. Kull had used them many times before under various aliases.

He placed another call to the hotel and he had a room reserved, too. Taking Exit 99 off I-85 South, Kull made a right onto Jimmy Carter Boulevard. His destination was less than a quarter of a mile on the right before Buford Highway. Normally jammed with traffic every day, he cruised down the empty boulevard of long warehouses and silent strip plazas squinting through half-closed eyes for his turn off. A minute later, he spotted the Public Storage facility sign next to a 24-hour Dunkin' Donuts bakery. A slow right into the entrance and he came to a median and a fork. On the left was the lit up donut shop and hotel. To the right was the storage facility building.

He veered right and parked on the side of the storage facility's dimly lit main building in front of a side door keypad entrance. No one else was around. *Perfect.* Shutting down the engine and turning off his lights, Kull leaned his head back and closed his eyes for a temporary rest before unloading and entering the facility.

▼

Dunkin' Donuts

Four young Latino men sitting inside the Dunkin' Donuts couldn't help but notice a silver Lexus pull into the Public Storage entrance and park at the side of the building. Their eyes widened and they shared whispers. With a nod to the others, the oldest—a ripped, heavily tattooed, twenty-five year-old, completely bald on top but with a black goatie around his mouth—got up and motioned for the others to follow.

"Time to go shopping, *muchachos*," announced Alejandro "Angel" Hernandez as he quickly headed to the door. His platinum "grill" flashed when he spoke. A grill was a removable covering made of silver, gold or platinum and worn over the front teeth as jewelry to indicate wealth or luxury. Angel wore his grill on his lower set of teeth creating an impression of a flashy, snarling dog.

He was a hardcore member of the most violent gang in all of metro Atlanta: Sureños-13. And he was also the second in command, the right hand man or *Mano Derecha*, behind *El Jefe* (the Boss), who was back in Mexico coordinating a large shipment of drugs into Atlanta. Angel was also the designated enforcer who imposed discipline on the forty other members. Just last night, he tortured a fifteen year-old boy in a local drug house because he thought the teen had talked to the cops about the gang. The torture lasted five hours as he beat the teen and broke two of his fingers. He also shoved a gun in the kid's mouth and burned him with a hot butter knife before letting him go. No one fucked with Angel or betrayed Sur-13.

Members of the gang lived and operated along the Buford Highway corridor paralleling the north side of Interstate 85. Their gang territory stretched from Norcross, outside of the I-285 perimeter in Gwinnett County, all the way south to the Lindbergh area in the city of Atlanta. A highly commercialized, industrialized, and densely populated corridor, it was made up predominantly of Hispanic immigrants and illegal aliens with heavy concentrations of Asians and Blacks in between. It was one of the true melting pots of ethnicities in Atlanta.

An illegal himself, having come over the Mexican border with his uncle when he was eleven, Angel had worked in local restaurants as an undocumented worker before being recruited into the gang in his early teens. Convicted for aggravated assault and marijuana possession over three years ago, but set free under deportation orders by the Department of Homeland Security's Immigration and Customs Enforcement division or ICE, he ignored deportation and had lived openly ever since.

Local law enforcement knew he was around, but their hands were tied by partisan political ICE policies meant to be sensitive and non-offensive toward Hispanics. In the cops' eyes the lenient immigration policies, in direct violation of national law, allowed criminal elements like Angel to roam free in exchange for Democrat votes from Latinos during elections.

All four of the young men were from broken homes, with little money, and low levels of education. Each wore some type of blue and gray clothing with Atlanta Braves baseball branding. With the exception of Angel, the other three members also wore Atlanta Braves baseball hats. This attire distinguished them from other major city Sur-13 chapters who also took on the athletic colors of their home sports team. Still, all chapters were required to wear blue. All chapters paid allegiance to the original Southern California-based Mexican Mafia prison gang as foot soldiers, as signified by the thirteenth letter of the alphabet, M for Mafia in their gang name.

Sureños-13 gang members were basically rabid human wolves who preyed on the most vulnerable of society: the law-abiding sheep. The gang was involved in major violent crimes including homicides, kidnapping, domestic violence, armed robbery, drug trafficking, and human trafficking. Angel had done it all in his short career. This early morning he would stand back and provide overwatch for his training officer and two new young recruits.

A wiry, nineteen year-old with a thin mustache, named Enrique "Toro" Ramirez, was Angel's lieutenant. He and two youngsters, both fourteen, left their donuts half-eaten on the table and followed Angel outside. Gray hoodies were draped over their heads and ball caps. The two youngest were designated as "pee wees," and part of a unit known as the "Tiny Locos," made up of new recruits. Toro was in charge of their training.

The skinnier of the two pee wees was Freddy "Flaco" Peña and aptly nicknamed so. The kid was subdued, but when pressed he had out of control anger. He was Angel's nephew from his older sister and already had a police record for robbery and terroristic threats. The other kid was a handsome, little guy named Hugo Aguilar. His big mouth and even bigger attitude earned him the street name "Chente." His run-ins with the law began when he was just eleven and included battery and fighting in school. Both punks wore their pants sagging low with boxer underwear hanging out the rear. Each wore thin, silver rope necklaces over their Braves t-shirts. Under their ball caps they wore blue bandanas.

Over the last few months, Toro had been teaching the Tiny Locos how to properly mark Sur-13 graffiti in the gang's territory, how to steal property and cash through robberies, how to be lookouts for rivals, and how to commit acts of violence against rival gang members. Summer vacation from school for the two kids was all about more criminal action in order to gain respect in their peer's eyes.

Toro would introduce them to carjacking on this dark morning. He explained to the pee wees that jacking a car was a much easier alternative than actually trying to break in and steal the vehicle because of the increased complexity of anti-theft security devices. But Angel—as senior consultant on training—strictly advised them to leave the person driving it alone. Their time for a hit—a stabbing or a shooting—would come later as they progressed in their training. Toro emphasized they would just grab the car for a joy ride. They'd steal the stereo and then ditch the vehicle after they drove it around for awhile.

Toro took the lead and quickly closed to the Lexus not thirty feet away. Under the glow of a security lamp on the side of the storage building, he could see the driver resting his head back on the seat's head rest. Cloaked in darkness, he stopped under a tree on a landscaped median separating the storage facility and hotel. The two pee wees were at each of Toro's shoulders. Angel took up the rear, tapped Chente on the arm, then slipped a Glock semi-automatic pistol into his hands for the training op.

"Okay my little *niños*, remember how we do it," Toro said in thickly accented Spanglish. "Chente is gunman and demands the keys. Flaco, you *get* the keys. Me and Angel will be right behind you in case the sheep goes *loco*. Wait until he gets out and shuts his door then point your gun at him.

. . comprende, Chente?"

"*Sí*," Chente whispered back, fumbling with the Glock.

"*Vamos a hacer esta mierda,*" said Flaco. (Let's do this shit.)

"But I'm driving that Lexus," emphasized Toro with a laugh.

Angel smacked him on the arm. "Sshh, he's getting out. Get ready."

▼

Who they were, where they came from, what they looked like, how many there were he never knew. It all happened so fast. As soon as he had shut his car door and slung the backpack with stolen goods over his shoulder, he heard several pairs of footsteps approach him from behind. All Kull heard was, "Hey, *hombre*," in a Spanish accent and they struck. He was too tired and too slow to turn around in time and was cracked on the back of the head with something hard. It knocked him out instantly.

He awoke about ten minutes later sprawled face first on the parking lot, his head pounding in severe pain. With a moan, he spat out a piece of gravel from his mouth and reached back to feel where he had been hit on his skull. There was mushy wetness on his scalp. Drawing his hand in front of his face, he could see in the dim light he had been bleeding, but luckily the gash had clotted on its own.

Kull slowly turned over and sat up, wincing in even more excruciating pain. He groggily looked around him and noticed a blue bandana rag lying next to him. *What the . . ?* Looking up, confused, he saw that his rental car was gone. That meant his personal travel bag and burglary kit were lost, too. His iPhone was missing as well. Usually he carried it on his hip in a little belt case. Fortunately, he did still have his wallet in his front pocket. As a thief, he knew never to carry it in his back pocket, like most men, because it was the first place pick pockets stole from.

Searching around some more, he then realized the worst: the backpack holding the Nazi baton, pistol, and McPherson's hat—with waybill stuffed back inside—was missing, too. He searched all around him to no avail. Closing his eyes, his shoulders sagged in defeat. He had lost everything in an instant. The job he had risked everything for was completely blown.

I'm fucked.

Not sure what to do or where to go, he snatched up the blue rag and pressed it on the back of his head then got up and staggered over to the side keypad entrance to the storage building where he could at least see better under the light. Obviously, he had been carjacked and robbed. He figured the blue bandana may have been a calling card from who clocked him. He also assumed no one witnessed the crime at this early hour in an isolated parking lot, otherwise the cops would have been there already.

Actually, he thought, that was the only positive outcome he could think of besides still having his wallet with credit cards, IDs, and cash. In his current bloody condition, he couldn't go to his hotel room just yet as the night manager would probably call an ambulance on him for his own good.

No transportation, no phone, bloody, exhausted, and out of options, Kull slumped down in shame. After a minute of self-pity he looked up slowly and subsequently noticed a surveillance camera on the corner of the building pointed toward the parking lot.

Well, whaddya know?

It also dawned on him he had the storage facility code to get into the building and his pre-paid locker. Tapping in the code and unlocking the keypad door with renewed vigor, he entered a hallway filled with five foot high locker closets along both walls. Turning a corner, he also found a restroom reserved for patrons. His luck was improving.

Taking a few minutes to wash off the blood and grime, Kull then sat down on the toilet to mull things over. Elbow on knee, chin on fist, eyes closed, he thought his options through. The pounding in his head was replaced with deep, vengeful anger.

"Of all people, I get robbed," he said to himself in a mumble. Then he screamed, "*Unfuckingbelievable!*" That certainly didn't help his head feel any better. In fact, he nearly doubled over from the piercing pain.

And then it dawned him. His iPhone had all of the photos on it from his museum recon the day before the theft. It also had the lone cropped photo of the waybill map he had sent to his broker. *Why didn't I delete all those pictures?* His stomach turned and he became nauseous once he realized the implications of how that phone could incriminate him. Every job had a screw up and this was his.

But it wasn't just the pictures. The phone contained information on his true identity, his network of professional contacts, and other identifiable and fraudulent data on his many aliases. *Should of bought one of the throw-away phones. Stupid. Stupid. Stupid.*

Never one for violence he now knew it was definitely in his playbook to get his phone and his loot back at all costs. And that meant killing for it.

Where to start? He wasn't even sure if the carjacking was a random act or a planned one related to his theft. But first he needed to use his skills to track down the robbers. Looking at the surveillance camera tapes of the parking lot where he had been jumped was the first step. He would find out who did this.

Then track the motherfuckers down.

"Wait a second," Kull said, just realizing that having his iPhone stolen was actually a Godsend. It was installed with an Apple GPS tracking app called Find My iPhone that would pinpoint its location and in all likelihood, the robbers, too, that is *if* they didn't delete the program.

In order for it to work he needed an Internet-enabled computer to log into his iCloud account. As a security expert himself, he knew a facility such as this would have their playback equipment, monitors, and a computer in the manager's office somewhere near the front entrance. But that lobby and office area was walled off from the back storage locker section where he now was. The front office was probably under a motion detector alarm system linked up to a private security company and the local police. Smashing the common locked doorway to enter that front section would surely set off alarms and bring the cops within minutes. That direct, bold approach was out of the question.

However, climbing up inside the ceiling structure and over the wall was not. It was something he had done many times during burglaries. It was a much exploited weakness in architecture. Plus, it would be hours before the morning crew came into work so he had more than enough time to put on a spider act.

He'd have to crawl across the girders and drop ceiling to find the right room, then slither down to see what he could find in equipment.

Time to get to work.

The Phoenix would rise again.

▼

The joyride of the stolen Lexus lasted only fifteen minutes once Angel was finished bitch-slapping Chente in the backseat for disobeying training orders. The kid was a crying mess with a bruised face and busted lip after Angel had finished beating him. It had to be done to keep recruits in line. He needed to be ruthless in front of the others when a fuck-up happened. The gang couldn't afford rogue actors. They needed discipline and team cohesion for survival, like any fine tuned infantry unit. They relied on each other in the heat of crime and when arrogant little punks aren't put in their place early on in their careers they tended to get themselves and members around them jailed, or worse; killed.

Angel did ease up on the kid though. He didn't hurt him too bad. In the end, he patting Chente on the knee and praised him for knocking the white dude out with one blow to the head. He told him he was impressed with his strength and technique at least, which made all the difference for the fragile little recruit. Chente smiled back with bloody teeth and they all laughed off the beating.

Flaco, the other pee wee, was in the front passenger seat while Toro drove. Angel allowed him to keep the iPhone he found on the sheep as a reward for staying disciplined. He followed the rules, even down to leaving the signature calling card of his blue bandana on the victim. The kid was thrilled with his new phone. It was the latest Apple model and had all sorts of cool apps. He was already downloading a popular game called Candy Crush when Toro told him to put it away. His uncle cracked him on the back of the head to listen up.

"Flaco, sell the phone right away to make some money for yourself," Angel said from the backseat. "You can get $200. But sell it on the street or at a some flea market. *Efectivo* (cash). Not a pawn shop. You know why?

"No."

"Toro, tell him."

Toro explained. "Because pawn shops record the transaction to the state. They require an ID, they take a picture of you, and the shit your pawning. Simple as that. Stay away from pawn shops. Go to a flea market. They don't ask no questions, *comprende?*"

Flaco answered by nodding.

"Get rid of it by tonight," Angel ordered.

"*Esta noche*," reiterated Toro, looking over at the kid.

Flaco stashed the phone in his pocket. He wouldn't let his uncle down. He then rifled through the glove compartment and found paperwork that the Lexus was a rental car picked up in Philadelphia, the white man being an out-of-town traveler. When Angel saw this he told everyone they'd have to ditch the car sooner than expected. Toro knew why and proceeded to explain it to the trainees.

"If the *gringo* already called Twelve (the cops) and notified the rental company of the theft they'd probably locate this car with a LoJack. We can't take any chances."

"Ahh," said Flaco, understanding.

"Chente?" asked Toro, looking in the rearview mirror.

"*Sí?*"

"You know what a LoJack is?"

"*No.*"

"It's a tracking device installed on luxury cars," informed Toro. "So rich people can locate their stolen *mierda*. The LoJack tells Twelve where the car is located by GPS. You know what GPS is, Chente?"

"*Sí*, Global Positioning Satellite," Chente said, proud with himself for one-upping his buddy. "They got it on Call of Duty on my XBox."

"Shut the fuck up, Chente," admonished Angel, sitting next to him. He raised a hand as if to hit him again. Chente flinched. "Listen to Toro. Learn something you stupid fuck. Twelve might even be on to us already. Twelve shows up we all bail out and meet up back at my house, *comprende?*"

"*Sí, señor, comprende,*" Chente said.

"*No problemo,*" agreed Flaco.

The fun was over.

They didn't even have time to sift through the white dude's backpack that sat on the backseat floor between Angel's legs. Angel told them they'd take all of the guy's shit and look at it back at his house. He wanted the car ditched immediately. He placed a phone call to make things happen as Toro continued to drive south on Buford Highway.

A few minutes later, Toro pulled the Lexus into a parking lot across from the Latino American Association building in the Lindbergh area. Another Sur-13 gang member in a crew cab Toyota Tundra pick-up truck was waiting for them. After finding a couple of duffle bags in the trunk of the rental, they transferred the stolen goods into the Tundra's bed and all piled in.

Within minutes they had arrived at Angel's house. It was a non-descript 1950s ranch his late uncle had left him on Shady Valley Drive in a nearby residential neighborhood. There, he and Toro lugged the backpack and two duffel bags inside while the young recruits were driven back home by their associate before their parents woke up for work.

Toro pulled out a cigarette and sat down on the living room couch with one of the bags. Angel went in the kitchen and grabbed a couple bottles of Negro Modelo Mexican beer from his refrigerator while Toro started in on the sheep's shit.

"Pants, shirt, socks, underwear, deodorant . . ." Toro rattled off the person belongings of their victim as he simultaneously smoked a cigarette and pulled the items out of the travel bag. "Man, this is bullshit stuff! Garbage." He inhaled on the cig, blew out smoke then tossed the bag aside and grabbed the other heavier one.

Angel entered the room sucking on a beer. He placed the other bottle on an end table next to his lieutenant as he unzipped the next duffel bag. He, too, had a cigarette dangling from his mouth. Mumbling, he said, "Next run we do I'll give my nephew the gun. He listens. But Chente's a little bronco that needs to be broken."

"I hear you, *hombre*," replied Toro as he pulled out a short crow bar followed by a small sledge hammer and a hack saw. He looked over at Angel who was sitting on a chair watching him while drinking and smoking. "This fucking *gringo* a carpenter?"

Angel merely shrugged his shoulders with a flashy, platinum smile from his grill. He reached for the remaining backpack.

Next, Toro pulled out what looked like a Halloween mask and held it up. It was an old white man's full head mask and had a realistic look and feel to it with wrinkly, droopy skin, and gray hair. "*¡Qué chingados!* (What the fuck!)

After tossing the mask on the couch, Toro pulled out a case of women's make up. "This guy some kinda serial killer? Some weird *mierda* this *gringo* got." He reached for his beer.

Angel placed his cigarette on an ashtray and unzipped his backpack. Out came a piece of clothing. And another. He pursed his lips. "Ah, man. Clothes, too." His hand then grasped something wool-like and black colored. He squeezed the top of the material and yanked it through the backpack opening. Partially crushed, it clearly was a hat. And old, tall one at that with a wide brim.

Angel looked the hat over, glanced inside at the sweat-stained inner band and silk material, then shrugged his shoulders. He placed it on top of his smoothly shaven, bald head and stroked his black goatie. Toro let out a whoop and doubled over in laughter.

Angel chuckled back and reached in the bottom of the backpack with both hands. He pulled out a small wooden box, gave a frown, and set it on his lap. Next he pulled out a long rod that had some significant weight to it. Once the rod cleared the bag it glimmered in the lamp light.

Gold eagles and crosses sparkled down the length of the shiny, foot-long, white shaft. It looked like some type of baton a marching band leader would use, only this one was fit for a king because on the end caps were hundreds of tiny diamonds.

Angel's mouth opened, but he didn't utter a word. His eyes met Toro's and they both knew they had something of major value. Angel laid the baton across his knees as he fumbled with the box on his lap.

Flipping the hinged lid, this time he did speak. "No fucking way, *hombre*. No fucking way." He pulled out of the black velvet-lined box an exquisitely engraved, gold pistol. It fit in the palm of his hand. Next, he extracted a short, gold magazine of six bullets and clicked it in place inside the pistol's handle. Grabbing the baton, too, he stood up. The box dropped on the carpeted floor with a thump, a gold cleaning brush popped out.

With an old hat on his head and waving a loaded golden gun in one hand, a diamond encrusted baton in the other, Angel danced around the living room in glee. Toro laughed and laughed, kicking his legs up in the air as he leaned back into the couch uttering joyful Mexican obscenities.

"Get a vid! Get a vid!" Angel urged his lieutenant.

Toro immediately fished out his smart phone and started shooting video as Angel pimped various poses. He tipped his hat down and looked angry, pointing at the phone with the gun. He crisscrossed the gun and baton across his chest and threw his head back flashing his grill. He then flipped the hat up on his forehead and raised both objects up for the camera.

In his best Spanish redneck-accented, Forrest Gump impression, Angel said, "Life is like a carjacking. You never know whatcha gonna get." Toro stopped the recording and they laughed like school children opening their best gifts on Christmas morning.

Angel handed Toro the baton to check out while he inspected the pistol more closely. His eyes suddenly widened in all seriousness as he noticed a certain symbol in an elaborately engraved inscription in a foreign language on the body of the gun. It was an icon recognized throughout the world.

The Nazi cross.

▼

Nathan Kull's early morning monkey act of climbing through the ceiling and over a common wall inside the storage facility had gone much easier and faster than expected. Once through the Styrofoam tiled drop ceiling, he climbed up into the roof support infrastructure and made it over to the office and lobby side of the building. Hanging above the false drop ceiling, he removed tiles and looked down into several rooms quickly finding the security surveillance room in the small office area.

Seeing there were no motion detectors inside that room, he jumped down and went to work. First priority was finding out where his phone was. Fortunately, an Internet-enabled computer was available in the same room and did not require a password to log in. Typical human nature, he thought, who would secure computer access inside a security room?

Entering his Apple ID and password, he logged into his iCloud account on a web browser and chose the Find My iPhone app. The program immediately started tracking his device. A slick compass icon twirled on screen while the data loaded.

Kull drummed his fingers on the desk.

Within twenty seconds, a Google satellite map filled the monitor screen and a small, 3D, green ball appeared.

He smiled.

Gotta love technology!

He zoomed in on the map and wrote down the name of the street on a Post-It Note; Pleasant Trail. It was located off Oakcliff Road near Buford Highway in the area of Doraville. The location looked to be inside of a large complex of duplex townhouses from all satellite indications.

Using Google Street View, he mined deeper on the map. High resolution 360° camera angles from ground level made it easy to find the exact duplex. They all were narrow, two-story homes with brick and vinyl siding. The backs of the duplex buildings faced Oakcliff Road and were blocked by a long iron fence. The front entrances faced a parking lot as did all of the townhouses in the complex. Kull saw that his phone was located in the third duplex southeast from the main entrance on Oakcliff. If he faced the front door of the duplex from the parking lot, his phone was located in the left townhouse. Moving the Google Street View icon slightly back north, he came to a view of the front entrance to the complex and saw a sign that read Cambridge Square Townhouses. There was no security gate, no guardhouse. One could drive in at will.

Finding his current location of the Public Storage on the map at Jimmy Carter and Buford, he allowed Google to run a directions and distance calculation that told him the Cambridge Square townhouse he wanted was exactly 3.3 miles and 7 minutes away.

He loved Google.

It had made his career as a thief so much easier over the years.

A quick search gave him the location of the closest rental car agency.

Just around the corner, not two blocks away in a strip plaza on Buford Highway, was an Enterprise-Rent-A-Car.

He smiled again.

Making sure to delete his browsing history, he closed out the computer program. Next, was the storage facility's surveillance tape to find *who* robbed him. Having installed the same type of equipment himself many times before through his legitimate company, he easily found the side entrance camera feed and rewound the hi-resolution color video to view his assault. It wasn't pretty.

The attackers, four in number, all wearing hooded sweatshirts, had run up on him out of the dark. A smaller individual had leaped in the air and hammered him in the back of the head with an unknown object. Watching himself hit the pavement face first was surreal. Seconds later, he saw what the object was that knocked him out.

A handgun.

He watched as the initial attacker was now pointing it at his prone motionless body while a second, skinnier individual grabbed the car keys that had fallen out of his hand and chucked them to the third individual who immediately went for the car. The fourth player, a stocky well-built individual, flung off his hoodie exposing himself as a mid-twenties, Hispanic male with a bald head and black goatie. He walked up to the smaller male holding the weapon and smacked him on the back of his head, like a parent cracking a wise-ass child. Words were exchanged. The gun-toter cringed then handed the weapon to the obvious leader of the crew. The reprimanded attacker ran to the car, headlights already turned on.

Kull raised his eyebrows as he watched his backpack torn from his limp, rag doll body by the same skinny male who took his keys. The backpack was given to the man with the gun who pointed toward the rental car, indicating they should leave. At that moment, his phone was stolen off his hip and his back pockets searched. The skinny male stood up, took off his hoodie, and revealed a baseball hat underneath with a large script font A on the front indicating the Atlanta Braves baseball team. The male looked to be a very young teen. He took off his hat and underneath was a blue bandana. That's when he flung the bandana on Kull's back.

Both the teen and the leader then jumped in the rear of the sedan and it reversed out of the parking spot and took off.

Kull played the tape several more times, burning the scene of the attack into his mind. He raged with revenge. Finding a USB Flash mini drive in a desk drawer he made a digital copy of the assault scene and saved it to the tiny, portable pocket drive. He erased that section of the surveillance tape from the time his car had pulled into the parking lot, to when he had entered the building. He turned off all surveillance cameras throughout the facility, climbed back up through the drop ceiling and roof supports to the locker room side, and walked out the side entrance.

A quick hike to the Enterprise-Rent-A-Car location and Kull waited outside until they'd open. He needed transportation and supplies for a stakeout. Soon it would be time to recover his prizes.

Clutching the blue bandana calling card of the punks who robbed him, he glanced up into the morning glow of a deep purple sky.

The sun was coming up and Hermes, the mythical God of Thieves, he thought in jest, was smiling down on him, giving him an opportunity for redemption. But it wasn't divine intervention that drove him.

To have those priceless Nazi treasures in his clutch be snatched away so quickly by mere street thugs, gave him all the motivation he needed to retake them. To hell with the McPherson hat his broker had contracted him for. It didn't compare to the dreams of grandeur he conjured up based on cashing in on the Nazi prizes. He had earned that "take" with his superior cognitive skills. He had thought the West Point Museum theft through to the minute detail, executing it flawlessly. He deserved them. Not some punks.

He would get them back no matter what.

And he would do it with severe payback.

11

J AKE AND RAE BOTH HAD INDULGED WAY TOO MUCH
in drink last night. They hit the bed after their respective night caps
and were instantly lights out. However, in the middle of the night Jake
remembered being awoken in a rather pleasant manner with Rae's lips and
tongue exploring between his legs. They both then indulged in a little sexy
night cap of their own before falling back asleep.

Waking up early with his hard body pressed against Rae's naked
backside, his hand stroking the firm curve of her hips, they held each other
for many minutes of intimate whispers before arising with groans. Hot
showers and aspirin, to alleviate their headaches, soon got them back up to
speed and in the game.

After letting the early bird Nurse Holden know they were slipping
away for breakfast while they awaited Sergeant D'Arata and the CID's
call, the couple took a long walk from Cherokee Manor all the way down
to River Street via Bull Street. Over fourteen city blocks, through some
of the most beautiful squares, past historical monuments and sculptures,
they walked hand-in-hand getting themselves up-to-date on last night's
respective conversations.

At one point they got a bit confused at Chippewa Square standing
in the shadow of the towering statue of the colony of Georgia's founder,

General James B. Oglethorpe. Jake was looking at his illustrated map trying to find the bench that Forrest Gump sat on in the popular comedy/drama film. Only the bench wasn't where it was supposed to be. Flowers and plants marked its spot instead. At the same time a tall, clean cut man in a crisp, dapper, seersucker suit and a yellow bowtie, complete with a white straw Panama hat, led a group of tourists over to the very spot Jake and Rae were standing. After eavesdropping on the tour guide's explanation of Gump's bench, they soon discovered a replica was actually sitting in the Savannah History Museum.

As the tour guide passed by Jake, he stopped, glanced down at Jake's Masonic ring, and said with a wide smile in a deep Southern accent, "Good to see a fellow Traveling Man." The two shook hands the only way Masons knew and the guide strode away at the head of his tour group.

While continuing South along Bull Street, Jake informed Rae of their new *side* mission and she was completely thrilled and on board as expected. As his right hand woman, she couldn't wait to talk more with Tommy once they returned back to the house. She wanted the details, leads, angles, direction.

Rae then explained to Jake what she had learned from Becky over their bottles of wine last night. It was all the gory details of the scandal that rocked Savannah some thirty years ago. Tom Black, then the thirty-something insurance salesman son of Tommy, had been secretly stealing from the family's extensive Civil War and military artifact collection inside Cherokee Manor. According to the gossipy Holden, the ancestor room at that time was chock full of every kind of artifact there was. Black had simply dug deep into the pile and started stealing and selling off pieces he didn't think his father would miss.

"Apparently," Rae said, as the pair stood in front of the gold domed City Hall waiting to cross Bay Street, "He was taking orders from an arms collector in Charleston."

Jake had his illustrated Savannah map unfolded and was looking to see where they were.

Rae cracked him on the arm. "Are you listening?"

"Yes, yes, Honey," said Jake, still looking down at the map. "Arms collector in Charleston. Tommy mentioned to me last night Black was stealing from him. But did you know, according to this map, that the dome of City Hall there is covered in gold leaf from Dahlonega? That's gold from north Georgia. Up where we're headed."

Rae folded her arms across her chest. She hated when he did that. He was always doing trivia, exploring, always pre-occupied with something when all she really wanted was for him to listen to her. *Men, all the same. Never listening.* She smirked, although not too terribly upset.

"Really, Indiana Jones?" she answered, hands on hips. "I would never have guessed."

Jake looked at her and folded the map. "Got me. I'm sorry, Gingersnap."

Another smack on the arm.

Several cars and a motorcyclist dressed in black leather passed by them as they waited at a crosswalk. The motorcyclist had actually slowed down and looked at the pair before accelerating away.

"Any ways, what I was getting to was that the FBI botched the whole investigation. Some technicality got Black off and he walked after spending six months in jail before trial. Tommy never did recover the stolen items and the arms collector also went free. But that's what got Black disowned by his father. He's been a cast off ever since."

"Ah, so that's what happened," Jake said, grasping Rae's hand as they crossed Bay Street into Salzeburger Park. "No wonder he doesn't trust the FBI and the Feds. That's why he wants our little hunt for the *Map of Thieves* to be kept on the down-low."

The couple made their way across a small park filled with tall palm trees and sprawling live oaks. The park honored some of Savannah's first settlers in 1734, a persecuted religious group known as the Salzburgers from present day Austria. The pair stopped in front of one of Savannah's most visited buildings along the waterfront. In front of the building was a circular fountain and a beautiful terra cotta griffin—a winged lion sculpture with water spouting from its mouth. The griffin, a mythological guardian for a city of treasure, stood on the edge of the fountain pool surrounded by a ring of bright green bushes and an elaborately designed, circular wrought iron fence. They walked up to the fence and took in the beautiful sculpture.

Behind the sculpture, over the building's terra cotta main entrance façade, was the name Savannah Cotton Exchange. This architectural gem had served as the main administrative office for cotton brokers who set the price of cotton on the worldwide market during Savannah's late 19th century cotton run. After Eli Whitney's invention of the cotton gin in 1793, Savannah turned into a "King Cotton" boomtown, creating many wealthy families and luxurious mansions throughout the city. At that time, Savannah was the #1 cotton seaport on the Atlantic coast and was often referred to as the Venice of the South. Under the building's name were two more words displayed in an arch: Freemason's Hall.

"This is Solomon's Lodge No. 1," Jake exclaimed. "How cool is this?"

Many years later the building was occupied by the same Masonic lodge Tommy belonged to, started by General Oglethorpe back in 1734, a Freemason himself.

"I know something you don't," challenged Rae.

"What's that?"

"Becky told me that Tommy's grandfather, the one who shot McPherson, resettled here in Savannah after the war was over."

"I was wondering how the Waties of Arkansas ended up in Savannah."

"He was wounded during fighting in Jonesboro, south of Atlanta, was hospitalized in Macon and then evacuated here to Savannah retreating from Sherman's March-to-the-Sea campaign."

"Really? Well, listen to you Miss Military Historian." Jake leaned on the wrought iron fence and stared at the building entrance.

"Yep, that's when he fell in love with a young nurse," Rae continued. "He got out before Sherman entered the city. I guess he went back to the Indian Territories after the war, but after a year he pursued his love and returned to Savannah. He became a member of this Masonic lodge."

"Very cool."

"And then he took that young nurse's hand in marriage. Her name was Annabelle. Sweet story isn't it?"

Jake turned and winked at her. *Women, all the same. Always hinting at marriage.* "It's a wonderful story, Rae."

She thought so, too. "I guess the Waties were involved in the lumber and railroad business here at the port, Becky said. That's where all their old money comes from. Very wealthy family and pretty much all that's left is Tommy."

"That's interesting," Jake said, preoccupied with the Masonic Hall. "Whaddya say we go inside and check out the lodge?"

"Noooo," Rae whined and tugged at his arm. "I know you could spend a day in there, but I'm hungry and my feet ache. Let's get some breakfast!"

She tugged again, this time a bit more forceful and Jake's whole body moved with her toward the right. At the same instance, he heard a loud pop, like a firecracker and felt his ear burn, saw the fountain's griffin head lose an eye in a shower of terra cotta, and knew a bullet had been fired at him from behind.

They bolted for cover toward the right as another bullet narrowly missed him. A massive, live oak tree with thick, spidery branches hanging low with Spanish moss provided their best opportunity.

Rae jumped behind the tree first. Right behind her, Jake glanced back to where he heard the shots. Slow motion seemed to kick in, his senses fine tuned for survival. He keenly saw a helmeted figure dressed all in black sitting on a motorcycle on the other side of Bay Street. The shooter panned his aim as Jake sought cover.

Jake's own weapon, a Beretta M-9 pistol, was already out and just as he was raising it to fire back he noticed a group of people scattering on the far sidewalk in front of a tall gray building directly behind the shooter. One miss and he'd kill someone. His urban combat experience kicked in and he held his shot.

For a split second.

The motorcyclist fired again and hit the huge tree trunk just before Jake slid behind it, bark splintering in his face.

"Shooter on motorcycle! Twelve o'clock," Jake yelled.

Rae emerged from the other side of the trunk, dodged behind a parked car, and took aim with her Ruger LC9 pistol toward the twelve o'clock position. She spotted the motorcyclist. Behind the target were people scattering about in a frenzy in front of a massive Neoclassical Revival style granite building with vertical bay windows and huge Doric columns. The shooter saw her at the same time and re-aimed. Rae took that hesitation and fired low into the shooter's motorcycle, avoiding the bystanders behind the target. Lead down range was all that mattered.

It worked.

Her bullet hit square in the thigh. The shooter cringed, looked down at his leg for a split second, then holstered his weapon. He spun around and shifted his motorcycle into gear to speed off.

That exchange gave Jake the chance he needed. Popping back out from the tree trunk, he now had a clear shot with no pedestrians in his field of fire. Just as the motorcyclist cranked his handle accelerator back and spun his rear tire, Jake fired. And advanced. And fired again.

He crossed Bay Street now, gun outstretched and fired again. A car slammed its brakes coming to a screeching halt, inches from hitting him. Jake paid no attention. He fired again.

The first bullet had plowed right through the helmet and entered the shooter's temple. The next bullet entered the side of the target's chest. The bullet after missed and shattered a huge bay window in the building behind the target. Jake's last bullet struck the shooter's arm.

As the motorcycle fishtailed uncontrollably away with the shooter slumped over the handle bars, Jake stood in the middle of Bay Street and fired three rounds into the target's back. A bystander screamed.

Rae was at Jake's side now, her pistol aimed at the shooter. The motorcycle sputtered on for another five feet, jumped the curb on the right, and crashed to one side, pinning the shooter underneath. The body landed at the doorstep of Savannah's official tourism agency offices.

The target was down, blood puddling like a faucet left on. Jake walked up and double-tapped the would-be assassin in the helmet.

He then looked up at the glass entrance door to the tourism office. A horrified woman had her face pressed up against the inside glass. Above her read a visitor's slogan:

Welcome to Savannah, your journey has just begun.

12

TOM BLACK'S BIRTHDAY KEPT GETTING WORSE. AND, of course, none of it was his fault. He was the victim and others were to blame. Jaconious Johnson's hired help for starters, the so-called professional criminals. The way this whole charade was going, it crossed his mind more than once that his chief of staff may have even been conspiring against him. Hell, he thought, he was offering up piles of cold hard cash and no one seemed to want to collect on it. *Imbeciles.*

As he sat on a leather sofa in his Roswell mansion study—a combination library and home office—he fumed at Johnson who was pacing back and forth across the room. While he spoke he held down the Bowie knife in his lap with his right hand, thumb bandaged, while rubbing furiously with a pencil on a piece of note paper draped over one side of the knife blade. He was making a copy of the engraved symbols and words as an added backup in case anything happened to the knife.

In a disparaging voice, he asked Johnson, "How in the *hell* does an ex-Atlanta cop get nine bullets shot into him? You *assured* me your guy was the cream of the crop. That he'd take care of that couple. But apparently *you* hired another stupid, incompetent motherfucker just like that thief!"

The first bad news that had hit them was Johnson's fixer calling this morning saying the broker had lost contact with the West Point thief. The last time the broker had heard from the thief was around 2 a.m. as he was coming into Atlanta. The hat and waybill, expected to be delivered this morning, were now a complete bust. Either the thief had been tracked down, arrested, and was being held by authorities or, as the fixer speculated, the thief said the hell with delivering the contract item now that he had a couple of priceless Nazi treasures in his possession. Either way, Black was going paranoid and had blamed Johnson all morning.

Then the next pile of shit hit the fan. They had just found out on national news that an ex-Atlanta police officer was gunned down in Savannah by none other than the *Battlefield Investigators* themselves; Army Lieutenant Colonel Jake Tununda and Private Investigator Rae Hart. The dead man was the guy Johnson had hired just before they flew back to Atlanta from Savannah last night.

After fleeing Cherokee Rose Manor, Black and Johnson had remained in the historic district listening in on the disguised pen bug all night long as Tommy Watie and Jake Tununda drank and talked. Black was floored at learning the full legend behind the waybill and knife. If he were to possess that *Map of Thieves*, as Tununda named it, he would wield such incredible power within the Federal government he could write his own ticket to the top. But once he had heard Tununda had taken on his father's secret mission to go after him personally and the same treasure he coveted, too, he knew what proactive measures needed to be taken.

He provided the money, Johnson provided the means. Jake Tununda and Rae Hart were the first targets on the assassin's list. The Army special agent with the Italian last name and the nurse were next if needed.

Black would leave his father for last after all the nasty things he heard him say about him to that Tununda. His father called him a bastard son, a rotten, spoiled, useless child, even a pacifist pussy. He brought up all the bad things he did when he was younger. *Oh, you wait, dear old dad. You fucking wait.*

"You're the one who started this whole goddamn mess!" Johnson fired back, standing in front of his boss, pointing a finger. "I'm the one trying to figure out how to keep us both out of jail. Don't you *dare* blame me!"

"Don't you talk to me in that tone, *boy*!" Black blasted back, rising to his feet. The paper rubbing floated to the floor. He waved the Bowie knife in front of him. "I'm a U.S. Congressman. *No one* talks to me like that!"

"Screw, you, *Congressman!*" Johnson retorted. He had lost all self-composure. His normal calm demeanor was thrown out the window upon hearing the news that their hired hit man was the one killed instead of the intended targets. "You're gonna take both of us down over some fucking Cherokee Golden Horse and some goddamn map. What the hell are we hunting gold for? It's not like you *need* any more money, do you? It's all just to spite your father, isn't it?"

"Enough of your attitude!" Black slammed the knife into a wooden coffee table in front of the sofa. It stood upright, wobbling next to an open envelope of $50,000 in cash meant for a bonus payment to the thief. A gulf of silent defiance stood between the two men. Neither one would give in as they stood not five feet from each other. Black finally turned his back on Johnson, hands on big hips, and walked toward a fireplace in the study. He huffed loudly then turned back around.

"Who was this guy you hired? You said you knew him personally."

"That's right," Johnson spat, still rebellious. "I *did* know him personally. I used him in the past. He was living down in Brunswick. Was close by so I called on him. He cleaned up a loose end I had up here in Atlanta about five years ago. Some punk threatened to kill me over a girl. My man popped him in the head. End of story."

"Was that the fatal attraction bitch you beat the shit out of?" Black asked, his voice lower. "The one that pressed charges against you?"

"Dat be da ho," Johnson said arrogantly, arms folded across his chest. "She refused to testify against me after that. Case closed."

"What do you think happened down there in Savannah? How'd your man mess up?"

"Don't know what to tell ya, Tom," Johnson said, a bit calmer, dropping his arms, looking down. "My dude was bad-ass. Atlanta SWAT. Killed a few *suspects* throughout his career. But the FBI caught up to him about ten years ago. Nailed him and a bunch of other cops for taking bribes to protect gang drug deals in the Bluff. Did three years in prison then started doing hits and collecting drug debts for big dealers after he got out. I guess that colonel and his bitch just got the jump on him."

"But *we* are good though, right?" Black asked, fear glazing his eyes. "The cops can't trace anything back to us, right? You got rid of that cell phone you called him with, right?"

"We're good, Tom," Johnson assured him. "No worries. That phone was a pre-paid disposable model. His own phone records will show that number as a dead end. They can't identify us. Besides, he's dead, too, so he can't turn on us."

Black sat back down on the sofa with a deep sigh of relief. He gathered up the paper rubbing on the floor and resumed his pencil marks now on the other side of the blade. After a couple of minutes, he finally finished and admired his handiwork. One side showed a sentence written in the Cherokee language. The other side showed some strange symbols and more Cherokee words. It was all foreign to him and he knew he'd have to somehow get it translated. He folded the paper and placed it in his shirt pocket for safekeeping.

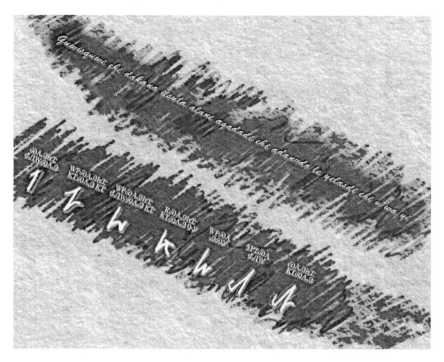

Next, he reached for a UPS Express box laying next to him that had just been delivered. It was from an order he had placed online Friday night after thinking up his plot. Inside was an XXL-sized costume he ordered for seventy bucks. He purchased the full outfit with the exception of the general's hat. That would be coming soon, hopefully, he thought before tossing the box aside.

"Wish to hell our little spy pen didn't crap out," he complained. "You think they found it?"

Johnson shrugged then reached in his pocket for his cigarette pack. "All I know, based on the conversation your father and that Tununda guy had last night, is he can't do shit without the waybill and knife. The waybill is coming to us and you have the knife, so we're in the driver's seat."

"I'm not taking any more chances. Any obstacle in our way of finding the *Map of Thieves* is worth snuffing them out. We cannot let that map fall into the hands of simple-minded peons like my father and this dumbfuck Army soldier and his stupid girlfriend. They can't handle the importance of acquiring such a tome of power with what that map contains. It's the reason why people like me are the 1% who pay all the taxes that run this country and make the grown-up decisions for the millions of ignorant minions out there. It's why we know what's best for the nation. You understand?"

"Completely."

"Do you understand what we can do with it *personally*, too? You and I, Jaconious? It's not about the money. It's about the absolute control of a national treasure and how we can dole out that power to those who we see fit. That's why this matters. Now, I want you to line up another contract on them. Swat those flies away so I have no distractions."

"I've already got some people in mind," Johnson said, lighting up a cigarette with a silver Zippo lighter and inhaling.

"Who?"

"You don't need to know." Blue smoke exhaled from his nostrils.

"Humor me."

Johnson took another drag on his cigarette and smiled. "Some of our finest constituents in the heart of our district. A nasty fucking crew called the Bluff Boyz. They'd kill their own sister for five hundred bucks."

Black raised his eyebrows and nodded, very pleased.

"If this Tununda fool decides to come to Atlanta, well—" laughed Johnson, "Statistically, he'd have a much higher chance of survival going back into combat."

Black smirked. "Perfect."

"The Boyz have some family down in Savannah. I'll have them put your pop's house under watch. Gather intel, you could say. The moment he and his girl leave, we'll know. If they head up here, then we've basically got a small army at our disposal."

"Have a few of them around, outside my birthday party tonight, too. But I don't want any of that scum allowed in," Black demanded. "Just have them keep watch outside."

Johnson said he'd get on it. He then switched to another delicate subject. Black's real job. Or lack thereof. "You know there's a high profile budget vote in DC slated for real early tomorrow morning? I'm talking like 3 a.m. is what they're saying now. The Democrat minority leader's staff has been all over my shit saying you must be present, that you've been missing too many votes already and your absence is quote-unquote, unacceptable."

"Unacceptable, my ass!" Black huffed. "She's been buzzing my cell phone all day long, too. I've just been ignoring the bitch."

"Yeah, well she left a rant on my phone as well. She's pretty much demanding you get back to Washington, Tom. Said she needs every last vote to overturn the opposition. Should I arrange a flight out after the party? We've got to leave by midnight I'm thinking, no later."

"Screw her—the cunt nugget. It's my birthday. And tonight I'm celebrating."

"Tom, we're playing in a different league now. She's a major power player who can open doors for us. You just can't blow her off."

"Shut up, Jaconious. Just shut up. I was the largest fundraiser of her reelection campaign, so she can bite me. Why in the hell do you think I got a seat on the House Finance Committee. It's because she needed my cash influx because no one had confidence in her anymore. We're staying put until I get my fucking hat and waybill." Black glared at his chief of staff. "All you gotta do is tell her I'm having family issues—that I'm emotionally upset that my father had a heart attack and that I'm providing support for his well-being. Okay?"

"Fine. Whatever, Tom."

"Fine. Settled. Now be a good boy and call our fixer back. I want an update on where my hat is so we can hand over this cash," motioning to the envelope of money on the table. "And on to hunting gold. Cha-ching."

"I'll call him. But first I need a drink."

"Get me one, too."

Johnson gritted his teeth and started walking out of the room.

"Oh, and get me a big piece of that key lime pie in the fridge, too, I'm famished."

Fucking pig ate just a half hour ago, Johnson thought as he left the room. As soon as this father-son fiasco ends he was updating his resume. He was done being Black's bitch laundry boy. With his foot in the door, it was time to move up the Capitol Hill ladder to bigger and better political machinations in some other elected official's staff whether it was Democrat or Republican. He didn't give a shit, they were all power hungry hyenas just like himself. The damn thing was that Black had the golden handcuffs on him so tight with an enormous paycheck and under-the-table quarterly cash bonuses that he couldn't imagine walking away from the piggy bank. Grin and bear it, he told himself over and over again, thinking of his four different baby mamas he had to support with cash. *Grin and bear it because maybe this* Map of Thieves *is real.*

Black farted loudly as soon as his chief of staff left the room. Sitting in his own odious mist, he then cracked a smile knowing it was going to be a long, fun night with him the center of attention as the birthday boy. He reached for the UPS box again and tore it open to view the Yankee general's costume he had bought.

This would be no traditional birthday party like the one he had last year with his Atlanta field office staffers and the handful of friends he did have. Instead, this was his own private affair with some key men in his district who wanted to pay and play. They knew the game. Pay Black in money or fine gifts and he would make things happen in their favor.

One was a top Democratic party superbundler donor to his campaign now seeking a cushy, no responsibility, high-paying government appointment. Another was a private businessman wanting Black to introduce a bill in his favor to quash his competitors. There was also a lobbyist for a coalition of churches in the Bluff seeking millions in grant money for rebuilding their properties. Lastly, was a persistent prick of a father of a high school student wanting to attend the Air Force Academy who was seeking his signature on a reference letter. All would bring exceptional gifts for the Congressman hoping to get an audience.

After all, he thought, he was now *General Carpetbagger* of the district and in order for him to act on his constituents' needs he required a bit of groveling on their part. But while they waited, they would be rewarded with a burlesque show of Black's favorite Asian prostitutes. Hmmmm, he moaned, thinking of all the raunchiness he'd soon be indulging in himself.

Patting his pocket he made sure he had a Viagra pill to stay up the rest of the night.

▼

Savannah

Once the cops had arrived on scene of the shooting, Jake and Rae were confronted with drawn pistols pointed in their faces. Their weapons had been confiscated, they were frisked, placed in handcuffs and immediately transported down to Savannah-Chatham Metropolitan Police Department headquarters adjacent to Colonial Park Cemetery. Their arrest was expected. They had waited for police to arrive. But the number one rule they both agreed to before being taken into custody was absolutely, under no circumstances, were they going to talk to the police. They would invoke their Fifth Amendment rights under the Constitution and only utter one phrase: self-defense.

Even though the killing of the man trying to assassinate them was a clear cut case of self-defense, Rae had learned from firsthand experience during her eleven years as a trooper and investigator with the New York State Police, that cops legally can lie to you, manipulate your statements, and twist the facts even if you are 100% innocent. She had done it on her own. Jake, too, had learned that lesson while being questioned by cops up in Rochester, New York, during his escapade on the hunt for British gold over a year ago, when he and Rae were rivals working together. He also knew the ways of military political correctness, too. And, lastly, how the news media whores could change their story to fit their own biased narrative.

The double-tap Jake gave their would-be murderer was witnessed by many people on the street. Making sure your enemy was absolutely, unequivocally dead was what combat warriors were taught. It's what he trained the soldiers under him to do. Problem is that type of excessive force may be fine on a battlefield among soldiers, but not on a public street in the most romantic city in the U.S., not even in self-defense. Jake knew to keep his mouth shut.

Later at police headquarters, the Savannah lead detective showed Jake and Rae a surveillance camera recording from a nearby business that caught the whole shooting on video—clearly exonerating them both. Even then, they refused to speak. A half hour after that the same detective switched on the television and somehow that same video was playing over and over again on a local Savannah news station.

Jake knew he could all but kiss his military career goodbye.

Cops don't like it when you invoke your right to remain silent, especially from Yankees.

The crucifixion had begun.

Jake and Rae were held in separate interrogation rooms, or as the cops called them, "interview" rooms, for three hours refusing to talk while detectives and the local prosecutor decided their fate. They were allowed to use their personal phones however, and Jake contacted Tommy Watie to have him send the best criminal lawyer in Savannah to represent them both. Within thirty minutes upon arrival of their defense attorney, the couple was released under their own recognizance, with no charges filed against them. For the moment, they were warned.

Rae and the defense attorney were allowed out a back entrance where they immediately headed back to Cherokee Rose Manor, while Jake remained in custody pending transportation by the Army. In due time, he was escorted by the cops out the front door and released to the custody of two young MPs from Hunter Army Airfield's 3rd Criminal Investigation Division, as denoted by their "CID" arm band insignia.

Jake fully expected to see Special Agent Marco D'Arata there to greet him, but he was nowhere to be found. Instead, standing behind the two MPs was Colonel David M. Perkins, the commander of CID himself.

Never having met the full bird colonel, Jake did, however, recognize the name from conversations with D'Arata. The distinguished-looking black colonel, with a long, bony face, was dressed in ACU's and sunglasses. He looked like a rock statue, emotionless, unwavering, and pissed off. The colonel then barked an order to the MPs and, to Jake's utter dismay, they handcuffed him on the spot. With the Colonel in tow, they led him into a Humvee for a silent trip back to Hunter. The CID's commander and the Savannah police chief made sure they had coordinated the reverse "perp walk" under a full display of whirling media cameras.

Military law enforcement commanders don't like it when active duty officers gun down civilians on their turf.

After the leak of the street shooting video, it instantly played out on national news outlets because of the semi-celebrity status of the two *Battlefield Investigators*. MSNBC, a decidedly liberal leaning, anti-military, so-called news channel on cable television, splashed a provocative headline of: "Battlefield Investigators Brutal Breakfast Barrage." Jake was disparaged as a violent bully in the edited video, pumping two rounds into the motorcyclist's helmet as the supposed victim lay trapped under his bike. One of MSNBC's usual bloviating, anti-gun pundits condemned Jake as a jack-booted Army thug because he and Rae used a "disproportionate" level of force in shooting nine bullets into their attacker. Of course, the talking head glossed over the fact that the couple were the ones being targeted for assassination. They then ran the video of Jake being taken into custody by the Army, their character assassination complete.

On the flip side, a local news outlet had been the first with a reporter on scene. She interviewed a group of eyewitness tourists who saw the shooting right in front of their eyes. It was clear, according to their live, raw emotional portrayals, that Jake and Rae not only saved themselves in dramatic fashion, but were held in high esteem for checking to see if no bystanders were hurt after the incident. The worst damage done was a broken plate glass window and a small cut on a little girl's cheek from some shattered glass.

While defenders of the Second Amendment's right-to-bear-arms applauded the use of self-defense, and left-wing liberal pacifists called for more gun confiscation laws, Jake sat silently the next hour in a military holding cell at 3rd MP Group Headquarters. Sergeant Marco D'Arata was still no where to be found. Jake felt the special agent could clear things up in a heartbeat and get him the hell out of there. He requested that D'Arata be contacted, but was denied by Colonel Perkins. His fury raged at the treatment he was getting by his own Army counterparts, an Army he had served and risked his life for over a career. He asked several agents in the office who the assassin was but they stonewalled him further. He asked to see his new defense attorney. Perkins stalled again. After another half hour of futility, Perkins finally revealed the reason he was being held; the broken window.

He was facing misdemeanor property damage charges from when his stray bullet had shattered the bay window at the former bank building that housed Savannah's Chamber of Commerce. It was a historically irreplaceable window, the original from 1914. A costly window in more ways than one.

And then Perkins said he was also recommending Jake for the Selective Early Retirement Board, saying his kind had no place in the Army.

Jake was thinking about slugging the smug Colonel to get that early retirement fulfilled when he was handed a phone by one of the MPs. It was the director of the Military History Institute. His boss ordered him to cease and desist his services on the West Point investigation. Furthermore, in rather loud colorful language the director explained he had officially been put on administrative leave because of his reckless actions. CID and Colonel Perkins would be conducting their own internal investigation into the shooting. When summoned, Jake was ordered to appear in front of the Colonel.

He was finally released, driven under escort to the main entrance at Wilson Boulevard, and discarded off base like a fast food wrapper on a windy day. It was a five mile walk back to Watie's house, a walk he cherished to clear his angry head.

13

FTER RENTING A NEW CAR WITH ONE OF HIS STOLEN debit card identities, Kull had gone on a morning shopping spree to re-supply himself before going after the culprit who had his iPhone. The first and most important stop was at an AT&T store where he bought a portable, Internet-enabled, iPad mini tablet with the hundreds in cash he still had left in his wallet. This allowed him to instantly log back into his iCloud account to see where his iPhone currently was. Fortunately, it hadn't moved from the residence and was still actively pinging its location on Google Maps.

One of the first apps he downloaded was Police Scanner +, a radio frequency scanner that allowed him to keep tabs on local law enforcement and emergency dispatches.

A local Army-Navy surplus store equipped him with sundry hardware tools, a backpack, blanket, gloves, brass knuckles, a tactical knife, a monocular, duct tape, sunglasses, an extra set of clothes, and some personal toiletries. At a Dick's Sporting Goods store he bought a blue New York Yankees baseball cap and a white Atlanta Braves cap. Lastly, an aluminum baseball bat. They never break.

Especially when you're teeing up someone's knee.

Which was exactly how he beat the little punk down. It ended up being as easy as whacking a piñata, without the blindfold.

When Kull arrived at the parking lot across from the target house, he waited in his car a good distance away under the shade of a tree. His iPad mini was plugged into his lighter port giving the device full battery power. The green dot of his iPhone's location didn't move for two more hours even though he had watched through his handheld monocular as a chubby, middle-aged Hispanic male and a thinner Hispanic woman carrying a baby exited the house and entered a minivan. The male didn't fit either of the four carjacker's descriptions from the surveillance tape.

That video was running in a different window on the tablet from the USB mini-drive he had copied it onto at Public Storage. He knew he'd be looking for two younger teens and two males possibly in their twenties. The iPhone signal still pointed to being inside the house as the minivan drove away. Which one of the carjackers had it in there, if any of them, Kull didn't know. He waited.

It wasn't until 11:30 a.m. that his target exited the townhouse. He knew because the green dot moved on his zoomed-in screen map. He recognized the person as one of the teens, the skinny one who had actually tossed the bandana onto his back as he lay unconscious in the parking lot.

The kid walked nonchalantly across the parking lot toward him, head down cradling Kull's iPhone with both hands, tapping away as if playing a game. He wore earbuds and was oblivious to any surrounding noise. The teen was dressed in a Braves ballcap, gray hooded sweatshirt and baggy jean shorts. As Kull scanned his surroundings for any witnesses, the kid walked right past his car never even noticing him sitting in the front seat. The parking lot was virtually empty as most people were at work. That's when he decided to make his move.

Throwing open his driver's door he moved quickly, dragging the aluminum bat in his right hand. Strutting up ten feet right behind the teen, he double-fisted the bat and gave his best Alex Rodriguez impression.

Except, instead of aiming high, he swung low and nailed the boy on the outside of the right knee with a loud aluminum-on-bone clang.

The boy immediately crumpled to the pavement as his legs swept out from under him. He landed on his side, head bouncing off the parking lot, the iPhone clattering away. Kull had already raised the bat over his head and swung down with all his force connecting on the kid's back. The sound was a mixture of cracked ribs and a dull wallop. The kid howled like a wounded dog. One more swing of the bat, this one deliberately a tad bit lighter, connected with the boy's head.

Three strikes and he was out.

Kull picked up his iPhone, pocketed it, then grabbed the rag doll teen by his hood and dragged him back to the car. He opened the rear door, tossed the bat inside, then picked up the teen by the back of his sagging pants and tossed him in face down like a bag of garbage. Several pre-ripped strips of duct tape were waiting for him on the back of the seat cushions. He pulled the kid's arms behind his back, yanked a length of duct tape and tied his hands up tight. He did the same with his ankles. Next, he pulled the blue bandana from a pocket, yanked the kid's head back by his hair—jaw dropping open—and stuffed the rag in his mouth. He then applied a piece of tape over his mouth, carefully allowing his nose access to breath. A blanket covered up his body.

His quarry secure, Kull slammed the door shut, jumped in the front seat, jammed the car into drive and took off with a squeal of his tires.

While monitoring the police scanner for any traffic of a kidnapping, he drove around until he found a secluded abandoned warehouse area at the end of Oakcliff Road. He backed into the corner of the weed-infested, cracked pavement parking lot surrounded by trees and transferred the teen to the trunk of his car. The hogtieing continued. He taped his arms to his body along with several strips around his knees. When the kid was totally immobilized Kull splashed some water on his face and slapped him.

He came to, gagging in terror on the rag jammed in his taped mouth.

Kull allowed him to struggle, cry, and hyperventilate to the point of almost passing out. Once the kid wore himself out, he spoke to him softly holding up his iPhone. The boy's watery eyes grew large.

"You and your boys carjacked me last night. I came to get my shit back. All of it! When I take the tape off your mouth you will tell me where it is. You understand?"

The boy nodded.

First things first. Kull deleted all of the museum photos. But when he got to the waybill image that showed only a small portion of the much larger map he had found, he paused. That cropped image was the only one he had of it. No one would know what it was. It was safe to keep it on the phone. Might prove valuable if anything. Finished purging his phone, he looked down at the kid.

He ripped the tape off his mouth leaving one side still attached to his cheek. He then fished the soaked bandana out of the teen's throat and allowed him to catch his breath.

"Where's my stuff?" Kull demanded from behind his Yankees cap and black sunglasses.

"I don't know nothing, *señor!*" The kid groaned. "I wasn't there."

"Liar!" Kull punched him in the mouth with brass knuckles. Two front teeth broke in half. Blood spurted from a gashed upper lip and filled his mouth as he moaned in renewed agony.

"I saw you there in the security camera. You're the skinny little fuck that stole my phone and tossed this bandana on me after you're little faggot boyfriend hit me with the pistol. You lie to me again, I hit you again. I will do this all day long until you tell me the truth. Understand?"

The boy whimpered then licked his chipped teeth in pain. "*Sí señor, sí.*"

"What's you're name?"

"Freddy Peña, *señor.* They call me Flaco."

"Good start, Flaco," Kull hissed. "How old are you?"

He groaned. "Fourteen, *señor.* Fourteen."

"Lying punk!" Kull pulled back for another punch to his face.

"Honest. Honest. I'm f-f-fourteen," the kid stammered, cringing and closing his eyes waiting to be hit. "I go to Chamblee High School. I'm a f-f-freshman. My wallet. My wallet. School ID."

Kull lowered his fist and looked around him to make sure no one was watching. He then flipped the bloody-mouthed teen over who squealed in pain and fished out his wallet. He also found a cheap cell phone, which he pocketed. From the wallet, he took out a school ID. The kid *was* telling the truth. He flipped the boy back on his back.

"Where's all the stuff you took from me? Where's my car? I want names. Who's planned this? Who's the leader? There were four of you."

Flaco was having trouble breathing. His cracked ribs had actually punctured part of his lung when Kull had hit him with the bat. "Ever hear of the gang "Sureños-13?" The name came out with crisp, arrogant pride. He paused to catch his breath. His watery eyes and baby face then turned demonic. "My uncle's gonna fucking kill you, *hombre!*" He spat a gob of blood at Kull.

Enraged, Kull punched him square in the nose, flattening it. Blood oozed out and spread across Flaco's cheeks. "Kill *me?*" Another full force crack with the brass knuckles clocked Flaco above the eye, cutting the brow open. More blood and instant swelling. Flaco's eyes rolled in the back of his head.

Kull had never felt this much adrenaline-filled, violent anger before. He knew he could beat this little dog to death. It was so easy, so unfair. He couldn't think straight. This wasn't like him. He had crossed the line entering a new territory of criminality all fueled by an inherent desire to repossess his rightful stolen trophies. But he stopped. Having a dead boy would do him no good in getting his goods back.

He jabbed a finger in his victim's forehead. "I will cripple you for life. I will beat your little fourteen year-old head in and then break your fucking arms and legs. You like that baseball bat I hit you with? Felt good, huh? Just like when your faggot friend hit me from behind. Wanna feel that bat again?"

Tears and blood streamed from his eyes. He moaned and begged. "No, no, *señor. No mas. No mas.*"

"Then start talking. Who took me down? Who's your uncle? I want names and addresses of the other three. Where is my stuff?"

"If I snitch, they kill me!" He sobbed.

"That's it. I'm getting the bat." Kull moved away from the trunk and Flaco immediately yelled for mercy. He broke easily after that, crying like a baby in fear of being beaten further.

"I only kept your phone. My Uncle Angel has all your other stuff. He sent me a text with a video of what he found. Like a gold gun and some diamond wand. It's on my cell phone. I don't know where your car is, *señor.* Honestly. We left it in some parking lot down Buford."

Kull flipped open Flaco's cell and viewed his text messages. One of the most recent ones showed a time stamp early in the morning from a contact listed as Angel. It was just after he was carjacked. A video attachment to the text showed a man he presumed to be Angel posing with his prizes. Angel smiled with a flashy mouth grill, McPherson hat on his head. His heavily tattooed arms were crisscrossed over his chest with gun and baton in hand. He was the same buff built Hispanic male with a black goatie who was the leader in the security video. Kull remembered him smacking the boy who hit him with the pistol. Kull ran the video. It was short.

Angel flipped his hat up on his forehead and raised both trophies up then said in a Southern redneck accent tinged with Spanish, "Life is like a carjacking. You never know whatcha gonna get."

Kull was furious. "Where does your uncle live?"

Flaco whimpered and closed his eyes. "N-n-no, *señor*. I can't say—"

A hand smacked him across the face. The kid whimpered.

Kull punched him in the ribs.

After several minutes of painful crying, Kull punched him again, demanding answers.

Flaco gave up the whole enchilada.

14

DRESSED IN A BLACK CIVILIAN SUIT AND TIE, TYPICAL attire for a CID special agent, Sergeant Marco D'Arata entered the parlor of Watie's Cherokee Rose Manor where Jake, Rae, and Tommy had gathered. He had driven an unmarked black sedan and parked it down the street so as to not attract any undue attention at the residence. After allowing him in, Rae pulled a set of red velvet drapes across the windows so no one could see inside the house.

Tommy had given Nurse Holden the afternoon off but she was still on duty just a phone call away. After a consultation with their defense attorney, Jake and Rae were so shot out from the whole affair they hit the bottle. Rae was halfway through a bottle of Riesling and had already smoked a half a pack of cigarettes—the first cigs she'd had since quitting over a four years ago. She refilled her wine glass and took her place back on the couch, crossing her legs.

Jake had grabbed a bottle of Zubrowka—Bison Grass Polish Vodka— on his walk back to Tommy's and was drinking it on the rocks. He was on his fifth glass, attempting to play a game of chess with Tommy. That's when D'Arata unexpectedly knocked on the front door. It was the first they had heard or seen of him all day long.

"Special Agent D'Arata," Jake slowly announced, his drunken voice tinged with anger. "You've got some big balls coming here. What other trumped up charges does your commander have up his fucking ass?"

"S-sir," D'Arata stammered, moving into the parlor, "I-I apologize for how they treated you. I caught a Black Hawk to Atlanta early this morning to get the DNA results at Fort Gillem and I just got back."

Jake ignored him. He instead tried to focus on the Civil War figurine chess game, strategizing several moves ahead in order to capture Tommy's wicked queen who was depicted as Confederate General Robert E. Lee. He needed to at least immobilize Lee or better yet, take him out altogether. Jake moved a knight—one of his Union cavalrymen—to box Lee in, then slowly turned his head and stared at the special agent.

D'Arata held out his hands. "I learned how it all went down about an hour ago and I raced over to the base but just missed you being released. Believe me, I would have raised holy hell with whoever pulled that perp walk stunt, including Perkins himself. It was complete bullshit."

No response from Jake. Nor smoking Rae, nor Tommy.

"Sir," pleaded D'Arata, "They don't know I'm here. I'm risking my job just coming to speak with you."

Jake sprung out of his chair, causing D'Arata to take two steps back. Rae even flinched. "You're risking *your* job?" he shouted drunkenly, pointing at his younger subordinate. "How about *my* fucking career being over?" He tapped his own chest. "All because *we* defended ourselves from being gunned down like dogs!"

"Sir, I'm sorry."

Jake was livid. "Over twenty goddamn years I served! Wounded twice and the Army nails me over *broken glass?*"

D'Arata bowed his head. "It's Perkins. He's a by-the-book asshole. The real reason he's spinning you is he hates that you've got Army celebrity status because of your *Military Channel* show, is what I was told."

Jake slurred his words. "This is bullshit. My best friend was the Army and it stabbed me in the back. I've given the Army everything and now they want to take everything away. What the hell do you want with me? Why are you even here?"

D'Arata looked up, trying to keep his cool. "I heard they pulled you from the case."

"Yep. I'm on indefinite paid vacation."

"Screw 'em, Colonel. I still want you both involved. Off the books," D'Arata said sternly. "It's not right what Perkins is doing to you. I'm not playing his fucking politics. I came here to give you my full support. I came here to give you an update on the DNA test and some new developments out of West Point. And if it costs me my career, too, for being in contact with you, so mote it be. Lost jobs can be regained. Brothers cannot."

Jake didn't say a word. Their bond as combat soldiers and Masons was strong. He bowed his head and merely held out his hand. D'Arata shook it and Jake pulled him closer touching chests. "Marco, I'm sorry. I tend to overreact," he whispered in his ear.

D'Arata pulled back and winked at Jake. "No shit, Jake."

Jake smiled. "Asshole."

Tommy asked what the DNA test results were.

"Mr. Watie," D'Arata said, breathing easier, "It's good and bad. Sort of a gray area. All indications are that you were correct. It seems it *could* be your son and in all likelihood it is. The DNA matched yours."

"I knew it," Tommy said. "His smell was all I needed."

"But," D'Arata held up his hand. "I was cautioned not to assume this fully by the technicians. It won't stand up in court. Yet. Reason being is we do not have any visual evidence or eyewitnesses that place Tom Black here. They said if he had a son of his own, for instance, then it's possible that person could have been here, not him. See what I'm saying?"

Tommy nodded. "Well, he's definitely got no offspring. He's sterile."

"Thank God for that," Rae mumbled from the sofa.

"But we still need more evidence," D'Arata cautioned. "Physical evidence. Brass told me this. They still need clear probable cause to approach a federal judge and apply for wiretaps against a sitting congressman."

"Pfft!" spat Rae. "But for everyday citizens they just contact the NSA."

"Aww, hell fire!" said Tommy. "Always some technicality. Always some rule and regulation we gotta play by that the criminals don't."

"Not me, anymore," Jake said. "I'm technically now a criminal."

"We both almost had our brains blown out," agreed Rae, puffing on her cigarette and massaging one temple with her index finger. "I'm ready to get the son-of-a-bitch back, by all means necessary."

"We know he cut his hand, right?" D'Arata asked, more as a statement. "Pretty good blood loss so it's not a cut he can hide. We need evidence of that wound to further mesh with our story of how things happened. The more circumstantial evidence that fits the crime, the better our chances for a search warrant. With that said, we need our own eyes on his movements to be one step ahead of him. Especially since you both were targeted earlier this morning." He paused and rubbed his chin. "He must be on to us somehow. Maybe he even saw us arrive here yesterday."

"We raised that same issue with our new defense attorney earlier," said Rae standing up. "How the hell did Tom Black know about us? We thought either there's a mole in this investigation or some type of surveillance equipment embedded in this house. Or maybe even both. We know Black stole from here in the past, probably had a key made to break in so easily, too. We thought something had to be in this house that he may have planted before he left yesterday. We think our near miss in catching him in the act spooked him into targeting us."

"We can sweep the house," urged D'Arata. "The equipment you need can be bought at any Radio Shack. Maybe we should talk outside, huh?"

Jake held up a hand, urging him to hold up. "Our defense attorney enlightened us on Black's criminal background. Turns out during his recent election his opponent accused him of also planting a listening device in her office." He then waved his hand at Rae.

Rae smiled and walked to a chair in the corner of the room where her purse was. She reached in and pulled out a gold ballpoint pen.

"Already done," she said, holding it up for D'Arata to see. "Our lawyer knew exactly who to call. We had a crew come out and they swept the entire place. Found this just before you got here." She handed the pen to D'Arata. "Battery's out. It's disabled. It's compromised as possible fingerprint evidence though. Too many people already handled it."

"Where was it?" D'Arata asked, inspecting the pen.

"In the ancestor room," Rae answered. "Tommy verifies he mistakenly placed it back in the cup on his desk after he knocked it over yesterday, never realizing it was a brand new pen he'd never seen before."

Tommy grunted his disgust at having been trumped by his own son. He pursed his lips, bowed his head, and studied Jake's last chess move with the Union knight.

D'Arata handed it back to Rae. "So Black was privy to all conversations in that room?" he asked.

"Everything," Jake slurred, taking a seat again at the chess board, and refilling his cocktail glass with a bit more vodka. "What about the other developments from West Point?"

This time D'Arata grinned. He pulled a notepad out of his inner coat pocket, flipped several pages deep and sat down on the sofa. Rae joined him. Leaning forward, hands on his knees he started reading. All eyes in the room were on him.

"Our main suspect's nickname is Phoenix. He is one of the most prolific master thieves in the country. We pulled fingerprints from evidence we found at the West Point Museum that link him directly to several high profile, unsolved burglaries on the FBI database." D'Arata turned to Rae. "You remember the theft of the Andy Warhol painting from Jaquizz Marshall's estate down in Miami? The Dolphins' showboating wide receiver? About five years ago?"

Rae furrowed her brow, thinking. Her green eyes then lit up. "Oh yeah, yeah. The burglar posed as a pimp or something, right? Con artist."

D'Arata nodded. "That's our man. The fingerprints pulled from that case matched several other burglaries, too. Problem is this Phoenix guy has never been arrested. Prints attached to a real name aren't in any law enforcement database. So we don't know *who* he is. Can't match a fingerprint to a real identity."

"How'd you get his prints at West Point then?" Jake asked.

D'Arata smiled. "The old vet with the cane."

Tommy looked up from the chess game with eyebrows arched.

Rae cracked D'Arata in the arm. "It *was* him. I told you!" She glanced at Jake and he pointed at her with a look admitting she deserved full credit.

D'Arata read from his notes. "Okay, so here's how Lieutenant Colonel Paxton explained how it all went down. The bulk of their findings happened all last night. He moved pretty damned quick to get where we are a day later." Then he looked up at Jake. "By the way, Paxton's just as pissed off at what Perkins did to you, too. Those two have had a bad history together. He's on our side. Call on him if you need to, he said."

Jake nodded back.

"Rae, he took your advice and they followed the vet on the security cameras." From his notes, D'Arata read; "He was present in the sub-basement gallery when the first smoke grenade went off. Fedora, cane, overcoat on, wearing full head mask of older veteran disguise and glasses. He was then caught on camera double-stepping it up to the basement balcony gallery, cane in hand, limp gone. Limp reappears on the balcony gallery. Another smoke grenade goes off from where he had disappeared behind a corner. Subject runs upstairs again to first floor gallery. Another smoke grenade goes off near restroom. Fire alarm pulled. We got him on camera doing that. Last seen, he was in front of McPherson's display case as smoke obscures all cameras throughout interior of facility. Subject's fedora later found on head of McPherson mannequin. Broken wooden cane found outside shattered Nazi display case. Fingerprints later pulled from cane. Subject's eyeglasses found on floor, too. Fingerprint on lens indicate match to cane. Subject is picked up on camera outside rear emergency exit. No cane. No fedora. Overcoat in hand holding object presumed to be McPherson's hat under coat. Nazi items unseen. Subject's limp switches to other leg. Baton possibly stuffed in pants due to bulge. Subject seen running awkwardly to bus parking area. Lost in trees."

Rae started laughing. "Baton in pants due to bulge? Oh, my freakin' God." She held a hand up to her mouth and snorted.

Jake and Tommy snickered, too.

"I am *not* kidding you," D'Arata shrugged with a sly grin. "Probably the best place to hide it." Reading more, he continued. "Canvassing of local Highland Falls businesses on Main Street reveals several surveillance camera angles outside main entrance of museum. Subject picked up on McDonald's camera feed, entering West Point Inn & Suites. Minutes pass. New subject exits dressed in black baseball cap, sunglasses, gray hooded sweat shirt, tan cargo pants, black backpack. Described as white male, approximately five seven to five nine. Thirty to forty years old. 170-180 pounds. Enters blue four-door car with Alamo rental sticker on rear bumper. License tag unreadable."

"Uh, oh," Jake interrupted. "A rental. I sense a screw up coming by our Phoenix."

"10-4, but not just yet. He's a clever one," nodded D'Arata, eyes on his notes as he flipped a page. "Ahh, oh, fingerprints taken from hotel room match those on eye glasses and cane. The room was booked late Saturday morning and paid in cash for a two night stay, according to the manager who also verified the description of the man exiting the establishment." D'Arata took a breath.

"The Alamo rental car was purchased in Highland Falls with a debit card under the name of Jason Stevens of Manhattan. Now we get to Philadelphia International Airport. We traced the car there, arriving just before 3 p.m. yesterday."

"About the time we arrived in Rochester to catch our flight down here," Jake added, sipping his drink.

D'Arata read on. "On scene investigators were able to impound the car before it was cleaned and prepped for a new rental customer. Subsequent search revealed fingerprints matching those at West Point. Same guy."

"Who? Jason Stevens?" Tommy asked, eyes still on the chess board, no move made, but still listening intently to the conversation.

"Nope," D'Arata shook his head. "Dead end. Our team had tracked Mr. Stevens down by that time and he said the purchase of the Alamo was an unauthorized purchase. He had family in for the whole weekend from out of town and his alibi checked out. Nowhere near Highland Falls. Confirmation came when his fingerprints didn't match. Determined his bank account had been compromised. He wanted to deactivate it but we convinced him and his bank to keep his account open."

"Wow," Rae said. "You guys are good."

"It's Paxton cracking the whip. Not allowing anyone to sleep. Called in extra manpower. Oh, so get this." D'Arata looked up to Jake and Tommy while pulling his smart phone from his coat. "A handwritten note on West Point Inn & Suites stationery that our suspect apparently dropped, as it was wedged between the seats in that Alamo rental at Philly. The note was sort of a code we thought at first." He tapped the phone's screen and did some scrolling to find the right image before handing it to Jake. "Had most of us stumped, but Paxton deciphered it. It turned out to be flight information to Berlin, Germany, written so close together it looked like a code. It also contained a contact person our subject apparently is or was supposed to meet up with there."

"Ahh, yes," Jake said while staring at the image. "I see. It means a 5 p.m. flight from Philadelphia, to London, Heathrow, and on to Berlin. And he's meeting a Sebastian von Blücher." Jake handed the phone to Tommy.

"Blücher is an antique dealer in Berlin," D'Arata added.

"The fence for the Nazi artifacts?" Rae surmised, getting up and taking the phone from Tommy after he gestured he was done looking at it.

"Yep, you got it," D'Arata nodded. "We've already got Interpol set up with surveillance around Blücher's office address on the note and his home. It's a total flight time of ten hours or so from Philly to London to Berlin, so it's possible our subject is already in Europe somewhere. Problem is we don't know who *he* is. Plus, the last I've heard is that Blücher is actually on vacation with family in Spain."

"This thing has gone international now," Tommy said, a bit exasperated.

"Any indication he actually got on the flight at Philadelphia?" Jake asked. "I mean how'd he get on board with the stolen goods? Hitler's gold pistol would never make it through security scanners."

"Right," D'Arata said. "As a carry on. But if he checked his luggage it would make it on fine. The pistol, baton, and hat. TSA doesn't check every single piece of stowed luggage."

Tommy perked up with a sour look on his face. "Big risk allowing those treasures to leave his hands. Luggage gets stolen or lost all the time. Had my suitcase lost for an entire week once going out to Arizona. If I went through all this cloak and dagger trouble I sure as hell wouldn't be leaving priceless artifacts in the hands of those dumb-asses running our airports."

"Yeah, plus he would have to use his own identification too," added Rae, giving the phone back to D'Arata. "Our Homeland Security is so tight with identities that a stolen ID or credit card would surely be flagged. It would be like he was walking right into the hands of the authorities taking a risk like that."

"Not if he used his real identity, though," Jake countered. "It'd be legit."

"Right," D'Arata agreed again. "Thing is, we still don't have a confirmed ID on who this guy is. So, we don't know who we're looking for exactly. All we do know is we have the flight list of names on that Philly to London bound flight. And of all the males on board who fit our subject's description, our team is in the process of narrowing down who's who."

"So, he's gone to Berlin," Jake said, scratching his chin. Defeat permeated his eyes. "Dealing the Nazi artifacts back to the Fatherland where they would fetch the highest bidder. That means our McPherson hat and the waybill is either with him in Europe, too, or stashed somewhere in the States or delivered to someone between the time he left West Point to his flight in Philly. Heck, Tom Black could have been waiting for him as soon as he finished the theft."

"Yep. We've speculated on several different scenarios involved. We're trying to ascertain Black's movements in the last few days and running into brick walls. But!" D'Arata held up his hand. "You mentioned the Phoenix screwing up, right?"

Jake nodded back. "Yep."

"Well, get this. We just got a hit this morning around 8 a.m. on the stolen debit card being used again. It was the same one used to rent the Alamo rental car in Highland Falls. Guess where it popped up now?"

"Berlin?" Rae asked, as she lit up another cigarette.

"Nope."

"London?" Jake asked, sipping his drink.

"Nope. I'll give you a hint. It's four hours away."

"Atlanta," Tommy answered, moving a Confederate colonel with a raised sword—his bishop—diagonally across the chess board to take one of Jake's rooks—a cannon with an American flag.

"Yes, sir."

"Where Tom Black lives," stated Jake as he watched Tommy smile while taking Jake's rook off the board.

"Where the McPherson hat and waybill are probably supposed to be delivered," speculated Rae. "If he drove all the way down from New York."

"Where my Bowie knife is, too," added Tommy.

"The debit card was used to purchase a rental car in Norcross, Georgia. Our subject's preferred mode of transportation. It was a red, four-door, Toyota Camry from Enterprise-Rent-A-Car. Same Mr. Jason Stevens account that was used at Highland Falls for the Alamo."

Jake smirked. "That's his screw up."

"Yep, but frankly we thought it was going to be in Europe somewhere. So this jumbles the deck of speculation. We really don't know if he's in Europe or not. Or had others go to Europe for him. And where the stolen goods are, we still haven't a clue."

Rae asked if there was a LoJack device on the rental. D'Arata shook his head, but said they did have its tag number and that all law enforcement agencies in Atlanta have been notified with a BOLO.

Jake stood up, wavered a bit, and began pacing. "Well, I tell you this. CID's got Europe covered. Our personal interest lies in the McPherson hat and Tommy's knife. We know Black was in this house yesterday. DNA proves it. We know Black lives in Atlanta. We know why Black wants the hat. It's because of the waybill and knife connection with Cherokee gold. It's his motivation to steal this dream from his own elderly father for being disowned by Tommy many years ago. Remember, Tom Black has been a thief all of his life, too." Jake caught Tommy nodding out of the corner of his eye. "We also know he probably targeted us for assassination based on what we've revealed through the spy pen."

Rae stood up, too, nodding, wine glass in hand. Her words were slurred somewhat, the wine clearly getting the better of her. "We know the thief headed south on his escape from West Point, right? He could have taken a flight from any international airport close by. New York, Boston. So why risk going three hours to Philly? Like being pulled over by cops for speeding, right? And his car searched. Also, why risk going directly to an airport into the arms of law enforcement and the tightest security around, trying to pass stolen goods on to an airplane? Art thieves lay low for years." She gestured wildly with her free hand. "They don't blindly risk it all up front. I may be wrong, but timing is everything. Our episode on the hat came out Friday night."

This time Tommy stood up. "And who happens to call Tom Black by mistake that same Friday night? My own nurse. That's who. Tells him how some Civil War hat caused my dadgum heart attack. Even told him the name of the show: *Battlefield Investigators*. I ain't never told Becky one stinkin' word about a McPherson hat or my ancestor or what secrets the knife holds. Any of that. So we know it ain't Becky working for Tom Black. She's as innocent as they come."

Jake cut in. "And the very next day a room is reserved in Highland Falls, hometown to the West Point Museum where that same hat was sitting after we *told* our audience this in the show."

"The thief takes the McPherson hat *first* in the museum, Nazi trophies second," Rae added. "The real trophy always comes first."

"Seems our road is leading right back to Atlanta," Jake stated. "Where our episode first began. It's likely that's where this Phoenix is now. Maybe even meeting with Tom Black as we speak. If the Army isn't going to watch Black's movements then we'll get on his ass." He gulped down the rest of his drink.

D'Arata winked at Jake. "Officially we aren't watching Black. Unofficially, I've got eyes on his home in Roswell and another set on his district office in Atlanta."

Jake nodded with approval.

"Is the FBI involved?" Tommy asked.

"No, sir," D'Arata answered. "This is a CID show. All Army."

"You're a smart man, Sergeant," praised Tommy.

D'Arata shut his notepad. "Well, it seems my road is back to Atlanta, too, then. I'd offer you a ride in the sky, Jake, but I don't think you're too keen on the Army right now."

"I want nothing to do with Army at the moment and don't want to jeopardize your position either. We'll catch up with you when we arrive and set up shop somewhere."

"Anything I can do to help you out before I leave?"

"Find out who hired that poor sap we killed."

"I'll try," nodded D'Arata. He said his goodbyes and hustled out.

Jake sat back down at the chess table and Tommy joined him. "I've got a truck here you can drive up to Atlanta with," the old man offered. "And a couple of . . ." He made a motion with his thumb and index finger indicating shooting a gun.

Rae's eyes widened. "Good. I'm feeling naked without one."

Jake nodded, pleased he'd soon be rearmed again. He glanced at the chess game and tried to remember Tommy's last move, but at this point he had lost all interest.

Tommy cleared his throat grabbing Jake's attention. "There's something y'all are gonna need to pick up first when you hit Atlanta. It's a major piece to the puzzle that us Watie men compiled over the last century. You're gonna need it, believe me."

"Ahh, Tommy, you've been holding back on us," Rae playfully chided.

"Since my mutt of a son now has my knife we're gonna move to Plan B," Tommy told them with a twinkle in his eye.

"And what's that?" Jake asked, leaning back in his chair, arms across his chest.

"Y'all are gonna have to go to a place everyone is dying to get into," Tommy said with a wry smile. "Even if my evil son has the waybill right now in his hands . . . well, let's just say he's got to find all those wayfinding arborglyphs and petroglyphs *first* in order to use that knife as a key. And most of those symbols out there on the land have long since disappeared from urban sprawl and development."

"Never considered that," Jake said. "So the knife is almost useless for him is what you're saying?"

Tommy nodded and stood up. "Come on you two. Let's take a walk out back among the roses just in case they missed a spy bug in here and I'll tell y'all about this little thing. I trust you two. You've proven your worth."

15

Monday. 5:30 p.m.
Abandoned warehouse parking lot
Doraville

FLACO GAVE UP FULL NAMES AND ADDRESSES, NOT only of his uncle, but each of the other three assailants, too. Kull even had to take notes. Flaco told where their hang outs were, meth and heroin labs, drug distribution houses, even down to what cars and trucks they drove. He was desperate and pleaded for his life, all the while asking for his *mami.*

"Did you look at any pictures on my phone?"

"*Sí* "

"What did you see?"

"Like a museum. Weapons. Old uniforms for soldiers."

"You see that gold pistol? Same one Angel had?"

The kid nodded.

"What else?"

"That diamond wand, too. They both were in some glass case or something."

"Did you look up any of my personal information on the phone?"

He nodded again.

"What's my name?"

"Nathan Kull."

Kull closed his eyes. The kid had sealed his fate.

"You tell anyone else my name?" The kid shook his head.

After the trunk interrogation, he allowed him more water as a reward. Using Flaco's own cell phone he snapped a picture of the boy's bloody and bruised face along with his body duct-taped up in the trunk. Flaco warned Kull that the gang was all around them. Once Angel knew he was kidnapped, he'd send out scouts looking for him. He tore the tape off Flaco's mouth. He couldn't tape him again because his nose was broken and clotted with blood. If he taped his mouth again, he'd suffocate from the unbearable summer heat stewing inside the trunk.

He closed the trunk, but not before issuing Flaco a warning that if any of the information he gave up about the gang was false he would pull out his fingernails as punishment.

Kull drove south down Buford Highway toward Angel's residence and monitored the fire and police scanner to see if a missing person or a kidnapping had been reported off Oakcliff. Nothing. Still in the clear. He grabbed some lunch and more supplies along the way. Texting his broker, he said he had run into some minor obstacles, but that he was in Atlanta and would still be delivering the contract item. Just needed to lay low for a while first. He ignored her frantic return texts.

He had already driven past Angel's address, a small ranch style house on Shady Valley Drive, and saw his big, white and chrome, crew-cab F-150 Platinum pick-up truck. Now sitting in his car, parked under tall pines in the small parking lot next to a basketball and tennis court in Shady Valley Park, Kull was readying to make the ransom phone call. He would use Flaco's own cell phone. If he used his own iPhone, then Angel would have his number. He didn't want that.

He called. At first, the gang leader didn't pick up. But after repeated ringing a male voice came on the line.

"Angel?" Kull asked.

"Flaco?" A pause. "Who's this?"

"Remember the carjacking last night, Angel?" Kull asked in a smooth serious voice. "You've got some things of mine that I want back."

"Eh?"

"And I've got your sister's son, Flaco—"

"*¡Vete a la mierda!*" (Fuck off!)

The call ended abruptly.

Kull was prepared.

Images of the bound, beaten fourteen year-old nephew were sent to his uncle Angel's phone, accompanied by a carefully crafted ransom text:

Alejandro Hernandez of 113 Shady Valley Drive. Uncle of Freddy Peña, your sister Maria's oldest child. You like what I've done to Flaco? I think I broke his leg when I hit him with a baseball bat. Definitely broke his ribs. He can't really breath that good. The bat made one hell of a clang on his head, too. And then when the little brat mouthed off to me, the brass knuckles made him talk. Oh, and talk he did. You want your nephew back in one piece? Then return to me the three items you were wearing in your video. You return my goods, you get Flaco. And you stay out of jail as a bonus. No cops involved. We deal de hombre a hombre. Flaco's lost a lot of blood and is fading fast. Reply back soon and you might get him to the hospital in time.

Minutes later, Flaco's phone vibrated with a text. It read: *You bullshit,* gringo. *Fuck off!*

Kull immediately texted Angel back threatening to contact his sister, the mother of Flaco. He'd turn up the pressure by using the parents.

A text back from Angel read: *Drugs matter more to her than Flaco. You get nothing back. Hitler shit be mine. Keep Flaco as pet. Adios.*

Obviously Flaco's uncle cared more for the treasure than his own family or even Kull's threats. The mother would have no sway either. Allowing Flaco some air and water from the oven-like trunk, Kull told him no one would be rescuing him. Not any of his gang members or even his own family. The kid was devastated. For Kull, the boy bait was now of little value. In fact, he thought, Flaco was better off dead knowing what he knows now.

Kull shook with rage at not being taken seriously. He wanted so bad to attack Angel's home head-on, but he knew the place would be defended like an armory and he was only one person without weapons. Plus, they'd see him coming through their network of scouts. So he upped the ante. When money matters the most to these thugs, then it's time to hit their profit-making machine.

Securing his victim and taking off in his car, he wasted little time in targeting one of the gang's meth labs tucked away in a quiet residential neighborhood a couple of miles away off Dresden Drive. It was one of the addresses that Flaco had given up during interrogation. At a nearby gas station, he easily created six Molotov cocktails of gasoline in tossed away glass bottles and found a piece of clothing in the trash which he shredded in strips with his knife to serve as the ignition rags.

Kull reconned the target split level, two-story home with an attached carport. A lone, late model shiny blue pickup truck sat under the covered car parking area. Driving by several times he coordinated his plan of attack.

The house itself was tucked between two other residential homes with lots of tall pine trees separating the properties. Nobody seemed home at the adjacent houses next to his target. Feeling like the opportunity was ripe, he drove up to the house, parked on the shoulder, jumped out with four Molotov cocktail bottles and ran down the short sloping driveway.

He set the bottles down in the grass, quickly lit the first rag and flung the liquid napalm weapon through the home's front bay windows. A large fireball exploded in a shower of shattered glass, burning drapes, and wood framing. A man screamed inside.

The next firebomb he smashed against the front door blowing up the awning-covered, small entrance way. The lone drug dealer—heavily armed according to Flaco—now had no immediate escape or means to quickly counterattack.

The third bottle hit the truck under the carport. It smashed through an open rear cab window and blew up inside of the truck itself covering the entire interior with flames. Kull's baseball aim was spectacular.

The last Molotov cocktail he flung back through the gaping, burning, smoking hole that was once the front windows of the house. When the glass bottle shattered inside, it exploded in another huge fireball in the front living room.

Kull never stuck around to watch his handiwork. He bolted to his car and sped away. As he rounded a bend, he heard a huge explosion go off behind him. He drove west on Dresden past the Metro Atlanta Rapid Transit Authority (MARTA) Brookhaven-Oglethorpe University station, then made a right onto Peachtree Road Northeast, not really sure where he was going because his adrenaline was so jacked up. He saw a fast food joint on his left and pulled into the parking lot for a breather.

Out of his right side window a plume of black smoke rose into the sky from the neighborhood he had just left. On his fire and police scanner he listened to the frantic response of 9-1-1 dispatch as calls came in from his terrorist arson attack. His heart thumped faster in his chest.

Immediately across the street, just past the high concrete wall topped with barbed wire fencing that held the MARTA train tracks, he saw a large billboard: Brookhaven Self Storage and an arrow pointing down to its facilities. He assumed it was hidden beyond a tree line of tall pines. To Kull, this was the blinking neon sign that meant "Safe House."

He backtracked to Dresden, made a quick left onto Apple Valley Road and followed the signs to where it dead-ended at the storage company. Using his own phone and one of his stolen credit cards, he sat in his car outside the main office and made arrangements for a full-sized garage storage unit back in the secure, fenced-in row buildings beyond the main gate. After getting the access code, entering it into the back gate, and driving towards his remote garage, he again turned on the scanner to see what was up. He learned the fire department had called in extra units to help fight the blaze. The house was fully involved with the possibility of people trapped.

Kull swallowed hard, but he remained emotionless.

Entering a new code for his garage, he swung the metal door up, hopped back into his air conditioned car, and pulled straight into the narrow, empty, corrugated metal chamber. Shutting the car down and stepping out, the heat inside the garage felt like someone had left a furnace on all day. He flicked on a single overhead light then closed the garage to the outside world.

And opened the trunk.

The taped-up kid was motionless, his head turned to the side. He looked dead. A slight rise from his chest indicated he was passed out from the trunk's heat. Remorseless, Kull grabbed his blood-caked pale face at the jaw and turned it upwards. He then slapped the little bitch several times until his eyes stirred opened. A mixed sigh of relief blew from Kull's mouth. *Thank God my bait is still alive.* He needed him.

He sent a friendly text to Angel on Flaco's phone telling him of his handiwork at the meth lab house, reminding him that he had many more addresses on the list if he didn't get his three items back.

The scanner squawked again from the iPad on the front seat. Kull left the trunk open and leaned back into the car to hear better. A series of alert tones indicated an important new broadcast. What the female dispatcher said next hit him like a kick to the nuts.

BOLO to all police units. Be on the look out for arsonist in connection with the Briarcliff structure fire. Last seen driving a red, Toyota Camry. License tag number BRU-4967. That's Baker, Robert, Uncle, Four, Nine, Six, Seven. This is an Enterprise-Rent-A-Car booked with a stolen credit card. Suspect was seen tossing bottles of gasoline at house by a neighbor.

Additional information on suspect follows: Yesterday, at approximately 1000 hours, the suspect was involved in a theft and arson attack at the West Point Museum in New York State. The suspect is considered armed and extremely dangerous. The suspect is described as a Caucasian male, 30-40 years-old, almost 6 feet tall, 180 pounds, wearing a blue ball cap, black t-shirt, and tan pants.

The dispatcher repeated the message again.

Nathan Kull sat down in the front seat, stunned. The cops now had a BOLO out on him. He took off his Yankees hat and brushed a hand through his hair, sighing deeply. Questions raced through his mind. *How did I screw up? How did they trace me to Atlanta so fast? Was it a credit card I used?* He had three or four of them in his wallet. Between being knocked out from the carjacking and his relentless mission to recoup his stolen goods, he had forgotten all about not using the same credit card twice. This would create a trail of bread crumbs any law enforcement rookie could follow. He had broken his own rules.

The Stevens debit card. I used the same one for the Alamo at West Point as this one. "Dammit!"

He had stolen the man's debit card account two years ago along with nearly 1,000 other people's accounts at Bank of America branches throughout New York City. It was another one of his ingenious scams that provided a supplemental source of income. He made nearly $100,000 worth of income since his scheme went into effect. And the majority of accounts he hadn't even tapped into yet.

It was called skimming. On an ATM, he'd affix—with double-sided tape—the skimming device along with a pinhole camera on a small panel painted silver to match the color of the machines. This panel was directly below the card insertion slot and was noticeable only as a lip. In essence, its disguise was virtually undetectable. While the pinhole camera recorded the customer's pin, the skimmer recorded the information on the magnetic strip of the card.

On a typical day he would leave the devices in place for about five hours at a time. Once he obtained the cards' info, he'd use it to encode blank cards to make purchases and cash withdrawals. He would also sell the stolen debit card accounts to customers in his nefarious network to be used in other states for more purchases.

If the Stevens card was the problem, this also meant the authorities had probably tracked him from the museum to West Point Inn & Suites where he entered the Alamo car in their lot. Without wearing any latex gloves during his operation, surely his fingerprints would have been picked up in his room. They'd also be on the Alamo rental. The cops most likely traced that car to the Philadelphia airport, too. Obviously then, if they were looking for him here in Atlanta, they didn't bite on his ruse for the flight to Berlin.

His saving grace was that he knew he had never ever allowed any agency to obtain his fingerprints his entire life. They weren't in any national database and therefore, even if his prints were picked up on this latest operation— let alone the hundreds and hundreds of jobs he had done throughout his career—nobody would know his true identity.

What was telling, was the dispatcher didn't give his name as a suspect. She only gave a general physical description. Kull quickly shed his clothes and dressed in his spare set. He also changed his blue ball cap to the white Braves cap. That would help somewhat. Most importantly, he knew his true identity was still intact. No one knew who the real Phoenix was.

Except for the little piece of shit in the trunk.

Flaco had admitted knowing Kull's full name and even saw the stolen Nazi items on his phone's photo stream. If Flaco ever told his name to the cops, they'd arrest him, fingerprint him, and he'd be implicated in not only the kid's kidnapping, but the arson, the museum theft, plus all of his past crimes where his prints may have appeared.

He was screwed and he knew it.

A fist pounded the dashboard in fury. In the trunk, he heard Flaco crying softly and moving about. *Sureños bastards!* Kull got up, went back to the trunk, and slugged Flaco in the jaw, knocking the kid out cold.

"Back to sleep, bitch!" He slammed the trunk shut.

A minute later Flaco's phone rang in his pocket. Kull answered.

Angel was on. He sang a different tune now and begged Kull to leave his drug houses alone. He agreed to return the stolen merchandise and wanted Flaco back after all.

Perfect timing, Kull smiled. He told Angel he'd text him back with instructions in two hours.

Now, how to make the swap was all that was on Kull's mind. Where would he be able to obtain his items without Angel's many gang members trying to watch, capture, or kill him? He pondered several scenarios. And then it hit him. He had actually driven right past it while coming to the storage company.

MARTA. It was just a half mile away.

With the rental car and Flaco staying put, he'd use the public train station to make the swap in the middle of a crowd and make a clean escape. Donning a rag, he wiped down the rental of any stray fingerprints, shut the engine off, and secured all of his possessions in his backpack.

In the trunk, the kid was still unconscious. Kull pulled out his tactical knife and unfolded the four inch blade into the lock position.

He plunged it into the kid's chest three times, piercing his heart.

Flaco's eyes never even opened.

16

I T WAS STILL DAYLIGHT AS THE THINNING RUSH-HOUR
crowds exited the train station, but the lights around the rapid transit
facility had just blinked on. Nathan Kull was on edge after he had shopped
for his latest disguise and had gotten into position. Donning his white,
Braves baseball cap pulled low over sunglasses, he adjusted his false beard
and shuffled about with the backpack over his shoulder. His new set of
clothes also made him look physically heavier than his normally fit build.

This was it, he thought, checking his watch. Angel had texted him back
five minutes ago agreeing to his last set of instructions. It was make or break
time for the thief-turned-killer as he stood in a darkened corner on the
second level, open-air platform, keeping an eye out for his adversary. The
concrete platform overlooked a small parking lot on one side, designated for
MARTA buses and taxi cabs, while an expansive parking lot on the other
side catered to thousands of commuters. A tunnel ran between the two
lots under a set of freight railroad tracks running parallel to the MARTA
commuter tracks.

Kull watched diligently from his birds-eye-view as a diverse mix of
day laborers from downtown Atlanta exited the tunnel and headed in one
direction; to their vehicles and home for the night. He was on the lookout
for the opposite; an approaching vehicle coming into the lot. That would be

Angel's truck.

But the gang banger was three minutes late. Kull began to fidget as he looked around for any suspicious Hispanic males mulling about in the station. Angel surely must have dropped off some scouts before his drive in. Could be why he was late, Kull figured. But he had the advantage. He knew what they looked like from the storage company's surveillance video. And if they had gotten a good look at him, too, during the carjacking, his precautionary disguise would throw them off for what he had planned next.

The disguise also hid his true identity under the bubble security cameras throughout the train station. Along with several armed MARTA police officers on foot patrol at the main entrance, he also observed a white MARTA police van patrolling the parking lot at regular intervals. They might prove a life and death deterrent if the gang took any violent action should his cover be blown.

No punks fit the bill at the moment as another train pulled into the station, crept to a loud hissing halt, and engorged a new set of commuters. Kull blended in with the rush of people exiting the train and feigned following them down the concrete steps to the main exit toward the tunnel. Instead, he veered off before the stairwell and walked to the other end of the raised platform keeping an ever watchful eye on the parking lot with a small monocular scope clutched in his fist.

Two minutes later a vehicle entered the far end of the lot with headlights on. It was a pick-up truck. A white, Ford, crew-cab, Platinum model like Angel's. It flashed its lamps three times per Kull's instructions. Kull's heart raced. The gang thug was actually following his orders.

The truck drove up to the tunnel entrance which was designated as a Kiss-n-Go drop off point. During his earlier recon, Kull observed how vehicles would drop off passengers and their luggage at the curb, a kiss and a hug goodbye from loved ones, and the vehicle would drive away within a minute. And that was the basis of his plan.

The vehicle parked at the curb just down from the tunnel entrance, which was obscured from his vantage point. A diminutive-sized teenager jumped out of the front passenger seat holding a red backpack, according to plan. Kull recognized him as the little punk who had pistol-whipped him during the carjacking. He watched as the boy disappeared behind the raised railroad tracks into the tunnel area, then reappeared moments later without the backpack. He re-entered the truck and it sped off. Not until he was certain it left the parking lot with the rest of the flow of traffic did he make his way down the platform steps.

At the bottom of the stairs, Kull waited briefly behind a businessman in line, then mimicked him and swiped his recently purchased MARTA Breeze Card on the exit turnstiles and pushed his way out. As he exited, two young Hispanic males with Atlanta Braves baseball caps were swiping their card several turnstiles away to enter the platform.

Kull's sphincter tightened.

Both punks looked about, completely suspicious. One had a cell phone up to his ear. That kid looked about nineteen or twenty, somewhat recognizable as another one of his carjackers when he passed by Kull. Luckily, neither one of them paid any attention to him. Near miss. They double-stepped up the stairs to the second level. If they were part of Angel's team cutting off his getaway, then all was still going according to plan.

Ahead of him was a parked MARTA bus accepting passengers, and a line of six taxis with Middle Eastern drivers standing about. Kull walked toward the taxis, pointed at a Pakistani driver and gave him a thumbs-up. The driver nodded vigorously happy to have a new fare. Kull then gestured with a raised index finger and told the driver he'd be right back in one minute, that he had to grab something. The anxious driver nodded, understanding. Down another set of concrete steps to his left, Kull entered the wide tunnel heading toward the commuter parking lot on the far side.

Halfway into the tunnel, with several people walking in front of and behind him, he came into a dead zone where there were no security cameras watching. To his right, leaning against the wall, jingling a red plastic cup with some coins in it, was a disheveled-looking black man in a dirty, olive drab Army jacket, obviously a homeless man looking for a few handouts. Held in his hands was a piece of cardboard that read: "Still Hoping for Change." Kull walked towards him reaching for some seemingly loose change in his pocket. The gnarly man smelled like dead fish as he got closer. The man then shoved an index finger up his nose and twisted it.

Kull glanced past him toward the end of the tunnel about thirty feet away. He could see a dusky, blue sky and a well-lit parking lot beyond. Hanging from the ceiling was a large bubble security camera which he wanted to avoid. Directly below the camera were two circular marble benches serving as vehicle barriers. On each side of the benches were three massive, bowl-shaped, ceramic planters further filling up the entrance to the tunnel. The furthest planter to the right was pushed up against the tunnel wall, and there, in the gap next to the wall, sat a red backpack.

Kull winked at the homeless man and dropped a rolled up $100 bill into his cup: the man's cue.

Homeless Vet dropped his sign and strode away as Kull took his place and leaned back against the wall. He pulled out his cell phone for a rather loud, fake phone conversation with his supposed wife and how he was running late. He glanced about making sure no Hispanic punks were near while lowering his own backpack at his feet and unzipping the top. Seconds later, the homeless man arrived back with the red backpack and placed it on the ground between them and unzipped it.

Kull ordered the Vet to look away as he pocketed his cell phone. He then reached inside the red backpack and grabbed an old black wool hat. He immediately stuffed it into his own open backpack. Next, he saw a small wooden box, which he opened. To his satisfaction he saw Hitler's gold pistol, magazine, and cleaning brush all in their proper velvet insert. That too went into his backpack. Lastly, he reached in and grabbed Göering's ivory and diamond baton wrapped in a cloth. Making sure the Vet and no one else was watching, he quickly transferred it into his pack as well, then zipped it up. The last thing he did was take his Braves baseball cap off and shove it in the red backpack as a big "fuck you" to the gang and their brand identity.

The deed was done. He cleared his throat and the Vet reached out with his plastic cup again. Kull deposited another $100 bill and his Breeze Card. The Vet snatched up the red backpack and headed up the tunnel toward the main platform. Kull waited a few seconds to allow several people to slide in between them then headed in the same direction.

The Vet walked up the stairs and made a right towards the turnstile entrance while Kull walked up and continued straight ahead toward the taxis. He watched as the homeless man passed by a MARTA police officer, swiped his Breeze Card, and entered the stairwell up to catch a train.

Nodding to the waiting taxi driver, standing outside of his cab with a rear door already open, Kull jumped in the back seat with his backpack and shut the door. The driver hustled around the front and slid in behind the wheel. A tap of his meter and he drove off asking his passenger where he was headed.

"Ritz-Carlton hotel," ordered Kull. "Buckhead. Had a long day." As he spoke, he fished inside his backpack for McPherson's hat and pulled it out. Fingering the liner aggressively, he felt the waybill still stashed inside and blew a sign of relief.

"Indeed, sir," acknowledged the driver in a Pakistani accent. "That's less than two miles away. We'll be there shortly."

As the taxi pulled away from the station, Kull lowered his sunglasses and glanced out his right side, rear passenger window up toward the open-air, second level platform where he could see passengers waiting for the next train to arrive. He watched as the homeless man with a red backpack and $200 cash was forcefully being escorted away to the far, dark end of the platform by the two Hispanic gang members.

Befriend and betray, Kull thought with a shrug.

And it only cost him two hundred bucks.

Extracting the waybill from the hat and unfolding it on his lap, he took a digital photograph of the entire piece of paper with his iPhone camera. That would be his insurance copy. The taxi cab was now clear of the station and accelerated south down Peachtree Road toward Atlanta. He refolded the waybill and stuffed it back inside the liner, stowing the hat away.

And now to make the call he had been waiting for. Time to contact Mona to find out where to deliver the godforsaken hat that had gotten him in this jam in the first place.

▼

Monday. 11:00 p.m.
Atlanta

Kull had booked a $300 per night room at the Ritz-Carlton, Buckhead's iconic luxury hotel. This time the room was under a different stolen Bank of America debit card owner's name—a one Henry Hodgson of Harlem, New York. After securing his stolen items in the room safe he hit the hotel lobby and checked the remaining balance of the account at an ATM. Three thousand bucks to play with, he went shopping across the street at the prestigious Saks Fifth Avenue in Phipps Plaza. It was time to indulge a little and wind down.

He had purchased a new Armani Collezioni outfit consisting of a shawl collar, black cashmere sportscoat for $1,300, trousers for $365, a dark gray dress shirt for $250, and Versace leather loafers for $500. Back at the Ritz-Carlton he spent the next hour and a half melting away the horrible day at their ninth floor spa with The Executive Massage for another $200. Showered, shaved, primped, and gelled, he dressed in his new digs and enjoyed a fine dinner at the The Café lobby restaurant which ran him an additional $75 on his credit card. Finally, it was time for the drop of the hat.

Grabbing another taxi out front, and with his hat inside a boutique bag, Kull proceeded to downtown Atlanta. He was told by his New York-based broker on the phone, after she coordinated the final drop with the client representative, that he was to simply place the McPherson hat on a certain mannequin in some weird French cabaret-style private events room. The client himself would be there celebrating his birthday. This room, Le Maison Rouge, or The Red Room as translated in English, was attached to a large antique store called Paris On Ponce.

Paris On Ponce, as it turned out when he was dropped off out front, was actually a 50,000 square foot, sprawling, brick warehouse located on Ponce de Leon Avenue just east of downtown Atlanta in the Historic Fourth Ward District. This famous Atlanta treasure trove of antiques sat diagonally across from the tall, old, massive former Sears factory now being renovated for high-end loft apartments.

Le Maison Rouge itself, at 692 Ponce de Leon Avenue, was actually a smaller two-story former ammunitions storage warehouse from the 1920s. It was located on the slope of a railroad spur embankment, now turned into a beltway walking and biking path. In the mid-fifties, the 4,000 square foot building housed the original Colgate Mattress company, which supplied Sears until they moved out for expansion. Subsequent companies filled the space in the following decades. On the first floor is where Paris on Ponce began as the original antique store in 2001, until their success allowed them to expand into the large adjacent warehouse facilities many years later. The vacant second floor was then turned into Le Maison Rouge as an events room for rent, furnished in the style of a seductive French cabaret. The red room was so famous that it was booked a year in advance.

There was no street access to the cabaret. The first floor entrance had been sealed off. All invited party guests, Kull was told by Mona, would enter Le Maison Rouge through the antique warehouse from its parking lot side entrance, however, there was an outside smoking area off the rear loading dock on the top of the embankment facing the old railroad tracks. Kull was told to slip in discreetly from that rear access, he was expected, and the password, when asked by armed bodyguards, was Birdseye, after General James B. McPherson's middle name.

All the while, since he left the MARTA station, Flaco's phone kept vibrating with Angel's desperate phone calls and texts asking where his nephew was located. Kull never responded and the pleas for an answer escalated. Soon they turned into hollow threats if Flaco was harmed. Angel then texted Kull that one of their gang members was killed in the house explosion and that they would be hunting him down like a dog and would torture him for many hours before decapitating him.

Kull knew it was now time to frame Angel. His use for the piece of trash and the Sureños-13 was over. Dropped off on the curb a block away from Le Maison Rouge, the dapper dressed Kull clicked confidently down Ponce de Leon, and using Flaco's phone he dialed 9-1-1. He lowered his voice giving his best Hispanic accent.

"Atlanta 9-1-1, what's your emergency?" asked a fast talking black woman on the other end of the phone.

"¡Hola! I have information about the house explosion in Doraville this

afternoon," Kull whispered in Spanglish. "I know who did it. It's the same *hombre* that stole the stuff from the West Point Museum yesterday. I need to remain anonymous. I fear for my life. Am I being recorded?"

"Yes, you are, sir. Please go ahead with your information."

"The Sureños-13 gang put out a hit on the dealer in that house for stealing drug profits. I have names and addresses of the people involved. The person who ordered the hit is named Alejandro Hernandez of 113 Shady Valley Drive. Goes by the street name of Angel. He's illegal alien. There are also two others involved—" Kull gave the names of Enrique Ramirez and Hugo Aguilar along with their addresses. "The three of them also kidnapped a fourteen year-old boy being held for ransom by Angel. His name is Freddy Peña. Goes by Flaco. Angel gave me Flaco's phone to hold on to. I'm calling from it. Are you getting all this?"

The dispatcher said she was. She asked him how to spell some of the names and to repeat some of the addresses again as she typed furiously.

Kull got overly dramatic on purpose. "You recording this, right? They put the boy in the trunk of the stolen car. It's a red Toyota Camry is all I know and it's hidden in one of the storage companies in the area. I don't know which one, though. Angel might have already killed this boy. He's gone *locos*. You guys gotta get Angel!"

"I'm dispatching the police right now, sir. Tell me about the West Point Museum."

"He's the one who stole the Nazi shit from that museum yesterday! I saw a video of him with the gold pistol and that long, diamond wand thing and that hat on his head. He was showing off like he always does."

"Can you repeat that?"

"Angel is crazy. He took the shit, *señora*. I have a video of him he sent to Flaco's phone. He's supposed to use the shit as collateral for a large drug shipment coming here from Mexico. Don't underestimate him," Kull continued, exaggerating as much as he could. "He has many illegal weapons at his house and lots of drugs and laundered cash there, too. If you send a SWAT team he will shoot at them. He has nothing to lose he told me personally."

"Yes, sir. Are you also affiliated with the gang."

"I am. I want out. Angel's gone too far this time. He's totally out of his mind. He'll kill me if he finds out I was talking with you."

"I understand, sir. Can you send us this video? Can you text it to our detective unit? I can give you a phone number."

She played right into his hand. Kull paused, faking that he was thinking it over. "Okay, I'm cool with that."

The dispatcher gave him a phone number and he said he'd send it, then he ended the call. In a few minutes the incriminating video was sent to the detective's number. A reply text indicated the detective received it.

And with that, the trap was set. He took the SIM card out of the back of the cell phone, snapped it in half, and tossed the pieces in the gutter. Out came the battery which flew over his shoulder. The phone case followed, smashing in bits. He then headed toward the rear parking lot of the antique store to finally finish his weekend transaction.

As he approached, a couple of young black men stood at the corner smoking cigarettes, but they paid no attention to him. Upon arriving at the already full parking lot, he noticed some giggling guests walking up, too—women, girls, smaller in stature, dark-haired and scantily clad in sexy costumes and high heels reminiscent of New Orleans Mardis Gras or Brazil's Carnival. They wore gilded face masks, flamboyant hats, long feathers, and glittering necklaces of beads. They jibber-jabbered in some Asian language.

A burly, white bouncer manned the entrance and checked the guests' names on a list. Kull nodded to him and walked by, going around to the back, darkened alley toward the rear smoking lounge on the loading dock. Another young, black punk was up ahead at the end of the alley. They passed each other and the kid eyed him suspiciously and moved on.

Turning the corner, Kull shuffled up some steps onto the long cement loading dock. He saw in the darkness ahead a few women smoking and drinking outside of a rolled-up, overhead garage door. Their smoke was cast in a haze of red from flickering interior lights. They laughed and puffed as music spilled out from the cabaret.

A man stepped out of a doorway, flicked a glowing cigarette butt out onto the ground and approached Kull.

"That's far enough, bro," said the firm voice of a buff, black man wearing a ball cap backwards; another bouncer. He held his hand up to stop Kull, even going so far as to place his palm on the thief's chest with a slight push backward. "All guests are supposed to enter from the main entrance back around where you came from. I'm sorry, but you'll—"

"Name's Birdseye," interrupted Kull in a most pleasant tone, brushing the man's hand off his chest. "Just dropping off a birthday present." He raised the small shopping bag.

"Ah, yes, Mr. Birdseye," the guard said, lightening up. "As expected. Not a problem at all, sir. You're most welcome to enter through here." He then reached inside his jacket and pulled out a shiny, silver-colored, plastic eye mask with matching satin ribbon ties, and handed it to Kull. "Everyone inside is required to be masked, though. Here's an extra one if you need it."

"Thanks, man," said Kull as he placed the mask over the top half of his face so only his blue eyes shone through. Several strands of his blonde hair fell across his forehead and he followed the security guard inside, nodding to the smoking young girls as he passed. One of them whistled at him from behind, telling him he was hot.

He said, "I know."

17

THE RECORDING STOPPED PLAYING. RAE PULLED THE old Maxell C60 compact cassette tape out of the dashboard player and re-inserted it to play Side B. Both her and Jake were mesmerized as to what they had just heard on the first thirty minutes of recording.

"My God," Rae gasped. "Can you believe this?"

Jake just slowly shook his head, hands stiff on the wheel of Tommy Watie's vintage, 1957, fire-truck-red Chevy pick-up truck he had lent them. Rear taillights of a tractor trailer loomed ahead in the right hand lane as he drove at a high rate of speed.

"I can't believe how many murders took place in the Cherokee Nation back then," he finally said. "What did Corporal Watie say, some forty murders were committed between the Watie and Ross factions?" He depressed the gas pedal and the rebuilt, 350 V8 engine roared even faster.

"Come on," Rae pleaded, seated right beside him in the middle of the bench, shoulders touching. "It's dark. Slow down! You're still probably buzzed from the vodka you drank." She braced both hands on the dash board as Jake cut into the left lane, no blinker, and raced past the tractor trailer going about 95 miles-per-hour. "If you don't stop, I'm going to throw up all over you."

"Okay, okay," he laughed, slowing back down to 80. "Can't help it.

This beast has a mind of its own. Probably hasn't gone this fast in some 40 years! Go ahead, hit play, Hon." He nodded to the old, 1980s-era cassette recorder, custom installed at the time, in the dash of the classic truck.

They had just finished listening to the high-pitched, deeply southern voice of Corporal Thomas Black Watie Jr. of the Confederate States of America's army. At the time of the recording, in late 1949, Junior was one-hundred-five years-old and bedridden in a Savannah hospital room, on his last leg. He would die two months later. Two other southern voices were present in the recording: his seventy year-old son, Thomas Black Watie III, and the grandson, Tommy Black Watie IV, a twenty-three year-old World War II vet who was slated to take over the family business in a few short years. Tom Black was just a newborn infant at the time. The Watie men's voices were accented so thick with the southern drawl that Jake and Rae had to reverse the tape backwards several times and replay it just to understand what they were saying.

The rare, 1949, first-person interview recording of the aged Civil War veteran was made possible by the grandson, Tommy, who had learned of a new technology called magnetic tape recording. Discovered by American soldiers in WWII who confiscated Nazi recording devices, they brought back the technology to the States, refined it, and manufactured it for the radio broadcast market. A few years later, tape recording machines were made available to the public. Tommy convinced his father, who in turn convinced his own father—the Confederate vet—to share his Civil War experiences for posterity's sake. Most importantly, they wanted him to pass on his knowledge of the secret mission he had been given by General Stand Watie so young Tommy could continue the hunt and, in turn, pass down that information one day to his own son, who could hear his great granddaddy's genuine voice.

That original reel-to-reel tape recording sat in a secure drawer in the Watie ancestor room for many years until compact cassettes were invented. Upon his own father's passing in 1968, Tommy had dubbed, or transferred, the old recording to a cassette tape that lasted an hour. Cassettes were the latest technological rage at the time, with the introduction of the portable cassette tape recorder/player, allowing people to record their favorite music and play it back wherever they went.

After their talk in the backyard of Cherokee Rose Manor and outlining to Jake and Rae what needed to be done next in Atlanta to help their quest, Tommy had given them the almost fifty year-old cassette tape to listen to as background intelligence. And, as promised, he allowed them to take his antique pick-up truck for transportation. He also insisted they take a wad of five thousand dollars in cash for miscellaneous expenses. Lastly, both were outfitted with new weaponry before they headed north toward Atlanta.

For Rae, Tommy produced a Smith & Wesson LadySmith .38 Special revolver. It used to be his late wife's for personal protection. For Jake, a 1939 Luger 9mm semi-automatic pistol, a classic of WWII. Tommy had snatched the Luger off a dead German officer on the battlefield. Both guns were in pristine condition, neatly maintained over the years.

The first half hour of cassette recording was Watie explaining how he was bent on revenge against Chief John Ross for the murder of his own father back in 1845 and for how Ross had betrayed the Cherokee Nation by siding with the Union after allying with the Confederates. He talked about his exploits in the Indian Territories under General Stand Watie's Cherokee Mounted troops and the circumstances behind his uncle giving him the mission to Georgia in 1864.

His capture and release at Adairsville came next, followed by rejoining the CSA under Govan's Brigade and his front line skirmishing. All were explained with incredible detail and emotion. The Battle of Kennesaw Mountain was a particularly life-changing event for young Corporal Watie as he described the horrific slaughter at the Dead Angle and how he observed the Masonic signal of distress from enemy troops.

He had just started talking about the Battle of Atlanta and how he had General James B. McPherson in the target hairs of his Whitworth's scope when the tape ran out on Side A. As the old cassette tape squealed and crackled to life once again on Side B, a ghostly voice from the past continued his tale:

Corporal Watie: It was the biggest mistake of my life getting caught by McPherson's troops in Adairsville. I thought I lost the waybill for good all stashed away in his hat. Had to get it back or die trying. And lo and behold who pops up in my Whitworth's crosshairs not two months later but the man himself. I was up in a tree. A loblolly pine to be exact—

Tommy IV: Wait now, Granddaddy. You even remember the kind of *tree* you were in?

Thomas III: Didn't I tell you, son, his mind is fresh as a your mamma's apple pie. Now don't interrupt him.

Corporal Watie: Tommy, I sure do. I remember everything that day.

Tommy IV: I'm sorry. Please go on.

Corporal Watie: It was July 22, 1864, and General Hood gambled big. Marched us troops some twelve miles to flank the enemy. At night, too. The attack got off real slow that next morning. Them officers were having a tough time coordinating the jump off and we lost hours. Plus, the terrain through the thickets, woods, and ravines was tough. And you top it all off with the devil's heat of another Georgia day, and our go at it was simply unbearable.

We were in Hardee's Corps, Cleburne's division, on the right flank and were ordered to hit Sherman on his left flank at Bald Hill and push him up all the way to the Decatur Road to cut off his supply train, which would then be attacked by Cheatham's Corps in the center. Hood was aggressive. Was going to be a pincer strategy. And we followed him, but by golly we were beat up and tired when we attacked.

But attack we did. Hit em hard. Rolled their skirmishers right up. I was pickin' them off left and right. Then we charged and blasted through the lines of Union's 16th Iowa. We took their cannons and lots of prisoners. That's when things got all tangled up.

You see, I started out with Govan's 2nd Arkansas Brigade with my boys in the 1st/15th Arkansas, but then done got split up, and took in with some dismounted 24th Texas Cavalry and some beat up 5th Tennessee Infantry on my right, and we kept on attacking. Nonstop. Pushed up into some woods along a small wagon road. Little did we know we had gone through a gap and were behind enemy lines. I was ordered to hold back a bit and cover our advancing troops up that road, so I took up into one of them there loblolly pines with the wide branches.

I was just getting comfortable and I see this Union horseman come barrelling down the road toward our hidden infantry just up ahead of me, about 40 yards away it was. Was McPherson himself alright. Recognized him with his long, bushy, black beard and round handsome face. He had a pudgy nose and thick black eyebrows. He was right in my scope boys, and I about shit my drawers. Then our infantry jumped out and a captain done waved his sword and told the general to halt and surrender. That's when the rest of the general's staff come galloping down the road behind him, and what in God's name does McPherson do having twenty or so Johnny Rebs pointing at him?

Tommy IV: What he do?

Corporal Watie: The balls of that good man. He took off that dadgum hat of his and waved it like he was greeting the finest lady around, and then wheeled his horse and took off like son-of-a-bitch. His staff followed suit and they skedaddled back up the road, riding like the wind.

Tommy IV: Good Lord.

Corporal Watie: And that's when I shot him. Square in the back. Not a second before our boys opened up on him. But only one shot got him— mine. Two of his men got their horses shot out from under them, but I got McPherson alright, I tell you, and don't let no one else tell you otherwise. You know when you bring down a man when he's in your scope. I had no choice. No choice . . . no choice, I tell you.

There was silence on the tape. Jake and Rae waited with bated breath. Rae clutched Jake's right hand in both of hers on her lap as she snuggled closer to him. Suddenly, they heard weeping on the tape. Corporal Watie was crying and his seventy year-old son and grandson were consoling him, telling him it was okay. Rae's eyes teared up and she sniffled. Jake stared straight ahead down a dark highway.

Corporal Watie: I know. I know. I'm okay. I'm okay. Poor bastard. I hated doing that. I just wished he would have never taken my waybill. He didn't know what it meant. Not a clue. But dammit, I needed to get it back and that was my only chance. So, when he got shot he fell off his horse, and I saw in my scope that damn hat of his fly off his head and get stuck hanging in some branches. I hustled down my tree and started to make my way through them prickly woods to get to him. And when I got to him—

Thomas III: Wait now, Daddy. Don't forget to tell Tommy about who you met in those woods first, before you got to McPherson.

Corporal Watie: Oh, yeah, yeah. Those two staffers of his that got their horses shot out were taken prisoner and were being escorted back to our lines. One of them was Colonel Robert Scott. Son, you tell him. I need some water.

Thomas III: Sure, so Scott was taken prisoner, but then exchanged during a swap a couple of months later. And then toward the end of the war he became a general. He was also the first governor of reconstructed South Carolina, but years later, on up in Ohio where he was from, he ended up killing his son's friend and went to trial where he was acquitted of murder. The public was outraged. They said—

Corporal Watie: He got off Scott-free!

Thomas III: And that's where we get that saying from.

Tommy IV: Well, isn't that something.

Corporal Watie: The other prisoner was McPherson's orderly named A. J. Thompson. He witnessed and signed the receipt for my waybill when they let me go in Adairsville. That man was a no good bastard the way he treated me in front of the general. Threatened to hang me as a spy. Any how, he recognized me and I asked him straight up if the waybill was still in McPherson's hat. He said he believed so. He was crying like a baby, said I killed the best man in their Army. That hurt. I never forgot what he said.

Jake paused the recording. "Check out my phone, Rae. Go to the camera roll. I took a picture of that receipt for the waybill in Tommy's ancestor room."

Rae fumbled with Jake's smartphone and flipped to his picture library.

"Find McPherson's hat cord. The receipt should be after that," Jake said, while glancing in his rearview mirror as headlights came up behind him in the left lane. He signaled and guided the truck over to the right lane to let the vehicle pass. A bit paranoid, he eased up on the gas pedal and hovered his foot over the brake pedal letting the truck drift. It was a technique allowing him to maneuver quicker in case this fast-mover meant business. He had already done this several times before with other vehicles that seemed suspicious during their late night four-hour trek up to Atlanta; just in case someone else tried to target them.

"Here it is," said Rae, tapping on the photo which zoomed in on the old paper receipt.

"Check out the signatures on the bottom," Jake said, keeping his eye on his driver's side mirror. Then, as the vehicle approached, he watched out of his driver's side window. It was a shiny, metallic green Crown Victoria with tinted windows he couldn't see into and oversized chrome wheels, typical with inner city youth showing off their ride. Freakin' pimp mobile, Jake thought as the car rushed on past.

Rae expanded the image with her fingers and looked at three signatures. "James B. McPherson, A. J. Thompson, and Thomas Black Watie Jr." She looked up at Jake. "Wow!"

"How cool is that?" Jake followed the road signs to where I-16 ended and turned into I-75 to Atlanta. He stayed in his right lane, crossed the dark Ocmulgee River and made the connection heading north. He then hit play on the cassette player and floored the truck's accelerator.

Corporal Watie: . . . and then I finally done got to McPherson's body, but these two Yankee privates were fighting over it. One of them had his elbow all blasted away and was arguing with the other who was stealing paperbacks from the general's pocketbook. I took my Arkansas toothpick up underneath that Yankee thief's chin and kicked him in the ass out of there. He pissed his pants, I remember. But that other fellow—with the wound—he was an honorable soldier. He was protecting his general.

Tommy IV: But where was all of our own infantry?

Corporal Watie: They took off already. Continued the attack. Pressed on up the hill into the woods. This Union private was a wounded straggler trying to get back to his own lines and came across McPherson's body. He was hiding in the bushes and saw how our boys rifled the general's possessions and then left on the attack. I do believe that boy's name was

Private George Reynolds. He was one of the most resolute, loyal soldiers I've ever come across, the way he wouldn't leave McPherson's side. He even tore off the general's gold buttons and shoulder boards to hide the fact he was an officer if someone else came along and wanted to strip him down further.

He was no threat to me so I started looking for the general's field hat. You know, the one with my dadgum waybill in it. But by Lord, it was nowhere to be found. That private then told me he witnessed one of our Johnny officers with the infantry who done stole it. He said it was a captain claiming it was his war trophy and swapped out hats. I found that captain's torn up Kepi cap and the spot where the general's hat was and all that remained was the bullion cord. I guess that's when I picked it up and must of shoved it in my pocket. I forgot I even had that cord until the battle was over and I escaped back to our lines.

But anyway, Reynolds told me our boys took McPherson's field glasses, his watch, his sword-belt, and some of his papers before leaving. They left so fast they never even took off his gauntlets. I found out many years later his diamond ring was still on his little finger when his body was recovered.

Thomas III: But Daddy, McPherson wasn't dead at that point, right?

Corporal Watie: Right, Thomas. He was shot through, but still alive. Got knocked out cold from the fall off his horse. He came to when me and Reynolds were there and first thing he asked was that private's name and told him he was a good man. He asked for water and we gave him some. I held his head in my hands, boys, and I gave my victim water on his lips. I knew his wound was mortal. He was gushing blood. I scared Reynolds off and then I had to ask the general before he died about my waybill. If it was still in his hat. And he recognized me. Said it was, wanted to give it back to me right then and there, but I told him it was missing.

His last words was asking where his hat was. God awful, boys, I felt God awful for what I had done. So bad. It's why I kept quiet for so long about shooting him. I was traumatized myself I guess you could say. Made me want to murder John Ross even more for having to take McPherson's life like that with a bullet in his back. It just wasn't fair.

Tommy IV: But you didn't know. You couldn't have known it would come to this. War is nuts. As vets, we all know that. It's simply nuts the shit that happens out there.

Corporal Watie: I felt so bad Tommy, I gave him my Cherokee protector crystal. My mamma gave it to me to keep me safe from Raven Mockers and I wore it as a necklace all throughout my battles. I put it in McPherson's inside coat pocket right over his heart.

Tommy IV: Dadgum! You did that? Dadgum.

Thomas III: He sure did.

Corporal Watie: And by the time I caught up to the infantry skirmishers I was with earlier they were all killed or taken prisoner up at the top of the hill. Never saw 'em again. Never knew their names. Not even that captain was who took my hat. For all I know he had his head blown off in some entrenchment. I knew I failed my mission right then and there. I was so close. But I didn't have time to feel sorry for myself, surviving was all that mattered. The Battle of Atlanta lasted until nine o'clock that night and then for the next month Sherman bombarded the city with artillery.

Tommy IV: Then came the Battle of Jonesboro at the end of August, right? Sealed the fate of Atlanta and should I say, of the Confederacy, too?

Corporal Watie: Can't disagree with you, Tommy. In hindsight, yeah probably so, because it got Lincoln re-elected that November. What with Sherman's March-to-the-Sea and taking Savannah in December, yeah, you're probably right.

Thomas III: But tell us about Jonesboro. It's where you got wounded.

Corporal Watie: That I did. Was another fierce battle. This time to hold the Macon & Western Railroad line supplying Atlanta from the south. It was our last artery into the city. Sherman swung his army south of the city at the Jonesboro depot. Hood sent only two corps to defend: S.D. Lee's and Hardee's. I was back with Cleburne's division, Govan's brigade. We were down to nothing. We attacked the first day and got slaughtered. The next day damn Hood pulled Lee's corps out of there to defend the railroad north of us, leaving us all alone. One corps versus four Union corps. We were at the apex of their assault holding the Warren House. There were just too many of them damned Yankees. They penetrated our lines, we fought hand-to-hand. An old, gray haired Yankee and I squared off. I took a bayonet in my side. Ended up clubbing that big Yankee's skull with the butt of my Whitworth. If you look at the stock it's how that crack got in it.

Tommy IV: My God.

Corporal Watie: They overran our position and killed many of us. Captured over six hundred in our brigade. The 1st/15th Arkansas lost it's regimental colors and then we retreated down to Lovejoy Station.

Thomas III: There's even a tiny little cemetery dedicated to General Patrick Cleburne's troops just north of the depot in Jonesboro, Tommy. Me and Daddy visited it many times over the years, placing Southern Cross markers at the gravestones.

Corporal Watie: That bayonet wound apparently nicked a kidney pretty bad and I was none too well. It got infected, I caught a fever and was near death, but somehow I held on. Don't know how. I was evacuated to Macon and then when we thought Sherman was going to attack Macon, they sent me on down to Savannah. I was barely alive. That's where I met your grandmammy, Tommy. Miss Annabelle, a beautiful Southern girl who was volunteering as a nurse at Candler Hospital. She was my angel. She captured my heart and nursed me back to life. But then when Savannah fell I was evacuated again, this time up river to Augusta, where I recuperated during the rest of the war. Never again saw my regiment. They were down to a skeleton unit and fighting in the Carolinas before they surrendered.

Tommy IV: Where'd you go after the war ended?

Corporal Watie: Right back to the Indian Territories—my home. I helped the family re-establish themselves and was on the delegation with Uncle Stand to negotiate a treaty with the Federals in late sixty-five. Lo and behold, but who shows up at the Grand Council at Fort Smith to undermine us once again? The most loathsome power hungry creature that ever fed upon the sewage of the dungeon: the politician John Ross.

I knew I had to act and act I did. I done got that old wretch with a witch's poison in his shot of whiskey and then I hightailed it out of there. My love was in Savannah and I came here and made her my bride. Started the lumber company soon after.

Tommy IV: What happened to Ross? I know he died the next year in Washington D.C.

Corporal Watie: That he did. The witch's poison was suppose to last an entire year and it worked perfectly. He suffered a long, miserable, torturous death and finally was terminated from this earth at the Medes Hotel on Pennsylvania Avenue. The most important part of my mission that Stand gave me was fulfilled. But Ross' waybill to the tunnel was still lost.

Tommy IV: But eventually you did end up hearing about the missing McPherson hat, though?

Corporal Watie: Not until many, many years later after the war when I read that article in the Confederate Veteran. What year was that, Thomas?

Thomas III: Oh, let's see. That was the 1903 issue, I do believe. I was about your age, Tommy. In my twenties. And when Daddy read that article, well, that was the flame that rekindled our fire.

Corporal Watie: Yes-sir-ee, that's when I read about one of those skirmishers—who tried to make McPherson surrender and shot at him— he claimed he shot the general. Mind you this was some forty years later and minds get hazy. But not mine. But in response to that article a Captain Beard of the 5th Tennessee wrote back saying it was someone else. You see this man was the most credible witness because he was actually the captain who raised his sword to McPherson to surrender and then watched as the infantry fired on him after he bolted. It didn't matter to me who took credit. All that mattered was that Captain Beard also witnessed Captain William A. Brown from Mississippi take the general's hat, too. Said it straight out in that letter. To me, this corroborated the story from that Union Private Reynolds. Beard said all of the skirmishers in his unit were taken prisoner and all of the possessions that they stole from McPherson were found and returned to his body. All except that hat. I never knew that.

Tommy IV: Now that is something!

Corporal Watie: Gave me a glimmer of hope, it did. You see it had no insignia on it, no bullion cords. It was just a black, wool, Hardee-style hat like many others worn in battle, so it makes sense the Yankees didn't take it back. They never knew it was a general's hat. Beard said Brown wore that hat all throughout his captivity at Johnson's Island prison up in Ohio and then back to his home in Mississippi after the war. Once I found out a name I was able to track him down.

Found out he died back in 1889 already. I asked his family members about the hat. They remembered it alright, but said Brown never mentioned he stole it from a dead general. They said he sold it to someone many years before his death, but no one knew who. I searched and searched. Placed newspaper advertisements. Nothing. Found nothing. Visited Clyde, Ohio, where McPherson was from hoping the hat was returned to his home. Nothing. It was lost.

It was pretty much my hobby outside running the family lumber business down here in Savannah. That and trying to find the Cherokee Tunnel up in the mountains. It's how we'd spend our vacations, until I physically couldn't do it no more. Until Thomas here took over the quest. He caught the bug. We ain't never found that hat yet or the tunnel yet, but by golly we sure did record lots of Cherokee carvings in our little wayfinding clue book now, didn't we?

Thomas III: That's right, Daddy. We sure did. And thank God, because people were farming heavily and clearcutting the land and we were afraid we'd lose out on the clues.

Tommy IV: How'd y'all know where to look for the Cherokee Tunnel though? You didn't have the waybill.

Corporal Watie: General Watie told me the location was somewhere on the Etowah River south of Ball Ground. That's what he heard from Ross's staffer who did the espionage and stealing of the waybill and knife. And the only thing I truly remember from looking at that waybill was this sorta curvy line on the drawing that was supposedly a birds-eye-view of the bends in the river. It looked to me like the profile of a turtledove to be exact. When I was doing my sleuthing I always thought that turtledove had significance because John Ross came from the Bird Clan of the seven clans of the Cherokee. And that clan was symbolized either by the eagle, the raven, or the turtledove. So, it can't be by coincidence that he chose that location.

But I never did record any of the symbols on the waybill to those on the Bowie knife. That was another dadgum blessed mistake I made. I should have written everything down ahead of time in case I lost something. Sure enough I lost it alright. Dumb, cocky boy that I was, I figured I had the knife as a key, right? And that's all I needed. That waybill was covered in all kinds of symbols that were supposed to guide me somehow to that tunnel entrance and I done lost it.

Tommy IV: I remember helping you two out with finding them symbols all through my teen years. I loved exploring those woods, the river banks, the cliffs. That was the best part of my life y'all. Then World War II came for me.

Corporal Watie: And thank the Lord you made it through, Tommy.

Tommy IV: Thank you, sir.

Thomas III: I tell ya though, Ross and his men must have made one hundred symbols out there in the woods. It confused the shit out of us. Remember? I wish we could find that McPherson's hat then we'd have all the pieces we'd need to find that tunnel, seeing as how we already got the knife as our key.

Corporal Watie: Yeah, well, life deals you a certain hand and it's what you make of it. But we sure had fun trying though, right? You know, boys, there ain't much difference in men now compared to men in the days of King Tut. No-sir-ee. Gold is their dadgum obsession. Gold, gold, gold. Sure as shit, there ain't been a patentable improvement on men in thousands and thousands of years and there won't be any in many thousands more. There's no explaining it other than saying it's a disease, boys, and there ain't nothing we can do about it. It's in our blood. And I think we made the best of it.

Thomas III: I know, Daddy. I know. I caught the disease, too, and it's all your fault. (*Laughter*)

Tommy IV: Yep, and thanks to you both, I now inherited it, too! (*Laughter*)

Corporal Watie: Oh, don't you know it, boys. Don't you know it. It was that one thing I desired all my life. Just to finish my mission and find that Cherokee Tunnel.

Thomas III: We did the best we could.

Corporal Watie: I know son. All that matters is our family legacy now. We persevered. We survived. We Watie's are tough workers, responsible, dedicated. We're upright men and Masons with good character. Now Tommy, you raise that little boy of yours with the same values and he'll make you as proud as I am of both of you. Carry on our name in good faith.

Tommy IV: That I'll do, sir. I promise.

Rae pushed a button on the dashboard player as the tape ended. "God, that's sad. No wonder why Tommy hates his son so much. They were a tight group of men who cherished their family reputation."

"Yep," agreed Jake. "They had high expectations. They were proud of their heritage—hardworking, successful, accountable. And Tom Black was the opposite of all that."

"He became a liar, a cheat, a lazy, arrogant know-it-all who spat on his family history," Rae summed up. "And spits on his country."

"No wonder he aspired to become a politician," stated Jake. "Fits right in with those corrupt bastards in D.C."

Rae changed the subject. "So, that little clue book that Corporal Watie and Thomas III mentioned is the same one Tommy told us about. The one we have to recover in Atlanta."

"Yep, and apparently they recorded the exact topographic locations of a whole bunch of carved symbols out there in the woods and along the river. All we have to do is get that clue book from Corporal Watie and then recover that damned waybill from Tom Black to find which symbols will take us to the tunnel entrance."

"I am not looking forward to this," lamented Rae. "Especially after just hearing Corporal Watie's voice. This is going to be really weird actually seeing him."

18

WHAT A RAUNCHFEST, THOUGHT KULL AS HE stepped inside Le Maison Rouge into a loud party of writhing, sexy bodies. Entering from the rear, he realized he was on the far end of the cabaret stage, separated by a couple of rusty steel columns decorated with flashy ribbons, glitter, and red drapery. Making his way down a few steps to the main floor he saw several circular tables with various costumed men and women looking up to the stage toward his right. They cheered and hooted amid the fast-paced, booming music and strobe lights as three, scantily-clad, masked women stripped down to thongs and high heels while feathers and bubbles floated around their scrumptious bare breasts. He had entered a modern vaudeville show.

To Kull's immediate left was a row of tables along a raised platform; the occupants hardly seen in the dark, crimson hues that filled that section of the room. He did notice a masked woman sitting on the lap of a well dressed, masked man grinding her ass against his crotch as he spread his legs to accept her.

To the back of the room was a fully stocked, mirrored bar filled with all sorts of crazily dressed mannequins, strange statues, exotic objects, blinking lights, brass music instruments, and rare antiques, all sharing a common color: red. In fact, that's what made this room so unique. Virtually every item placed here had some kind of red scheme to it; from red chandeliers hanging from the ceiling, plush red sofas and chairs, lamp shades, table cloths, candle holders, to walls decked out with long red frilly tapestries and French theatre posters.

But best of all was the glistening, covered, harem lounge couch in the far rear corner. Now that was pretty damned cool, thought Kull as he walked closer, taking in the scene. The transparent, peacock feather drapery over the couch suddenly flipped open and some masked, obese man dressed in a navy blue, Union general, Civil War uniform was sitting between two incredibly sexy, costumed women while eating a piece of chocolate cake. The large man's costume was complete with gold shoulder boards and buttons, navy pants with a gold stripe down the sides, and a red waist sash. Only thing missing was a hat.

The general laughed with a loud obnoxious cackle in the middle of the pillowed couch as one woman stroked his inner thigh while the other playfully unbuttoned his jacket. He even fed them cake off his fork. Above the harem couch was a banner that read: HAPPY BIRTHDAY CONGRESSMAN TOM BLACK!!!

"Jabba The Hut," Kull mumbled to himself and turned away.

"It's General Black," said a voice in his ear as a hand slipped under his arm and grasped the inside of his bicep.

Surprised, Kull looked down and laid his eyes on a short, gorgeous, black-haired beauty dressed like a 20s, speakeasy flapper. Her hair was done up with a sequin headband and feathers. Behind her black mask he could tell her eyes were oriental. As he moved his gaze down, he peered past a black feathered boa into the cleavage of her pushed-up bosom over a beaded neckline, and became instantly aroused. The rest of her short, black satin dress sparkled with lace overlays and sequins that finally ended in fringe at the tops of her fishnet-stockinged thighs. Kull swallowed hard. *Very dangerous.*

"How you know Mr. Tom?" the girl asked loudly in Asian twang.

"Friend of a friend," Kull yelled back. "Never met the guy. Heard of him on the news. I guess he likes his harem doesn't he?"

"Very much. Long, long time." She giggled and clung on Kull's arm, squeezing it ever so gently. "But I like you! We date tonight, okay? I not taken yet."

"Maybe so," Kull said, bending down to her ear, smiling. "But first I've got to drop off my birthday present."

"All presents in the Buffet Room. Back there," the girl said gesturing behind him as she leaned up so he could hear. Then she slipped the tip of her wet tongue into his ear and teased him. "I get us drink at bar. Whatchu you want, hot stuff?"

"Screaming orgasm, honey."

She giggled again. "Ah, you bad boy. I give you *that* later. Drink now."

The girl took a couple of steps forward then deliberately dropped her feathered boa on the floor. She slowly bent over to pick it up making sure Kull saw the full view of her black-thonged, tight ass under her dress. He swallowed again, shifting his leg to adjust his rising desire. The girl sauntered off toward the bar with a smile back at him.

Kull's radar told him to stay away, to focus on the swap no matter how much he wanted to screw the shit out of this little chick. He immediately made his way out another door with a red tinted window into the room she mentioned. This room was half the size and much quieter with big band jazz music playing in the background. But it, too, was full of antiques, costumed mannequins, lounge furniture, and posters, all with some type of red theme. The smell of hot foods turned his head to a self-serving hors d'oeuvres station set up with stainless steel heating bins. Another table held a multi-tiered chocolate birthday cake half dug into.

In one corner of the room was a red velvet, high-back chair that looked like it came from a European monarch. Behind it was a tall stage prop panel painted with red, royal fleur-de-lis. A masked couple sat in the chair while a photographer flashed his camera taking pictures. Nearby was a table with an array of various antique hats that guests would don as props for their portraits. A black fellow, seated in the chair in a red and green sports coat, had a colorful, extra-wide brim Mexican sombrero on while a young white woman wore a white, African safari hat and matching cape over her white feathered Mardis Gras attire. She placed a long, lean leg on the chair in his crotch and they chuckled it up posing for the camera.

On the opposite side of the room sat a red couch filled with wrapped birthday presents. Against the wall sat an antique piano and a couple of empty gold Victorian arm chairs on each side of a marble coffee table strewn with discarded drinks. Lastly, Kull noticed a costumed mannequin of a white faced, female harlequin clown in a silver and red court jester outfit sitting on a big red vase with a floppy hat on her head.

That's the mannequin he was looking for. The harlequin clown. And specifically the hat. He took its hat off and tossed it on top of the piano then reached into his bag. Out he pulled the McPherson hat and placed it on the mannequin's head. His boutique bag went into a nearby trash bin before he sat down in one of the Victorian chairs, and waited.

A half minute later the masked black man in the cheesy Christmas-colored sports coat stood up from his photoshoot and tossed his sombrero back on the table revealing a shiny, bald head. He smacked his girlfriend on the ass and she re-entered Le Maison Rouge. The photographer followed. The mocha-skinned man walked over to sit down in the chair opposite Kull. He crossed his legs and leaned back, criss-crossing his hands behind his dome, elbows high up in the air. They were the only two in the Buffet Room at the moment.

"Fucking sexy bitches, huh?" Mocha asked Kull with a pleasant sigh.

"You know it, pal," Kull said sternly, noticing the man wore small diamond earrings on each ear. His eyes behind his green mask were an unusual light blue with long eyelashes.

"I believe you are Mr. Birdseye, am I correct?"

"Perhaps. And you are?"

"Why, I'm the caterer who ordered General Tso's chicken for my client." He smiled with bleached teeth and nodded his head with a glance up over Kull's shoulder at the new hat on the mannequin.

"Pleased to make your acquaintance," Kull said with a nod. "Sorry for the delay. Had a rude welcoming committee when I drove into Atlanta late last night. Had to knock some balls out of the park first."

"Your timing is perfect, actually," laughed the fixer, folding his hands on his lap. "Birthday boy's about to open his presents," he winked. "May I ask, is the fortune still inside the cookie and fully intact?"

"It is. In the liner, under the sweatband. Look for the gap. And may I ask, do you have my—"

"Indeed we do, Mr. Birdseye," interrupted Mocha, reaching in his coat to extract a small piece of paper. He leaned across the coffee table and quickly handed it to Kull.

Several women, including Kull's apparent date for the night, entered the room engaged in loud conversation. They made their way over to the food station and helped themselves. His little Asian girl shimmied over and gave him a highball glass filled with a fruity red drink over ice with a wedge of lemon. She winked and rejoined her friends.

"Ahh, you've already met Malina I see? She likes to bounce on top."

Kull laughed and sipped his drink mixed with vodka, peach schnapps, crème de cassis, and orange and cranberry juices. He smacked his lips enjoying the fruity cocktail. Placing the drink on the table he opened the piece of paper. It read that an envelope with his bonus cash payment of $50,000 in one hundred dollar bills was sitting behind a desk in a private dressing room. He looked up at the fixer.

"Familiarize yourself with the contents." The man nodded toward a doorway off the Buffet Room. "I've kept it vacant for you. And once you're satisfied, there are several taxis out front for transportation." The fixer stood up and extended his right hand to shake Kull's. Kull also stood up and shook hands.

"And the balance?" asked Kull, referring to $700,000 he was to receive through a wire transfer to his Cayman Island account. "When?"

"Tomorrow morning by 10 a.m. Your broker will receive her commission of 15% and the rest is yours."

"Marvelous."

"One question. Why the other two items?"

"A man's got to have some insurance if he's messing with Uncle Sam. If you're going big, might as well go over the top."

"Can't argue with that. Have a fun night, Mr. Birdseye."

The rep snatched McPherson's hat off the mannequin, flipped it over and looked inside. Turning the sweatband down he inspected closely around the inner liner. Touching his fingers on the waybill, a smile formed on his face and he gave Kull a wink before tucking the hat under his arm and walking inside Le Maison Rouge.

Kull grabbed his drink off the table and skirted over to the dressing room. Several minutes later he emerged entirely satisfied, his drink finished and a thick envelope in his coat pocket. Waiting for him was the little Asian whore. She propositioned him again and he lied, telling her he was gay. She swore at him in some foreign language and then flipped him off as he turned his back on her.

Back through Le Maison Rouge, walking toward the smoking lounge rear exit, Kull saw that the strippers were off the stage now and dancing on the tables for the guests. He glanced over at the harem couch again, curtain pulled back. Two black men stood in front of it, one was the fixer he had just spoken with. Seated on the couch he could see Tom Black wearing the McPherson hat and holding the waybill in one hand while turning a long knife in his other hand. A dark skinned, masked man with a goatee and mustache dressed in a gray suit stood over him. He tapped into a cell phone.

Looks like the so-called Civil War collector, General Black, was as happy as a pig in shit, thought Kull. *Guess the fuckface completed his costume.*

Outside at the smoking lounge he enticed the bouncer with a $50 bill to escort him to one of the waiting taxis out front. He didn't trust any of those lone wolf black kids hiding in the shadows, especially with 50k in cash in his pocket. In minutes he was on his way back to the Ritz-Carlton to happily sleep off his weekend project. Come 10 a.m. he'd be on his way out of Atlanta with a bulging checking account.

19

J AKE'S PHONE RANG AT THE SAME TIME HE WAS backing the truck into a parking spot at the Six Feet Under Pub & Fish House, directly across from Oakland Cemetery on Memorial Drive. The pub was quite familiar to the pair as they had enjoyed a nice seafood dinner there many months back while shooting the McPherson episode on *Battlefield Investigators*. They both remembered the wonderful view of Atlanta's skyline from the pub's terrace seating, along with an incredible overview of the famous Oakland Cemetery right across the street. It was so wonderful it had spurred them into taking a guided twilight history tour of the cemetery that very same evening. Little did they know that their re-entry into Atlanta's largest burial grounds would come again so soon.

In the middle of the night.

And for much more ominous purposes.

"Hey, answer that will ya? I've got to straighten out," Jake said. "My parking sucks."

They were told about an hour ago on the phone by the extremely-irritated sexton of the famous Atlanta cemetery that he had agreed to meet them at 12:30 a.m. at the gated pedestrian entrance across the street. Jake had found plentiful, well-lit parking this late at night as most guests of Six Feet Under had already departed before it closed in a half hour. Checking out Jake's phone as it continued to ring, Rae assumed the call was from the sexton again. Instead, the incoming ID read it was from Special Agent D'Arata.

"What's up, Marco?" answered Rae, putting him on speaker. "Got you on speaker. Jake's having parking dysfunction."

"Some developments," said D'Arata.

"Shoot."

"The guy that tried taking you both out? Name's Blake Jesse Raymond. Georgia Bureau of Investigation is the lead agency on this one. My contact there said they tagged him as an ex-Atlanta police officer with SWAT. He was corrupt to the core. He accepted thousands of dollars to provide protection during drug deals. Was busted by the FBI and spent time in prison. The guy's apparently a known hit man—"

"Not any more," whispered Rae.

"Lived down in Brunswick, Georgia. His phone records indicate he was contacted late Sunday night from an unknown cell phone number, probably a chat-and-chuck. We're speculating that's the call to target you guys. GBI is still doing a search at his home. Sorry, but no good leads on who hired him yet. You guys took down one bad ass dude, though."

"Fucking punk," mumbled Jake, placing the truck's gear in park. "Keep on it, Marco. Find out who hired him, and then I'm going to do some private contracting of my own."

"Copy that," said D'Arata. "More bad news, though. I was told by Colonel Perkins we still can't get a search warrant at Black's home because Tommy Watie neglected to file a police report on his break-in and stolen knife. So, officially a crime has *not* been committed in the eyes of the law and there's no probable cause. Perkins said it is a civil matter between the father and the son, that it's all just circumstantial evidence for us."

"Unbelievable! Who's side is Perkins on?" shouted Jake as he turned the truck's engine off.

"I was afraid of that," Rae muttered. "We should have pressured Tommy to get the locals or GBI in there as soon as we knew a crime was committed."

"I know," agreed D'Arata. "I know. They're saying it's hearsay at this point. An elderly father's word against a sitting U.S. congressman. Who's going to win that dog fight? But the good news is we think we've got a damn good hit on our Phoenix here in Atlanta."

"No shit?" asked Rae.

"Our thief is a killer, too. He firebombed a residence up in Doraville with Molotov cocktails this afternoon. It was apparently a meth lab or something because it blew sky high and fried a known member of the Sureños-13 gang. I have no motive on this gang connection. We knew it was him because a neighbor spotted the car he was driving and the tag matched the rental we've been looking for."

"The red Camry from Enterprise?" asked Jake, grabbing two flashlights they had purchased earlier. He handed one to Rae.

"Copy that."

"Get a description of the suspect?" asked Rae.

"Yep, matched our boy from West Point, too."

"Damn!" Jake said, excitedly. "We're close to bagging him."

"Well, how close are you? To Atlanta, that is?"

"We're actually *in* Atlanta now," Jake said. "Undisclosed location, though. Private matter for Tommy we need to take care of."

"Understood. Listen, I followed Tom Black from his Roswell mansion down to the city earlier tonight, where he's throwing a birthday party in a private lounge. I found this out when I questioned one of his guests, who left early in total disgust. I guess Black has a room full of prostitutes putting on a show, and this guest was one of his constituents wanting a reference letter signed for his son's application into a military academy. Black's been putting him off for months now and stiffed him again tonight, so he caused a bit of a scene and got tossed out by some bouncers. I took the risk of approaching him and he opened up to me. He said Black's been in there a couple hours already. But, here's the best part: guess who just showed up at the rear entrance about five minutes ago and sort of slips in quietly?"

"The Phoenix!" replied Rae.

"I think it might be," acknowledged D'Arata.

"Where exactly are you?" Jake asked.

"I'm at the old Sears factory on Ponce de Leon just east of the downtown. I've got a camera covering the place across the street called Le Maison

Rouge. That's where Black's party is. Listen Jake, we've got to figure out some way to nail everyone, tonight, if you know what I mean."

"10-4," said Jake. "No rules. Especially after Black tried to kill us."

Rae nodded back as she quickly tapped in location and mileage directions to Le Maison Rouge on her own smartphone Google Maps app.

"I'm thinking this may be the final delivery of the hat and the two Nazi trophies to Black," D'Arata summarized. "We can't let this opportunity slip away. The problem is I don't have concrete legal evidence and probable cause to go in and bust up a private party, let alone any back up firepower. It's just me here, alone, with a fucking camera up my ass and my hands tied behind my back from Perkins. Man, I tell ya, we'd already be knocking down doors like we did in Iraq if this bastard wasn't a goddamn congressman."

Rae held her phone up to Jake so he could see the Google map showing how far away they were from D'Arata's location. "I hear ya," Jake said. "Listen, as soon as we're done with our business we'll rendezvous with you. It shouldn't take us too long. Everything's been arranged for us in advance. We're just three miles south of you. I'll call as soon as we're done. We gotta boogie."

"Copy that." D'Arata ended the call.

"And when we're done here," said Rae, pulling out her revolver, rotating the cylinder, and seeing that is was loaded. "We'll give Tom Black a birthday present he'll never forget."

Jake checked his Luger, chambered a round, and they exited the truck. They walked briskly across Memorial Drive to a wrought iron gate secured with a heavy, silver chain and a Masterlock. The entrance was set inside a six foot high brick wall that ran the entire perimeter of the cemetery.

Now they waited.

▼

Outside the main entrance vehicle gate on the west side of the cemetery, at Martin Luther King Jr. Drive and Oakland Avenue, a metallic green Crown Victoria with oversized chrome wheels slowly cruised by. It passed the entrance, then turned a sharp left onto empty Biggers Street, cut its headlights, and parked at the curb in an unlit section. Several minutes later a white Dodge Charger pulled up and parked behind the Crown Vic.

Two, black, twenty-something men from Savannah got out of the Crown Vic while two other similar aged blacks from the Bluff Boyz gang exited their Charger. Each gave a gripped fist handshake and a chest bump to their counterparts. They exchanged a few words and glances at their cellphones. The Savannah men pointed in the direction of the south end of the cemetery toward the row of restaurants along Memorial Drive. A thick wad of cash bound with a rubberband was passed to them by the Bluff Boyz, departing handshakes followed, and the Savannahians got in their vehicle and headed out of town.

The crew from the Bluff Boyz reentered their car and emerged several minutes later wearing red bandanas over the lower half of their faces. Hoodies were over their heads, rounded out with dark clothing and white latex gloves. One carried a Nighthawk .45 caliber pistol with a Ti-RANT sound and flash suppressor and an extended 15-round magazine. The other carried a fully automatic MAC-10 submachine gun with a suppressor.

At the corner of Oakland and Biggers was a chain-link fence butted up to the brick cemetery perimeter wall. Easily scaling the fence, the two thugs climbed over the crumbling wall and entered their dark hunting grounds.

The cell phone call from Mr. Johnson said it was a go. They were to locate the prey in the vast 48-acre cemetery.

Then quietly take them out.

▼

A lone, squat figure walked down the sloped asphalt lane in the moonlight heading toward the pair as they waited outside the gate on the sidewalk. He could easily be seen as he approached downhill from the slight rise in the middle of the property. His silhouette marked him against the glimmering Atlanta skyline looking north. Jake and Rae held their hidden weapons inside their coat pockets as the figure entered the dim glow of a yellow street lamp throwing light from across the avenue.

A none-to-pleased, short, portly black man in his late 50s greeted them at the gate simply asking their names and for ID. Jake and Rae slipped their wallets through the gate and the sexton returned them stating his name was Stanley Rogers as he unlatched the Masterlock with a key. As the large chain slid off the gate and the sexton pulled it open, Jake extracted a white envelope from his inner coat pocket.

"Mr. Rogers?" asked Jake, getting the head of the cemetery's attention as he walked in, "Tommy Watie wanted me to personally thank you for doing this on such short notice. We know you've got better things to do on such a late night and —"

"Yes, I do Mr. Tununda," snarled Rogers in a whiny monotone voice. He slammed the gate shut and started re-chaining it after Rae barely made it through. "My daughter is in labor with my first grandchild over at Grady Memorial Hospital. And my wife is all over my ass for being back here. I'd rather be there welcoming life into this world than disturbing the dead."

"Sir, we're very sorry," uttered Rae. "We didn't know—"

"Whatever," the sexton grumbled under his breath. He clicked the lock through the chain and jiggled it to make sure it was secure. Turning his back to the couple he ordered them to follow and started heading up the dark lane.

Jake grabbed his arm firmly and turned him back around. Before the man could say anything Jake flicked on his flashlight and displayed the envelope spilling with cash. "Maybe this will ease your annoyance." Jake spat. "It's from ninety year-old Tommy Watie as a thank you for allowing us to see his grandfather."

The sexton's eyes widened.

"Of course if you can do without the $2,000 donation we can wait until regular hours," cited Rae.

The sexton snatched the envelope and shoved it in his coat pocket. "I'm always happy to oblige a long time customer such as the Waties. Please tell him I'm very grateful. Now follow me, if you please." His tone and demeanor was incredibly more pleasant now.

Jake and Rae stole glances, rolling their eyes.

As the sexton led the way, Jake scanned behind him along the inside of the thick perimeter brick wall. He didn't like being locked in. He noticed to the right of the locked pedestrian gate were several steps leading up to a terrace of graves. That higher terrace butted up against the top of the brick wall leaving just a couple of feet clearance. It would make a nice escape route should they need to exit on a moment's notice and not be hindered by the locked gate. All they would have to do is simply step on top of the wall and jump down six feet to the sidewalk below.

"Corporal Thomas Black Watie Jr. is resting in the Watie family mausoleum just north of the Confederate Obelisk between the Generals and the Lion of Atlanta," said Rogers, heading up the moonlit lane. "It'll be up ahead on our right. It's one of the most elaborate mausoleums this cemetery has."

Jake and Rae followed behind, their flashlights panning left and right taking in the gravestones and thick trees while casting moving shadows along their walk.

"Probably best to shut those off," recommended Rogers, walking briskly. "The shadows play funny tricks on the eyes. Especially in a cemetery, late at night. Just follow me. The moon's nice and bright tonight."

They cut off their flashlights and let their eyes adjust to the night. Remarkably, the moonlight cast the cemetery in hues of deep blue and cold gray from the white grave markers, limestone mausoleums, marble vaults, sculptures, statues, and masonry work scattered throughout their field of vision. Only when they passed under one of the many leafy trees did darkness really overtake them.

Established in 1850 as a six-acre cemetery on the outskirts of Atlanta, City Cemetery, as it was known then, was designed as a rural garden type cemetery, a highly fashionable, aesthetically appealing alternative to the traditional overcrowded graveyards of the time.

Having taken the historic tour, Jake and Rae were somewhat familiar with the layout of the property. They knew straight ahead would be the high ground where the Bell Tower, visitor's center, and sexton's office were located. On that hill, on July 22, 1864, stood a two-story farmhouse where Confederate General John B. Hood observed the Battle of Atlanta raging to the east. Scores of his soldiers would be buried in the cemetery because of his miscalculations against Sherman during the Atlanta campaign. That same afternoon saw Corporal Thomas Black Watie Jr. slay General James B. McPherson.

By the end of the Civil War, there were almost 6,900 Confederate soldiers laid to rest at Oakland. 3,000 of whom were unknown soldiers from the heavy toll taken during the battles around Atlanta.

"This way, please," directed the sexton. He turned right, down another gray lane. "A little short cut through the Confederate burial grounds."

To Jake and Rae's left they started to see the rows upon rows of rounded top, white, marble markers denoting Confederate dead.

Skirting east and then north, up a narrow brick path, the grave markers now enveloped them on both sides. "Watch your step. These pavers are loose," warned the sexton. His cell phone rang and he answered it while walking, the display screen lighting up the underside of his face. After a mere ten seconds of listening he ended the call and stopped.

"My wife. She is *not* happy," Rogers told Jake and Rae nervously after being berated by his wife on the phone. "My daughter's about to give birth. Listen, I need to be there. I've never allowed this but I'm thinking I'll have to just unlock the mausoleum and you two can lift the slab off and pull the coffin drawer out on your own. Are you okay with that?"

"I suppose we'll have to be," Jake said.

Rogers continued walking. "Don't worry. It's easy. I'll explain everything once we get there. Either one of you have a knife?"

Jake told him he did, asked why, and didn't receive a reply.

After passing under several dense magnolia and oak trees on each side of their path, they saw the Confederate Obelisk directly in front of them. Several spot lights aimed upward from the base illuminated the four-sided, Egyptian needle. The glimmering, 65-foot tall, granite monument, dedicated to the patriotism and valor of all the Confederate dead, stood out like a beacon in the night. Now Jake and Rae could start to understand why Corporal Watie chose to lie in rest here under its shadow with so many of his fallen comrades around him from the horrific Atlanta campaign.

Around the circle that the obelisk occupied, and a zig to the left, they entered another brick path.

As Jake slowly walked ahead he glanced down the slope to his right at a large bright sculpture behind a tree. "Is that the Lion of Atlanta over there? To our right?" he asked, remembering the beautiful monument from his last visit.

"Indeed, it is. Even shines in the darkness, doesn't he?" replied the sexton, stopping and turning toward the rectangular block monument of a prone lion. "He guards the unknown Confederate dead buried in that field. Several thousand of them. The most visited and photographed monuments in the cemetery. The lion is wounded and dying yet he clutches a Confederate battle flag. Such a morbid expression paints his face." He was about to explain more when he extracted his phone from his pocket as it was vibrating with a text. Glancing at it his face soured. "She's relentless! Please follow me. Just past this magnolia on our left is where the Watie mausoleum is. I really gotta get outta here."

By the end of the Civil War the cemetery had expanded to its current 48-acres and was renamed Oakland because of the many prevalent oak trees. The years to come saw the emergence of beautiful family gardens with shrubbery and flowers, as they attended to the graves of their loved ones. Magnolia trees, dogwoods, and evergreens spread their branches over the deceased, trying to protect the quiet atmosphere as dense residential and industrial neighborhoods sprouted up beyond the cemetery walls. To the north were a set of CSX freight train tracks paralleling another MARTA commuter train station. Over time the cemetery would fall into disrepair due to vandalism and neglect until the late 1970s when it made the National Register of Historic Places. Soon after, the Historic Oakland Foundation was established to raise funds for its continued restoration.

A sharp left down another narrow, somewhat hidden path, past the Beerman family plot on their right, and a large above-ground structure loomed before them. The sexton announced they had arrived at the Watie Mausoleum. He extracted his own flashlight and turned on its wide LED beam to light the façade. Jake and Rae turned theirs on, too. The sight was magnificent as they panned up. The Waties spared no expense.

Set upon a terrace surrounded by a three foot high wall, the light gray, highly polished, quartz-infused granite mausoleum looked to be a miniature replica of the Temple of Solomon with heavy Masonic overtones.

Rectangular in overall shape, the outer walls no doubt held the crypts of the dead or treasures of the soul, while the inner chamber would replicate the Holy of Holies. The roof was flat. Jake noted that even the direction the mausoleum faced was in line with the Temple, where the head rested toward the west and feet faced east, when the soul would awaken and face the rising sun. The front doors of the porch were flanked by two freestanding pillars with carved spheres upon their tops, open to the sky.

As Jake viewed it from outside, the left, or southwest pillar, was named Jachin and symbolized the celestial, and standing eternal with God—the mental aspect of a man. The globe on top was carved with stars only, denoting the universe. The right, or northeast pillar, was named Boaz meaning strength, and symbolized the physical—knowing the Self. That globe was a representation of the earth.

Over the door and a circular window was a carved bas relief Freemason symbol with the square and compasses surrounding the letter G. Under the symbol was a message: We Enter The House Not Made With Hands.

Rogers immediately mounted a flight of stone steps up to the porch and narrow arched entrance with tall, windowless, double bronze doors fronting the walk-in mausoleum. The doors, adorned with decorative floral engravings, were now aged to a green patina. He placed his flashlight on the ground aiming upward upon the doors and then fiddled with a small key in a tiny lock hole.

"How many crypts are inside?" asked Rae, shining her flashlight beam on the block construction jutting out from the side of the structure.

"Eight to ten. Not sure," Rogers curtly replied, still jiggling with the lock. "Four on each side. Just look for the name of the one you need. Damn thing!" he shouted in frustration at the lock. "Hasn't been opened since Tommy's wife Margaret died ten years ago. I looked up the records. My God, I don't have time for this."

"Want me to try?" asked Jake, standing behind him on the first step, flashing his beam on Roger's back.

"No, I got it," Rogers huffed as he worked the key. "Now listen to my directions. There will be vertical, marble crypt slabs in the walls with handles on them. All you have to do is break the caulking seal around it at the joints. That's why I asked about the knife. Then lift the slab out and you'll see the coffin on a shelf inside. The entire shelf is on rollers and really easy to pull out. Get what you need and replace everything as is. I'll have the maintenance crew reseal the slab later on this morning when they come in. Any questions?" He didn't give them time to answer. "No? I didn't think so."

He pushed on the door now with his shoulder while turning the key. "It's just the damn lock that isn't catching. So many of these mausoleums need repairs," he complained, twisting the key some more. "But I've got to say the Waties were smart though. They built theirs with Stone Mountain granite. Most of the other limestone and sandstone mausoleums are just falling apart. Like melting away from neglect and old age." Rogers looked back at Jake and Rae as he spoke. "And then of course we had the direct hit from the F-2 tornado "Sherman" back in 2008 and still haven't recovered."

"Tornado *Sherman*, you said?" Jake asked, somewhat amused.

"Oh, for sure," replied Rogers as he pulled the key out and jammed it back in. "His path of destruction warranted it." Just then his cell phone rang. He left the key in the hole and answered it.

"Okay! Okay!" he said to his exasperated wife on the other end. "The baby's crowning? Shit. I'm leaving now. Son-of-a-bitch!" Rogers ended the call and stuffed his phone in his pocket.

With another shoulder into the door it finally sprung open, swinging inward with a squeal. "Yes! Got it." Rogers extracted the key and gave it to Jake. "Keep it for now. Lock up behind you and return it later. I've got to go!" He picked up his flashlight and turned to leave.

"How are we supposed to get out of the cemetery?" Rae asked. "We're locked in."

"Jump the wall," Rogers replied, already on the path heading toward the visitor's center. "People do it all the time. Bye. Bye."

"Don't worry, Hon," Jake said, grasping Rae's arm. "I saw an easy spot to get out at the pedestrian gate where we came in."

"That guy is an asshole."

"And two thousand dollars richer for simply opening a door. Come on. Let's see what's inside." Jake stepped aside motioning to the open door. He laughed. "Ladies first."

"Aww, is my little sugar plum afraid?" she chided, then stepped in first, her beam shining ahead. "What the—"

▼

Devonté "Dawg" Marshal and Ladarrius "Dare" Howard of the Bluff Boyz crew scampered southeast through the cemetery, hiding behind trees, vaults, mausoleums and grave markers. Venturing this far out of their "hood" on the other side of the city, they were cautious of their surroundings on another gang's turf. They made slow progress through the cemetery as they listened and looked for movement about, all the while pulling up their baggy pants which kept exposing their bright white Haynes underwear. Their main problem, though, was trying not to step on fallen magnolia tree leaves as the crunch made a horrendously loud sound under foot, like walking on a bag of Doritos chips.

Not sure if the security guard station was occupied, they hit that little shed near the main entrance first and found it was dark and empty.

Light flashed deep within the cemetery down the slope toward the east, several flashlight beams moving about. Both young men perked up.

"Dawg," whispered Dare in crude, ghetto Ebonics, "Dey be headt to da vistoors center."

Dawg mumbled from behind his bandana, the whites of his eyes wide in the moonlight as he scanned left and right. "Man, dis place be whackdt. Dese graves be givin' me chills. Like ghosts n' shit be watchin' us."

"Nigga, what you trippin' fo'? We bout to cap two cracka bitches," Dare laughed. "They be fittin' right in here. And we be gettin' good Benjamins from Mista J fo' droppin' em. Ain't no ghosts n shit. Come on. Follow me." He then hustled north up the brick gutter of the lane, hugging the low walls of terraced family plots for cover. Clearly spooked, his counterpart quickly moved in behind him not wanting to be left alone.

A couple of minutes later, they snuck up to the two story visitor's center and Bell Tower. Built in 1899, the stone building originally housed a chapel and the sexton's office, who lived on the second floor. Now the second floor was reserved for public meeting space and the Historic Oakland Foundation's offices. The sexton's office was now on the first floor.

Hiding behind one of the large mausoleums across from the Bell Tower, the pair noticed a light go out in a first floor window. The front entrance opened onto a dimly lit covered porch and a stubby black man stepped out in a hurry. He locked the door behind him and ran to his nearby car.

"Who dat?" Dawg asked.

"Shit if I know. Em-plo-yee?" Dare asked in a whisper. He extracted his cell phone from a pocket and touched the screen a few times to get the text from Jaconious Johnson. The bright screen lit up his hooded, masked face. The screen showed two face images. One was of a chiseled male with short dark hair, high cheek bones, and a prominent nose. The name Jake Tununda was under his picture. The other image showed a beautiful, younger woman with long, auburn hair and green eyes, her name tagged as Rae Hart.

"Ain't on Mista J's list. Fuck im."

"Where be da otha two?" Dawg asked, looking about as they watched the black man quickly drive around the crescent shaped lane heading toward the main gate.

"Flashlights," Dare whispered and pointed east, down the slope just two lane's over toward the Confederate Obelisk. "Let's go."

▼

Rae's heart leapt and she took a step backward. "My God! What is this?"

Jake moved past her with his flashlight beam hitting the narrow interior vestibule area. Straight ahead in a shelved alcove high up against a tall stained glass window was a gigantic brown bird with outstretched wings and open talons. Spider webs hung from its wings and claws.

"Whoa!" Directing the light beam onto the bird's head and open beak Jake realized it was a taxidermic golden eagle suspended from the ceiling. And an enormous one at that.

"Holy—" said Rae, brushing up next to him. The bird's rich, golden brown head reflected in their shifting light, two large, light brown eyes glimmering back at them. Its gray and yellow beak was open as if singing a song. And its deep brown, feathered wings displayed gorgeous hints of white, amber, and gold.

On each side of them, walls of crypts extended up to a marble ceiling. Four crypts to each side. Two brass handles protruded from each vertical, marble crypt slab, names and dates of the deceased carved in their faces. In a corner there was a rickety looking wooden chair accompanied by a small table with a purple crystal and a dusty Bible on it.

"It's a golden eagle," Jake said, staring up at the bird as he approached the rear alcove about ten feet away. His voice was loud inside the chamber. "Sacred to the Cherokee. The master of the skies flying at a higher altitude than any other bird. Thus, they are closer to the Creator than any other creature on earth and would carry prayers from humans to God."

Rae stared in awe, but was also creeped out and shivered a bit. She drew her beam below the bird, down the colorful stained glass window designed as a Cherokee rose, to a marble shelf about chest high. On it they saw old candles, wax melted down their sides, and an array of shiny quartz crystal rocks. An empty bottle of Southern Comfort held a tiny little Confederate battle flag. Just below the shelf were two more crypts set in the rear wall reserved for the original two interments.

The top one had another Freemason symbol carved into its marble slab. Below that was a Confederate States of America Southern Cross. "Beloved Soldier, Husband, Father, Thomas Black Watie Jr.," Jake read out loud. Below the name were his dates of birth and death. The crypt below his read: Wife, Annabelle Watie.

The door to the mausoleum suddenly opened inward behind them with a squeal. The pair jumped in surprise, Rae letting out a whimper. They spun around with their lights expecting someone to enter. Jake fumbled in his pocket for his gun. Rae followed a split second later after catching her breath.

A whispery male voice filled the chamber. "Eagles also protect against witches."

Rae backpedaled behind Jake and crashed into the little table, knocking it over, the Bible and crystal clattering to the marble floor.

"Show yourself!" Jake demanded, quickly extending his weapon and flashlight at arm's length toward the open door. He saw a shadow move. His heart pounded. "Or risk being shot!"

Three long seconds ticked off and no one appeared. He bolted forward and out the door onto the porch swinging his beam and gun left and right in one motion. All he saw were low bushes, flowers and the Beerman family grave sculpture.

Nothing.

Rae was right behind him doing the same, scanning for the intruder, trembling in utter fear from the ghostly voice.

Still, no one was there. No movement anywhere.

Jake whispered to Rae to go around one side and he'll hit the other. They both stepped off the porch and onto the soft grass and turned the corners of the mausoleum quickly sweeping the sides with their lights and weapons. Proceeding to the back corners they met again at the rear and found no one. Shoulder to shoulder they stood, their beams swinging wildly into the neighboring family burial plot showing a wide vertical grave marker bearing the name Northen along its bottom. Several more flat grave marker slabs for other members lay in front of it.

"You heard it, right?" Jake whispered. "It wasn't just me."

"Yeah, I heard the voice, too," Rae whispered back, searching in vain for the source. "Clear as day. Eagles also protect against witches, right?"

"Yes," agreed Jake, still searching with his flashlight. He even looked above him on the roof of the mausoleum.

"There's no one out here. You think it was the Corporal speaking to us, his ghost?" Rae asked, shaking.

"A ghost?" Jake asked in a mocking tone. "Sounded like a real person. I mean who opened the door then, Rae? It's not even windy out."

"I don't know, Jake! My God. I'm scared, okay? What the fuck! I feel like we're being hunted, so just lay off!"

"Okay, okay. I'm sorry, Hon. Just calm down."

"Don't tell me to calm down!" Rae sniped back.

"I'm sorry," Jake sighed. "Come on, let's just go back inside and get this over with and get the hell outta here. You cover the door just in case." Jake took the lead and led her back around to the porch, shining his flashlight on the ground ahead of him. Rae held onto the back of his coat. He turned the corner and re-entered the mausoleum through the open door.

As Rae stood guard, peering out from the nearly closed door, Jake inspected the rest of the mausoleum crypts. He found a total of nine out of ten interments, one apparently left empty for a future family member.

Thomas Black Watie Jr. (1844-1949)
Annabelle Marie Watie (1844-1949), Wife
Thomas Black Watie III (1878-1968), Son of Thomas Jr. and Annabelle
Sarah Ann Watie (1890-1972), Wife
Thomas Black Watie IV (1924-   ), Son of Thomas III and Sarah
Margaret Frances Watie (1930-2004), Wife
Thomas Black Watie V (1949-   ), Son of Thomas IV and Margaret
Catherine Julia Watie (1952-1967), Daughter of Thomas IV and Margaret

"Tommy had a daughter," Jake whispered. "She died at fifteen years old. Interesting, too, that his disowned son still has a spot waiting. They must have carved his slab before the big falling out."

"I wonder how she died."

Jake's phone vibrated in his pocket. He fished it out and saw that it was a text message from D'Arata. He read it out loud: "Phoenix on the move. I am tracking. Sitrep to follow once he lands. Go to Le Maison Rouge and see if you can get eyes on Black. Party seems to be winding down."

▼

The ghost of a man stood still and erect, pressed inside the black entrance way of the massive Grant Mausoleum overlooking the Bell Tower building. He listened as a CSX train loudly crept across the tracks behind him to the north, the silence of the cemetery being shattered with piercing metal-on-metal grinding. He watched as his hooded prey stupidly checked a brightly illuminated cell phone easily advertising their hiding spot across from the visitor's center. As the sexton drove his car off property his two would-be victims scampered from their cover, strutting slowly down the crescent lane toward the Watie Mausoleum. Both hit men had their weapons out, their white latex gloves and exposed white underwear contrasting sharply against their dark attire.

Stupid, little, baggy-assed angry birds.

Ghost Man moved out, quietly running due south along a parapet wall to intercept them. A thick, black-bladed knife emerged in one hand, a red-dot, laser-guided Taser in the other. He built up speed upon soft shoes, his black hair and coat flowing behind him.

At the intersection of two lanes where a circular fountain trickled water, the two hit men were attacked.

Ghost Man leapt from the wall into the air, arms outstretched like a bird of prey. Before he even landed a red dot appeared on one man and the Taser fired.

The powerful, law enforcement-grade Taser sent two small probes attached to 15 feet of insulated conductive wires into his victim's side just as the street thug was pulling up his sagging pants. The probes penetrated the hoodie and a shirt underneath embedding in the young man's skin. Instantly, an incapacitating charge transmitted between the two probes and overroad the sensory and motor functions of his nervous system. He lost all muscular control and dropped his pistol before his body hit the ground in convulsions.

Ghost Man had already dropped his Taser since its microprocessor was programmed to pulse a 30-second discharge—allowing him to free a hand to take down the other little angry bird. Pouncing on the other man's back, he slammed his knife into the base of the man's neck through his hoodie. A twist of the knife and the fierce collision of death ended with his victim's ragdoll body hitting face first into the asphalt. One last nerve impulse twitched the victim's trigger sending a burp of ten rounds from his suppressed submachine gun ricocheting through the cemetery.

▼

"What was that?" Rae whispered, perking up to a series of short muffled sounds outside the mausoleum. Her revolver was out, scanning with her flashlight outside the door. "You hear that, Jake?"

"All I hear is a train out there," replied Jake, having already finished cutting away the caulking around Corporal Watie's waist-high crypt slab. "Come on, help me pull this out. It takes two people. Grab that handle."

Rae pocketed her weapon and grasped one of the handles of the slab. Jake held the other and they pulled simultaneously. The slab easily slid out. Being only a couple of inches thick it was still quite heavy as they lowered it, then dragged and leaned it against a side wall.

A coffin lay inside on a shelf. Jake lifted one of the hinged side handles to the coffin, Rae the other, and with a tug they slid the coffin out horizontally on its retractable roller-drawer.

Jake wasted no time in prying open the top of the coffin.

Rae turned her head. "I can't see this." She made for the door and stepped outside.

And then let out a fierce guttural scream.

Jake was so startled he jumped, then dashed for the door.

Standing on the steps to the mausoleum was a man with long, jet black hair, his face turned down. He wore dark clothing and a long jacket.

Rae had her revolver aimed at him in the beam of her flashlight.

Jake raised his weapon, arms shaking, heart exploding.

The man stood still like an apparition, but his chest heaved up and down. Jake noticed a bloody knife in his hand and drops of blood on the granite step below it.

The man slowly turned his gaze upward at them, squinting in the flashlight beam with remarkable black, keen, restless eyes. He looked high, as if he were on drugs. When his shoulder length black hair parted, a strikingly handsome, taut, tanned, mid 30s face void of facial hair appeared in full. He clearly was of Native American ethnicity.

"Drop the knife!" Jake ordered, Luger bobbing slightly in his hands. The knife immediately clinked to the ground. The drugged look painted on the man's face was all too familiar to him. Jake knew what it meant. Combat. Death. This guy had just killed someone and he was now on the ultimate God-high.

"Where's the sexton?" Jake demanded, his gun aimed at the man's face.

"Raise your hands!" barked Rae after catching her breath.

Ghost Man slowly raised both arms. "Tununda and Hart?" The same earlier ghostly voice asked. "Sorry to scare you. I meant to knock."

A tattoo flashed on the underside of the man's right wrist as his hands went up. Looked like a bird, Jake thought for a split second. "Where's the sexton?" he asked again. "Did you harm him?"

"He's fine. I watched him drive out the main gate. The only ones I harmed were the two black punks about to assassinate you both. Unfortunately for them, they are now deceased."

"What?" shouted Rae.

The man's head tilted and he smiled at her. "They were sent by Tom Black's chief of staff."

"Who the fuck are you?" Jake demanded. "What two assassins? Where are they?"

"Colonel," the Ghost Man said, hands still raised, breathing coming easier. "We're on the same side. My name is Alex James Vann. I'm from Dahlonega, Georgia. I'm a member of the Cherokee Nation and am here to offer you protection at the request of my benefactor *Tommy Watie*. The two men I killed are floating in a fountain not a hundred feet away." He tilted his head toward the direction. "Let me prove it to you."

Rae stepped forward, flashlight beaming in his face. "Slowly back away from the knife. Keep your hands where I can see them."

Jake grabbed the tactical, fixed blade knife, ten inches in overall length. He pointed it at Vann. "Were you the one who whispered to us earlier about the eagle and the witches?" Now, being closer to the man, he stole another glance at his wrist tattoo. It was a stylized Native American eagle and a shield. Centered on the shield was a skull with a beret.

"I had to get you two out of there. You were sitting ducks."

"Turn around asshole. Show us where your victims are," Jake ordered. "Fuck with us and you're dead."

"Don't worry, I saw your video on YouTube today. You both have very good aim." With his hands locked behind his head, Vann led them to the scene of his slaughter. There they stepped between two pools of blood on the lane marking the kill spots of the victims. He then showed Jake and Rae a discarded pistol and a submachine gun, both with suppressors. Jake picked them up, checked their magazines and chambers then holstered his own pistol. He hung the submachine gun over his shoulder as it had a strap attached. Now holding the suppressed pistol of one of his would-be killers and producing his flashlight, he peered with Rae into the small, raised, circular planter fountain.

A cast iron sculpture of a cute boy and a girl with an umbrella over their heads stood on an island in the middle of the fountain. Two crumpled bodies floated in shallow bloody water, one face up, the other face down. The one face up had his throat slit almost severing his head. Curiously, he was wrapped in wires. The face down victim had a blood-stained hooded sweat shirt over his head with stab rips through the back of the hoodie.

"Jesus Christ," Jake whispered, noticing the victims even wore latex gloves to cover trace fingerprints or gunpowder residue when they fired their weapons. Given that fact, and their suppressed guns, these guys knew what they were doing.

And Vann wasn't bullshitting.

"Oh m-my God," stuttered Rae, staring at the bodies then back at Vann, who had lowered his hands. "Keep your hands up," she ordered, her weapon trained on him. Vann complied.

"I thought I heard muffled gunshots earlier when the train went by. Did they fire on you?" Rae asked.

"One fired off his MAC-10 when I took him down," Vann said. "The other one . . . see the wires? Tasered him. The Taser is inside my coat, so you know."

"So he was still alive," Jake stated.

"I interrogated then terminated him."

Jake and Rae glanced at each other.

"What do we do with the bodies?" Rae asked.

"My mess," Vann replied. "I'll take care of it. I'll weigh the bodies down with heavy stones so they'll sit under the floating plants. I'll toss some more vegetation on the surface to conceal the blood and hopefully it will be a day or so before they're discovered on the bottom."

Jake cocked his head. "Well aren't you efficient. Military?"

"1st SFOD-D," Vann replied.

Jake knew Vann was referring to the 1st Special Forces Operational Detachment-Delta. Better know as Delta Force. He was looking at one of America's most lethal and secret counterterrorism warriors.

During his many years with the 10th Mountain in Afghanistan, he had partnered with some Delta Force operatives in a task force on a manhunt for the top bad guys. Since Delta Force members were essentially always undercover, that would account for Vann's appearance with the long hair and civilian clothes, thought Jake. But he still wanted to test the killer's knowledge further, not ready to believe him just yet. "You still active?"

"Active, but on a month's leave. Timing was good when Tommy called me. Lucky me, right?"

"You always run side jobs like this?"

"Only when it matters. How about you?"

A real wise ass, thought Jake. "Tell me Alex Vann, what Army unit did Delta Force recruit you from?"

When Rae heard Delta Force mentioned her eyes went wide and she shifted her feet apart to steady her aim at Vann's chest.

"75th Ranger Regiment. Based in Fort Benning, Georgia."

"Your rank then?"

"E-5. I was twenty-five. Was right before the start of Operation Iraqi Freedom in 2003."

"What group were you assigned to?" Jake asked, familiar with the organizational structure of the elite shadow unit.

"F"

Jake paused. "So you were an operator?" The man nodded his reply.

"What's your rank now?"

"E-8."

"What squadron were you in, Master Sergeant?"

"A," Vann answered, keeping up with Jake's barrage of questions. "I was in a recon and sniper troop. I was the one who lasered the safehouse in Baquba in '06 when we took down that monster named the 'Emir of Al-Qaeda in the Country of Two Rivers.' You know who that was?"

Jake most certainly did. He was serving in Iraq at the time himself. It was the title given to most brutal terrorist leader their forces had come up against. "Abu Musab al-Zarqawi," he answered. The man responsible for beheading his hostages and most of the suicide bombings and IED attacks on civilians and military personnel during the outbreak of violence after the initial invasion.

"What kind of ordinance did you hit him with?"

"Damn, Colonel," Vann said, shaking his head with a smirk. "You know your shit. An F-16C rolled in and dropped two 500 pound bombs. One was a GBU-12 and the other a GBU-38. Satisfied?"

"Not yet." Jake knew a few more details surrounding al-Zarqawi's death. "Who else was killed in the blast?"

Vann looked away, his eyes blinking. "His wife and child."

"One more question." This one Jake did not know the real answer to as there was speculation and contradictions surrounding al-Zarqawi's last moments when he was pulled from the rubble still alive. "When you found him, did you guys beat him to death or did you administer medical aid?"

"We aided him alright. I'm the one who gave him a black eye before he was terminated. With all due respect, sir. Are we done?"

"We're done. Lower your hands," Jake said. "I believe we both owe you our lives." Jake extended his right hand to shake, which was firmly accepted. He then extracted their protector's knife and returned it to him, handle first which Vann slid into a belt sheath. "Take this, too." Jake placed the suppressed pistol on safety, turned it handle first, and offered it to the younger man as a sign of trust.

"Thank you," Vann nodded, his warrior glare locked with Jake's, knowing full well the importance of such a gesture.

Watching Vann hide the pistol in his coat Rae finally lowered and pocketed her own revolver.

Vann looked around. "Listen, you guys need to finish whatever business you have in the mausoleum and then we better get the hell out of here. We can talk later and I'll show you their cell phones and wallets and what I learned from the one I interrogated."

"Wash away this blood out here, too, if you don't mind," Rae said, pointing to the pavement. "Less evidence."

"Indeed I will, Miss Hart."

"Meet us back at the mausoleum when you're finished. Let's go, Rae."

Back inside the mausoleum Jake wasted no time. While Rae stood guard at the door, he popped open the hinged coffin lid and looked down at Corporal Thomas Black Watie Jr., or what was left of him. The corpse was dressed in a black suit and tie, his face decayed so severe it looked like yellow tracing paper was pulled tight over his skull. Strands of long white hair lay on his shoulders. A glimmering Masonic pin adorned one lapel on his tattered suit. On his breast was a pin and ribbon of the Southern Cross of the Confederate Army. His arms were crossed over his chest, the hands hidden under an old gray hat on his midsection.

The Civil War era slouch style hat had a black feather stuck in its headband. Jake raised a brow.

The Raven.

He removed the hat and set it aside to reveal Corporal Watie's skeletal hands, one folded over the other. Jake noticed a gold wedding band over a bony ring finger on the left hand. That hand clutched a crystal stone. The right hand held a sprig of Acacia—the Masonic symbol for everlasting life. Under the hands, sitting on top of a white, lambskin Masonic apron, Jake saw what they had come for.

"It's here."

Rae stole a glance out of the corner of her eye.

The item was a small, black, leather bound notebook about six by nine inches in size. Tommy said he placed it there when he last entered the mausoleum for his wife's interment. He had told Jake it was when he had completely given up on the dream of finding McPherson's hat, waybill, and the tunnel.

Jake delicately lifted the Corporal's hands and pulled the worn book from underneath and set it on the edge of the coffin. He carefully moved the hands back in place, then put the slouch hat back on top, covering them. About to close the coffin lid, he took one last look at the Corporal's face and shook his head. He needed to say something.

Jake placed a hand on the man's breast and uttered a message: "Your story *will* be finished, Brother Thomas Watie. I'll find the truth."

Stashing the notebook in his inner coat pocket, Jake closed the lid to the coffin, shoved it back into its crypt, and, with Rae's help, lifted the slab back in place. Vann showed up just as Jake was attempting to lock the door behind him.

Jimmying the key, he asked Vann his mode of transportation. The man replied he had driven down from Dahlonega in north Georgia earlier in the evening, but parked his vehicle north of the city and had taken MARTA downtown before entering and hiding in the cemetery to keep watch on the mausoleum. Jake offered him a ride and he accepted just as Jake finally locked the door.

Leading the way out of the cemetery, Jake showed them where to hop the wall near the pedestrian gate. Checking the avenue below for any watchful eyes or vehicles, the trio jumped down off the brick wall and nonchalantly walked across the street toward their pick-up truck. Within minutes, they were headed north up Boulevard on their way to Tom Black's party at Le Maison Rouge.

20

S PEEDING BEHIND A LIMO, A THOUSAND FEET BACK
on I-75/85 North were Jake, Rae, and Alex Vann squeezed on the
seat of Watie's old muscle truck. Having arrived just minutes before Black's
departure at Le Maison Rouge, peering through binoculars, they were
lucky enough to recognize the fat Congressman leaving his party with what
Jake noticed, in all likelihood, was McPherson's hat on his head. The hat
rounded out some cheap Union general costume he was wearing.

Two party girls had entered a limo with Black. Once it took off they
subsequently informed D'Arata, via text, they were giving chase. It wasn't
long before D'Arata replied back that he had lost the Phoenix's taxi on the
other side of the city because of a tractor trailer accident and that he'd failed
to observe the taxi company name after he took a detour.

"Should I ram the son-of-a-bitch off the highway?" Jake asked, motoring
at a high rate of speed to keep up with the taillights ahead in the distance.
Tall, highly illuminated skyscrapers hovered over the main interstate that
pierced the center of downtown Atlanta. They had just passed the Varsity
restaurant on their right as traffic in the multi-lane highway had dwindled
to just a few vehicles.

"Two innocent girls and a driver we know about are inside," Rae said.
"Let's be rational. What do we really want here?"

"The bastard sent three assassins for us in twenty-four hours," Jake replied. "I'm done being rational, Rae. I'm done playing by his rules of engagement. It's time we go guerilla on his ass. The thief escaped and this is our only chance now. Look, there's no one even out here driving either."

"He's a billionaire with unlimited resources," Vann said, sitting on Rae's right, leaning against the passenger window. "Are you willing to live the rest of your life always looking over your shoulder wondering who next is going to put a bullet in the back of your head? Your nine lives won't last long trying to be rational."

Rae kept silent, not responding to either man at her shoulders. Finally, after a minute, she said, "You're right. You're both right. He's not going to stop as long as we're alive. He knows we're working for the one person he most despises in the world: his father."

"Exactly," Jake said, keeping left behind Black's limo as the 85 split from the 75 and continued northeast.

Rae shifted between the two men. "So we go apeshit on him then. See, I thought it through, *rationally*."

Each man let out a snicker and Jake sped up.

"Listen, so we're on the same page here," started Vann. "I know all about Tommy's knife, the waybill, and the Cherokee Tunnel cache. And even the Guardians of Gold master map. Tommy said you call it the *Map of Thieves*. That's pretty fitting as I'm well-versed on the subject."

Jake and Rae both looked over at him, stunned he was privy to the secrets of their mission on top of being a highly lethal Delta Force operative. "What's your full name again?" Jake asked, his foot easing off the gas pedal.

"Alex James Vann. I've helped Tommy with historical research on the Golden Horse. He's been a mentor and a financial benefactor to me the many years I've personally known him. I owe him my life for all the things he's done for me. I fucked up real bad when I was younger. Was a knucklehead before I joined the Army and through his scholarship program he put me on the right path. Gave me a second chance. Wasn't until I was deployed overseas that I really appreciated how good this country is compared to the rest of the world. It's when I first felt real patriotism."

"All well and good, Sergeant, but the James Vann connection ain't no coincidence," Jake said, tapping the brake, remembering his late night conversation with Tommy. "You're ancestor was the last one to possess the map before he was murdered, right? Early 1800s if I remember what he told me the other night. Was the second richest man in the U.S."

"Yes, James Vann."

"Now that's just wonderful of Tommy," Jake sarcastically remarked, leaning in front of Rae to look over at Vann. "So he invites a James Vann descendant to offer us protection?"

"Tommy called me Saturday when he came home from the hospital. Well *before* he contacted you on Sunday morning asking about the hat. He tasked me to help him find it and to offer any of my services. I'm way more involved in this than you two but I was willing to join forces for the common good."

"I take it your main interest in this affair is getting that map back and having the Vann name be the richest in the nation again, am I right?"

Vann glared back at Jake. "Let's clear the air here, *Colonel*. I've proven my worth. My initiation with you is over."

Jake and Rae frowned at Vann as he chastised a senior officer. He didn't give them a chance to respond.

"You're gonna need me if you want to get inside that Cherokee Tunnel."

"How's that?" Rae shot back.

"Because legend has it there's a Raven Mocker guarding it. And I'm one of the few remaining Witch Killer medicine men in the Cherokee Nation to take it on. Only *we* know the black magic that can detect that invisible old witch."

Rae clammed up. She knew better than to question the validity of black magic and spirits from the other world that lurked among them. She had experienced it firsthand and it had changed her forever.

"From the oral history I've been told," Vann snipped with attitude, "when Chief Red Fox deposited the Golden Horse in the tunnel, he conjured up a Raven Mocker to stand guard over it, unbeknownst to Ross. Red Fox never trusted Ross either. And some say to this day the Raven Mocker's presence can still be felt up and down the Etowah from Canton to Hightower. You want to go at him on your own. Feel free. I'll pick up your pieces later." Vann leaned back, crossed his arms and stared ahead at the distant limo.

"Tommy told me about the Raven Mocker," Jake said quietly. "But he never mentioned we'd have to kill one to get into the tunnel."

"So, you're the golden eagle warrior protecting us against witches," Rae stated. She, too, had noticed his tattoo. "Is that what the tat means?"

"Yeah, sorta. Listen, I'm sorry but Tommy was supposed to call and tell you that I'd be making contact tonight so I didn't spook you. I don't know why he didn't. Christ, for all I know the old man fell asleep. Or maybe he deliberately didn't want to scare you off from continuing this mission. In any case, I guess he's looking for insurance to make sure we're all successful."

"And you're the insurance," Rae said.

"What do you want with the *Map of Thieves*?" Jake asked, getting back on point. He moved into the right lane ramp off the 85 to transition up Georgia State Route 400 North still trailing the limo.

Vann blew out a breath and began. "James Vann was an abusive, racist, drunken murderer. Hated blacks and whites equally. He was a highway robber who befriended white travelers along the Federal Road, then murdered them outright. Sure he was an entrepreneur of the highest means, but still, he was a selfish Dr. Jekyll and Mr. Hyde who exploited the map he was bequeathed with.

"Deserved to die the way he did. Ambushed in a bar by an unknown killer. He had many enemies. Some say one of his black slaves did it because he routinely beat and killed them, too. I say it was the Guardians of Gold that did it. The Guardians took the map back with extreme prejudice because they believed he was not worthy of managing that vast power generated by the wealth. And by God, if Tom Black gets a hold of that map and shares it with politicians and industrialists of his ilk, do you know how many more James Vann's it will spawn?"

"We agree with you on that," Rae butted in. "We have no intentions to allow the Federal government to ever see that map."

"I gave Tommy my word on that," Jake reiterated.

"I know. He told me that on the phone and thank God we're all on the same page. But I don't want the map to just be buried again from existence once we prove it's real. It needs to be used for something positive this time. And that is precisely the crux of the problem I face. I can't think of a way the Feds *won't* be involved somehow."

"What do you mean, what are your intentions?" Jake asked.

Vann stared ahead. "Patriotism is what drives me. Believe it or not I—we—me and Tommy, actually want to figure out some way it can be used to turn this bankrupt nation around. To get us out of the $20 trillion in debt the Republican and Democrat, ruling class elites imposed on us. To break our dependence from foreign nations. To make our economy roar again."

"Noble cause. You going to run for president on another Hope and Change platform?" Rae asked snidely.

"Ever hear of cerium, niobium, promethium, samarium or dysprosium?" Vann asked, ignoring her jibe.

"What-um?" she blurted.

"Nope," Jake said.

"These are all rare earth minerals," Vann explained. "There's seventeen of them. *Highly* sought after, *highly* valuable. More so than gold or silver or copper. These rare minerals are used in most high-tech applications in computers, aerospace, automotive, and the military. Things like lasers, night vision goggles, missile guidance systems, jet engines. Ah, let's see, stuff like laptop computers, cell phone batteries, hybrid cars, wind turbines, steel, magnetics, even medical tissue research. The list is virtually endless. And guess who has us by the balls in supplying all of these rare minerals essential for our nation's economic vitality?"

"Who?" Jake asked, looking over at Vann.

"China," Vann answered flatly. "They have 50 percent of the world's known deposits and they supply 98 percent to the rest of the globe. They *own* the U.S., not only by controlling this supply and demand, but they own us financially, too, with all of our trillions in loans we've taken out with them. Because of the demand of rare earth minerals and Chinese restrictions on exports, the prices have skyrocketed over 700 percent!

"You think the Middle East holds us hostage and exploits our consumers because of our dependency on oil? How about if the Chinese shut off the wicket to rare earth minerals? They could bring our economy to a grinding, fucking halt in a heartbeat."

"I'm still not getting how obtaining the map is a game changer," Rae said, shaking her head. "How's it supposed to get our nation out of debt?"

"While mining gold up in north Georgia, my ancestor James Vann also secretly explored many rare earth mineral sites that were indicated on the map as unknown elements. You see, the ancient Cherokee prospectors and miners and medicine men found this stuff but didn't know what it was. But according to James's notes they still recorded where these locations were on the map."

Vann again gestured with both hands as he spoke. "Here's the deal. These rare earth minerals are really everywhere all around us but it's like tossing a handful of sand on a pile of dirt and extracting each granule. It's all about the densely concentrated supplies that are the rarity and what's in huge demand and what's worth mining. There's only like three known highly concentrated sites in the world. We only have one active mine in California which is like a drop in the bucket. But James Vann essentially re-discovered major supplies of it here in north Georgia because of that map.

"And *I* am in *possession* of his samples. Based on his notes there is a *vast* concentration of these minerals in nine separate locations shown on the map in a cave-infested belt centered around Blood Mountain."

"Blood Mountain," Jake repeated. "I've hiked that mountain before. We did some Ranger School training there. It's on the Appalachian Trail."

"Right," said Vann. "It's due north of Dahlonega smack dab in the high peaks region. James Vann wrote that he found all nine of the sites where he was handling large nuggets of this rare earth stuff, not sand particles. I've hiked the shit out of that mountain and have only found dead end caves with no indication of rare earth. The real sites must be blocked off or hidden somehow. But I did verify and test some of his larger samples and he was right. It's all real. So, we're talking the mother lode right here in Georgia, if we get that map back."

"In terms of dollars what is considered the potential if these nine sites are tapped?" Jake asked.

"I've estimated the potential to be upwards of ten trillion dollars."

Jake gasped. "Trillion with a 'T'?"

"I shit you not," said Vann shaking his head, shifting in his seat. "In Afghanistan in 2010 a team of U.S. geologists and Pentagon officials found an untapped lithium deposit. Remember when President Obama promoted General David Petraeus as commander of the U.S. and NATO forces? You know, after McChrystal embarrassed him?"

"Loved General Stanley McChrystal," Jake said. "So true what he said. And so damn wrong what the CINC did to him . . . and to Petraeus a few years after for Benghazi. Secretary of State Clinton should have been the one fired, if anyone, for the murder of our four men."

"Tell me about it," Vann sighed. "Any way, one of the secret operations I was on with the Unit was to protect that geological exploration team. And when the *New York Times* announced the discovery of the deposit it was estimated as an untapped one to three trillion dollar potential. It would literally turn that country from one of the most backward ass nations in the world to one of the most lucrative mining centers in the world. A revolutionary game-changer. But to this day, Afghanistan and the U.S. are still squabbling over who exploits it and how the profits are divvied up. All because of politics and greed and the power it would bring."

"I see what you mean now. The same problem we'd face with our own government," Jake lamented.

Vann nodded. "They already own two thirds of the land in north Georgia and all around Blood Mountain, too. It's the Chattahoochee National Forest. Nothing will be mined on that land without the oligarchy's approval and without bureaucrats' pockets filled deep with the profits generated."

"Plus, you'll never get past the federal regulations and radical environmentalists to mine those sites," Jake added. "The bureaucrats will cause it to flounder in purgatory for decades. Look at all the oil this nation has. We can be independent from the Middle East in a heartbeat if the government loosened the restrictions for drilling and fracking on federal lands. Same will go for this mining map. They'll find some fucking exotic frog or owl that needs protection over a massive influx of revenue from our own natural resources to benefit the country as a whole."

"I know," Vann said with defeat, shaking his head. "That's the dilemma with this map. How do you keep it *out* of the hands of the bureaucrats and politicians, but make sure it goes to a worthy cause to say, pay down the debt? If you don't put strangleholds on that revenue, then politicians of both parties will treat it like an endless cookie jar, raiding all of the funds to finance their earmarks like pigs at the trough. Like they said they weren't going to do with Social Security."

Jake slowed the truck down to keep pace with Black's limo. He saw they had passed the Lennox Road exit off the 400 and knew they didn't have much time to act before Black made it home to Roswell. He still wanted to pursue the conversation with Vann a little longer to make sure they were doing the right thing.

"So to rediscover and mine the locations of each of these rare earth hoards," Rae surmised, "This nation could have independence from the Chinese monopoly on the market?"

"Exactly," Vann exclaimed. "We'd be the Saudi Arabia of rare elements. Know what that vast influx of wealth would do to our country?"

"It would provide an economic revolution to benefit all," Jake said.

"Or," offered Rae, "it could totally destroy us into a tyrannical state if completely controlled and regulated by the government. Sort of like the massive government health care boondoggle that took over one-sixth of our economy. The map needs to be kept in the right citizens' hands to make sure it's not controlled by political thieves."

"Precisely," said Vann. "That's where I'm at a loss. I'm not a CEO. I'm an operator. The map needs to be in the hands of someone or some group who shares our dream but knows how to game the federal system and run a major mining corporation. But that person or organization *must* have a watchdog to make sure they stay on course and don't get intoxicated from the map like James Vann did. Who better to keep watch, than sheep dogs like us? Us warriors, and law enforcement types—we who take their Constitutional oath seriously to protect the citizens against the wolves in sheep's clothing who would exploit the map for personal gain."

"Can't argue that," Rae nodded.

"But we need the *bite* that politicians and insiders really fear." Vann said without hesitation. "It used to be the mainstream media acting as the fourth branch of government that checked the corruption and caused politicians to resign or get prosecuted for wrongdoing; but now the media is firmly entrenched in the pockets of the politicians and their cronies. And if one of those investigative journalists does grow some balls to write a story that exposes their crimes, well the oligarchy calls in operatives like me to make their cars go boom."

"You're kidding me?" Rae said, taken aback.

"I shit you not," Vann said. "I'm tired of being a pawn for the country I love. I didn't become a patriot to spy on, exploit, and kill my fellow citizens at the hands of career politicians and bureaucrats."

"Instead, those political pigs that serve us, should be shitting their pants in *fear* of patriots," added Jake.

"Right now it's the reverse," Rae agreed. "The people fear and distrust their own government beyond belief. Congress is a broken institution. Their approval rating is like three percent. And the approval rating of the latest new empty suit in the White House is down to ten percent. But of course they both think they're doing a fabulous job."

"Federal law enforcement agencies have proven time and time again they don't respect the law, so you can't rely on them to be the watchdog," Vann said. "They turn the other cheek for their own political agenda since they're all headed by political appointees who protect their puppet masters."

"So your watchdog group would have to pull an end-around the Department of Justice," Rae said. "It'd have to be covert. You'd have to act in the shadows and bite when it counts."

"Who better to head that secret group up than a proven Delta Force operative," Jake said with the obvious solution.

"I know," Vann sighed. "I'd have to leave the Unit. I couldn't do both. I would dedicate my life to this cause—to this new mission."

"Unfortunately, I'm afraid you'll have to extort the extortionists to get it done," Jake continued. "Here's a scenario: what if a legitimate private mining company was formed and run by your bound and trusted individuals. They discreetly leak behind the scenes to the power players in D.C. about the potential revenues that can be generated from the rare earth sites and the positive ramifications for the economy. Plus, you entice them with the gold and silver mines, too. Those who secretly buy into the company then have a stake in making it successful. They won't be able to resist the lure of treasure and the power behind the map. Power is like heroine for them. It's highly addictive once they taste it on their lips. They do this all the time—that insider trading of knowledge. How do you think these Congressmen come into their seat making a modest income but by the time they leave they are multi-millionaires? You play *their* game. And then when there's enough support internally—"

"Then the land magically opens up for production to begin," Vann said with an arch of his brow. "Regulations are waived. New rules written."

"Precisely," Jake smiled, knowing he had him. "Once it goes public then there'll be a massive fever lust for treasure."

"Oh, you sly devil," Rae said, knowing where Jake was headed. "And once there are enough politicians and cronies deep in the company's pockets, then the secret watchdog has power over *them* and can bite back hard if they stray out of line and become corrupt."

"Then I'll impose my version of term limits," said Vann in a dark tone. "Give them a taste of their own medicine if they fuck up. Now you guys know why I got skin in this game."

Jake tapped the steering wheel, mind whirling. He noticed they were passing under the I-285 Perimeter at Sandy Springs. The next town north up the 400 was Roswell, where Black would likely exit.

"It's realpolitik," Jake said. "What the fuck, the cause is worthy." Jake clenched a fist and extended it toward Vann in front of Rae. "I'm with you, but I'm warning you, it will take years to get off the ground and there are lots of deadly obstacles along the way."

Vann bumped fists with Jake. "I know. Thank you, Colonel."

"What the hell," Rae said, reluctantly dropping her own fist on top of theirs. "Listen, let's just find the damned Cherokee Tunnel first and see if this treasure map even *exists*. And then later we can cross the bridge at Concord and revisit 1775. Okay?"

"Copy that," Vann said with a grin.

"And the one person who has what we need is in that limo," Jake pointed as he turned off his headlights and punched the gas pedal. "Balls to the wall, baby! We're going to pit him."

21

PANTS AROUND HIS ANKLES, TOM BLACK LEANED back against the limousine's rear seat and enjoyed the blow job he was getting from both girls. He was half dressed in his Yankee general uniform, coat off on the seat next to him, McPherson hat on head, waybill stashed back inside. Yet his shirt was fully unbuttoned, droopy man breasts and protruding flesh-mound of his stomach blocking the view of two Asian prostitutes sucking on his erect shaft, courtesy of Viagra.

Having left his chief of staff to organize the clean up and settle the bill for his party, Black staggered drunkenly to his waiting limousine to drive him the half hour back home to his Roswell mansion. Drink in one hand, he now moaned as the whores took turns teasing him. In his other hand he texted a garbled message to his personal financial manager authorizing a massive wire transfer of funds when his bank opened later in the morning.

Hitting send on his smartphone, he tossed it on the seat then looked down and admired the two hired lovelies playing with this jewels.

It doesn't get any better than this, he thought.

And that's when the limo was jolted from behind and sent into a spin. Black's hat flew off his head as he was whiplashed forward. His drink shot from his hand and smashed into the driver's window barrier. Both girls screamed and were tossed wildly about the back of the limo's floor while Black's naked legs flopped up in the air as he rolled off the rear seat.

Two screeching 360s and the limo smashed up hard against a guardrail on the shoulder of the empty three lane highway and came to a rest. The girls continued to scream and Black screamed back at them to stop screaming. The driver's window barrier then powered down and his staff driver, an elderly black man in a suit, leaned through asking if everyone was alright. Suddenly, he was pulled backward and tossed outside.

The limo's rear door opened, the interior light lit up and two men looked in, one short haired, the other with long, black hair, both wearing sunglasses and red bandanas over their tanned faces. A camera flashed. Everyone inside blinked. They raised guns, one aimed at the whimpering girls on the floor, the other at a half-naked Black, flat on his back with his blue uniform pants and large white underwear still wrapped around his ankles. His once Viagra-enhanced member was now limp as a deflated balloon.

"You two get out! Now!" ordered the short-haired man to the prostitutes, a voice Black seemed to recognize. Black raised his hands in the air, seeing that both men carried weapons with assassin silencers on them.

"Move it!" snapped the long-haired man in a deep voice as he pulled one of the scantily clad women out the door, throwing her onto the asphalt. "Give me your cell phones," he demanded. Black noticed an eagle tattoo on the man's wrist.

The short haired man then laid eyes on the McPherson hat that lay on the limo's floor near Black's legs. He snatched it up and aimed his submachine gun at Black's head. "Where's the waybill?"

"I'm a U.S. Congressman!" Black drunkenly slurred back, hands still in the air. "Don't know what you're talking about."

The submachine gun fired a burst over his head point blank in a suppressed rat-a-tat-tat. The windows shattered above Black's head spraying him with shards of glass. Screams from the girls came from outside. Another woman's voice told them to shut the fuck up.

"The waybill! Where the fuck is it?" ordered the short-haired man.

Black now realized the voice belonged to Army Lieutenant Colonel Jake Tununda. He was supposed to be dead and hidden inside Oakland Cemetery according to a phone text that Johnson had received just before they left the party. Shocked at being shot at, and, now, having his nemesis demanding his waybill at gunpoint, he started sweating profusely. Instantly giving in, he mumbled that he placed it back inside the McPherson hat liner.

Tununda pulled down his sunglasses, looked inside the hat, fumbled around with the liner and finally pulled out the folded waybill. He unfolded it, scanned it quickly, and, satisfied, placed it in his coat pocket. The hat went on his head. Seeing Black's cell phone laying on the floor of the limo Tununda grabbed that and handed it behind him to the long-haired man.

"Now, Congressman Limp Dick, where's the knife you stole from your father yesterday?"

"In my coat," Black readily answered, spotting it still on the seat.

"Push it to me."

"Can I pull my pants up first?" Black asked.

"Want your little dick shot off?"

Black shoved the Yankee general's uniform coat closer to Tununda who quickly opened it. The knife was wrapped in a cloth inside. He unwrapped a portion of it then handed it back to one of his cohorts telling them to get ready to go.

Black had managed to partially pull up his underwear and pants.

"Did I say you could do that? No!" Tununda roared. "Now turn over, motherfucker. Lay on your stomach." Black complied and flipped like a drunken walrus out of the water. Tununda charged the handle of his weapon to terrify his victim that he'd be executed.

"Please. Please God, don't kill me," pleaded the fearful, facedown Congressman, uniform pants at his knees, white underwear halfway up his sweaty, pimpled ass.

"Where are the Nazi trophies?" Tununda barked as he reached in his pocket and pulled out a long, gold object.

"I don't know. For real. He kept them." Black's breathing came hard.

"Who is *he*?"

"I don't know. Someone else hired him," the drunk, embarrassed legislator cried out. "His name was not given on purpose. It's the truth. His hire went through many layers. You know how the game is played. I plead ignorance."

Tununda fumed at Black. "Who hired him?"

"My chief of staff! Jaconious Johnson, okay? Please don't hurt me!"

The other masked man tapped Tununda on the back and whispered that they needed to go.

"Tell Johnson I'm personally coming for him next. And if you send one more hit on us I'll personally cut your nuts off next time. You go to the cops and I send naked pictures of you and a recording of this conversation to the Drudge Report. If you want to keep your job, *Congressman,* do *not* fuck with us!"

Black buried his head in the floor of the limo and cried that he understood everything.

Tununda then raised his arm and swung down forcefully, stabbing Black in the ass with the gold spy pen. It punctured his exposed right ass cheek two inches deep. Black screamed in agony and flapped about as blood spurted from his wound.

"A birthday gift from Daddy Watie!" Another camera flash went off and the door to the limo slammed shut.

Black heard a muffled shot outside and one of the tires blew out. The limo listed sideways. All he heard next was screeching tires and the deep rumble of a vehicle's engine pass him by. He shouted obscenities. When the door opened again, the driver and his two girls stood there in shock at the sight of him.

One of the Asian whores started laughing uncontrollably.

22

SHOTS WERE FIRED, THE VOLLEY OF BULLETS NARROWLY *missing Jake's head. He screamed for Rae to take cover, but she just stood there like a statue, a beautiful sculpture in white marble. Like a guardian. It didn't make any sense. He told her to get down but she was paralyzed in stone. All around them stood rows and rows of white grave markers. Fallen Confederate soldiers. More bullets pierced the air and Jake crawled between the markers, earth kicking up around him, fragments of stone chipping off graves with each bullet impact. Jake looked up for Rae. A charge of Confederate soldiers clad in gray came at him howling their rebel yell. He looked behind him. A similar line of Yankees clad in blue, advanced screaming back, their bayonets glimmering in the midday sun ready to run him through. Cannons fired off in the distance. Thick gray smoke, clumps of dirt and body parts rained down from explosions. Terrified, he lay prone, lodged between two clashing armies. Tried to flip over, couldn't move. Both of his legs were gone below the knee. How did that happen? I didn't even feel it. Blood gushed out from the stumps and he lay back face down, screaming in agony. But no sound came from his mouth. He tried screaming again but he couldn't breath. Black smoke and fire swirled over him. He flipped on his back, his mouth open, but this time the shrieking cackle of a raven came out. A black bird swept over him landing on one of the grave stones. It looked down on him still cackling, its eyes blazing red. Jake turned* *his head sideways and between the grave marker another body slumped down next to him. It was the motorcyclist assassin whom he had shot. The man's helmet was still on his head but the tinted visor was cracked showing a bloody face staring back at him. Jake thrashed his head the other way and two other bodies fell down in the next row of grave markers. The black gang assassins. One was wrapped in electrified wires zapping his twitching body. The other was simply a bloody mound with a hoodie over his head. The raven cackled again, throwing its neck back and flapping its wings. Then before his eyes it morphed into a hideous old man who laughed with the same cackle. He knew it was the Raven Mocker witch. The demon pounced on Jake's chest knocking the wind out of him, tearing away at his shirt to get to his heart. He tried to beat the witch off but it was too strong. He resorted to a last desperate plea, the Masonic sign of distress, waving his arms frantically in the mysterious magical gesture of the Craft. Suddenly the old man's face turned into his beautiful lover, Rae Hart. She touched him on his cheek. Oh, the comfort of her touch. He cried, tears streaming down his cheeks. Now he knew he was dying. Closing his eyes, he soon faded away to darkness.*

"Shhhh," Rae quietly whispered in Jake's ear as she stroked his cheek with two slender fingers. "It's okay, Honey. It's okay." She pulled his face to hers and gently kissed his lips. "Wake up, Jake. You're having a dream. It's just a dream."

She watched as Jake gasped for breath, blinked his eyes open, frowned, and looked about in a panic. Sweat droplets lay on his heaving chest, twinkling in the late morning sun rays that pierced through the window blinds of their upstairs master bedroom in Alex Vann's mountain home. He reached for his legs, found they were still there and crashed back down on the pillow gasping for air.

He wore a heavy chain necklace with a silver disk on the end that now lay askew off his chest. Grasping it, Rae readjusted the medallion and centered it gently back on his chest.

The medallion was about the size of a half dollar and made of hammered silver surrounded by a border of elongated white wampum shells common with Native American jewelry. It was an ancient broach at one time, worn only by guardians of a treasure. In the middle of the silver disk was an engraving of a buck with an antler rack, but inside of the deer's body was a small serpent. This was the mark of the White Deer Society, an ancient cult that protected the most important and powerful artifact of the Iroquois Confederacy: the *Crown of Serpents*. And after Jake and Rae had found the hidden crown deep in the caves below the Seneca Army Depot on their last adventure, they, too, both became unlikely guardians of the treasure.

They had also snuffed out the life of the man responsible for her father's death. Their personal bond tightened beyond their wildest imaginations and before they knew it they were madly in love. Rae, too, wore a matching necklace. She considered hers her good luck charm, crediting it with saving her life on more than once occasion.

"Where are we?" Jake asked confusedly, still breathing heavily.

"Alex's place. Remember?"

"Huh?"

"After we gave D'Arata the hat, we drove Alex to the MARTA station to get his Jeep and followed him up here to his home in the foothills? You remember any of that?"

"Somewhat." Jake sighed deeply, still catching his breath. "What a nightmare. My God."

"Figures. You hit the bed and were out like a light," Rae said, thinking he hadn't had one of these kinds of nightmares in about six months. He looked sapped. "And you snored like a chainsaw, too," she smiled trying to lighten the mood.

She was glad to be by his side, though, waking up in his arms to comfort him. His head swung from side to side taking in the room, his breathing finally calming. He smiled and kissed her several times, thanking her for waking him up and escaping the dream.

Rae kissed him back softly and asked what he was dreaming about. All he said was the Civil War. And a Raven Mocker. She kissed him again to ease his mind. And again. Then gradually she pressed harder on his lips before slipping her tongue out with a flicker to meet his. He gave a little sexy chuckle knowing full well what was coming next. Something he could never get enough of with her.

Under the sheets of their king-sized bed, she shifted a bare leg over his crotch, pressing her thigh into the smooth fabric that covered his soft bulge. He reciprocated by slipping his fingers under her silk panties grabbing her firm ass to pull her leg even tighter against him.

Rae straddled his leg and gently rocked herself against his solid thigh. She moaned in his ear and sucked on his neck, deeply inhaling his morning, masculine scent, feeling his bulge grow against her leg. Her heart beat faster, wetness formed in her vagina and absorbed into her panties as her rhythm increased.

"I want you," she whispered in his ear.

"I'm all yours, Honey," he whispered back, nuzzling her neck with light pecks from his lips and strokes from his tongue.

Rae glided her hand softly down his chest, over his medallion, touching his nipples, circling his belly button, and then followed his treasure trail down for her prize. She slowly slid her hand into his underwear and instantly found his thick and hard member. With a clench of her fist around his fully erect penis, he bucked as a jolt of energy rippled up through his body.

"Holy crap your hand is cold!" he laughed.

"And you're hot as hell," she said in an alluring voice, squeezing him.

One of his hands fully wrapped around her small ass cheek while his other hand pushed against the back of her head as they passionately kissed again. His ass hand then wandered to the front of her panties and pressed against her wet mound, finding the groove of her lips tight against the fabric. His middle finger slid up and down the slippery smooth channel as she opened her legs to receive his wanted touch.

They continued to play with each other for several long minutes until Rae couldn't take it any longer. She sat up and flung the bed sheets off her naked back. Beautiful, full breasts jiggled for her man to enjoy, her guardian medallion shining between them. She then reached for his black underwear and in one well-practiced motion pulled them completely off. They went flying off the bed, landing on a suitcase.

Wasting no time she positioned herself between his legs, bent over on her knees and started licking his long throbbing penis from the base to its glistening head. Her lover moaned out in delight. Back down his shaft she went with soft kisses and flicks of her tongue before coming back up and taking him fully into her mouth. This time she sucked hard on the head using her tongue to tease him in the right spot. Drawing him deeper in, with her lips clasped firm, she thrust her head up and down for several more minutes while at the same time tickling his smoothly shaven testicles. Jake arched his back several times trying to hold back. Finally, unable to last any longer, he shoved her away telling her he was afraid he'd cum too soon. Catching her breath and licking her lips she feigned disappointment and stood up beside the bed turning her back on him.

"Where are you going?" he pleaded.

Rae pressed a finger to her lips then slowly slid her white panties down over her gorgeous ass. As she dragged her panties around her knees, she bent over and arched her back, sticking her ass in the air so Jake could watch her full movements. Looking back, she smiled and winked at him as his mouth fell open, brown eyes twinkling with animal desire. Turning back around to face him, just out of arms reach, she ran her hands seductively over her breasts teasing him some more. He reached out to grab her but she pulled away and smacked his hand with a hard sting.

"You want some?" she asked teasingly, pointing down. "You gotta wait, Mister Tununda."

Jake merely nodded his head like an impatient kid in a candy store getting a taste and wanting more.

Down her hand went again, fingers dragging slowly against her tight abdomen until she reached her well-groomed triangle of light brown pubic hair. As Jake continued to drool over her racy little show, Rae pressed three fingers against her wet vagina and touched her clitoris in a slow gyration.

After a minute of the devilish exposé, Jake blurted out. "You're killing me. Get over here *now!*" He leaned over and grabbed her wrist pulling her back onto the bed. On top of him she went, squatting over his body so he could see everything.

Because she knew he liked to watch.

As he lay back, she immediately grabbed a hold of his penis and guided it against her vaginal lips until they touched. She pressed her body down against his until his full erection slid deep inside of her. They both moaned in ecstasy, eyes closing from the powerful surge they shared. Her nails dug into his chest as she slid upward and back down again.

Rae tossed her head back and rode him, her long auburn hair swinging wildly in the sunlight. Oh, he feels so fucking good, she thought. Jake started giving her an extra bonus thrust up as she slid down on him with every repetition. He placed a finger on her clitoris and rubbed while she bucked. She groaned deeply as juices trickled out and she climaxed, yet she still kept in perfect rhythm, waiting for her man. Some thirty seconds later Jake groaned loudly and shot his powerful load up inside of her.

Collapsing on his chest, both of them panting like dogs, Rae told Jake how much she loved him. He said the same through heavy breaths and kissed her while holding her close, still inside of her.

"Not a bad wake up call, eh, Big Boy?"

"It was below expectations," Jake said with a shit-eating grin.

She sat up and whacked him on the chest, then jumped off the bed. "I'm taking a shower!"

"Leave some hot water for me," he said as he watched her saunter into the bathroom. She even gave a little wiggle of her ass knowing full well his eyes were upon her. He couldn't help but laugh again. "God, I love that woman," he whispered to himself.

After showers, there was a knock on their bedroom door. It was Alex Vann speaking from the hallway. He said they should come down and bring the booklet, waybill, and knife, that their employer had just arrived from Savannah and couldn't wait to see them.

23

Black House
Roswell

DEFLATED ALL THE NEXT DAY, HIS EGO HAVING taken a knock out blow last night, Tom Black turned to food to regain his composure. Chomping away on his fourth piece of cheesecake while standing at his kitchen counter, he rubbed his ass injury again thinking how he'd exact revenge on Tununda. No one had ever physically assaulted him like that in his entire life—well, besides his father.

And thinking once again about the way that Army piece of shit did it, and what he said afterward as being a birthday present from his father, that set Black's blood on fire anew. On top of it all he had lost the hat, waybill, and the knife. His weekend gamble had been an embarrassing and costly blunder that he still had to pay for since he was the one who lost the goods. Another forkful of cheesecake entered his already stuffed mouth, crumbs of which fell down the front of his shirt onto his protruding belly.

After being accosted, Black had gone into damage control as soon as Tununda and his crew had sped off. His cellphone was left on scene so he tried calling an ambulance and soon found out all their phones were rendered useless, their SIM cards having been taken out. With the help of his on-staff driver the pen had been extracted from his ass cheek. The girls did the rest, applying pressure to the wound to stop the bleeding and then bandages from the limo's first aid kit. The driver meanwhile, had replaced the blown tire with a new one and had driven the group back to Black

House. After paying the driver and the girls thousands of dollars in hush money he ordered the driver to transport the whores home. Popping some sleeping pills, washed down with more alcohol, he finally fell asleep at 3 a.m., mostly pissed off that he never even got laid.

One of the first things he did upon waking up some nine hours later was call his chief of staff from his house phone to inform him that the hat and knife were themselves stolen, how the highway robbery occurred, the stabbing in his ass cheek, and that Johnson's life was now being threatened, too. Black told him he'd already started carrying his concealed weapon. Johnson reminded him that he was a vocal supporter of gun control legislation, and he would appear highly hypocritical to his constituents if they found out he secretly favored guns for his own personal protection, while denying it to others. Black scoffed, telling Johnson his views have "evolved."

After several more back and forth phone calls, Johnson had found out that the two Bluff Boyz gang members they had hired to kill Tununda the night before had gone missing. He explained that the last text he got from them was that they were inside Oakland Cemetery in Atlanta. From that point on Johnson was extremely rattled. He told Black flat out he wanted no part in his treasure hunt any more, that they had met their match.

Black couldn't blame him but he personally wasn't going to give up so easily after the experience of holding that knife and waybill in his hands. He tasted victory only to have it burned from his tongue. Furthermore, speculating that there was something important in the Watie Mausoleum at Oakland Cemetery, he knew his father must have had other secrets kept from him. It must have been why Tununda and Hart were dispatched to go there in the middle of the night.

With Johnson on the back burner he had then taken matters into his own hands. He placed a call to a highly lethal, personal security agency known as The Gladii, meaning "The Swords" in Latin. When a heavy player like himself needed protection—or even a lethal side job—they were at the top of the list in worldwide protective services. In retrospect, he knew he should have gone with them first instead of relying on Johnson's ghetto rejects.

Speaking directly to the company CEO, another golfing buddy and former bureaucratic hack, Black demanded an immediate team be dispatched. He got it. For an inflated fee of course. Four armed bodyguards—all combat veterans—were expected to arrive in Atlanta from their south Georgia base in several hours.

He was doubling-down on Tununda.

Although somewhat reassured, the crap still kept on flowing. Johnson had told Black that the Democrat Party minority leader just finished a morning press conference. It was about their party's one-vote loss on her important bill early this morning, and she publicly blamed the missing Tom Black as the reason why it didn't pass. Furthermore, she informed Johnson, not Black, on a furious voice message that the Congressman was being suspended from his seat on the House Finance Committee as a result of not showing up for such an important vote. He was required to meet with her face-to-face tomorrow in Washington.

All because of Tununda's meddling. It was all his fault, thought Black as more cheesecake filled his face.

Turning the television on in hope of finding news about what that bitch minority leader said about him, he was taken aback when FOX News aired an update on the West Point Museum theft.

"FOX News Alert now. Breaking news from New York. I'm Kelly Adams. We've just learned from a press conference by the U.S. Army Provost Marshal at West Point that one of the three stolen items from Sunday's brazen theft at the museum has been recovered. We repeat. One of the stolen artifacts from the West Point Museum has been recovered and is back in the Army's possession. It is the famous McPherson hat recently featured in the hit show Battlefield Investigators *hosted by Army Lieutenant Colonel Jake Tununda and Private Investigator Rae Hart. Yesterday both investigators were targeted for assassination in Savannah, Georgia, but they turned the tables and gunned down their would-be killer in a clear case of self-defense as captured by this surveillance video. Take a look."*

Video rolled of the shootout then switched to the perp walk outside the police station when Jake was handed over to the Army.

*Tununda was taken into custody by the U.S. Army's Criminal Investigation
Division but was later released with no charges filed against him. West Point
Provost Marshal Lieutenant Colonel Cliff Paxton credits the return of the
McPherson hat to Tununda and Hart saying 'their bravery and courage are
worthy of a medal.' He declined to comment on how the pair recovered the
hat last night but specifically went out of his way to praise U.S. Congressman
Tom Black of Atlanta's 15th District for his cooperation in the recovery effort.
As you know from earlier reports, Tom Black is in hot water for missing the
important vote last night. Our repeated calls to his district office for a comment
have gone unheeded. The whereabouts of the remaining two German trophies
from the Second World War are still unknown but they do have a suspect they
are pursuing. He is on the run and—"*

"You're a dead man, Tununda!" Black swiped his plate of cheesecake off
the counter. It hit the kitchen floor in shower of ceramic shards and sticky
cream. He roared obscenities at the television set knowing the *cooperation*
jab was a clear public threat for him to watch his next step. Pounding a fist
on the counter he knew he had been trumped. A hand rubbed his forehead
as he listened further.

*". . . multiple law enforcement agencies are hunting him down. We go now
live to our FOX News affiliate station in Atlanta for an update on who that
deadly suspect is. Todd Ashton, what's the latest down there?"*

*"Well, Kelly, this case is capturing the hearts and minds of American
patriots. Tununda and Hart have the Internet ablaze. Not only did they show
us why the Second Amendment continues to be so important in this violent
society we live in, but the outpouring of support from all across the nation
for the U.S. Army to recover our nation's war trophies continues to go viral,
especially from the remaining veterans of World War II. Here's what we know
so far about the suspect. Take a look at this exclusive video released by the
Atlanta Police Department.*

A ten second video showed a Hispanic male with a Civil War hat on his
head, gold pistol in hand, baton in the other, arms crossed over his chest.
In a mix of Spanish and Southern accents he said, "Life is like a carjacking.

You never know whatcha gonna get."

If that's not the smoking gun evidence I don't know what is. His name is Alejandro Hernandez. He is the enforcer of a brutal Hispanic gang called Sureños-13 and goes by the street name of Angel. Described as a Hispanic male in his mid-twenties. Approximately five eight, 180 pounds.

An ICE mug shot of Hernandez appeared on screen.

He is an illegal alien and was supposed to be deported by ICE many years ago but apparently slipped through the cracks of Homeland Security as so many of these criminals do. This brings to mind the Boston Marathon Islamist terrorists not too long ago.

According to law enforcement officials here in Atlanta, who wish to remain anonymous, this Angel drove from West Point directly to Atlanta and was spotted throwing Molotov cocktails at a local residence here in Doraville yesterday afternoon. The house exploded. One man who was trapped inside perished in the flames.

Video of the fire filled the screen with firefighters dowsing flames on a smoldering, collapsed house. The scene was sure to include a zoomed in shot of a body bag being wheeled out on an ambulance gurney.

Incidentally, fire and police officials say the house was a known meth lab belonging to Sureños-13. Could this West Point theft be some kind of internal gang civil war? Our own investigative journalists think that may be the case. They are following up on a missing teenager associated with the gang. Fourteen year-old Freddy Peña was allegedly kidnapped by Angel yesterday morning according to a missing persons report filed by his parents. Doraville police have already taken into custody two associates of Peña and we understand they have lawyered up and aren't talking. One of them is a juvenile.

We also have unconfirmed reports from the Atlanta Journal Constitution *that a mask used during the West Point Museum theft was found in Angel's home during a search warrant execution in trying to apprehend him. If so this is more damning evidence.*

Kelly, bottom line is this case is taking many twists and turns and an alphabet soup of law enforcement agencies are trying to sort it all out. Right now the Army CID, the FBI, ICE, ATF, U.S. Marshals, GBI, Atlanta Police and Doraville Police have got their hands full in who's who and who's even calling the shots.

Regardless, we do want the public to know this Angel suspect is considered armed and extremely dangerous. He was last seen driving a red Toyota Camry, Enterprise-Rent-A-Car with tag number BRU-4967. If you spot this individual call 9-1-1. Kelly, back to you in New York."

Holy Christ, thought Black, transfixed by the rest of the news report. He was still irate over the obvious inclusion of his name into the investigation, but was more impressed by all of the death and violence he had set in motion. Instead of any feeling of remorse, he felt an exciting shiver up his spine. The absolute power he could wield and how easily he could continue to manipulate his little pawns was so very intoxicating.

All by the power of his almighty dollar.

He especially admired this Angel. *My little thief is a bad, bad Angel.* Very resourceful, he thought. One who has proven he can shed blood. One who delivers on a promise.

And then it hit him.

The waybill!

It meant everything to get in back in his hands.

While driving down to Atlanta the thief had sent a small cropped version via the fixer to Johnson's iPad. Maybe, just maybe, he had the *full* version of the waybill still saved as a digital file, Black thought.

After all, he had parted with a considerable amount of money to obtain it in the first place. Having the waybill would at least allow him to pinpoint the location of where the tunnel was, or so he hoped, once he really had a chance to inspect it. He didn't need the actual knife anymore since he had been smart enough to make a paper rubbing of the engravings on each side of the blade as his backup copy. With a digital waybill and a copy of the key, he could then decipher the exact location of the Cherokee Tunnel and head off Tununda and his father from every obtaining the treasures inside, including the map.

And then he would kill every single one of those motherfuckers who had thwarted his goals.

With renewed vigor he placed another flurry of phone calls and texts to Johnson again, begging him coordinate an exchange one last time. Compliant as usual, his chief of staff, in turn, called their fixer to ask the thief's broker in New York if he did have a full copy of the waybill saved on his phone.

About an hour later the broker said the thief was still in Atlanta holed up and trying to make arrangements for transportation out of the state. She confirmed he possessed a full digital copy of the waybill and that he would exchange it for a discreet flight down to Miami on a private plane. The broker explained that their thief felt all car rental agencies were on high alert, Hartsfield-International airport was out of the question, and bus and train stations were probably being watched too. She said that her man had his trophies still on him, which were hindering his choices for escape.

The fixer asked Johnson about the flight to Miami, who asked Black, who wholeheartedly agreed to the deal. Black said he knew of a private airfield south of Miami called Homestead General Aviation Airport and that he would arrange a flight out by tonight from DeKalb Peachtree Airport. Black had no intention of using his own plane. Instead, he would call in a favor of one of his political cronies to use their own private plane to transport his VIP guest no questions asked. The fixer would pick up their passenger to get him on the flight out. A direct phone number was left with the broker for the thief to contact him once the flight was arranged.

Never once did the broker let on to Black's fixer that the news reports about her man being Angel were a can of worms of misinformation and deception further lubricating his clean escape from Atlanta.

Black rubbed his hands together, somewhat satisfied that he was back in the game again. His phone buzzed once more. Jaconious Johnson again, the caller ID showed.

"Everything OK?" Black asked.

"Everything's all arranged," Johnson replied. "The fix is in. I'm headed over to the district office right now to start the spin machine with the media. There was a lot of damage done with the minority leader's statements this morning. And then I'm flying up to D.C. later tonight. I'll see you in the morning on Capitol Hill for the interview. Remember, blue blazer, American lapel pin. Put on your patriot face. And try not to ruffle any feathers tonight, okay?"

"I hired personal security. Four of them from The Gladii. Just in case."

"That's good thinking. Just stay in the house. Have some bourbon and a cigar. Nurse your wounds. We'll get that Tununda back in due time. We just need to lay low for awhile."

"Okay. Okay," Black sighed. "I won't do anything rash."

"Tom, we'll come out of this clean. No worries. Goodbye."

Black set his phone down on the counter. Within seconds it buzzed with another call. Not bothering to look at the caller ID, he figured it was Johnson again,

"What now?"

"Is this Thomas Black Watie, the fifth?" asked a sultry female voice on the other end.

Black hadn't heard his full name spoken in over thirty years. His heart fluttered. "That's me. Who is this? You a reporter? What do you want?"

"Did you find what you were looking for inside McPherson's hat?"

24

TOMMY WATIE'S EYES LIT UP AS HE PATIENTLY SAT at the long, wooden, country kitchen table. A smiling Rae Hart descended the stairs first, followed by Jake Tununda holding three items. Tommy spoke up. "Y'all get shot at, interrogated by cops, drive four hours, open up Granddaddy's tomb, and then commit highway robbery all in one day. Y'all don't pussyfoot around, do ya?"

"Mr. Tommy!" greeted Jake, shrugging his shoulders with a big smile. "It was merely a minor fender bender accident is all." He winked at the old man. "Now check this out. Have we got something for you." Jake held up the leather book from Tommy's grandfather's crypt, the knife in its snakeskin sheath, and lastly the waybill all folded up. Jake set the items in front of the old man as Alex and Rae crowded in behind him.

"Black had McPherson's hat," Rae said. "You were absolutely right, sir."

"I'm sorry, but I had to return it to the Army last night," Jake said. "Sergeant D'Arata has it. We can get you to see it when all this shit blows over, okay?"

Tommy waved his hand gesturing to not worry about it. Instead, he picked up the folded waybill. That's all that mattered to him. His hands shook and the waybill wavered when he unfolded it. "Oh, my Lord! I never thought this day would come!" he said loudly.

"Mr. Tommy, you okay in there?" shouted the voice of Nurse Becky

Holden from a first floor guest room. She poked her head around the corner to check on him. "Hey y'all!" She said, once she saw Jake and Rae.

"Hey, back at you," Rae replied, picking up some of the Southern lingo. "How was the drive up?" She gave Holden a hug as the nurse joined her patient Tommy at the table.

Holden rubbed the small of her back. "Six hours by the time we stopped for pee breaks, isn't that right, Mr. Tommy?" She placed a hand on his shoulder. Silence. "*Mr. Tommy?*"

Tommy was in another world. His eyes had already teared up as he lay the waybill down on the table and smoothed out the folds. He clapped his hands. "I can't believe it's real."

The waybill was an almost childlike drawing made up of many recognizable symbols, some alphabet letters. There was also a wide, flowing, curvilinear line. A complex rectangular shape on the bottom was most intriguing with its squared corners and many boxes.

For several minutes the group respectively gave Tommy the opportunity to experience his long sought-after artifact. He scanned the waybill, fingers dragging over the symbols, head nodding and shaking as he took in what lay in front of him. At one point he openly wept while addressing his grandfather by name that the waybill had finally been found.

Jake came around from the other side of the table and stood behind Tommy to join Rae, Alex, and Becky in reviewing the waybill for the first time, too. When they had arrived at the lodge last night they had deliberately decided not to review any of the items. They did get a hold of Holden to announce the good news to Tommy before catching some sleep. They had agreed to wait until the pair arrived to give Tommy first dibs at really inspecting it.

Jake couldn't take the silence any longer and finally interrupted Tommy's concentration. "I've got a question, Tommy," he said, treading lightly. "Why didn't you tell me about Alex Vann last night? He met us in Oakland Cemetery and, well . . . it would have been nice if we had a little forewarning."

Tommy selectively didn't hear Jake. His head was drooped, still too busy absorbing the waybill in front of him.

"Mr. Tommy slept all last night after y'all left Savannah," Holden said in his defense. "Had me look up Alex's phone number for him, but he fell right asleep after they spoke on the phone. He was fixin' to call y'all for sure. Told me so."

"Yes, yes, sorry about that, Jake," Tommy said, looking up at him. "Completely slipped my mind." He bowed his head back down to the waybill again. "Hope your introductions went well."

Jake and Rae smirked at Alex. Alex simply shrugged his shoulders and placed a finger to his lips indicating they shouldn't let on to what went down in the cemetery.

Tommy reached for the leather book, opened it, and fanned some of the pages until he found a topographical map of the Ball Ground, Georgia area along the Etowah River. Once unfolded, he spread it out on the table and placed the waybill on top of it. Overly excited, his heart rate was increasing by the minute.

"Y'all look here now," Tommy said, pointing to the waybill. "This curved line is supposed to be an overhead view of how the Etowah River flows." He then tapped the topo map to show them how the curved line matched the curves of the actual river.

"Ahhh," Holden said, staring at the waybill.

Alex nodded. "There's a Cherokee word at the end of the curve: ᎤᏳᏔᎸ. Pronounced 'u yv tlv.' It means 'EAST.' So the map orientation fits."

Tommy agreed. "All Granddaddy remembered from the waybill before he lost it in '64 was this river curve because it reminded him of the head and wings of a bird. Could hardly remember any of these other symbols, though. That curve is all we had to go on when we were hunting for the arborglyphs and petroglyphs."

Rae creased her eyebrows. "I remember from the tape we listened to that your grandfather said the curve looked like a turtledove, which was one of the symbols of the Bird Clan that John Ross belonged to?"

"That's right, young lady. Was no coincidence by Ross that he chose this area to dig the tunnel."

"You had a general idea of the location of the tunnel all these years?" Alex asked.

"That's about it," Tommy explained. "General Watie told Granddaddy it was on the Etowah somewhere south of Ball Ground before he left from Arkansas. Took him just two days to get to Georgia. Didn't have much time to memorize the map, nor did he have the means to make any copies or anything of that sort. Years later, when he realized the McPherson hat was really lost, well, he figured maybe he'd just start looking for signs out there along the Etowah anyway, thinking it might lead him to the tunnel one day. All he had to go on was those engraved symbols on the knife. He thought maybe they'd be out there in the woods or something, but those knife symbols never did appear."

Tommy was revved up. He spoke faster. "The turtledove was in his memory and that fit the Etowah the best right here at a little place called Gober." He touched the topo map again in the upper left corner. "That's where he started looking with my daddy. Got permission from landowners to walk their property because, after all, we were in the lumber business and interested in logging. Or so he told them." The old man laughed.

"But they never let on," Tommy continued to explain. "They started finding lots and lots of symbols. Well over a hundred. That's what all of these numbers on the topo map are. Each and every symbol we found we recorded it in this here master book with a description of what it was, where, and when we found it." He grasped the leather book and turned to a page inside where he showed them an example. A symbol was pencil-sketched and accompanied with a written description of where it was found, whether carved on a rock or a tree. Lastly, a map reference gave its location.

"When I became of age I joined them in the hunt. Scoured every damn inch of land in that entire area, seems like." Tommy pointed to the switchback curve of the river on the far left of the map. "But without the waybill we didn't know the meaning of any of them there symbols. We were in the right area we knew. We did all the leg work, but we were still *lost*."

Like a child with a new toy he was proud of, Tommy kept on talking. "Now lookee here, this circle in the upper left symbolizes earth. Or the ground. Every dadgum Cherokee knows that. And this here arrow attached to it means you cross an obstacle." He tapped the waybill over and over again. "So, that's telling me the ground location of the tunnel is pointing across the river. Never did much explore there, though."

"On the south bank?" Rae asked.

Tommy quietly nodded. He seemed sad all of a sudden.

"What do you think all these boxes are here on the bottom, Tommy?" Jake asked, pointing to the rectangle shape at the bottom of the waybill.

Tommy squinted. "I'm pretty sure that is sorta like a floor plan of the tunnel, best I can determine. It was said to be 200 feet long. See how this circle and cross appear again? That's an indication of the entrance being in the earth. So I think these might be steps or a ladder once you go down inside the tunnel. I'm guessing these little squares and the longer shapes may be the family vaults. Hell if I know for sure, though."

Tommy looked up at them with raised eyebrows. "What do y'all say we figure out what these seven symbols on the waybill really mean?" Not waiting for their answers, he fanned the leather book's pages.

"Mr. Tommy, this map thing ain't none of my business," Holden interrupted. "I'm already lost with all this symbol talk. All that matters is you're happy and healthy now, so I'm gonna head on down to the local store to stock this here empty refrigerator, if y'all don't mind? Will do some cookin' later."

"Honey, that'd be great. Thank you much," Tommy said. The others, too, expressed their appreciation for her polite discretion.

After Holden headed out, Tommy pulled the Bowie knife from its leather sheath and placed it on the table. In the book he found a two-page spread near the front. One page showed a sketch of the side of the knife blade containing characters. The other page showed a sketch with a long sentence written in Cherokee and nothing more.

Tommy took a pen out of his shirt pocket and glanced back and forth from the waybill to the knife symbol sketch. He explained. "We already knew what these seven individual characters on this side of the knife meant."

"Huh?" Rae asked.

Tommy looked up at her. "They're the numerals one through seven written in the Cherokee language. The language and these numbers were created by Sequoyah, except these specific seven characters were *not* officially adopted by the Cherokee Nation. They were rejected. John Ross commissioned James Black to create this knife so he more than likely used the rejected numerals because no one else would."

"They were in essence a secret numbering system?" Rae asked.

"That's right," Tommy said, smiling. "Granddaddy figured it out. Here's the numbering scheme that he wrote down." Tommy showed the trio the notebook scribblings.

1 = ᏉᎠᏚᎯᏓ ᏛᏁᎳᏬᏉᎠᏕ [180]

2 = ᎳᏈᏬᏉᎠᏚᎯᏓ ᏦᏬᏉᎠᏕ ᏦᏙ [233]

3 = ᎳᏈᏬᏉᎠᏚᎯᏓ ᏛᏁᎳᏬᏉᎠᏕ ᏦᏙ [283]

4 = ᏦᏬᏉᎠᏚᎯᏓ ᏦᏬᏉᎠᏕ ᎣᎩ [334]

5 = ᎳᏈᏬᏉᎠ ᏚᏬᎩ [25]

6 = ᏌᏈᎵᏬᏉᎠ ᏛᏁᎳ [78]

7 = ᏉᎠᏚᎯᏓ ᏦᏬᏉᎠᏕ [130]

Alex picked up the knife and twisted it in his hand to reveal the engravings reflected in the light. "So you two understand," he said to Jake and Rae, "these Cherokee words above the secret numerals are also numbers themselves. But they *are* the official Cherokee language numbers. That's for sure. But why two different sets of numbers? Ross had to have a reason for both numbers, that's the mystery that has befuddled the Waties and me ever since Tommy showed me this knife some years back."

"Wait a second, let me see that knife," Jake said to Alex. The operative handed the long blade to Jake who bent over and compared the knife blade etchings to the waybill symbols. A thick black eyebrow raised. His eyes darted back and forth from the blade to the waybill. "You see what I see?"

"I do," said Rae.

"The seven numerals on the knife are an exact match to the characters above each of the seven symbols on the waybill," Jake said, showing Tommy and Alex. "Now we can clearly see why one item couldn't function without the other. It's why they were a pair."

"Oh Lordy, Lordy that's the key, Jake!" Tommy burst out. "Ha. Ha. It fits. It fits!"

"Huh?" Jake asked, perplexed. "How does it fit? What about the official numbers above the seven characters? It still doesn't make any sense."

"I'm not quite getting this either," Alex said.

Tommy grabbed the knife from Jake and turned it over to show the other side of the blade with the long sentence engraved in Cherokee. He then handed it to Alex and pointed to it with a smile. "You remember this little riddle I showed you a long, long time ago? You remember what it said? Read it out loud. Translate it again."

Tommy placed a hand over the knife sketch in the book, covering the notes so no one would cheat by looking at the already written translation. "I already know what it means. Granddaddy was the first one to translate it."

"I think I remember." Alex cleared his voice and read the Cherokee inscription. *"Guwisquwi ehi dakana itsula alani agadadi ehi adanvdo le yelasdi ehi u wa yi."* He closed his eyes and thought deeply, lips moving, words forming. His eyes popped open and he said, "Well, I remember that Guwisquwi is John Ross's Cherokee name. It means rare or mythological bird. The rest of the sentence reads as follows: Guwisquwi is guided with land stealer in heart and knife in hand. Was that how it was?"

Tommy raised his hand on the notebook and read to himself to compare the meaning. He nodded and smiled at Alex. "You are spot on, son."

"What's a land stealer?" Rae asked, hands on hips.

"Why, it's a surveyor's compass!" Tommy said, acting as if she should have known.

"Indians considered surveyors as land thieves," Alex said. "And the instrument of their theft was the surveying compass."

Tommy nodded profusely. "And this second set of numbers above each of the seven characters refers to—"

"A compass heading," Jake said, finishing his sentence.

"And now we have the seven symbols on the waybill finally matched with their compass heading on a map," Rae stated. "The key unlocked it."

"Indeed it did," Tommy said, head nodding happily. "Indeed it did." He fanned the notebook and showed them pages and pages of sketched symbols the Waties had found carved on rocks and trees. Each sketch had a corresponding map coordinate location.

"Now we just find the seven waybill symbols in this book among the hundred or so we referenced. Then we plot their exact grid location on a map, mark their compass heading from the knife, and pray to God the seven waypoints aim to where the tunnel is."

"May I?" Jake asked, his hand out for the notebook. "Let me look them up." Tommy handed the book over and Jake sat down across from him. Rae pulled up a chair next to Jake to assist him.

Alex spun around and went for his personal laptop computer sitting on the kitchen counter top. "Hold up. Let me open up my topo map program. I have all the digital grid maps for Georgia. That way we can draw the correct compass bearing from each of the waypoints located on the map. And then I can download those coordinates to my GPS receiver." He placed the laptop on the table and sat next to Tommy who watched him intensely.

Jake tore a blank page from the notebook and wrote down each symbol description followed by their one through seven designated number and their compass bearing. He handed Rae the pen and paper.

"Okay, Honey, let's start with number one: the Turtle," Jake said, already scanning the pages of the notebook, looking for the matching pencil sketch of the symbol out of one hundred and twenty that were listed. "You write down the map grid reference when I say it out loud for Alex. That will give us a master list of the seven we can track from." Within a minute he found the Turtle symbol.

"Number 89. Turtle," Jake began reading. "Found on August 19, 1914 by TBW Jr. Carved on a large quartz stone, turtle head pointing south. This symbol is located west of the Etowah River turtledove head shape up on a slope, just north of East Cherokee Drive."

By the time he was done, Alex said he had pulled up the Ball Ground topo map on his screen. Tommy's eye's widened as Alex zoomed in on the turtledove curve of the river.

"You ready for the coordinates?" Jake asked. Alex gave a nod. He read the map grid reference out loud as Rae also jotted it down on their master list. "Latitude is 34 degrees, 18 point zero, eight, three feet, North. Longitude is 84 degrees, 23 point nine, zero, three feet, West."

Alex repeated the grid coordinates back to Jake for accuracy as he plotted a waypoint on his topo map software program. A small purple diamond appeared on screen just above the Etowah River on the north bank. He labeled it 'TURTLE.' "I'm ready for the compass bearing."

Rae cleared her throat. "Compass bearing 180 degrees."

Jake was already thumbing through the notebook for the Snake, while Alex repeated the compass bearing. He chose the compass tool on the map menu and placed his cursor directly on top of the diamond waypoint. An icon appeared and he moved the icon a couple of inches due south on the map, watching a small window showing him the correct 180° compass bearing. Satisfied, he let go of the icon with his mouse and a red line appeared on screen with an arrow pointing south.

"I found the Snake," Jake said, holding the notebook page open. "Number 38. Found on December 9, 1938 by TBW III. Carved on a beech tree. Located on the river flat inside the turtledove head of the Etowah. South bank. It has a grid coordinate of—"

Jake, Rae, and Alex repeated the process again for the Snake. When

Alex drew in the new, red compass line of 233° it intersected the Turtle line. Tommy gasped. It showed the intersection on a steep hill overlooking the Etowah on the south bank.

For the remaining five symbols, the trio repeated the procedure again while Tommy bounced impatiently on his chair not saying a word. He looked afraid, even sad as he watched Alex finish drawing seven intersecting lines on the topo map. All seven intersected at the same exact spot. Alex kept glancing up at Jake and Rae over his laptop screen, eyes swimming just like Tommy's, in anticipation to reveal the long lost location of the tunnel.

Once Jake and Rae completed their data list it now showed:

Turtle   1 = 180° from 34°18.083'N, 84°23.903'W
Snake   2 = 233° from 34°17.983'N, 84°23.617'W
Humps   3 = 283° from 34°17.749'N, 84°23.564'W
Hand   4 = 334° from 34°17.552'N, 84°23.773'W
Bow/Arrow   5 = 25° from 34°17.576'N, 84°24.045'W
Cross/Dots 6 = 78° from 34°17.752'N, 84°24.232'W
Triangle   7 = 130° from 34°18.013'N, 84°24.179'W

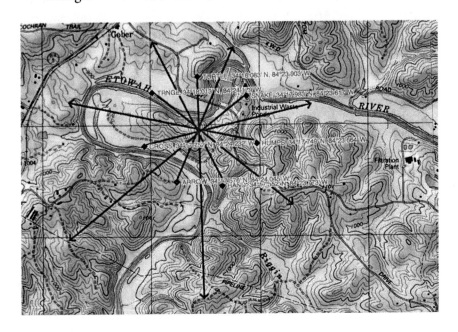

"Okay, are you guys ready to see this?" Alex asked. He turned the laptop computer around on the table to display the screen to Jake and Rae. "We've got our location!"

"Shit, yeah!" Jake said.

Rae squeezed his arm in delight. "That is awesome," she whispered.

Alex was already busy connecting his handheld GPS wayfinding unit to his topo map program to download the information, while Tommy wiped his eyes.

"What are the map coordinates for the final location?" Jake asked Alex, not noticing Tommy.

Alex clicked on his waypoint tool again and read out loud. "34 degrees, 17 point eight, one, nine, North. Longitude is 84 degrees, 23 point eight, nine, six, West. Gotta be in that area somewhere."

"10-4," Rae said, adding 34°17.819'N, 84°23.896'W to their master wayfinding list. "Tommy, you ever visit this property before?"

She never got an answer so she looked over at the old man. His head was turned down and his shoulders shook. He was crying.

"Tommy?" Rae asked, getting up and moving over to his side. She placed a hand on his shoulder. "Tommy, you alright? What's the matter?"

"My baby girl Catherine died there," he said sniffling as he pointed shakily to the location of the tunnel on the laptop screen. "She died right there. Same exact spot. Fell off that cliff and drowned in the river." Tears rolled from his eyes and down inside his hollow cheeks.

Rae wrapped her arm around his shoulders and hugged him. "Tommy, I'm so sorry," she whispered in his ear. "I'm so sorry."

"She was only f-fifteen years old," Tommy stuttered. "F-fifteen. I was down on the river bottom just south of the knoll looking for symbols. I left Catherine with Tom. He was s-supposed to watch her. He was s-s-supposed to be responsible for her. But he went off smoking dope! I never forgave that boy for what he'd done. Never! That irresponsible, no-good piece of—"

Jake and Alex stared at each other across the table, both knowing this was the true source of the early animosity between father and son. It was over the tragic death of Tommy's daughter. Jake thought back to her crypt at Oakland Cemetery. He remembered she died in 1967.

"Tommy, I'm sorry," Jake said, knowing there was no coincidence between his daughter's death and the location of the Cherokee Tunnel. He knew better. Coincidences don't just happen. They are meant to reveal destiny. "It's important I ask this, Tommy, but how did she die exactly?"

"My boy said she looked like she was pushed from behind and just jumped off the cliff. He said she committed suicide. He had no basis to accuse her of that. She was our little girl and the happiest creature on earth. It was that boy who was jealous of her. He was stoned out of his mind. I done accused *him* of pushing her. I accused him of *murder*. I beat that boy silly that day. We were never the same after that. You never expect your beloved child to grow up to be such a demon like he was."

Alex placed a hand on Tommy's shoulder. "Jesus, Tommy, I never knew. I'm real sorry, my friend." He let Tommy cry some more. "I'm real sorry."

Something didn't seem right to Alex, though. After a minute he spoke again. "Tommy? If she was pushed as your son claimed and we now know the Cherokee Tunnel is on that same exact spot, there's more than fate working here. I think there's something else that may have been responsible."

Tommy looked up at Alex with bloodshot, glassy eyes. "Don't you say it, boy! Don't you say it!" He clenched a fist in the air and shook it at Alex. "If it's one of them, I will drive a spear through its head myself!"

Rae glared at Jake shaking her head, confused at what Tommy was talking about. Jake quietly mouthed back the words: *Raven Mocker*. Her eyes went wide.

"I think it's one of them, Tommy," Alex said. "It must be. I think she just got too close to the entrance and . . . well, do you remember ever feeling anything in that area? Any type of presence? I know it was a long time ago. But—"

"That was the only time I was on that land," Tommy said, calming down. "It was old man Jacob Steiner's property. He had a big farmhouse and farmfields on the river flats on that there peninsula. I knocked on his door to get permission, but he wasn't home. So we were trespassing that day is what the police said. But Steiner never pressed any charges because he was sad about what happened.

"You see Granddaddy and Daddy had marked in that book there that they found some symbols along the north bank of the river way back in the early 1900s, and I wanted to see what I could find myself on the south side of the river. Catherine said she wanted to climb up to the top of the hill to see the view so I let her, telling Tom to keep watch over her. I never knew it'd be the last time I'd see her alive. I was devastated. My poor wife was never the same. That was tough on us. So tough. So tragic. She was so young and beautiful." He cried again.

Rae placed her hand on his and held it. "Tommy, were there any witnesses besides your son? Where was this farmer Steiner at the time?"

"Police said he claimed he was up in Ball Ground getting supplies at the time. Was nowhere near my kids. Tom said no one was around but him, and he said it looked like she jumped on her own. He couldn't tell because he was high on dope. Why would she jump?"

Tommy sighed deeply and wiped his eyes. "I remember hearing Tom scream," he recounted softly. "And I climbed as fast as I could up that hill. By the time I got there I saw her body floating down river, and Tom just standing there doing nothing to help that child. He was a frozen coward. Was the worst day of my life."

"I'm sorry, Tommy," Rae said again. She sat down next to Jake and placed a hand on his thigh. Jake held it.

Thick silence overwhelmed the room.

Scratching his chin, Jake spoke up, finally breaking the ice. "How much daylight do we have left?"

"About five hours," Alex said, knowing exactly where he wanted to go. He pulled his smartphone out of his pocket and tapped the screen while talking. "What kind of gear you two bring with you? You guys prepared to go into the woods and maybe even underground?"

"Negative," Jake said. "We're gonna need to do some shopping first." He squeezed Rae's hand under the table to comfort her after feeling the extreme nervousness radiating off of her. Last time they went underground they barely made it out alive.

"No worries. I've got everything we'll need in my arms vault," Alex said, staring at his phone. "But we got one problem." He turned his phone so the others could see. On his screen was a weather radar map showing a line of clouds colored in red and orange interspersed with green. "Severe thunderstorms headed east toward us. It's that time of year again when these things come barreling through here. But this one is coming with a tornado, too. It hit a town in Alabama already."

"Shit," Jake grunted. "How far away are we from the tunnel?" he asked, pointing to the laptop screen.

Alex waggled his head back and forth taking a moment to estimate the mileage from his home, then responded they were about a half hour away.

Jake asked him when the storms were due to arrive in their area.

Alex replied it would take two to three hours before the line of storms arrived from the Alabama border.

Jake knew it was risky but said, "Still enough time to gear up and go. We can at least do a recon and try to make contact with the land owner."

Rae asked, "What about Becky?"

"We can't wait for her," Alex said. "We need to move out now if we're going to beat this storm."

"No!" Tommy said. "I ain't going nowhere without her. We wait."

"I agree. I'm worried about Tom Black still," Rae said. "He's been one step ahead of us this entire time."

Jake patted her leg. "We've got him by the balls. There's no need to worry about him. He won't make a move tonight."

Alex backed him up. "With the leak we made to the media, he's in political damage control right now for sure. By the time he recovers in the next couple of days, we'll have terminated any unseen obstacles and breached that tunnel. We're good. Don't worry."

"We can't underestimate him," Rae warned. She then turned to Tommy. "Now we know why he risked everything to steal McPherson's hat. I bet he wants to get you back for your accusations so long ago about causing Catherine's death."

"I know," Tommy said quietly, bowing his head. "It's revenge *against* the father now. Pathetic, isn't it?" He paused and swallowed. "But Rae's right. Catherine didn't sacrifice her life, and Daddy and Granddaddy didn't do all this work for some ungrateful black sheep of the family to waltz in and steal our dream."

"That's why we need to move fast on this," Jake urged. "Go on the attack tonight, gain the objective before he gets back in the game. That way we can find out what's in there. We can cut a deal with the property owner that he can't refuse, then secure or transport off site what we can and figure out a way to guard the place. Lock it down."

"Can we get D'Arata to keep tabs on Black's movement?" Rae asked. Give us a warning if he's mobilizing anyone?"

Alex agreed. "He'll cover our ass just in case. Considering there's only the three of us and two non-operatives, we're a skeleton crew."

"I'll call him and see what he can do. I'm not even sure if he's in Atlanta still," Jake said. "What do you say we go over an equipment list and then check your vault?"

"One question, Alex," Rae said, "does Tom Black know about you? Are we even safe to be in this house here?"

"Completely. Black has no idea who the hell I am."

"Good."

Jake nodded.

Alex slapped him on the back. "Let's rock and roll."

25

PROFESSOR MARISSA MORGAN—A DROP DEAD gorgeous look-a-like of actress Halle Berry—sauntered around her desk and extended a hand to greet Tom Black. After taking a brief tour of the Native American cultural center that she headed up at Reinhardt University, Black had been awaiting her arrival from a class she was teaching, and had just entered her office. Short, stylish black hair framed a beautiful, cream chocolate-hued, thin face with long lashes and stunning brown eyes. At half his age, Black knew she was one of the prettiest black women he had ever laid eyes on.

She wore an open white blouse with ample cleavage and a thigh-high, gray mini skirt and heels to model her firm, sexy legs. He shook her hand but could not control his eyes from wandering down the front of his shirt.

"Congressman, it's a pleasure to meet you," Morgan gushed. "Thanks so much for driving up here so soon, considering how busy you are with all the news and such."

At the sound of her silky voice Black was over-the-top smitten, wanting instantly to ease a hand up that short skirt. He checked for a ring on her finger and found none.

Not that it ever mattered to him.

To Morgan's visible dismay the door to her office was abruptly shut by a burly looking, cropped hair, fiftyish white male with a big walrus style mustache in a dark suit and sunglasses—one of four of Black's new armed bodyguards. They had escorted Black to the college, shadowing him, and staking out the Native American heritage center. Since Black was meeting after hours there were no more public visitors, only a blue-haired ticket-taker going off-duty who had directed them to Morgan's office.

Black wore tan slacks and a plaid shirt thinking he'd play the part to fit in up in rural Georgia, where he only traveled to play golf. But instead, the man looked like an obese Patagonia clothing catalog reject as he spoke to the professor.

"Pleasure's all mine, Dr. Morgan," Black said. "You have a nice facility here. It's good to get out of the office every now and again. Besides, the media vultures were already starting to circle my home."

"Please, sit down," Morgan urged with a smile, gesturing to two chairs and a small meeting table with a vase of white Cherokee roses gracing the table top.

As she led the way over, Black stared at her ass in the tight skirt. No panty lines, she must be wearing a thong, he fantasized. Or better yet, commando. Already he was aroused and losing his train of thought. She sat and crossed her legs, he trying to catch a glimpse of what might be waiting for him in between.

"Actually if you don't mind, I'd prefer to stand. Took a fall last night and hurt my back a bit." He rubbed his lower back and hip for effect.

"Ooh, sorry to hear that," Morgan said sincerely, blinking her lashes a bit longer than normal. She leaned back and lifted her chest ever so slightly.

Black smiled, holding back drool.

"What's your Ph.D. in?" he asked.

"American Studies with an emphasis on Native American and African American southern regional cultures. My dissertation was on the relationship of the Cherokee and the slaves they owned. In particular, one James Vann from the early 1800s. I had a biography published on him in 2013."

"Never heard of him," Black said bluntly.

Morgan's eyes flickered from the brush back. She crossed her arms. "He was only like the richest Cherokee at the time," she spat in a bitchy tone with wiggle of her head. "Second richest man in the United States. With a famous Cherokee last name such as yours, Congressman, I would think you would have learned your history. Especially the Waties having been slave owners themselves."

Fucking bitch, thought Black. "The name is Tom Black," he said sternly, looking down on her arrogant gaze. His attraction to her started fizzling. "Dropped all association with the Watie family many years ago. I despise that name, so do not utter it again."

"I see, Congressman Black."

All patience gone he asked, "You said on the phone you knew about what's inside that McPherson hat?"

"Yes, John Ross's waybill from 1838. It leads to a legendary tunnel of gold deposits."

"How'd you know? Who told you this?"

"I've done my research over the years," Morgan laughed. "When you dig in the past you never know what you might resurrect. Now, my question to *you* is: was the waybill really in that hat you just returned to the Army?"

"Let's just say I returned it unwillingly."

"Contrary to the media reports of your kind cooperation?" Morgan grinned sarcastically. "I didn't think so, Congressman. It's one of the reasons why I called you. Thought we could help each other out. So, what about the waybill?"

"*If* it was in that hat, what's it mean to you?"

"If it leads to the Cherokee Tunnel, it means financial reparations for my slave ancestors who were owned by the Cherokee elite."

"You mean you want to cash in for yourself," Black stated matter-of-factly while crossing thick arms over his fat chest. "Feel that you're entitled to all the gold, huh? Because of your family's slave past? Well now, aren't you the entitled righteous one?"

Morgan uncrossed her legs and stood up to face him. "A page out of your own playbook," she countered, pointing at him. "Do you have it?"

Black had it alright. Johnson had received the full digital copy from his fixer on another email drop from the thief right before he took off on the flight to Florida. The thief had kept his bargain. Black received it on his personal computer from Johnson and then copied it to a flash drive now snug in his pocket next to the folded up piece of paper of the knife blade rubbing.

"Maybe," answered Black. "Depends on if you can help me with some Cherokee translations. You see, the waybill requires a key to decipher the symbols on it and I can't read this key. You know the Cherokee language?"

Morgan smirked. "Of course I do. Let me take a wild guess that this key you speak of is actually an old Bowie knife, correct?"

Black's eyes lit up. "Smart *and* incredibly good looking."

She ignored his compliment. "You have this knife key on you, too?"

"I have a *copy* of the key. The real key was, again, forcefully removed from my person recently."

"Did those *Battlefield Investigators* Tununda and Hart from the news reports have a hand in its repatriation, as well?"

Black nodded. "Plus some other long-haired Indian with them, too. They all wore bandanas over their faces like common thugs. I knew who they were except that other guy. I did notice a tattoo on him, though."

"Really?" She touched her chin. "Where?"

"Wrist."

"A wrist tattoo?" Morgan placed a hand on her hip. "Of what?"

"Looked like an eagle with a skull."

She fumed. "A skull on a shield?"

"Yeah. I think it might even had a beret on from what I remember."

Morgan bowed and shook her head letting out a depressive, sinister snicker. When she looked up her face had turned dark red, upper lip curled.

"What? You know that guy?"

"I do," she spat. "I fucked him for ten years! And then he dumped me like a used condom." She spun around and walked away.

"His name is Alex Vann, direct descendant of James Vann," she said, backed turned. "I did a genealogy search on the Vanns while researching my book and tracked him down. We hit it off instantly."

Black rubbed his chin. "Oh, I see."

Morgan turned and faced Black again. "But what if I told you where we can find Alex Vann and subsequently the Cherokee Tunnel? We wouldn't even need to use the key to decipher the waybill."

"You cut a deal with him last night after they robbed me?" Black bellowed angrily. "You been talking to Tununda, too?" He reached into his pocket and extracted a palm-sized, black, Ruger .22 caliber pistol.

Morgan didn't even flinch. "Put that tiny thing away," she ordered. "I haven't spoken to Alex in over a year. But I did receive this bouquet of Cherokee roses this morning from him. He's wanting to get back together with me. Says he misses me . . . *the fuck* . . . and he said this . . ." Morgan handed Black the card that accompanied the delivered roses.

Pistol back in his pocket, Black read out loud: *"Marissa, ride the Golden Horse with me. I'm about to lay my hands on it. I was so wrong to let you go. I beg you, please take me back. Let's make history together. Watch the news today and call me. Please. I miss you. Alex."*

"He's no poet. Did you call him?"

"Fuck, no."

"The Golden Horse is supposed to be in that tunnel," Black stated, eyebrows scrunched. "I know what secret the horse holds. Do you?"

"Damn right I do!" Morgan snapped. "Alex shared all his secrets with me when we were together." She snatched the card from Black's fingers and shredded it, the fragments trickling onto the floor.

"I was so in love with him," she said, tearing up. "Thought he was my soul mate the way our past ancestors were so connected. Thought it was destiny and all that bullshit. But in his mind, his duty to the country came first. I was second fiddle. So fuck him!"

"What did he tell you about the horse?"

"There's a highly valuable mining map hidden inside of it that his ancestor James Vann used to possess. It's what made him filthy rich."

"Tell me everything you know about this map."

"Well, it was first drawn by a Spanish cartographer employed by Hernando de Soto. This is the mid-1500s we're talking. The Spanish had heard the legends of cities of gold here in the New World and they were right. You see, the ancient native tribes had been mining gold for hundreds of years before the Spanish came. Some speculate the ancients were direct descendants of a Mayan emigration from the Yucatan to the North Georgia mountains, bringing their knowledge of gold and silver mining with them and eventually passing those skills down to the Cherokee.

"The Spaniards enslaved the natives and threatened to kill their families if they didn't reveal the source of their great wealth—their ancient mines. With their slave labor the Spanish started pulling out huge loads of gold, silver, copper, gemstones, you name it. And they started mapping these locations, too."

This confirmed what Black had overheard on the spy pen when he listened in on his father and Tununda's late night conversation. "Stunning. Absolutely stunning. Please go on. Tell me more."

The professor was in her element sharing her knowledge and expertise to a captive audience. "But the Indians rebelled. According to Alex Vann, their high priests conjured up a witch that slaughtered the Spanish soldiers. It was the most terrifying of all evil spirits, called . . ."

"A Raven Mocker?" Black asked.

Morgan stepped back, eyebrows arched, arms crossing her chest.

"My father told me stories of the Raven Mocker when I was a child," Black said. "Used it against me as the Boogeyman when I wouldn't listen to him. Never did any good."

"With the Raven Mocker's help the Indians sent the Spanish fleeing right out of Georgia," Morgan continued. "In commemoration of their victory, one of their goldsmiths crafted the Golden Horse. Along with their victory came the spoils of war. They captured de Soto's original mining map and even kidnapped the cartographer who had been working on it, too. That's how they first came in possession of it.

"The Spanish cartographer was now *their* slave and over the years he taught the Indians the art of mapmaking. He was adopted into their tribe and lived with them the rest of his life teaching young apprentices how to draw the landscape. Over several generations, the Cherokee expanded on the map and protected it from the white man by forming a secret society."

"You're kiddin' me?" asked Black.

"Nope," said Morgan. "Finally, Chief James Vann, a tribal leader and warrior, was given the map in the late 1700s as he was one of the ruling elite who could be trusted. Or so they thought."

"Tununda called this mining map a *Map of Thieves* because of how many times it was stolen," commented Black.

"He's right," nodded Morgan. "James Vann was murdered in 1809 and the map was stolen yet again. Vann ended up being a wicked, murderous man who killed any fellow Indians that crossed him, any of his own black slaves that looked at him wrong, and scores of white men who traveled up and down the Federal Road. He especially took sporting pleasure in killing the whites. Basically, the guy was a cruel, sadistic, slave-holding, racist, alcoholic. Which leads me to my own family's connection to this map story. It's why I started researching James Vann in the first place."

This time Black did take a seat, mesmerized by this woman's tale.

"The night Vann was murdered he had just come into Hightower, where he owned a farm and a ferry. It's due east of here about 25 miles as the crow flies. Right on the Etowah River. He brought with him a chest of gold powder in pouches from one of his mines, about $40,000 worth."

"That's a *shitload* of money back then," Black said.

"Sure was," agreed Morgan. "But get this: he also had the mining map in that chest, too. He knew people were out to get him. Knew that they wanted to take the map back for the terror he had become to his own people, so he kept it near him at all times. For safekeeping that night, he blindfolded two of his slaves, had them carry the chest from the farmhouse, down the hill to the outer edge of the river bottom field, and under a large oak tree he made the slaves dig a hole and bury the damn thing. He planned on digging it back up in a couple days to continue on to his mansion up at Spring Place near Chatsworth."

"No shit."

Morgan nodded. Pacing now. "One of the slaves lifted his blindfold to figure out the location. Vann saw him do this and bashed his head in with a shovel. The one who didn't peek survived. Billy Morgan." She paused. "I'm a direct descendant of that slave."

"Ahhhhh," said Black, sitting back. "There's the connection."

Morgan smiled. She wasn't finished. "Later that night, when Vann was getting drunk at Buffington's Tavern there in Hightower, he was lured outside and shot dead by an unknown assailant. He died with a bottle in one hand and a drink in the other. Was forty-three years old. Someone got their revenge. To this day no one knows who did it, but everyone celebrated nonetheless. Vann's body disappeared and to this day no one knows where he's buried."

Black opened his mouth to say something, but Morgan raised her hand for him to hold off.

"Billy Morgan took Vann's son, Joe, and whisked him away that night back up to his mansion at Spring Place. Joe inherited a vast fortune. People started calling him Rich Joe Vann. President James Monroe even visited him when Joe turned twenty. Fast forward a few years later and Rich Joe gives Morgan his freedom for saving him the night his father was killed.

"Soon after Morgan was approached by several Cherokee associated with the secret society that gave the mining map to James Vann. The map that was buried in the chest in Hightower. You with me?"

Black nodded and waved his hand in a twirling motion for her to continue.

The professor went on. "They explain to Morgan they know he was the last slave to be with James Vann the night he was murdered, and they are looking for a certain mining map given to Vann on loan and would pay huge sums of money in order to recover it. Morgan agreed to the deal. You see, he knew exactly where that chest of gold containing the map was because he also peeked out from under his blindfold while Vann was beating the other slave to death. He had kept that secret until he became a free man and now the time had come to cash in."

Morgan took a breath. "Billy Morgan secretly dug up the chest, kept Vann's forty grand in gold dust, and returned the map to their rightful owners. After receiving his reward, he moved up to Chicago as a very rich black man. And that's how the map made it back into the Golden Horse and deposited in the tunnel in 1838."

"Incredible," exclaimed Black. "Now I see your personal motivation."

Morgan smiled, pleased with herself. "Of course I never knew the Stand Watie and John Ross connection to it with the waybill and knife until your father then filled me in."

Black flinched. "My father?"

"Yes. Alex introduced me to Tommy down in Savannah because of my book research on James Vann. Your father sure is a talker," she smiled. "Liked to reminisce of the many what-ifs. But your father also spoke of *you*. And that's the other reason why I contacted you today."

Morgan wagged a finger at him. "Because I know damn well you two hate each other with a passion. So when your name was associated with the McPherson hat in today's news, I put two and two together. You see, I've been glued to the news ever since it was stolen on Sunday wondering if either one of you Watie men may have had a hand in its theft. And then the note and flowers arrive from Alex and it's your name that pops up in the news. And look who bites on my phone call. Why, it's Congressman Black."

"You're sly, I've gotta hand it to you," Black said, rising out of the chair as his ass wound started to flare. "What do you want out of this?"

"All I want is to get credit for the discovery of the tunnel and what's deposited inside the vaults. You, of all people, don't need the gold. But you can certainly have the Golden Horse and whatever's inside of it—that *Map of Thieves*. I want nothing to do with it. People tend to get killed over it. You see I'm all about the short term gain. You, I imagine, are all about the long term. Just think what you can do with the power that map holds, Congressman. All the people you could *influence*. Why, I wouldn't even rule out a presidential run in your future. Hell, I wouldn't even mind an ambassadorship overseas in a tropical climate in order to keep my mouth shut." She winked at him. "As one of your key fundraisers, of course."

This hot smart bitch certainly was persuasive enough but Black was no pushover. He knew she was stroking him. And he liked it well enough. He extended his hands palms up, playing coy. "I could do a helluva lot better than the retarded amateur in office now. So, that's the deal then? You lead me to the tunnel. You get what's inside and credit. I get the Golden Horse and the mining map. That's it?"

Morgan smiled something evil. "Well, I do have one extra favor to ask, since you have the means and the muscle you brought with you." She nodded to the closed door.

"What's that?"

"Make Alex Vann disappear for good."

"Oh, I'll do that alright. Tununda and Hart, too. And anyone else who stands in my way."

"Excellent."

"So it seems both our needs are met then?" Black asked.

Morgan nodded.

"Sorry, but I'm going to require some down payment from you," Black said, undressing her slowly with his eyes.

She knew what he wanted. Knew his reputation. She even dressed for it. Exploited it. No matter how much it disgusted her she knew she had to whore herself out to the fat bastard to get what she wanted. She approached Black aggressively, invaded his space, and placed a slender hand on his chest. She moved it slowly downward over his enormous belly until she found his growing crotch.

A slight squeeze and Black's heart almost leaped out of his chest. No need for Viagra this time, he thought. "I guess you know what I want."

Morgan stared into his eyes and in a low teasing voice said, "Don't you worry, Congressman. I'll suck and fuck you short of a heart attack."

With that she dropped to her knees and got down to business.

26

THEY APPROACHED THE ETOWAH RIVER FROM THE south among the rolling foothills that started the Appalachian Mountain chain. Heading out from Vann's Dahlonega hideaway in two vehicles—Tommy, Becky, and Alex leading in his black Jeep Rubicon and Jake and Rae following in Tommy's red Chevy truck—they caught Route 400 South for ten miles. Then west onto Matt Highway/Hightower Road they traveled several more miles until they found East Cherokee Drive, where they wound their way north toward the objective.

Dotting the lush landscape up East Cherokee Drive were beautiful estate homes, some with fenced equestrian areas. These large residences were fast becoming the norm as wealthy Atlantans continued to expand north with urban sprawl from the state capital. As the road descended toward the Etowah River, other homes ranged from well-kept, mid-sized country cottages to low income trailers amid this heavily wooded section of Cherokee County. The last few miles coming from the south to this particular, dove-shaped bend in the river, saw no residences at all. The main reason was the large Waste Management landfill and the constant rumble of trash-hauling tractor trailer traffic up and down the curvy country road.

Dropping further in elevation the closer they came to the river and its valley, Tommy pointed out to Alex a large hill up on their left. Somewhere at the top of that densely wooded summit was the location of the Cherokee Tunnel according to their map findings. The hill was one of the tallest in the area, offering views in all directions for many miles. Just beyond it, out of sight from a bend, sat the Etowah River where the road continued across on a high concrete bridge. They wouldn't be going that far, however, as Tommy excitedly wanted Alex to hang a left into the woods just before the bend.

Waiting for a large trash truck to pass them by in the opposite direction, both the Jeep and the Chevy turned left and entered an almost hidden, weed-filled, dirt road. The entrance was squeezed between an embankment and the encroaching forest. Just up that narrow road and out of view from the main drive, the vehicles came to a sudden halt at a barely visible gate blocking their route.

Their stop at the gate also gave a bird-like tracking drone, secretly flying above them, a chance to orient itself and re-acquire them after breaking contact when the two cars entered the woods.

Alex and Jake exited their respective vehicles, donned gloves and approached the fence through waist high grass, smothering weeds, and bushes with thorns that nipped and tore at their clothes. Fortunately, Alex had directed their group to dress properly for the occasion with long sleeve shirts, rugged cargo pants, hiking boots, hats, and thin mechanic's gloves.

The afternoon light waned and the purplish sky began graying with large cumulus-type clouds rising on the western horizon. Temperatures were in the upper eighties with high humidity as the trees around swayed from a warm, light breeze. Alex's earlier warning of approaching thunderstorms was soon to become reality as his smartphone weather app chimed with a notification a tornado watch was in effect for northwest Georgia counties.

Reaching the gate, Alex looked up and caught a glimpse of a large bird passing overhead before disappearing above the trees. A glint of sunlight reflected off the bird and he frowned, thinking it unusual. Jake cracked him on the arm, interrupting his train of thought.

"This place has been abandoned," Jake remarked. "For a long time."

The rusty, old wooden gate was enclosed within barbed wire fencing that ran well into the woods on each side of it. An old padlock and chain held it in place. Several faded "No Trespassing" signs hung from a post amid the weeds. Another torn sign showed a spray painted name in black of the property owner, Jacob Steiner, and an accompanying phone number. Up past the gate they could hardly make out that the road even existed since the undergrowth was so thick. Mother Nature had reclaimed the land. If not for tall, older growth trees draped over the gap, forming an eerily shadowed tunnel, the road would have never been noticed by passers-by.

"What do you want to do?" Alex asked. "This is the only access in."

"Well, try the phone number for the hell of it," Jake pointed toward the sign. "Never hurts to ask permission first."

Alex dialed the phone number on the sign and immediately got a loud, repetitive dial tone alert that the number no longer existed. "Number's dead. Gotta Plan B?"

"Sure do," Jake smiled. "We trespass."

▼

Remotely controlled by one of The Gladii contractors about three miles away in their Mercedez-Benz SUV, the bird-sized surveillance drone flapped its reflective robotic wings and dove in altitude to about 200 feet. The solar-powered, remotely piloted aircraft, called a Robo-Raven, then zig-zagged across the sky. A live video feed caught its targets on camera again just under cover of the trees at the entrance onto the property. Two men with hats stood outside of a gate.

Barely discernible in air from an actual bird, Robo-Raven mimicked the aerobatic flight maneuvers of a real bird. Independent, digitally controlled wing flaps allowed it to roll and flip as needed. Its flight was so realistic that even hawks and eagles—birds of prey—had attacked it on occasion.

Engineered and manufactured at the University of Maryland's Robotics Center specifically for the U.S. Army back in 2013, this particular Robo-Raven model fell into The Gladii's hands and was reconfigured for their type of highly deceptive, silent, illegal surveillance operations—mostly against U.S. citizens.

Robo-Raven's video feed was instantly relayed to a remote control laptop operated by one of the agency's bodyguards. He directed their team to pull into the small Dwight Terry Park just a mile or so up East Cherokee Drive where they waited for their targets to make the next move. The park held two little-league baseball fields and a playground. It was empty. Not a car in the parking lot. Their two vehicles parked behind a row of large trees in the corner of the lot hidden from the main road.

Pulling up next to their Mercedez, was Tom Black driving his two-seater luxury Camaro convertible. The top was up and air-conditioning was blasting from the vents.

Beside him was Professor Marissa Morgan, who sat patiently having already played out her major contribution. Now, as she crossed her legs and smoothed her hiking pants, she just needed to stay the hell out of the way of all these testosterone-filled brutes. After their fling in her office, she made a quick stop at her nearby home to change into more appropriate clothes, then led Black and his men to the location of Alex Vann's mountain house. The security unit parked nearby and had flown the drone up Vann's long driveway. They luckily spotted their five adversaries loading supplies into an older model red pick-up truck and a newer model black Jeep.

Recognizable in the drone's hi-def camera feed, were Watie, Tununda, Hart, Vann, and a large-set black woman assumed to be the old man's nurse. For the last half hour they had then tracked the two vehicles with the drone as their targets traveled south from Dahlonega.

Black powered down his window and leaned out with an elbow, ready to consult with the lead operator in the Mercedez. Realizing where they were on his Camaro's dashboard GPS navigational system, he had become visibly agitated.

One of the bodyguards stepped out of the Mercedez and provided protection. He faced away from the Camaro and scanned the empty youth ballfields. The contractor-in-charge of the security unit then stepped out, too. He was an overpowering figure as he approached Black's window to speak to his client.

Harry Smithson hailed from a career in the British Special Air Service or SAS, the United Kingdom's elite commando force where he first saw combat in the 1982 Falklands War between Great Britain and Argentina.

· 316 ·

He liked to brag the SAS were even better than the U.S. Navy SEALs. Well into his fifties now, the imposing man stood six foot, four inches but still had the barrel-chested built of the aggressive rugby player he once was in his early twenties. Bald and bull-head with no neck, he wore a thick salt and pepper walrus-style mustache on his butt-ugly face. After almost twenty years in the military, he retired as a major and immediately went into contract work in the States. He was one of the tough-as-nails veteran combat leaders The Gladii so coveted for their global customer base.

Ten years with the agency, amid postings all over the world, and he was pulling in a couple hundred thousand a year on salary alone. His side jobs of assassinations and kidnappings drew even more money. And now, with his new client Tom Black promising enormous sums of cold hard cash—off the books from his agency—for their current clandestine mission, the former SAS commando was quite happy indeed to be back on another hunt for the most elusive creature out there.

Man.

And based on Tununda and Vann's backgrounds, from what his ex-girlfriend and the lone American in his unit had told him, they would be up against two of the best combat vets the U.S. Army had to offer.

Smithson stood outside Black's Camaro, hands on hips. The high heat and humidity already had caused sweat to bead on his dome. He spoke quickly in a thick British accent. "We lost connection to Google Earth on our drone laptop. The SUV's nav system crapped out on us, too. And our phones have no signal either. How's yours?"

"The Camaro's phone is down and I haven't had service on my cell either since Dahlonega," said Black, looking up. "Also, I lost the on-board nav system. We must have entered a dead zone for satellites."

Morgan checked her cell phone, too, and shook her head. "No service."

"Good news is we still have a live radio aerial feed on where they are," Smithson said. "Looks like your mates drove into the woods on the left about a mile and a half down the road just before the bridge crossing."

Black's eyelid twitched uncontrollably. He knew this nightmarish location from his teens, but had never been back after his sister's death. *Was the tunnel connected to her death somehow?*

Smithson stroked his mustache. "We've detected a cut through the woods that indicates an old road. It ends in some flat fields along the river. But to the north is a good sized hill with what looks like cliffs along that portion of the river. Any idea where they're headed? Do you know who's property this is? Are we going to come across any civilians once we move in and do our business?"

Black tried to clear the lump in his throat. Memories raced back. His eyelid twitched faster. Up on that hill was the beginning of the end for his relationship with his father so many years ago. It was the root of the evil he knew he had embraced ever since. Sure he was stoned on pot at the time, but he was coherent enough to see Cathy was pushed off the cliff from behind.

Though no one else was around.

Black remembered that day clearly. That image of his sister's limp and unnaturally twisted body half on a rock, head submerged in the water after she fell. It had been burned in his memory forever. He screamed for his father rather than climbing down to try and rescue her, even though he saw movement in her legs. He was paralyzed with fear. Too shocked. Too high on dope to act. He let her drown upside down.

When his father finally arrived and saw his daughter below, she had just slipped under the water's surface and the current carried her downstream. His father slapped Black across the face for doing nothing to save her, when it was possible for him to climb down the rocky cliff at a less dangerous section. And that's when the bag of weed fell out of his pocket. The old man immediately blamed him for her death, but Black blurted out she had jumped on her own—suicide.

After hearing that unspeakable accusation, his father went ballistic on him. He chased his son along the cliff's edge up to the summit and around several piles of white, quartz rocks. His father had even picked up one of the stones and threw it a him, catching him in the shoulder and knocking him down. Then the punches flew. They fought each other until Black escaped and ran all the way back downhill through the woods and into the farmer's grassy, cattle-grazing fields.

When his exhausted father caught up and tackled him and finally saw all the blood flowing from his son's broken nose, only then did he back off, realizing the horror of all that had happened. Black remembered the last vestiges of his Daddy as a crying, broken man dropping to his knees, screaming and howling like a dying wolf in the middle of the windswept, green grass. He did however, help him retrieve Cathy's body as it floated down river to where they were.

Not surprisingly, he had a profound lack of remorse that his sister had really died. He didn't shed a tear at her funeral. She was the spoiled younger brat that had always gotten her way, while so much was expected of him. Maybe that's why he never tried to rescue her, he thought. He remembered vividly how thrilled he was as the only child left to receive all the attention, along with the family business and inheritance, one day.

But that attention and coddling never came.

Four years of cold paternal neglect and deep morbid feelings of insecurity, inferiority, and humiliation is what followed. It came during his college years at the University of Georgia in Athens. His mother even shunned him. Except for his summer warehouse job, he stayed away from Savannah as much as he could, and they in turn, didn't even attend his graduation. His parents had wanted him on his own and out of their lives.

Those years had sent Black on a path to reverse the negative image of who he was by choosing a course in life to achieve wealth and power by any means. Every chance he could get, he stuck it to the old man that had caused him so much personal pain and animosity. This included lying about and taking credit for running his family's successful logging business on some puff piece for the college newspaper.

He had developed an extreme hatred for his own Watie family history and all things associated with their military service, as well as anything with Cherokee heritage.

And then came years of stealing precious artifacts from his father's coveted ancestor room.

When his father finally caught his son the thief, he disowned from the family and the will.

"Congressman Black?" Smithson growled, leaning down to the Camaro's open driver's side window. "You with us?"

Black snapped out of his stupor. "They're going to head uphill to the cliff overlooking the river. That place, uh, has profound significance to my father. His daughter—my sister—was, uh, killed up there. She fell off the cliff."

Smithson's mustache stroking stopped. Morgan's lips parted. The bodyguard glanced back at the Congressman for a split second.

"I see," Smithson said. "Anyone you know of who lives on this land? Satellite imagery showed no visible structures before we lost the feed. And our drone doesn't see anything manmade either."

"I remembered an old farmhouse in the woods somewhere," Black replied, shrugging his shoulders. "God knows if it's even still standing. That was 1967."

"Well, I'm hoping no one lives there," Smithson said. "Now I just gotta pull a bloody plan out of my arse on how we're going to infiltrate the property. To make matters worse we've got thunderstorms approaching from the northwest with a possible tornado, too. Check your car radio."

▼

Alex acted fast. Making his way back to the rear of his Jeep, he extracted a bolt cutter and wasted no time in snipping the rust-weakened padlock. Jake pulled the chain off and yanked heavily on the old gate through the weeds to get it open far enough. Alex drove his Jeep up; and Rae followed in the truck, while Jake shut the gate behind them and re-secured the padlock and chain to look as if nothing was touched.

They were in.

As Jake walked back to the truck to rejoin Rae, a bright glint above in the air caught his eye and he looked up in time to see a large bird flap its wings and fly by before disappearing in the trees overhead. Several squawking black birds—ravens or crows as best he could tell—gave chase. A mosquito then bit him on the cheek. He squished it and hopped back in the pick-up truck.

The two vehicles slowly drove less than a quarter of a mile down a rut-filled road until they encountered a fork. The left fork of the road, bending southwest and heading further downhill, seemed clear, while the right was more or less a path that headed uphill. Fifty feet up the path a large, rotted oak tree was felled blocking the way. Three ravens sat on top of one of the twisted dead branches that formed the barrier. They cackled wildly at the new visitors before flying off.

Alex shouted back to Jake and Rae that they needed to park there at the fork and head up the path on foot.

Everyone got out and gathered around the two vehicles as Jake and Alex discussed plans. A loud chorus of rattle-like hissing and rhythmic chirping from cicadas and katydids erupted all around them as the grasshopper-type insects started communicating with each other. Tommy wasn't listening though. He kept looking behind him, off the dirt road, into the woods to the south. Finally he pointed.

"There! Steiner's farmhouse," he shouted. "I knew it was around here somewhere near this fork."

The group peered into the shadowed woods and at first only saw a lush, dark green curtain of kudzu weeds reaching up to great heights. Upon closer inspection, the form of a two-story farmhouse took shape in the kudzu camouflage. It looked like something from the 1800s it was so warped. The rusted, tin roof was partially caved-in with an old tree fallen on top, its weed-infested branches draped like a green death veil. Thick vines and vegetation grew out of the shattered windows. The dilapidated wood structure leaned to one side and looked highly unstable.

"I guess the Steiner's aren't home," said Jake.

"God, that place gives me the willies," Becky said, wrapping her arms about her chest.

Rae stepped forward through the brush to get a closer look. There seemed no way in. Where the front door should have been a sapling tree grew right out from the inside open hole. Inspecting the rest of the façade, she shook her head. Glancing up through a second story window she thought she saw something move in the deep shadows. A figure. She stumbled backward, tripped, and fell on her butt.

"Something's up there," she whispered in fear, pointing to the window. Just then a large raven tore through the weeds surrounding the window frame and jumped into the air flapping its wings. Four more ravens followed, darting low over the group who ducked for cover.

"Jesus Christ Almighty!" shouted Becky, as she hid behind the Jeep.

Alex and Tommy stood their ground defiantly.

The birds flew away disappearing over the trees, laughing at the rude, surprise welcome they gave their intruding guests.

"Alex, Tommy?" Jake asked after nearly pissing his pants. "Think we need to go in and check it out?"

"Waste of time, those fucking birds," replied Alex. "They ain't what you think they are, Jake. When we see You Know Who, we'll know."

"Besides," added Tommy, "That place is likely to collapse on us. We've gotta storm coming, too."

Alex checked his smartphone to get an update but there was no connection. "Phone's dead."

"Mine too," Becky said, holding hers in her hand.

Jake and Rae's phones also had lost all connection.

They were in an apparent dead zone between cell towers.

They quickly gathered their backpacks and weapons and had thoroughly applied insect repellent on their exposed skin. It was decided that Tommy and Becky should stay at the fork with Rae keeping guard. She would have one of their two-way, handheld radios while Jake and Alex would hit the path up the hill and recon the supposed location of the tunnel entrance. If there were no obstacles and they did happen to find the actual entrance, they would radio back to Rae to lead the old man and his nurse up. They were mindful of the approaching storm and knew they had just a couple of hours or so before it would hit. The good news was the top of the hill was a mere quarter of a mile away up through the woods.

Within minutes, Jake and Alex had skirted through the forest around the old downed oak and were hiking up the overgrown, narrow path toward the summit. As the skies grew darker, the woods began to quiet except for the increased wind ruffling the leaves and the several ravens circling overhead above the canopy of trees. Their cackling sounded like old women laughing.

"Radio check. Come in, Rae. Over." Jake keyed on his two-way radio once they lost view of the two vehicles.

"I'm here. Read you loud and clear. Over." Rae radioed back with some slight static. "Be careful up there and keep an eye on the weather."

"Copy that. Out."

Alex pulled a small glass vial from a pocket, popped the little cork off, and downed the contents with a grimace. He uttered a Cherokee phrase under his breath, cringed, and shook his head as the liquid hit bottom.

"Whaddya got there?" Jake asked kiddingly. "Shot of booze?"

"Shot of ancient black *ooze* to be exact," Alex said in all seriousness. "This shit allows me to see those witches in visible form. Has hallucinatory effects, but gets the job done."

Not questioning him, Jake remained quiet allowing Alex to walk point about fifteen feet ahead. Alex's head swiveled slowly to the left and right, and up and down. He was dressed in tan, multi-pocket law enforcement style pants and a long sleeve black shirt with a matching black boonie hat over his ponytailed hair. A black, fully-filled, water hydration backpack stuffed with tools, supplies, extra ammo, food, and medicine man essentials was strapped on his back. A holstered Glock 9mm side-arm with a silenced barrel was strapped on his right thigh.

On his left hip was his fixed-blade knife. Scanning in front of him he held a compact, recurve crossbow with a thermal imaging scope mounted on top, and a rail flashlight mounted on the side. It was painted a tactical matte black for stealth.

A bolt was already cocked and in the ready-to-fire position, but on safety. The tip of the bolt was replaced with one of Alex's custom-designed, razor blade heads made of pure silver. These bolts were specific to his duties as a witch killer should any Raven Mockers be present. A quiver of four more silver-tipped bolts was mounted parallel on the crossbow and within easy reach. Vann was a close-quarters, stealthy, killing machine ready to take on anything Cherokee black magic could throw at him.

Jake was dressed similarly, except for a black baseball cap turned backwards that Alex had given him. He carried the two weapons from the dead Bluff Boyz: the suppressed .45 pistol with its extended magazine and the suppressed submachine gun. Alex had also loaned him a .38 revolver strapped in a concealed ankle holster as back-up. He had already returned to Tommy his Luger for his own protection down at the fork. Lastly, Jake carried the Watie "Arkansas toothpick" in its sheath strapped to his belt.

The other item he donned was especially important. It would record tonight's exploration for history's sake—and for a possible new episode on *Battlefield Investigators*. Jake had inquired with Alex if he had any video cameras before they left his home, and he was quite surprised at what the Delta Force operative produced.

Clipped to the chest strap of his backpack, was the world's smallest recording device: The Micro Camera HD. It was a mere two inches long by just over an inch wide and recorded sound and video in high definition for up to three hours with its 6 GB card. Its screen was even date and time embedded for accuracy. Jake turned the device on.

After several minutes the weed clogged path seemed to be coming to an end as a dark wall of forest loomed in front of them. A silent, closed-fist hand signal from Alex stopped Jake in his tracks. Alex pointed up to a tree straight ahead.

Hanging from moldy, old rope off a low branch about ten feet up, was what looked like some kind of blackened figurine made of sticks. There were seven sticks with grass bundled around each end. It was a simple design of long twigs bound together to form the shape of a human, but with what looked like an extra pair of arms.

Alex looked back at Jake and whispered, "Not good, bro. It's a Raven Mocker warning to stay the fuck out. I've seen them in North Carolina, too, on a job I did. No doubt about it."

Jake stared at the figure as mosquitoes buzzed around his face. He then noticed movement in the shadows about five feet above it. Sitting on a branch was one of the largest ravens he had ever seen. It cocked its head slightly, opened its beak and looked down at the intruders. Jake slowly aimed his submachine gun at the bird.

Alex spun back around, made eye contact with the beast and raised his crossbow, flicking the safety off. The big silent bird unfurled its wide wings, bent its legs, and was ready to fly off. In the blink of an eye, Alex pulled the trigger to let loose one of his silver bolts.

The bolt shot direct through the raven's breast and then sliced through one of its wings, protruding out the other side of its body three quarters up the bolt's shaft. At 380 feet per second the bolt would have penetrated clean through if not for the wing. The raven gurgled and cackled loudly, screaming in agony, then fell to the ground in a heap of black feathers.

Alex was upon it instantly, his knife already drawn. Grasping its still-twitching head in one hand, he severed it from its body. The beak opened up several more times in a spasm of death before the raven's red eyes bulged out. Alex placed a foot on the wing and body and pulled the bolt clean through to use again.

Before Jake could even utter a word, Alex had already placed his foot through the crossbow foot stirrup and was re-cocking it by hand. It took incredible strength but once the string was cocked he placed the bloody arrow back in and flipped the safety on.

"Have I mentioned that I hate ravens?" the Delta op asked Jake in jest.

"I take it you're not a member of PETA then?" Jake replied with a grin. He then glanced back up at the stick man figure. The extra set of arms meant it could fly, he now realized. His radio squawked.

"Jake, come in," Rae demanded over static. "SITREP. We heard a scream."

"We're good," Jake responded to her demand for a "situation report." "Alex just bagged a raven warning us to stay the hell away. Over."

"Roger that, okay," she said with relief in her voice. "We've got several of them circling us down here, too. Over."

Alex grabbed the radio from Jake. "They're harmless. Just messing with your mind is all. Keep Tommy calm, okay? Over."

A pause and then Tommy's voice came on the radio. "Copy that. I'm alright, son. You just keep going and find that tunnel."

"Will do, Old Man! Out." Alex replied with a smile.

Tommy radioed back a static filled comforting laugh.

27

S MITHSON HAD BEEN DROPPED OFF WITH TWO OF
his men just before the road entrance onto Steiner's property. They
made a quick dash into the woods before another trash carrier came up the
road and spotted them. The remaining bodyguard was sent back to Dwight
Terry Park to protect Black and Morgan and to control the Robo-Raven.

Smithson's hasty plan was to head west through the woods until they
hit the Etowah River, then follow it until they reached the lowland grassy
fields where they would then strike due north up the hill back into the
woods to flank their enemy. He glanced at a hand drawn map he made for
himself that roughly outlined their strike route. It included terrain features
he'd seen before their Google Earth connection was lost.

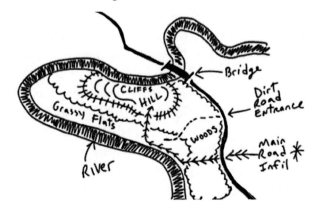

Smithson's orders from Black were to observe and track first. Make no contact. The mission objective was to allow Tununda's team to find the entrance to an apparent tunnel. Once the tunnel was confirmed, only then was he allowed to engage and terminate the opposition.

Except for the old man.

Black had more sinister plans for his father.

The trio had penetrated the woods but were immediately stopped by a twenty foot wall of deadfall logs and branches covered in a deep green veil of kudzu weed. Opting not to scale the tangled barrier, they instead diverted south until they found a gap through a rusted, barbed wire livestock fence that had been long since toppled over. Making up lost time, they experienced sparse ground cover of dead leaves and broken branches. Their biggest challenge was the heat, humidity, and the relentless buzzing and biting of flies, gnats, and mosquitoes. They had come completely unprepared with no insect repellent.

Smithson, call sign Wolf One, carried an assault rifle with a suppressor barrel attachment. Wolf Two wielded a military grade shotgun, while the third operative, Wolf Three, held a silenced sniper rifle with a powerful, night vision infrared scope. Each man also carried a sidearm. Bulletproof vests rounded out their camouflage attire. When darkness fell they were even prepared with night vision goggles.

Smithson keyed his radio headset mic to Wolf Four, the Robo-Raven operative back at the park. "Wolf One to Wolf Four. Any sign of the targets yet? Over."

"Affirmative, Wolf One. They were last seen heading up a path toward the ridge. But trees are too thick to maintain visual contact," radioed back the operative in his own headset. He was in the front seat of the company Mercedez controlling the Robo-Raven from a remote control unit while Black and Morgan remained holed up in the Congressman's Camaro.

Wolf Four's laptop sat on the front passenger seat displaying video from the drone. The video suddenly shuddered and the drone dropped in altitude. A black shadow passed over the screen and it momentarily turned to static. Wolf Four regained the drone's controls and steadied the flight. The screen flickered back on catching a large, dark bird on camera. The drone had been attacked by a real raven.

"The drone just got nailed by a big raven," added Wolf Four. "Sustained some damage. Almost lost her. Over."

"Copy. What about the others? Have they left their position? Over."

Smithson's transmission was experiencing interference. Wolf Four could hardly hear him. "You're breaking up. Repeat last. Over."

After making out Wolf One's repeat communication, he answered, "Negative. Still at the fork. All three are milling about. Over."

"Roger. Keep the bird on them." More static jumbled his words. "Let us know if they move. We're about to make it out of the woods and come up on the river. Wolf One out."

Wolf Four immediately programmed the drone on an automatic orbit above the targets at the fork but a troubled frown appeared on his brow.

Sebastian Schroeder, a former U.S. Army Ranger with a decorated combat history, was the only member of the unit that was from America. The other two men under Smithson were former Israeli special forces soldiers. Both were certainly qualified to fly the Robo-Raven. Schroeder suspected Smithson had kept him back from the infil precisely because he *was* former U.S. Army. And knowing both Tununda and Vann were both Army heroes who also went through Ranger school, he might waver in their operation.

Smithson would have been correct.

Schroeder initially had jumped at the extra money when Smithson proposed the job to his team after their client Tom Black changed their responsibilities from a simple protection mission to a termination op. It never bothered him that he'd be taking someone down. He'd been involved in "mission creep" before with Smithson and The Gladii and he was damn good at it—a very reliable killer.

He hadn't known the targets that the Congressman wanted gone nor what he was seeking up in the woods. Only when he was informed that Army Lieutenant Colonel Robert "Jake" Tununda and an Army Delta Force operative named Alex Vann were the targets, did his usually suppressed good conscience decide to wake up.

These men were Army rock stars. Real bad-asses. He knew both of them. Not personally, but by their actions in battle. Schroeder worked indirectly with Tununda in Afghanistan when the Rangers would use the 10th Mountain Division as a quick reaction force in case they got in a jam. Tununda was a combat legend with the Mountaineers, and a ruthless one at that based on what he did at the Mazar-i-Sharif prison during the invasion of Afghanistan. More importantly, his reputation as a soldier's officer was highly respected. Tununda went through Ranger school himself, loved the men he led, and they loved him back. Even on his new television show Schroeder could tell how much Tununda admired the U.S. Army and its storied history. The guy was charismatic and hard not to like.

Master Sergeant Alex Vann he had known from reputation only, too. In their world of special forces, the elite warriors' names were secretly whispered, and Vann's was one that crossed many lips. Also starting out in the Rangers, Vann was recruited into Delta Force. His legend grew in Iraq under multiple deployments and on several occasions working directly with Schroeder's own former Ranger unit. Vann's unwavering devotion to fighting America's enemies in the darkest corners of the earth was something most envied by the usually selfish operator Schroeder.

Both Native American men—these true American patriots—were the quintessential brother-in-arms Schroeder simply could not have any hand in killing. The bond and camaraderie of being a Ranger was too strong. He wasn't morally bankrupt enough to take these guys out for any amount of money. And especially for a congressman with a known reputation as a fat, lazy, greedy, sexist motherfucker who cared nothing for his country, and especially loathed the military in his many public statements since becoming a Democrat.

Fuck Tom Black, thought Schroeder, his inner voice screaming at him. He finally realized he needed to compromise the mission and somehow get word to Tununda, Vann, and their friends that they were about to be eliminated. He needed to give them a fighting chance. But how?

As he watched the video feed from the drone circling above the targets, he realized Robo-Raven, and the many real ravens that had been attracted to it, was his answer.

28

S ERGEANT D'ARATA SAT STRAPPED IN NEXT TO THE loadmaster in the rear cargo bay of one of the Air Force's new C-130J Super Hercules workhorse lift aircraft. He wore a flight jacket to keep warm and played the addictive Candy Crush puzzle game on his smartphone to while away the flight time. He was somewhere over central Georgia near Macon and heading due south trying to catch his prey.

He had gone with his gut, plus a valuable tip from Tununda the night before, when he had received McPherson's hat from him—no questions asked. While the media went berserk all day long on some gang thug named Angel Hernandez being the West Point Museum thief, D'Arata didn't veer far from the Army's original suspect; Phoenix. Tonight, he was sure he'd finally nail their man and recover the stolen trophies.

Tununda's tip was to follow Black's chief of staff, Jaconious Johnson. With no specifics on where he got his information, and knowing better than to ask, Tununda told him that it was Johnson who hired the West Point thief and was doing Black's bidding in order to insulate the Congressman.

D'Arata had started on Johnson's trail after the head staffer left his luxury midtown Atlantic Station condo late that afternoon. He went straight to Black's congressional district office in the heart of the Bluff.

Literally crossing the tracks and entering the forbidden zone west of Atlanta's luxury high rises, D'Arata couldn't help but be transported back to some of the most run down Third World ghettos he had seen on his many overseas deployments. Less than a half mile from Georgia Institute of Technology, one of the finest engineering schools in the United States, the terrain changed to garbage-strewn, weed-infested, pot-holed streets lined with vacant houses, some burned to the ground. The homes that did manage to survive all had burglar bars in their windows.

Black's office was located at the abandoned English Avenue Elementary School. His was the sole tenant of the once beautiful, sprawling, 1910 three-story, brick public school house that had since succumbed to the all-too-familiar boarded up windows, spray painted gang graffiti, and a surrounding chained linked fence topped with concertina wire.

In the crumbled asphalt parking lot sat several media vans and a gathering of local news reporters who immediately accosted Johnson for news about Tom Black. After receiving a bland, boilerplate statement outside the front door, the media scattered like rats looking for more cheese. Johnson's official business over, he hit the road and D'Arata followed again.

Just a few streets south, Johnson had a very curious meeting that ultimately sent D'Arata on another tangent. After parking at a corner store called Yaril Grocery, Johnson strode across the street toward a gathering of young black men who greeted him with familiarity. They were dressed in typical street attire of baggy shorts and t-shirts and drank alcohol from paper bags while smoking blunts; cigars hollowed out and filled with marijuana. They stood in front of a old, massive, two-story, peaked stone structure.

At the corner of Brawley Drive and Alexander Boulevard stood the ruins of the old Saint Mark African Methodist Episcopal Church. All that remained were its four, thick stone walls. There was no roof. The windows were either smashed out or boarded up. Where rows of pews once welcomed worshippers, now overgrown weeds, vines, and saplings had since taken over. One tree even grew right through an open window frame as a reminder of how many years the church sat in neglect. D'Arata thought the church belonged in a bombed out European town during World War II instead.

The sergeant parked and discreetly watched from a distance through his binoculars and tinted windows. Soon Johnson broke from the group with another black man, this one nicely dressed, bald, and sporting double diamond earrings and eyes with long lashes. And that was D'Arata's epiphany.

For he had noticed this same man enter Le Maison Rouge the night before when monitoring Black's party. Right before Phoenix had arrived.

To meet with Johnson, the very next day, was interesting indeed. Both men struck a serious demeanor and walked from the crowd to talk in private around the corner. Each man checked his watch—something was up. An envelope was passed from Johnson to his counterpart and the man departed. At that moment, D'Arata made his decision to risk breaking Johnson's trail to pursue the new lead. It was a decision that soon paid dividends.

Following Baldy to his parked luxury sedan just down the street, the tail was on. Up I-85 and into Buckhead some fifteen minutes later, Baldy turned into one of Atlanta's finest hotels; the Ritz-Carlton.

A well-dressed, thirty-something, white male donning a ball cap and sunglasses entered his waiting vehicle outside the lobby entrance. The man also carried a backpack. He had a striking resemblance to the same subject caught on the McDonalds security camera exiting the West Point Inn & Suites in Highland Falls, New York, just after the museum theft.

D'Arata's tail continued for another four miles north to Dekalb-Peachtree Airport, a private airfield catering to Atlanta's corporate and wealthy elite. By that time he had called local law enforcement with the tag number of the vehicle he was following. Dispatch returned with the address and name it was registered under: a one Antoine LaMar of 792 Donald Lee Hollowell Parkway. A Google search on D'Arata's smartphone revealed that LaMar's address was also the law office of attorney Antoine LaMar & Associates, LLP. The guy was a lawyer who resided in the Bluff, Tom Black's adopted neighborhood. The dots were connecting.

The target car entered Flightway Drive on the north of the airfield and then, at the end of the road, turned into one of several private flight clubs. LaMar and Phoenix strutted confidently inside. D'Arata kept his distance and monitored the club with binoculars. Twenty minutes crept by.

His smartphone received a FOX News alert: *Angel Has Fallen*.

D'Arata tapped the alert and was redirected to his web browser for the news story. It read:

Atlanta FOX News correspondent Todd Ashton reports that the lead suspect in the West Point Museum theft, a gang enforcer by the name of Alejandro "Angel" Hernandez, has been shot and killed by a fugitive task force during a raid this afternoon. According to a high-ranking law enforcement source, an anonymous tip took the FBI-led task force to a remote drug house in northeast Atlanta where they engaged the suspect in a firefight during their initial breach and search. Hernandez was subsequently gunned down in a hail of bullets after allegedly firing on officers first. One officer was wounded during the exchange and was transported to the hospital where he is listed in stable condition. Hernandez was also a suspect in yesterday's firebombing of a local residence believed to be a meth lab where another gang member died in the blaze. The search continues however, for missing Freddy Peña, the fourteen year-old allegedly kidnapped by Angel just before the deadly arson attack. More on this story tonight as it develops . . .

"It's not him," D'Arata muttered to himself shaking his head, trying to overcome the confusion of the news report.

A minute later, LaMar exited the hangar and made for his sedan, minus the man he had picked up at the hotel.

Staying put, D'Arata watched LaMar drive off. Soon after, the club's hangar doors opened and a Cessna Turbo Skylane 4-passenger aircraft taxied out. D'Arata could see only two people in the small plane's interior. Through his binoculars, the pilot looked to be an older white man in his sixties. The other person sitting next to him he believed to be the real thief. D'Arata marked down the plane's "N" ID number and other distinguishing features. He was able to snap several photos with his camera before the flight departed the field and flew due south.

At the same time, a call had come in from Tununda asking him to put eyes on Black, but D'Arata denied the request saying he was following the main suspect. He entered the flight club, flashed his badge, and asked the manager about the Skylane, its pilot, and passenger. At first the manager demanded a search warrant, but after D'Arata explained the gravity of the situation and possible links to the West Point Museum theft, the manager opened up and revealed that the pilot didn't even know who the passenger was, a name was never given, that he was doing a favor for a friend.

And that friend, D'Arata learned, was Tom Black.

The manager excused himself to the restroom on purpose, leaving his flight plan book open for anyone to read should they so choose. Seconds later D'Arata had found the Skylane pilot's flight plan.

Destination: Homestead General Aviation Airport in south Florida.

He made immediate emergency arrangements to get a flight out of Atlanta and found himself at Dobbins Air Force Base twenty miles west in Marietta. Within the hour he managed to finagle his way onto a C-130J Air Force transport plane headed down to Homestead Air Force Base in an effort to head off the thief's escape flight. Accompanying him was an Air Force special investigations officer who would coordinate with air assets and ground security forces at Homestead to eventually intercept the private flight in the air, redirect it to the closest military air field, and escort it down onto the runway where the plane and its occupants would be detained once on the ground.

Upon arrival D'Arata would give Phoenix a sizzling welcome that would burn his wings for good.

Some more taps on his puzzle game and D'Arata lost all interest. He yawned widely and is eyes slowly drooped shut. Within minutes, he was snoring loudly, in tune with the roar of the aircraft's engine.

▼

Reverse slope
Steiner property

Caught in a slight drizzle, Smithson and his two cohorts made it across the grassy, wind swept fields and into the woods. They hit the reverse slope of the ridge and headed north up the easy, gradual rise. Lightning, thunder, and heavy winds soon slammed into them as the fast moving storm gained power overhead. Knowing he would soon intercept his prey, Smithson slowed down and gave a hand signal to each of the former Israeli Defense Force soldiers to stop.

Protected from the woods somewhat he paused to reassess his situation.

"We're in a helluva clusterfuck now, boys," Smithson said to each man at his side as they dropped to one knee. "Storm's right on top of us and we're headed to the highest spot around."

"Lightning sure to find us," Wolf Two added in a thick Israeli accent.

"If it doesn't, the tornado will," replied Wolf Three in a similar accent. They had just found out about the confirmed tornado on the ground from a weather report relayed to them from Robo-Raven operator Wolf Four.

"Exactly," Smithson said. "Murphy's Law boys. It's what we get when a dumbass client throws us into a hastily planned mission. Everything's bound to go wrong."

After the weather report, Wolf Four had informed Smithson he couldn't control the bird due to the wind and would try to fly it back to the ballpark. That was his last transmission as all other radio communications went full static with the thunderstorm interference.

"What'll we do, sir?" asked Wolf Two.

"Well," Smithson started then hesitated, "how bad do you want your money is the real question? Worth the risk? Or we pussy out? We've got the advantage. We can intercept our targets under cover of this weather. They'll never expect it. Plus, these weather reports are usually always exaggerated. Especially when it comes to these little tornados. This ain't Kansas. I say we go with surprise, take them, and force them to tell us what they're looking for up there. Then waste their asses and make it look like an accident."

"I'm in," nodded Wolf Two.

"Show me the money," added Wolf Three.

"Okay," said Smithson. "Let's spread out and head up. As soon as you see movement, radio me."

Both men nodded and took their positions about ten yards separated on Smithson's flanks. As a unit they moved uphill.

29

Steiner property

THE WIND HAD PICKED UP SIGNIFICANTLY AS JAKE and Alex continued their slow ascent through the woods. The sky, barely visible through the canopy of trees, was half dark-gray with low billowing clouds and half dark-purple in the clear toward the east. They were on the leading edge of the approaching line of thunderstorms from the west and needed to act fast before it hit.

But the thunderstorm was the least of their worries.

Instead, they were more concerned when and where the Raven Mocker would make his appearance.

With virtually no heavy brush under the dense, dark trees, their footsteps were light. Alex was again in the lead as they softly skirted their way across the mulched forest surface of warm, rotted leaves and mossy dead branches. He looked back at Jake and stopped.

Jake moved up next to him as Alex raised his crossbow's thermal imaging scope up to his eye to scan ahead. The scope could easily pick out heat signatures in any terrain, including fog, smoke, dust, and foliage. Here in the woods, on the hunt for a different type of predatory creature, he was hoping the Raven Mocker's thermal signature would show up bright white on the black and gray background of the woods.

Jake whispered and asked if he could see anything. Alex grunted a no.

He continued scanning all the way around as Jake, too, peered through the increasing darkness with his own eyes.

"Fucking hot as hell out here isn't it?" Jake remarked, wiping his dripping brow with a sleeve.

"Welcome the South," whispered Alex.

"Eleven o'clock," Jake whispered back. "I thought something moved in the shadows."

Alex swung back around and looked uphill. His field of view showed a wall of trees with bright white leaves in the upper portions contrasted against black trunks and a gray-to-black shaded ground. White indicated areas that had absorbed the most heat and were letting off a "hot" signature.

Suddenly, a wide white thermal image appeared from behind one of the thicker dark trees about fifty feet away. With a push of a button Alex zoomed the scope in for a closer look. He blinked. The shape shifted again, appearing to have outstretched feathery wings. Another blink and his eyes seemed to play tricks on him. The wings then folded inward as the silhouette formed into the head and broad shoulders of what looked like a tall, upright standing demon.

Alex's heart beat faster. His lips parted as he struggled to press another button on top of the scope. The shape moved from side-to-side, advancing closer as he depressed the freeze frame button to capture a static image of the target.

"I've got him," Alex whispered back. "Jesus, he's big."

"Where?" asked Jake as he raised the MAC-10 up to his chest, pointing the barrel toward the woods where Alex aimed his crossbow.

The crossbow answered as a bolt fired.

The bolt narrowly missed the shape's head and whistled away deep in the woods.

Jake opened up with his submachine gun, strafing the woods with short suppressed bursts at the unseen target. Alex immediately re-cocked and loaded another bolt to re-fire. A guttural bird-like scream echoed through the woods. All Jake could see was a rippling shadowy figure quickly rise upward into the tops of the trees. In an instant it was gone.

Heart pounding, Alex readjusted his scope on where he last saw the shape. It had disappeared. "You wounded him I think," he said.

Back to back, breathing hard, both men scanned and listened for another minute. No movement except for blowing leaves and branches and the sound of wind cutting through the leaves above them.

"All clear," said Alex, fiddling with the buttons on his scope.

"Ditto."

"Holy Christ, check this out, Jake," Alex urged, holding his crossbow up to Jake's face. "In the scope. My God, I captured it in a picture. This has never been done before."

Jake took hold of the crossbow and peered down the scope. At first his eye blurred, then focused on the monstrous shape of the demonic looking man with a body that flared out into what looked like a cape of gray feathers reaching to, and blending in with, the dark ground. He pulled back, almost losing his breath. The still image of the creature scared him beyond belief. After a moment, he placed his eye back on the scope and inspected the image again.

Caught looking from behind a tree was the distinct shape of a tall man with an elongated skeletal head and wide shoulders. The face had clearly defined features of an extremely old man. Two deep, dark holes marked his eye sockets while high cheeks and a narrow jaw presented the face as a mere skull with a sheen of white skin pulled over top.

"Fuck me," mumbled Jake, face glistening with sweat. "It looks like the Mothman." He was referring to the legendary creature of West Virginia, spotted by numerous people back in the late 1960s, and turned into a movie starring Richard Gere in 2002.

"Mothman and the Raven Mocker are one in the same," Alex said as the wind howled faster. "Ancient Cherokee witches. That one in West Virginia was killed by the medicine man who mentored me."

"Come on, let's keep going," Jake ordered.

The men stepped it up knowing they had scared the Raven Mocker off momentarily. They knew they were about to summit soon and were trying to beat the oncoming storm.

A few more minutes of climbing they finally reached the edge of the woods where it met steep cliffs. The sky was a deep, dark slate with bulbous cloud formations swirling about. Flashes of lightning and the distant rumble of thunder—as if God was tossing bowling balls down the sky alley lane—marked the fast approaching thunderstorm. They could feel a light mist of rain upon their faces as they gazed north over the open rolling hills from their elevated position.

"There's the Etowah River below," announced Alex as a gust of wind from the west hit them hard. The river was a muddy brown color and looked to be at a high level from the many days of rain the area had experienced. Its frothy, fast current carried branches, logs, and sundry debris downstream from their right.

Alex pointed to the far right. "There's the bridge. East Cherokee Drive." He wiped his shirt sleeve across his face to get rid of the sweat.

Jake nodded pulling his counterpart back from the edge. "Come on. Let's summit and do a quick recon. Then we've got to get back down before this storm hits."

"Copy that. I'll take lead," Alex said as they plunged back into the woods behind them and continued up.

They noticed white quartz crystal rocks protruding from the ground as the terrain became rockier at the thinly soiled top of the ridge. The trees were much older with thick trunks and low hanging branches. Dominating were old oaks and beech trees. Within moments the slope flattened and they had reached the summit.

The cliff and river were on their right and the ridge, sloping away back downhill, was on their left. The light was a bit better on the cliff side and almost black in the deep woods down slope. Jake produced his flashlight. Alex turned on his own rail light as both clutched weapons to conduct an initial sweep-through search.

More white rocks appeared on the ground. Or so they thought. Upon closer examination, under the beams of their LEDs, they found dirty moss-covered animal skulls and scattered bones strewn about. Several large cattle skulls with broken horns hung from trees, a hornet's nest embedded in one. Rib, spine, and large leg bones dangled from branches and danced in the wind. Soaked with sweat from the humidity they continued across the summit where Alex pointed out three more Raven Mocker stick figurines spinning wildly.

Jake also noticed several cairns or mounds of larger, white, quartz stones among the old trees. Alex pointed out a few more up ahead.

"What is this place, an animal graveyard?" Jake asked. "Ever seen anything like this?"

"In lieu of humans, this is how the witch stays alive. Feeds on anything with a beating heart. But I've never heard of one burying his kills under quartz crystal cairns before. This is strange." A blinding flash of lightning momentarily lit up the woods around them. A second later an incredible crack of thunder stopped both men in their tracks.

"Reminds me of artillery," shouted Jake, his adrenaline rising, loving every minute of it.

At first the quartz piles seemed random but as they moved forward they felt as if they were suddenly circled by these landmarks. Some were higher than others as a few had crumbled down to just a weed covered mound. Jake counted them between the trees, his flashlight beam wheeling about.

A pitter-patter of rain drops on the tree tops could be heard as the wind began a steady drone. Leaves and small branches cut loose from above and drifted to the ground.

"I count seven cairns," Jake said, his voice raised. "That's not a coincidence. I don't think these are burial mounds. They're more like waypoint markers."

"This is it then. We're in the right spot," Alex replied, spinning around in a circle as the rain increased. They couldn't yet feel any drops as the canopy above provided good protection below. But another flash of lightning and rumble of thunder told them their time was about up. "Intersect the cairns' line of sight with each other."

Their flashlight beams traced each rock pile across the summit until they all seemed to meet at an invisible point centered around one of the largest oak trees not twenty yards ahead of them. Its trunk was as wide as a car and its low hanging, thick, spidery branches were draped with more skulls, bones, and stick figurines that flipped around in the wind.

The pair cautiously approached the tree from the east, the rain and wind escalating in intensity. Heavy drops soon penetrated the trees and started striking their hats and shoulders with dull thumps. More hit the ground making overlapping, ever-increasing patterns of "white noise."

They directed their beams upon the trunk and noticed two old carvings embedded in the bark. Moss had grown in the cracks almost camouflaging their readability. Jake reached in a cargo pant pocket and extracted the waybill map protected inside a plastic Ziplock freezer bag. He flipped it over to a drawing he had made on notebook paper back at the house showing how the seemingly random waybill symbols lined up 360 degrees around a compass. It mirrored the same seven line intersections they had plotted on the topographical map. As rain struck the plastic bag, Jake glanced at his drawing and then back up at the carvings while Alex directed his light outward into the woods conducting overwatch.

"Two humps and a snake on the east face. Fuck me, it's a match!" Jake shouted above the din of the storm.

Excitedly but methodically, he inspected the circumference of the trunk in a clockwise motion and another two symbols appeared on the southern

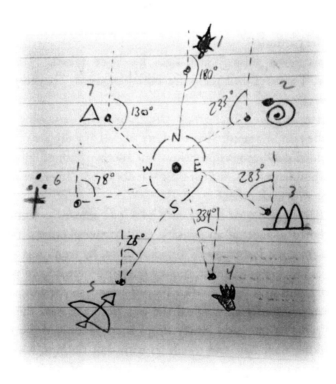

face. These were the hand and the bow and arrow. A smile grew on his face as the carved symbols again lined up with the correct compass headings.

Quicker now, as the rain started coming down in heavier quantities, he moved to the west face and found the cross and three dots as well as the triangle. Tripping over an exposed root, he stumbled to the northern face and found the last one—the turtle—nearly undetectable in the moss.

"They all match, Alex!" Jake shouted. "All seven symbols. This tree is the entrance. It must be."

The deluge slammed into them. All at once the skies opened up as dense sheets of rain poured out of the clouds and struck the trees above in powerful gusts. In an instant they were drenched and could hardly hear themselves speak it was so loud. Jake jammed the map bag back in his pant pocket. "Son-of-a-bitch," he shouted.

"We've got to get the hell out of here now!" Alex said.

"What?" Jake shouted back.

"We're sitting ducks up here. We gotta go!" Alex felt the hair on the back of his neck tingle.

As if to accentuate his warning, a lightning bolt sizzled through the air and struck a tree in a mighty explosion down the ridge to their west. The resounding crack had drowned out all other sounds. Both men flinched and ducked for cover, for in that instant they were both back in battle again. They turned just as a fireball flashed through the woods marking the exact impact spot of the lightning.

Jake keyed his radio and announced they were returning to the fork. He wasn't sure if Rae had even heard him but he did hear the ping of a reply and some static. Clipping the radio back on his belt, he donned his flashlight and double-stepped it past the cairns heading down slope.

"Follow me!" Alex said, bypassing Jake in a leap. His crossbow flashlight beam crazily bounced off tree trunks pointed ahead.

Jake ran as hard as he could, dodging trees and rocks while trying to keep his balance in the now slippery leaves. His baseball cap got tangled in a tree branch and he stumbled forward cutting his cheek on another branch that had whipped in his face. He tripped and sprawled flat in the wet, dirty leaves losing both his flashlight and his hat.

Instantly, on his knees, he found the light shining under the leaves, grabbed it and his hat, and stood back up cursing. Alex was still running down slope, probably thinking Jake was right behind him. Soon his battle buddy's light was lost in the woods.

He panned around and could barely see. As lightning lit the sky, peeking through the trees on his left, he could see he was close to the cliff's edge. Thunder cracked again after another flash. Leaves and branches fell all around him as he advanced. But worst of all, he started hearing a new noise gaining in the distance—a deep, continuous roar.

And now a different type of fear enveloped him. One that never showed mercy. He started running downhill, for Mother Nature was coming full force to suck him up.

A dark force came from his right. He was blindsided by an impact that hit him like a professional football tackle. Both the MAC-10 and his flashlight were launched out of his hands. He flew to the ground and slammed on his back in severe pain.

A black shadow swept over him with a sinister, loud cackle. Jake felt the brush of feathers on his face but there was nothing there. It was unseen. And then the grasp of heavy, claw-like hands wrapped around each of his legs. And pulled.

The Raven Mocker.

Dragging him toward the cliff.

Terrified beyond belief, Jake screamed.

Like never before in his entire life.

30

R AE HEARD THE LOUD CRACK OF LIGHTNING AND
the enormous explosion up on the ridge just as the storm rolled
in with major intensity. Several seconds later she heard Jake on the radio
briefly say they were returning. Thank God, she thought, nervously flinging
her wet hair aside as the wind gusts peppered her with ice cold rain.

Tommy and Becky were already holed up inside Alex's running Jeep.
It was the best place for protection against lightning instead of standing
among trees. After sending back a quick radio reply, she too joined them
inside, sitting in the driver's seat while wiping her face.

The radio was tuned into a local news station giving severe weather
reports by the minute.

"They're headed back, is all I heard," Rae announced.

"It ain't good, sister," Becky said from the back seat next to Tommy.
"Wind gusts up to 75 miles per hour. This is one bad ass storm coming."

What Rae heard next chilled her to the bone.

The distinct alert tones of the Emergency Broadcast System message
warned them even something worse was coming. Sure enough, it was
a confirmed report of a devastating tornado that had ripped through
Reinhardt University in Waleska and was on an easterly course moving
at forty miles per hour headed toward the Cherokee County Airport and
the tiny crossroads of Gober along the Etowah River. The message told

residents to seek immediate shelter in basements and interior rooms if in a structure or ditches if caught outside. It also warned people to stay away from any high elevations.

Referring to Alex's road gazetteer map, Rae fumbled to find the right page of where they were located in reference to the last known location of the tornado.

"Gober is just across the river northwest of us not a few miles away," Tommy said, knowing exactly where they were.

Once Rae pinpointed Waleska to their west she plotted the tornado's projected path to the airport and Gober and saw they would be taking a direct hit.

"Shit," she said before keying the radio for a transmission. "Jake. Jake. Come in. Tornado. Seek cover. Seek cover." All she heard in response was static, not knowing if he heard her warning. She knew she had to trust his training and experience, that he was well aware of the threat, but it killed her just the same knowing she was impotent to offer any kind of help.

Looking out the rain-drenched window as the windshield wipers flipped back and forth, a sinking feeling swept over her. Helpless and not knowing what to do next, she stared ahead watching the gusts of wind batter and shake the Jeep, waiting.

And then it hit her.

Shattering the windshield.

A large, metallic object had dive bombed into the front window, spiderwebbing it upon impact. All three occupants screamed out. Luckily, the laminated glass held together perfectly to keep the deadly object from penetrating the interior. Some glass splinters blew on Rae's face and she sustained minor cuts, but fortunately she was saved from severe injury.

"Good Lord, Rae!" Becky shouted. "Are you okay?"

"I'm good. I'm good," she replied, catching her breath as blood trickled down her cheek. Looking up at the object sticking through the windshield, she cocked her head. "What the hell is that?"

Tommy leaned forward from the rear seat. "Looks like some type of mechanical bird."

Rae touched the head of it and realized it was a shattered video camera.

Stepping outside in the rain with her flashlight she then inspected the rest of the object and found what looked to be two bird-like wings made of lightweight aluminum. A small logo on one of the twisted wings caught her flashlight beam. She peered at the mark and read: Robo-Raven. It was a surveillance drone.

Back inside the Jeep, she yelled at Tommy and Becky it was a spy drone, that they had been tracked and were in danger. The Jeep was useless from the window being shattered, so she ordered them to grab their gear and to make for the Chevy.

As the old man and his nurse gathered backpacks and scrambled outside, Rae sent a final radio plea that Jake and Alex would understand in military terms. "Come in, Jake. Mission compromised. Abort. Abort. Possible ambush. Possible ambush. Out."

The three soaked individuals made it over to the Chevy pick-up and were just getting in their seats with the doors still open, when a bolt of lightning struck a large tree not thirty feet away. Their hair stood up for a moment from the close electrical shock as an ear-piercing crack of thunder filled the air and rattled the truck. Becky screamed again.

Suddenly, they heard a different type of cracking as the tall pine tree that was struck came crashing down toward them.

"Oh God! Oh God!" Tommy cried in the middle front seat. He covered his arms over his head just as the thick tree slammed directly onto their just-evacuated Jeep, crushing it completely in a enormous earth-pounding thump of glass and wood. Smaller pine branches even peppered the hood of the pick-up. Becky was praying out loud and Tommy was motionless, still covered up.

Lightning flashed up above followed by another rip of thunder.

"We're good! We're good," Rae happily shouted. "It missed us." Catching her breath once again and knowing the Chevy was now completely unsafe from more falling trees, she knew they needed better cover.

"This is a deathtrap," Rae shouted. "We gotta get inside Steiner's farmhouse. Like now. Come on, get out." She grabbed a backpack and her flashlight and jumped out of the truck.

"Mr. Tommy!" Becky said, pulling her client outside to the rear of the truck. "You're going to ride me piggy back." She slammed down the truck's tailgate and snatched the little old man up from his feet and placed him in the bed of the truck.

Tommy's eyes widened, his long white hair soaked flat on his face from the onslaught of rain and wind. Becky backed her butt into him and ordered him to "Hop aboard." He straddled her wide hips with his thin legs and slouched over her shoulders holding on for dear life. She clutched his legs with strong arms and pressed him into her body, then jogged toward the farmhouse.

Rae took the lead and plunged into the kudzu weeds surrounding the dark farmhouse. She trailblazed a path to a set of stairs and an open front door, tearing down vines and prickers to make entrance. Becky and Tommy plowed in right behind her and up into the front room.

As rain poured in from leaks and rotted holes in the second-story ceiling, they took in the interior of what was suspected to be the front living room. Spider webs glistened with wetness over moldy walls sporting a floral wallpaper design. Strewn about were busted, old wooden furniture pieces, garbage, and rotted cushions from a collapsed sofa, its rusty springs exposed. The wooden plank flooring was barely visible under their feet as it was covered with a thick layer of dirt, leaves, weeds, and pieces from the ceiling above. The place was a hideous, abandoned dump.

A boxy, overturned television set from the early 60s, with a shattered glass tube covered in mold, sat in one corner. Some furry critter jumped out from inside the guts and scurried away to Becky's chagrin. The nurse then happened to look up through a hole in the ceiling with her flashlight and was petrified as several ravens peered down at her, their black eyes glistening in the beam. One squawked, as if admonishing her for trespassing. She nearly fainted.

Way up above the black birds, the structure's unstable roof groaned with the battering winds. Small pieces from the ceiling fell and the whole house seemed to shift. The birds disappeared in an upstairs room cackling away in their own fear.

The trio started to hear a frightfully low roar outside in the storm, like a hundred freight trains fast approaching. What they feared most was coming—the tornado.

"We've got to find a basement or get down under the foundation," Tommy demanded. "Look for a basement door. Through there." He pointed straight ahead with his flashlight toward what seemed like the kitchen.

Rae took the lead batting away more vines that were growing down from the ceiling. Tommy was shuffling along right behind her, clasped onto her belt loop. Becky held him steady by the elbow and took up the rear.

A doorless opening appeared on Rae's right and a narrow wooden stairway led down into darkness. "Found it! Let's go. Let's go," she said as the house shifted again. Something large crashed down behind them. Wasting no time she took the first few steps and determined they were strong enough for support.

Down all three went as the stairs creaked under Becky's added weight. Each tread held until she was down all the way onto the muddy, wet stone floor. As they squeezed through a stone passageway, the storm's roar above them was slightly muffled. They turned the corner to seek shelter deeper in the basement.

Stepping into a wider room about six foot in height, the three stopped in utter terror, hearts bursting out of their chests. Not from the tornado they knew was upon them, but from what hung from hooks attached to the ceiling.

Five, decomposed, human skeletal remains stared back at them.

Becky vomited.

Tommy took a step back, clutching his heart.

And Rae swooned on her feet in sheer horror.

9:30 p.m.

MICHAEL KARPOVAGE

31

Cliff overlook

JAKE YELLED AGAIN AND PUNCHED AT THE DARK shadowy force dragging him toward the abyss over the cliff. He felt his fist connect onto a solid body and heard a grunt, but the witch's hold didn't falter. Closer to the cliff he was dragged, through the pouring rain.

He lunged outward and grasped a handful of what felt like wet feathers. With his other hand he drew his sidearm in a quick motion, sat up slightly, and just started firing.

The witch let go of his legs after the third shot. As he pulled the trigger again, the pistol was knocked from his hand and he was slugged square in the chest. The overwhelming force had hit him in the solar plexus at the base of his sternum, knocking the wind out of him in dramatic fashion.

As he writhed on the ground pelted by rain, desperately trying to catch his breath through throbbing intense pain, Jake heard another loud cackle-like screech, only this time it sounded injured. Hoping he wounded the thing, he fought through his injury and turned on his side to slowly stagger to his feet. He looked toward the cliff just as lightning flashed in the sky.

With the illuminated sky acting as a backdrop, a rain-coated silhouette formed of a half-bird, half-man-like beast standing at the edge of the cliff. Its almost transparent wings were outstretched, but it appeared to be slumped over. Thunder roared overhead.

Several more flashes of lightning created a strobe-like effect as the thing limped toward him. Jake shook with fear. Then he remembered the back-up pistol in his ankle holster. He reached for it, keeping one eye on the witch coming at him.

He stood up and took aim with the .38 revolver. The air near his head split as a bolt zipped by. A silver crossbow bolt struck deep in the chest of the Raven Mocker and pushed it back with a howl. Red eyes lit up on its now visible skeletal face, its toothy mouth wide open.

Jake emptied all five high capacity rounds into the beast's body. The crack of his pistol was virtually drowned out by the rumbling, crashing roar of trees being uprooted and smashing through the woods. The witch staggered back to the edge of the cliff, but still wouldn't go down.

Jake threw his empty gun at the thing, then reached for the Bowie blade on his hip as a last defense.

Alex ran up next to him, hat gone, ponytail billowing, crossbow extended, eye to scope.

And fired again.

The bolt found its mark in the middle of the creature's forehead. The incredible force of the hit snapped the witch's head back and pushed its body over the edge of the cliff.

Both men ran up and watched as the black winged beast slammed into the jagged rocks then splashed into the raging river below.

It never surfaced.

Alex grabbed Jake by the shoulder and pulled him back. "Follow me," he screamed. "Tornado's coming. I found some cover!" He flicked his crossbow flashlight back on to lead the way downhill.

A massive jolt knocked the crossbow right out of his hands. He skidded to a stop to retrieve it, wondering if there was another Raven Mocker about.

Jake bent down and snatched the weapon. As he stood back up to hand it to Alex, the air split right between the two men with a firecracker-like explosion hitting the tree behind them. They knew all to well what had come their way.

Sniper fire.

"Cover!" shouted Alex, jumping behind the nearest tree.

Jake pointed the crossbow down to the ground, realizing the illuminated flashlight was giving the hidden shooter a bullseye. He hid behind a thick tree and fumbled with the toggle switch to shut the light off. "Shot came from downhill," he shouted to Alex, tossing him the crossbow. "Must be suppressed. No report."

Another bullet slammed into Jake's tree, the movement of his arm giving away his position. Then it dawned on him. The shooter must have night vision capability, just like Alex's crossbow scope. "Don't move! He's got night vision."

Through the heavy downpour Alex noticed his crossbow cable was hanging loose, damaged from the first shot. But he was still in the game. Easily detaching the scope from the rail system, he discarded the crossbow on the ground and shouted back to Jake. "Draw his fire again and I'll look through my scope as he reloads."

"10-4! On my mark. Ready? 3-2-1!" Jake moved out slightly from behind the tree exposing his shoulder and arm, then immediately drew back. The bark blasted off the tree right where he had stepped out.

Alex's thermal imaging scope was up, his eye pressed against it scanning through the woods downhill. He spotted the shooter about 50 yards away standing up against a tree, the bright red of his silhouette contrasting sharply against the black and white patterns of the trees between them. "Twelve o'clock downhill. One man!"

Alex watched as the sniper reloaded his bolt-action rifle and aimed for the next shot. A bright white flash came from the barrel just as Alex pulled back behind the tree for cover. The crack of the sniper's bullet zipped right past his head. "Fuck me!"

Alex was back out with his scope playing the deadly game of hide and seek. This time, as the sniper reloaded, he saw there wasn't just one white silhouette of an armed man, but now three. The other two were crouched next to him, weapons in hand. He pulled back, not willing to chance his head being taken off.

"There's three of them now! All armed."

"I only got a knife," Jake shouted back, the wind whipping rain now sideways through the woods. Small branches and leaves fell from above.

"I've only got my Glock," Alex said, his silenced pistol already out.

Just then the roar of the oncoming tornado made its presence felt.

"We're fucked either way," Jake shouted back. "We need to make a run for that cover."

"Wilco! Follow me," Alex yelled, then made a mad dash to his nine o'clock.

Jake was right on his tail. Five steps later he felt a white hot sting on his thigh. Down he went, stumbling in the leaves, but it wasn't enough to stop him. He regained his footing and staggered forward to keep up with the Delta Force operative.

As the EF2-sized Finger of God flattened a path through the forest behind them, larger branches dislodged and crashed all around jeopardizing their desperate escape. One branch struck Alex in the shoulder, bouncing him off a tree. Jake helped the tough man back on his feet and they both continued downhill and away from their deadly pursuers.

Finally, Alex slid around a large outcrop of rocks and tumbled at its base. Jake followed suit. "This is it," he screamed. "Get underneath." He pointed under a narrow ledge along the ground, barely able to fit one man.

Jake shimmied his way in, back against rock face, ledge above him, leg in fiery pain. Alex was next and the two men pressed against each other like spoons in a drawer. Jake held his counterpart tight in a bear hug. A tree came crashing down right in front of their hole with a crushing impact that shook the earth and bounced them off the ground, slamming their bodies up into the overhanging ledge.

Within two minutes, the tornado was now rolling right over them, trying to suck them up its vacuum shaft of deadly spinning debris. Trees literally blew apart sending lethal fragments ripping through the woods at high speeds. Entire swaths of thick, one-hundred foot tall pine trees toppled over in front of them like a game of dominos. It was incredible and utterly terrifying at the same time as the excruciatingly loud force of nature gobbled up all in its path and spit it out like a wood chipper. If not for the protection of the rock and its tiny ledge, both men would have been instantly swept away to certain death.

Downhill the tornado travelled toward the entrance to Steiner's property on East Cherokee Drive, shredding everything in its way. Within minutes the wind died down and the rain slowed to a drizzle. The loud unstoppable freight train of destruction started to fade.

Alex squirmed first, drawing a breath. "Is that a Bowie knife in your pocket or do you just like spooning me, *Colonel*?"

Jake released his grasp of the man and shoved him out of the hole. "Fuck you, you little Delta twink," he said, so happy to be alive. Alex crawled out next to the downed tree.

"Let me scan for OPFOR," he whispered, referring to their opposing forces in the abbreviated military term. Up on one knee, he peered through his scope in a wide swath. Jake slithered out next to him and inspected his thigh wound. He could feel a deep, wet gash. He applied pressure and grimaced.

After a minute Alex said, "There's no movement out there. In fact, there's nothing left standing." He stood up, still scanning.

Sitting up, Jake flicked his light on and assessed his wound. "I got hit when we ran."

"What?"

"It's a graze. See?" he said, showing him the leg wound. "That fucker was a good shot. I hope Mother Nature tore his ass up."

Alex helped him dress the wound and when both men stood up and panned their flashlights to survey the destruction of what once was a dense forest, their mouths dropped open. They simply could not believe their eyes. The clouds were fast moving away east and the night sky was lightening with bright moonlight casting the destruction in an eerie, wet, silvery glow.

All around them were shattered tree trunks snapped in half, their bark stripped bare, yellow wood exposed in deadly sharpened spears pointing to the sky. Clustered around the broken stumps were fallen, split logs all facing in one direction; downhill to the east. Branches and leaves lay strewn about, blowing and ruffling in the decreasing wind. And covering everything was a red-colored mixture of Georgia clay and brown mulchy leaves sucked up from the forest floor.

All was quiet. Not a bird chirped. It was as if they survived a World War I artillery barrage in the Ardennes Forest. To add to the surreal, no-man's land battlefield scene, a siren went off in the distance. Stepping on top of the tree that had crashed in front of their cover, they stood up for a better view, panning their flashlight beams in all directions. The cliff edge, the summit of the ridge, and the twinkling stars of a dark, royal blue sky were clearly exposed now. There was hardly anything standing as they looked west.

They did however, see a bright glow of flames on a ridgeline about two to three miles further west where they knew the county airport and the small town of Gober was located. It's where the tornado had come from. An explosion then went off in the distance and a bright ball of orange and red lifted into the sky.

Jake pulled the radio from his belt clip and toggled the microphone. He was worried their enemy had found the others. "Rae, come in. Rae, come in. Are you guys okay? Over."

Having received no response, he repeated his message again. Still nothing, he nervously told Alex they needed to get back down to the fork.

The men immediately proceeded to hike their way back down through the devastation, all the while keeping an eye out for the unknown armed individuals who had shot at them. The going was treacherous, though. There wasn't a clear path nor a firm foothold anywhere. Downed branches stuck out at every angle. The rain, mud, and wet leaves made it slippery to even walk.

Debris of every variety was scattered among the woods, too. Anything and everything that was light enough to float in the tornado from the residential areas near Gober was now discarded among the flattened woods. In their flashlight beams they saw torn clothing, shredded paper, pink insulation, roof shingles, bent metal parts, busted Styrofoam, a small freezer, a basketball hoop, even the twisted remains of a horse from a nearby farm, its bloody, broken body punctured with shafts of wooden shrapnel.

Other dead animals were tossed about, too. They noticed half of a deer carcass like a crude trophy mount, sitting upright against a stump. A dead dog hung from a tree and mangled birds of all sizes lay strewn at their feet. Even the ravens weren't spared.

At one point they came across a large airplane wing, most likely from the county airport. Crumpled in a ball, they even discovered one of those super compact, electric Smart Cars. Luckily, no one was inside.

But soon enough, as they made their way down the reverse slope of the ridge, they did find a body. It was a decapitated male. But what set the two men on edge was what the victim was wearing. He was dressed as a paramilitary contractor with a bulletproof vest. And he was still armed with an elaborate, yet damaged beyond repair, sniper rifle strapped across his back.

"Looks like Mother Nature did her job," remarked Alex.

Jake took the man's sidearm and extra magazines. His wallet indicated he worked for the global security protection firm called The Gladii. His identification indicated he was an Israeli citizen.

Both men knew very well that The Gladii was a firm based out of south Georgia near Fort Stewart. They took in a lot of ex-military personnel to act as VIP bodyguards or conduct other nefarious missions for the government and private enterprise. This told them Tom Black was on to them and had upped his game significantly to take them out with prime opponents.

Alex stripped the headless corpse of its bloody bulletproof vest and snapped it on over his own chest as a precaution.

Jake continued trying to raise Rae on the radio, but to no avail. The further downhill they hiked the further his heart sunk. With both men sweating profusely, they finally reached what they thought seemed like the road cutting through the property and decided to turn east until they found the fork.

They first came upon Alex's Jeep and saw it was crushed into a flattened hunk of metal. Quietly, they peered inside and to their relief it was empty. The Chevy pick-up shared a similar fate under a large sweetgum tree. Again, no one had been trapped inside. Which begged the question; where did they go?

"Hey Jake, come here," Alex whispered, back at his destroyed Jeep. He was bent over looking at a highly reflective object embedded in the front windshield. "It's a fucking military drone. The Gladii were tracking us."

Jake raised his newly loaded sidearm, courtesy of the dead contractor, and panned around with his flashlight. "Be on guard," he told Alex. "There's got to be more of them."

With his Glock and hand-held, mini flashlight, Alex, too, looked about.

Turning around, he noticed the Steiner farmhouse had been struck by several large trees nearly flattening the structure. It still remained standing however, although its roof was completely crushed in.

"What do you think?" he whispered. "Maybe our people took shelter inside. Let's check it out."

Jake moved closer to the abandoned home and swung his flashlight inside the front door. Part of the second floor had collapsed down into the main room. He stepped inside briefly and whispered loudly for his girlfriend.

To his delightful surprise he heard a muffled reply from an interior back room. "Jake! Jake! We're in the basement!"

Becky screamed out her excitement. And the older voice of Tommy chimed in, too.

Jake almost cried he was so happy. "Are you okay?" he asked, crouching down in the front room under the collapsed ceiling. Their voices came from the rear of the house where there must be stair access below. He inched forward and pieces from the damaged ceiling drifted down on him. A wounded raven fell from the ceiling, its blood-drenched wing broken. The black bird was barely able to render a cackle. It startled Jake at first, but then he just swatted it away. There was no room to go any further and it was too unstable to risk crawling in.

"We're good," Rae said loudly, seemingly just around the corner. "How about you and Alex?"

"Banged up a little, but we both made it," Jake shouted back. "Barely."

"We're trapped down here." Rae advised. "The basement stairs broke apart when we were trying to get out and the outside basement door is locked or something. Go around to the back side and see if you can open it for us."

"Wilco," Alex said, from behind Jake. "Be right back."

At the rear of the house Alex saw a downed maple tree across the slanted double-door entrance to the basement. There would be no way to move it. Instead, he re-entered the farmhouse from a back door and carefully made his way into the kitchen. Once Jake saw him directly ahead, he backed out the front door and rejoined Alex in the rear. They now had access to the basement hole where the others were.

Alex produced a rope from his pack and started making foothold knots in it. He then anchored it in the kitchen and tossed a length below. Jake took hold and made the quick jump down. He landed where the old set of wooden stairs now lay busted and his leg gave way. Rae helped him up and they hugged for a moment and kissed.

"Listen guys, Black is on to us again. We were shot at it. I was grazed in the leg." Rae bent down to look at the wound. "I'm fine. There were three shooters up at the summit tracking us. We found one of them dead. Decapitated from the tornado. We traced him to a security firm called The Gladii . . . "

"That explains the Robo-Raven drone that dove right into the Jeep's front window," Rae said, interrupting him. "I didn't think it was coincidence. I sent a radio warning to you guys. But then the tornado was bearing down on us and we took shelter in here."

"Yeah, we never heard the transmission. So you haven't seen any paramilitary looking guys, right?" Jake asked.

"No, no one."

Rae whispered in his ear to get the others the hell out of there right away and then she would show him what was in the next room. Jake was able to prop the stairs back up as a make-shift ladder and with the rope and Jake pushing from behind they were able to get the larger Becky back up first. Tommy was much easier. Rae stayed down.

Jake turned his flashlight on and entered the gloomy cellar.

They all heard his gasp—and then a slew of obscenities.

Up top, Becky told Alex what they had found and he immediately climbed down to join his counterpart. He had seen some of the worst atrocities on the battlefield. This ranked up there with the most heinous.

Hanging from ceiling hooks penetrating the five victim's necks, their skeletal remains were in various stages of decomposition. Three of the oldest victims were simple skeletons covered in moss and rotted old clothes. It was unknown what their sex was. The other two victims, one a male, the other a female, were murdered much more recently, although still it seemed they had been there for at least five years based on their level of deterioration. All victims shared one thing in common, though; their rib cages were sawed down the middle and spread wide like crude open heart surgery. The insides had long since been eaten away by maggots or rodents.

Or something else.

Jake knew what it meant. He hadn't shared the details that Tommy had given him to Rae about how a Raven Mocker sustains his immortality for fear of her bowing out of the mission or talking him out of it.

Alex joined Jake's side, taking in the sight. He remained quiet with a deeply disturbed look on his face as he walked up to each victim and inspected their corpses.

Rae held onto Jake's arm. "I've taken numerous photos of each victim with my phone. I also went through their remains and found some form of identification on all five. Three of them had wallets or papers saying who they were. One even had ID from the 1850s. Once I took pictures I placed the items back where I found them. These are missing victims thought never to be found. The Steiner family and this property need to be investigated to find out who the murderer is, so help me God."

"I can tell you right now, Rae," Alex replied softly. "You'll find only one person—I mean *thing*—responsible for this. It was the Raven Mocker."

"And we just killed it on top of that ridge," Jake said.

Rae folded her arms across her chest. "Be that as it may, these people had families wondering what happened to their loved ones. They'll want answers. I know it. I've dealt with this before up in New York. The most important thing in these missing persons cases is the family always wants to find the body for a proper burial. The least I can do is somehow dig into their history and to reunite them again."

"You're a good woman," Alex said. "Just spare the families the details."

Their ultimate fears were well founded when Rae pointed out a submerged fire pit filled with rancid water and bugs. A long, rusted metal rod was positioned horizontally on two metal supports. It was a rotisserie spit used for roasting meat—the kind humans *weren't* supposed to eat.

"Oh Christ," Alex whispered. "I hoped I'd never see this again."

"What is it?" asked Rae.

"It's where the witch cooked his victim's hearts and ate them."

She turned away gagging.

"Sick, evil, twisted creature," mumbled Jake. "Thanks for saving my ass, Alex. . . again."

"Come on, let's get the fuck out of here," Alex said.

Rae turned. "Agreed."

With that, they climbed back up the rope and broken steps and pulled themselves onto the kitchen floor where they rejoined Tommy and Becky.

Back out front, standing near the crushed vehicles, all flashlights extinguished, they regrouped to discuss what to do next given the new threat from Black.

Out of nowhere something grunted and snapped a branch. Everyone clicked their lights on and found the source. They were dismayed at what they saw. Struggling toward them was what looked like a giant zombie paramilitary man from The Walking Dead. An assault rifle slung over his shoulder, the ugly man's bald head and wide blanched face were caked with blood and mud. He had a bushy walrus style mustache also covered in blood from a flattened nose. He limped on a wooden staff, his pants shredded and bloody, one boot missing, foot caked in Georgia clay. His upper arm had a large piece of wood protruding right through the bicep that bled profusely. If it wasn't for his body armor he probably wouldn't be alive, not that he had much longer to live as it was.

Every single one of the five had weapons aimed at him as he staggered closer and closer.

Rae took the lead. "Drop all your weapons or we drop you. NOW!"

The large man stood in shock, flashlights blinding him, not comprehending the order. Rae barked it again and he blinked several times, still not cooperating.

So Rae shot him once in the chest with her .38 Special.

Becky screamed.

The brute staggered back, but didn't lose his footing. He looked down, confused as to the blow that slammed against his bulletproof vest.

"Drop your weapons or the next one is in your head," Rae ordered again, moving closer to the man and taking aim at his face.

This time he complied. He let the assault rifle slip from his shoulder to the ground and then unsnapped his sidearm allowing that to fall off, too.

Jake snatched up both weapons and checked for ammunition. Both were set to fire with full magazines and one in the chamber. He handed the suppressed assault rifle to Alex.

"That your drone over there?" asked Jake, pointing his flashlight onto the twisted Robo-Raven sitting on the hood of the crushed Jeep.

The man looked over, nodded, paused then laughed. "Isn't that the bloody ticket—our drone ending up in one of your cars." His accent was British and he spoke slow and in pain. "I knew the Ranger wanted no part of this mission."

"Who the hell are you?" asked Alex, his silenced Glock in the man's face. "What Ranger? Who owns this drone?"

"Name's Harry Smithson, mate," the defeated man replied through labored breathing. "Former Major with the SAS. I work with The Gladii now. Or did. Doesn't matter, though, I'm a dead man walking. Lost a ton of blood. Artery severed in my arm. Leg gashed bad, too. And now a stinging sensation in my chest thanks to the looker here. Ain't gonna make it."

"How many contractors you got out here?" Alex asked after Smithson confirmed who he was.

"Three of us. Heard you firing. Gave away your position. We had you pinned down good didn't we? Was moving in to take you out before that bloody tornado hit. We had no place to hide. Both my men are down. One crushed under a tree, the other decapitated. Found his head. Nothing else."

"We found the rest of him," Jake said.

"You got no one else out here?" Alex asked.

"There's a former Army Ranger who's all that's left. Was flying the drone and probably crashed it to warn you about us coming. I knew he wanted no part in killing you Yanks. I was right so I left him with the client."

"So you came to kill us all. Who hired you?" Tommy asked, stepping forward, his WWII-era Luger aimed at the man's face.

Smithson's legs gave out and he collapsed on the ground. Grunting, he managed to sit upright against a fallen tree trunk. "Well, if I'm not mistaken that would be your loving son, Congressman Tom Black. He hired us *today* in fact. Spur of the moment. Why? I haven't a bloody clue."

Tommy lowered his weapon and cursed. "Where is he?"

Smithson coughed up blood. "We left them with the Ranger back at some little ballpark to the south about a mile and a half away. Haven't had contact with him since." He fumbled with a radio on his belt loop. "Here. You try calling him, old chap. Channel three." He tossed the radio to Tommy.

"Oh and by the way he's with some good looking black broad, too. You might know her, mate," he said, pointing at Vann. "A professor at Reinhardt University ring a bell? From what Black told me after they met up this afternoon she sucks like a vacuum cleaner and fucks like a jackhammer."

Alex kicked the man in the mouth. A gasp went up from Becky. He then stormed away realizing what he had done in contacting his jilted lover. All eyes and flashlights were now on him. "It's how you found us and tracked us here, isn't it?" Alex asked in a rage. "She sold me out, didn't she?"

Smithson spit a tooth out as blood trickled down his chin. "She sure did. Hooked up with Black and sold her soul." He smiled with bloody gums then coughed. "Love at first sight. You should have never sent her those make-up flowers this morning, Tonto. Just goes to show you that centuries-old quote is still so true today."

"And what would that be you fucking ball-busting, Limey bastard?" Alex asked, using the derisive term Germans called Brits in World War II.

The lead contractor slumped to one side and spoke slowly. "Heaven has no rage like love to hatred turned, nor Hell a fury like a woman scorned." He coughed again. "She wanted you dead, son. I'd watch your six."

"Who is *she*, Alex?" Jake asked, confronting his counterpart.

"Marissa Morgan, isn't it?" Tommy demanded.

Alex nodded, completely embarrassed and humiliated. "I wanted us back together again. What with finding the waybill and all, and the book she did on James Vann, and helping us out, Tommy. I wanted her a part of the discovery."

"You dadgum fool!" Tommy shouted at him. "Talk about timing. You think you could have kept it in your pants until *after* we made the discovery! Boy, you done put us all in danger. Well, I guess you got your answer didn't you now? That'd be a big ol' dagger in your back, wouldn't it?"

"I know. I know. I'm sorry, sir."

"Why are you telling us all this?" Rae asked Smithson. "Why'd you come seek *us* out now? You want our help? You want us to save you from bleeding to death? Well, screw you." She spat on him.

Smithson was breathing much slower now and had trouble talking. "Because I didn't want to die up there in a pile of garbage under some tree not knowing if it was all worth it or not. Black said you were looking for a tunnel. He said to track you. Find out what you're up to. Then eliminate all of you. Except for Old Pops here. The son wanted the father all to himself." Smithson coughed again, very weak. "I just want to know one bloody thing." He turned his gaze up to Tommy. "Tell me why this tunnel's so bloody important your son is willing to kill you over it."

Tommy cleared his throat and stepped over to the dying man. He bent down on his hands and knees and looked him in the eye. In his quiet, deep, slow Southern accent he spoke. "When the unknown becomes known, the unobtainable obtained, the unreachable reached it all boils down to the final thrill of actually holding it in your hands. Boy, there's an ancient Cherokee map hidden underneath that hill that holds the locations of untapped wealth beyond your wildest dreams. Believe me when I tell you, it's worth killing someone over. I can give you 4,000 reasons why on the Trail of Tears. And my great granddaddy as 4,001. For whoever owns that map may do what he will in this world. Now you go and close your eyes now, alright? It's time for you to sleep."

Smithson nodded to the soft spoken elderly man and closed his eyes as he suggested. "Sounds worth it, sir. Thank you. I'm glad you told me the truth." His head soon slumped down, breathing even slower. Within a minute he fell gently against the ground.

Nurse Holden checked his pulse then shook her head. "He's gone. Bled out. White as a ghost."

No one said a word after that. Jake went over and straightened out Smithson's body as best he could then took off his bullet proof vest. He gave it to Rae to wear. Alex went through his wallet, found one of The Gladii business cards, and pocketed it.

"What do we do now?" Rae asked to no one in particular.

"We survived the twister and these men," Tommy answered. "I say we go find the treasure before my son does? Ain't nobody going to know we're out here with this destruction all around us."

"And no one has access anymore given all the downed trees," Alex added. "It's a perfect window of opportunity."

"And we know exactly where it is, too," Jake said to Tommy. "Right before the tornado hit, we found seven quartz cairns surrounding some type of animal cemetery at the summit, and seven symbols on an oak tree that intersected those rock piles. All seven symbols matched those on the waybill and knife."

"But the tree is probably gone now," said Alex.

"Only one way to find out," Jake replied.

"And what about the Raven Mocker?" Tommy asked.

"He took an arrow to the chest and one in the head," Jake said. "Alex saved my life, Tommy. We got split up and that thing came out of nowhere and knocked me down. Started dragging me off the cliff. Alex killed him. It fell down the rocks and disappeared in the river. We both saw it hit. Listen, we all make mistakes. Don't be hard on him when it comes to women. They have a power we can never resist. Isn't that right, Rae?"

She clutched his hand.

Tommy's eyes teared up. He went over to Alex and hugged him. Then Jake, too. "Come on y'all. Let's get on back up there."

"What about Black?" Rae wanted to know.

"What about him?" Tommy snapped back, shoving his Luger in his side holster. "If he wants the dream let him come get it on his own."

"Let me see that contractor's radio, Tommy," Alex said. "I've got a better idea. Anyone see any ravens still in the house?"

Jake nodded, "I saw one that was wounded. Why?"

"Think we can capture it?"

"I suppose."

"Perfect," said Alex. "Now, everyone listen up. Here's what I'm thinking. We're going to set a little booby trap for the fat, Black cat congressman. Something his curiosity can't resist."

MICHAEL KARPOVAGE

32

B LACK, MORGAN, AND THE LAST OF THE GLADII
emerged unscathed from the concrete block building that housed
the ballpark's concession stand and restrooms. They had taken refuge inside
when the tornado passed by not a mile down the road. The very first thing
Black did was check to see if his coveted Camaro was damaged in any way.
Except for some leaves and a small twig that had blown on its hood, it, too,
survived unharmed.

Unable to make any contact with the other operators, former Ranger
Schroeder knew his colleagues must have taken a direct hit from the
tornado. Their chances of survival were slim.

Black ordered Schroeder to drive them all down to the river to ascertain
what damage was done, what became of Smithson and his contractors, and
of the mission itself. All three piled into the agency's SUV and headed out
slowly across the debris strewn parking lot. Schroeder then received a radio
call in his earpiece.

"Come in, Ranger. Come in, Ranger. Over." It was a British accent for
sure, Schroeder thought, but didn't exactly sound like Smithson. Plus, using
"Ranger" as his call sign was strange. *He'd never say that. Maybe he's injured
or in distress.*

"Wolf One? This is Wolf Four. Is that you? Are you guys injured? Over."

"Wolf Four, is this a private communication? Over," the British voice said again.

Schroeder paused. Highly unusual question. Black and Morgan certainly could not hear what was being said in his earpiece from Smithson, only what he'd reply back to him. But just in case, he placed the vehicle in park and proceeded to step out onto to the pavement.

Assuming it was Smithson, Black interjected from the backseat and wanted Schroeder to ask him about the five people they were supposed to take down. He didn't give a shit about if the contractors were injured or not. He only cared about *his* plans.

Schroeder held an index finger up to Black telling him to wait. He then slammed the door shut and walked in front of the Mercedez, illuminating himself in the headlamps. "Secure. Go ahead with your message. Over."

"Wolf Four, this is *not* Smithson," said the same voice minus the British accent. "He is dead. Same with your other two men. Killed by the tornado. But before he died Smithson told us your client Tom Black's plans. Over."

"Copy. Who is this?" Schroeder shot back.

"A former Ranger like yourself. Now in the Unit. Over."

He was talking to Delta Force operative Alex Vann. He started pacing in front of the vehicle, holding the earpiece tighter to hear better. "Listen, I wanted no part of this mission. I thought it was wrong. Over."

"We understand that. Smithson told us you probably flew your Robo-Raven into my Jeep to compromise the mission. Is that true? Over."

Schroeder looked into the Mercedez. The dome light was on and Black and Morgan were talking in the back seat. "Affirmative. Over."

A bevy of sirens could be heard in the distance. Emergency responders were out and about.

"You have our gratitude," Vann radioed back amid static. "We did not kill your friends, the tornado did. You, on the other hand, still have the choice to live or die. I suggest you abort your employment immediately from Black and make yourself *lost*. Understand? Over."

"Affirmative."

A door slammed. It was Tom Black. Not happy. He strode up to Schroeder joining him in the headlamp beams. "Affirmative, what? What the fuck is Smithson saying? What happened up there? I want answers. Let me talk to him."

Schroeder made sure to keep his mic on when Black was speaking so Vann could hear the conversation. He held another "wait" finger up to Black, turned his back and walked away, ignoring the prick.

Black stewed. No one turned their back on him.

Another door slammed shut. It was the professor.

Vann quickly responded in Schroeder's earpiece. "Tell Black that Smithson said he's WIA from the tornado, that his other two men are KIA, but he *was* able to confirm all five of us intended targets were killed, too, but not by the tornado. Tell him we were killed and mutilated by some evil birdwitch. That the five bodies are hanging in the cellar of an old farmhouse at the fork. And that Smithson is at the bridge and you've been ordered to pick him up alone. Then make your escape. Tell him all this now and lay it on thick."

"I understand, Harry. Listen, hang in there, okay mate? I'm leaving right now to come get you. Over and out," Schroeder said loudly, faking that he had ended the radio communication. Instead, he still had his finger pressed on his mic's toggle switch so Vann could continue to eavesdrop.

He turned around to Black, feigning a crisis. "Sir, listen to me very carefully. Smithson's down at the river bridge, but he's severely injured. Our other two men were killed in the tornado. And——"

"What about the others?" asked Morgan.

"All five are dead," Schroeder lied. "But not by the tornado. Smithson said he found their mutilated bodies in the cellar of a farmhouse there at the fork where they parked their vehicles. They were killed and mutilated by some type of birdwitch? I don't understand." He shook his head and shrugged his shoulders. "But that's how he explained it. Listen, I need you two to stay put right here and I'll go get Smithson and assess his injuries. If he's bad off I'll just go right to a hospital with him."

"Okay, go, go," Black said softly, confused from the news his adversaries all died from a "birdwitch." He wasn't even sure what that meant. "We will, um, be in my car when you get back."

Schroeder nodded, strode to his SUV and got in.

"Very well done," said Vann in his ear. "Nice embellishment. Now keep your mouth shut and don't ever come back."

"Affirmative, Mr. Vann. And thank you for showing me mercy. Out."

Morgan stood frozen in the SUV's beams, stunned at the report everyone was really dead, especially Alex Vann, her only true love in life. His blood was on her hands and now she felt deep remorse at what she had set into motion. *I'm not supposed to feel like this.* She flinched when she heard the vehicle shift into gear and nudge forward. The Congressman eased her out of the way.

Seizing his opportunity, Schroeder hit the gas, drove over a curb and onto a grass median to avoid a tree that had fallen. Jamming his steering wheel back and forth to avoid more debris, he lumbered out onto East Cherokee Drive well out of the line of sight of where Black's Camaro was parked deeper in the park. Just to be sure, he cut off his lights. And instead of turning left to meet the ghost of Harry Smithson, he made a right and headed south, as far away from Tom Black and his Black Widow as he could.

"Smithson saw a birdwitch kill everyone," a troubled Marissa Morgan mumbled, just getting into the passenger seat of the Camaro. "That means it was a Raven Mocker."

Black squeezed himself behind the wheel and looked over at her crazily. "Professor, why would a Raven Mocker be at that location?"

Turning on the car's ignition with a chest pounding rumble from its supped-up engine, a blast of air conditioning blew out of the vents and onto their faces. Lowering the AC, Black fiddled with the GPS navigational system to no avail—still no signal. His onboard hands-free phone system also showed no service.

"Guarding the tunnel I think," Morgan said, deeply shaken. "Alex told me that the chief who deposited that mining map summoned a Raven Mocker to guard over the entrance. It would kill anyone who got close."

"What?" growled Black. "Why the fuck didn't you tell me this earlier? A Raven Mocker's been up there all along?"

"I didn't think it was true," Morgan replied testily. "I don't believe in that shit." She hugged her arms around her chest. "At least I didn't," she said quietly. "Until tonight."

Black now realized what really killed his sister had nothing to do with him at all. That through his pot induced haze that day, he really did see her pushed by someone or something else. It was the Raven Mocker all along; and he had lived with this lie and the false accusation he was responsible for her death, all of his life. Now he finally found out what really happened up there on top of that hill, and the feeling was utterly liberating.

And the best part was his own father was destroyed by the same witch. He couldn't have wished for a better ending. Mutilated and murdered for still pursuing that fucking treasure into his old age. The same obsession that got his own daughter killed. Black laughed out loud.

He reached into a compartment between the seats and pulled out a travel humidor from which he grabbed a small thin cigar. A click of the dashboard lighter and soon he was happily puffing away. He didn't even bother to crack open the windows.

"What do we do now?" Morgan coughed, powering down her window for some fresh air.

Black shrugged his shoulders and fished out his cell phone, still laughing. "Not really sure, Honey. Everyone's fucking dead." He puffed and laughed some more, then checked his own cell phone for service. Still there was no connection. "It all worked out better than I expected. We ain't got no blood on our hands."

Easy for you to say, thought Morgan.

Black tuned into a news station on the radio. A deep throated, fast-talking male news reporter was summarizing the top story:

AM 750, your news talk, traffic, and weather station for metro Atlanta. Late breaking news and live coverage of the devastating EF2 sized tornado that ripped through northwest Georgia this evening. We have reports of multiple deaths and injuries and widespread destruction along its path. Local fire and emergency personnel are reporting that Reinhardt University in Waleska sustained a direct hit when the tornado touched down. Seven people are reported dead there, many more missing. The tornado then continued due east bulldozing a path through mostly unpopulated forest areas until it struck the Cherokee County Airport and the small crossroads of Gober on the Etowah River. A reporter at the airport told us that every single plane on the runway was damaged in some way. In Gober, local firefighters are battling a raging fire with multiple explosions as a propane tank service company caught on fire. Further east we have scattered reports of power outages and downed trees. It seems the tornado has now died out with the worst of the damage concentrated from Waleska to Gober. We'll be right back with more after this brief pause from our sponsors.

Morgan mashed the button and turned the radio off. Waleska. It's where she lived. Reinhardt University. It's where she worked. Her whole life was there, her close friends, even her five cats, too. This treasure hunt can wait, she thought. They knew where it was now. Somewhere on top of that hill and only she and Black knew that. So the secret would still be intact, especially with a Raven Mocker guarding it. Alex Vann was dead, too. And honestly she felt extreme guilt and utter regret. She finally decided she needed to get home to find out about her friends and co-workers. She pulled out her cell phone and found it, too, had no service. Panic swept over her.

"Take me back to Waleska," Morgan demanded as Black continued to fiddle with his phone.

"What?" he exclaimed, placing his cigar in the dashboard ashtray. "The hell I will. Smithson will be back any minute. We need to find out what he knows and then we're going back in there. I want to see the bodies in the farmhouse and get my waybill and knife back and then we're going to find that tunnel entrance. Don't get your panties all in a wad and bail out on me now, *Professor*. We're too close."

"What, are you nuts? I'm not going anywhere with that Raven Mocker prowling about. The fucking treasure can wait, *Congressman*," Her voice rose with anger. "I've got to find out if my friends are okay first. Waleska took a direct hit and I have no way to reach them."

"No, little girl! I am *not* leaving here to take your sweet ass home."

"It's only fifteen miles away. The tunnel can wait," she pleaded. "We know where the tunnel is located now. And you're *Daddy* is dead. We can come back tomorrow in the daylight when we're more prepared."

"Don't you fucking tell me what to do, *bitch*. I'm staying right here," Black yelled back. "You want to get home so badly? You can *walk*."

"If you ever want to *fuck* me again," she barked, wiggling her head. "You will drive me *now*!"

"Fucking bitch," Black screamed. He backhanded her with a hard wallop against her cheek and left eye. The blow cut her brow instantly. "I'll *FUCK* you any time I feel like it. I own you, my little cunt slave. Now get the fuck out of my car!"

Stinging from the strike, the first thing that entered Morgan's mind was that no one had ever laid a hand on her. Not even Alex who was a violent warrior. The audacity of the act is what jarred her the most. It wasn't the pain, nor the disgusting obscenity he called her. *How dare he hit me!*

In a quick highly trained sweeping motion that Alex taught her, she reached to her right hip and extracted her Heckler & Koch P30 firearm from its holster. She flipped the safety off and pressed the pistol against Black's temple. "No! *You* leave. Or I blow your fucking brain's out, you fat motherfucker."

Black sat petrified, almost shitting his pants. As he blinked back some courage, his hand moved slowly up to his right pocket for his own pistol.

"Don't even think about it," Morgan hissed, eye swelling up, blood trickling down the side of her face. "Get the fuck out! Now!"

Black couldn't move fast enough. He popped the door and stumbled out of his car. Morgan jumped into the driver's seat then aimed her gun up in the air out the open door. She fired off two quick rounds and watched Black trip and fall. She jammed the Camaro into first gear, popped the clutch, and slammed the gas pedal, spinning the tires. The open driver's door swung shut as she accelerated away, bouncing over a large downed tree limb. A shower of ashes on pavement marked the spot where Black's cigar had been tossed out the window.

Within seconds she was gone.

Realizing he wasn't shot, he turned over and got up, then brushed away wet debris on his front side. Stewing with fury, he stomped on the pavement.

His $400,000 Camaro had been carjacked.

Nothing to do but wait for Smithson now, he started pacing.

Five sweaty minutes later, he wore himself out so he sat on the ballpark bleacher. Twenty more angry minutes later, he finally knew something was wrong, that Smithson and the contractor who had promised to get him, had disappeared. There was no way to reach either one with an unworkable phone. He speculated that Smithson's injuries were so severe he must have been driven directly to the hospital.

With no other place to go, he extracted his flashlight from his pocket, flicked it on, and set out in the darkness on his own. Down East Cherokee Drive he'd head, for the short mile and a half walk to the tornado ravaged riverside property where his sister had died so many years ago.

And where his father now finally joined her in death.

It was a satisfying feeling.

Tom Black whistled while he walked.

Dixie, to be exact.

33

HITLER'S GOLD PISTOL EMERGED FROM NATHAN Kull's backpack on his co-pilot's side of the Cessna's cockpit. He wasted no time in placing the barrel against the older pilot's ribs.

"What the—," said the pilot, a plump Italian-looking man in his sixties. He was sporting a black mustache and spectacles while dressed in a polo shirt and shorts. The plane swerved slightly as he looked down.

"Keep calm, maintain your course, and I won't put a bullet in your chest, capiche?" Kull said, still wearing his hat and sunglasses since they had left, even though it had gotten dark.

"Yes. yes. I understand." He regained control of the aircraft and leveled her out. "What's this all about? What'd I do?"

"You did nothing," Kull said, calmly. "Just relax. I need a favor from you and want to make sure it gets done is all."

"Anything. Just please don't kill me," the pilot pleaded. "I've got four kids and eight grandkids. Fucking Tom Black. I should have never agreed to this."

"Just be quiet and don't worry," Kull said, glancing out the front windshield to the dark, quilt-like patches of farmland below. He lowered his sunglasses. They were flying at about 3,000 feet with no cloud coverage, and great moonlight. "I just want you to drop me off at the Fitzgerald Municipal Airport. I believe we're coming up on it pretty soon, right?"

"Why y-yes, we are," the pilot stammered. "H-how did you know?"

"I ask the questions," Kull said, jamming the pistol harder into his ribs.

"Okay. Okay. Anything you say."

"Radio us in for a landing."

"Yes, sir." The pilot lifted his radio mic and called the control tower of the tiny little airport located in south central Georgia's farming country. That area was known for its peanuts and official state vegetable, the Vidalia onion. He received an immediate reply. Cleared to land.

"Take us down."

The plane pitched down and decreased in altitude. The nerve-wracked pilot began his landing procedure. He checked his radar display, GPS map, and other gauges for the descent. They were only five miles away from the small, one-runway four-building airport; but they both noticed it, as the runway suddenly lit up.

"What direction are we landing?" Kull asked after several minutes.

"They've got us coming in from the south. I need to circle around after we make a pass."

"Perfect."

As the plane passed the airport on its lower left, Kull leaned over and peered down in the barely visible light. The north end of the runway contained an empty parking lot with a single warehouse-type building. A lone vehicle was parked next to the building as noted by its headlights. He kept his eyes on the car. A bright flash came from the car. Then two more. He smiled.

Paralleling the airport, still headed south, Kull spotted the small terminal and a few more hangars that accommodated smaller aircraft. The terminal, too, was virtually empty except for a few twinkling lights. Their Cessna continued south then banked hard and swung around on a northerly heading, lining itself up with the end of the runway and its guide lamps. They were down to about 500 feet now, skimming over dark farming ponds and fields.

Kull pressed the pistol against the pilot's chest again to get his attention. "Now listen carefully. When we land I want you to stop at the north end of the runway. You will let me out. You will then turn around and take off again. Continue on all the way down to Homestead, Florida. I have associates there waiting to see if you arrive. If you do not, I will hunt you down and kill your family one by one, starting with your grandkids, understand?"

"I understand," said the shaken pilot. "Drop you off at the end of the runway. Then take off and head to Homestead as if nothing happened."

"Very good," smiled Kull, looking out forward from the cockpit as the land rose up quickly. "I was never here, right?"

"That's right. In fact, I just had a little engine trouble I needed to check on; that was the reason for the stop."

"Perfect," smiled Kull. "Now you got the hang of this."

The runway loomed large and the pilot landed the plane smoothly with not even a bounce. As they sped past the terminal on their right, Kull slipped low in his seat to hide. The plane continued up the runway slowing its speed. At the very end, near the lone warehouse, a dark colored sedan raced out onto the tarmac toward the plane.

Kull reached over and ripped the headset off the pilot's head then tore off the radio arm mic.

"What are you doing?"

"Shut up and turn the plane around!" He reached for the back up radio microphone on a cord attached to the dashboard, and pulled that out of its socket, too, in a fray of wires. The aircraft now had no communications.

Kull's getaway vehicle pulled up just behind the plane and stopped.

"That's good. Right here. Stop!" Kull ordered.

Grabbing his backpack, he opened the passenger door then stepped down onto the tarmac. He pointed the gun one more time at the pilot. "Now fly south and land at Homestead or else your family gets it. Go!" He slammed the door and ran for the waiting car, a BMW.

The plane accelerated down the runway and took off as Kull and his companion were already speeding away into the little town of Fitzgerald. Still holding Hitler's pistol, he followed the plane's blinking lights in the rear window and watched as it rose into the dark sky to continue its southerly direction. Satisfied, he turned around and greeted the driver.

Having only spoken to her on the phone during most of his career as a thief, he never imagined his broker could be so flat-out gorgeous. He took off his sunglasses to get a better look.

Although dark outside, her face was well lit from the dashboard lights. The brunette wore her hair long and stylish, sitting on her shoulders. A tight shirt cupped her well-formed breasts and a high cut, business-style mini skirt rode up her thighs. She looked mid-forties and an older version of the sexiest NASCAR driver ever to break into that boy's club: Danica Patrick.

Kull met her blue-eyed, blue-eye shadowed gaze and held his breath.

"Well, darling," she said through a glossy lustre on her lips in that sultry New York voice he knew so well on the phone. "Finally a pleasure to meet after so many years of working together. I never thought my master thief could be so handsome and would carry such a fine piece." She winked at him and glanced at his gold pistol as she extended her right hand.

Stunned at this cougar's beauty and boldness, Kull excitedly laughed saying, "Pleasure's all mine." He placed the gold pistol on his lap and took her dainty hand in his, raising it to his lips giving a soft peck. "Your voice on the phone has always intrigued me as to what the rest of you looked like. I must say you're incredibly attractive yourself."

His broker formed a sly grin and shifted in her seat causing her miniskirt to rise up slightly more on her toned upper thighs. "Well, thank you, Phoenix."

"Thanks for dropping everything and flying down here so quickly to bail me out, Mona."

"Aiding and abetting a fugitive, your success is paramount to my well-being, Sweetie. I caught the first flight I could to Savannah." She turned north onto Merrimac Drive not realizing the Fitzgerald city street had been named after the Confederate ironclad.

"Had a bitch of a time getting this rental in Savannah though, but I figured you'd like a little style in your grand escape."

"You know me well apparently."

"Can I see what you've got in . . . err, I mean, on your pants?"

Kull cracked a grin. Nothing subtle about this woman. He held up the pistol and handed it to her. "Don't worry. It's not loaded."

"Fucking wow!" Mona said, shaking her head in awe. "Adolf fucking

Hitler's golden gun." The car veered.

"Hey, eyes on the road," Kull said. "Don't want to get pulled over."

"Can I see your other piece? The long one."

Unfuckingbelievable, Kull thought with a laughing cough. He pulled the pistol box out of the backpack and replaced the gun inside. The box went back in the backpack and out came Göering's diamond encrusted baton. This time he held it.

"Oh. My. God," gasped Mona, trying to drive and view the priceless piece at the same time.

"Now you know why I couldn't resist."

"I see," she said, clearing her throat. "Let me hold it."

"No. Just focus on the road."

She gave sad puppy dog eyes, but did as he asked. "So, I got everything you asked for. The ammo can and liner, flashlight, and a trench shovel. Back seat." She made a right onto Central Avenue and headed east to the destination Kull had given her during their pre-planning.

Kull looked behind him. The olive green metal ammo can for 5.56mm cartridges would be just the perfect fit for what he had in mind. "Good."

"We're staying at The Bohemian in Savannah. It's a new hotel right on River Street. We have two rooms side-by-side, both under my name, Mona Lisa. A shuttle will take me to my 10 a.m. flight back to New York in the morning. You're on you own with this rental after that. It's all paid for in my alias. Be good."

"How far back to Savannah from here?"

"Took me about two and a half hours."

As they spoke she drove past the street names of Hill, Bragg, Gordon, and Longstreet, all named after Confederate generals.

"So what do I owe you for all these expenses?"

She brushed her hair aside and looked over at him seductively. "A. I will be the only one brokering a deal for these two trophies. You're gonna need me to find some very, very discreet buyers after the firestorm you caused."

"Okay. No problem."

They passed Jackson, Johnson, and Lee Streets, crossed Main Street and entered the Union sector of Fitzgerald.

"B. The Bohemian has a terrace-top restaurant called Rocks. I want a night cap with you after all the stress you put me through. Your treat."

Kull chuckled. This could be fun.

"And C," she said, placing her hand on his thigh. "You'll be spending the night in *my* room. Think you can handle *that*?"

Kull raised his eyebrows and grinned. Mona knew what she wanted. "I can't wait to find out," he said.

She pulled her hand back. "Good. First things first. You said Evergreen Cemetery right?"

"Yep, east side of town."

She drove on, passing Grant, Sherman, and Sheridan Streets.

"How the hell did you ever pick Fitzgerald? This is out in the middle of East Bumfuck."

"I needed a place on our flight path for a quick exit. Was basically a Google Maps search and then once I started browsing Fitzgerald's visitor's website I read up about how this town was formed after the Civil War."

They passed Thomas, Logan, and Meade Streets as he explained further. "A bunch of former Yankees and Rebels came together to live in peace here. And then I learned about Evergreen Cemetery and a certain grave where I'm going to bury these two trophies until we find a buyer."

"What's the name of the grave?"

"That, my dear, is my secret until you broker us a deal we can retire on."

The last roads Mona passed in the Union sector were Hooker Street and Monitor Drive.

"I've got to get rid of these trophies. Can't travel anywhere with them considering the publicity they have. They're radioactive." A right onto Benjamin Hill Drive and soon they approached Evergreen Cemetery.

"Turn left here on Evergreen Road," said Kull, remembering the layout of the cemetery from the tourism brochure that was posted online. With help from Google Earth satellite and street views, he had already planned exactly where he'd go in.

She complied.

"Now just pull over to the right shoulder when you see the farmer's fence after the cemetery fence stops. Then cut your lights. I'll jump out and

I want you to stay right there. Fiddle with your phone. If a cop happens to come up just pretend you're lost and looking on the map. If we get split up for any reason, I'll call you."

They passed the main gate drive in the cemetery on their right as they headed east. She parked the Beemer and turned off her lights as directed. Kull grabbed his backpack with the Nazi items, the ammo box, flashlight, and small shovel, then quickly jumped out. He jogged to the northeast corner of the cemetery's property where he found the juncture of a waist high iron perimeter fence and a farmer's triple barbed wire fence for livestock. He set the items over the fence onto the soft grass, then easily climbed over the iron portion and entered the cemetery.

Turning his flashlight on and off in quick bursts so as not to draw attention, he walked an empty grassy field until he came across his first waymarker, a dirt cemetery path named Lee-Grant Lane. Flat grave slabs and headstones started appearing all around him. He knew he was in the right spot.

Just to his right he spotted another intersecting lane and it's nameplate on a pole: General W. J. Bush Avenue. Now he had the right name. Just a matter of finding the famous grave. Another burst of light and more gravestones. He scanned each name. Finally, he spotted a large upright gravestone of the "BUSH" family plot.

Stepping behind the gravestone he spotted the horizontal graveslab of the man that would hide his treasure. Carved on the slab was:

GEN. W. J. BUSH
CO. B. 14TH GA.
C. S. A.
JULY 10, 1845
NOV. 11, 1952
THE LAST CONFEDERATE OF GEORGIA
"UNCLE JOSH"

Kull immediately began digging at the head of his grave, the most famous resident of the cemetery. His distinct honor in death was that he was the last of the 368,000 Georgia Confederate veterans to die. That's all Kull knew or really cared about because it would be easy to remember and easy to find again. He didn't even know what that strange square and compasses symbol with the "G" at the top of the slab meant. Instead, he peeled off a top layer of grass and started shoveling dirt.

General William Joshua Bush entered the Civil War as a private and served briefly in 1861 before being discharged that same year. He then reenlisted in 1864 and surrendered in 1865 after participating in four major battles, including the Battle of Atlanta. Bush achieved the rank of general only after the war, when he served in a veteran's group for the rest of his life. When he passed in 1952 at the ripe old age of 107, he was "The Last Confederate." The symbol meant he was a Freemason.

While digging, a loud airplane roared overhead. Kull looked up and noticed its distinct shape against a moonlit sky. It was one of those workhorse Air Force transport planes headed south. He paid no attention and continued shoveling.

He then started hearing weird clucking noises as the plane's engine died away. Grabbing his flashlight, he aimed it all around him and was shocked to see a flock of a dozen tiny brightly colored chickens running between the graves. These little birds resembled fighting game with their gleaming black tail feathers and brilliant yellow and orange ruffs. A rooster even crowed at him. And then he remembered Fitzgerald's other claim to fame. He had forgotten he read online that the town was overrun by Burmese chickens introduced in an agricultural project gone bad in the 1960s. Great, now I've got an audience, he thought.

But within minutes, Kull's foot deep rectangular hole was finished. He transferred the two Nazi prizes into the ammo can, carefully wrapping the baton in the liner cloth, then clamped the top shut. With the can sitting deep in the hole, he covered it with dirt and packed the soil down hard before replacing the top layer of grass.

The shovel he tossed into the farmer's field as he made his way back to the car, chickens clucking in tow. He climbed back over the fence and the chickens lined up along the inside wondering where their night visitor had gone. "No, y'all can't cross the road," he said in his best Southern accent.

Hopping back in the car with a shit-eating grin and sweat dripping down his brow, he told Mona to "hit it."

MICHAEL KARPOVAGE

34

THE HIKE BACK UP WORE EVERYONE OUT, ESPECIALLY Jake and Alex, as they took turns carrying one hundred pound Tommy on their backs, plus the extra gear they scavenged from the wrecked vehicles, and of course their weapons, too. Because of the mass destruction of downed trees, it took a good thirty minutes to make it to the top when normally it would have taken less than fifteen.

Becky Holden sat down hard on a felled tree trunk overlooking the cliff and river and could hardly breath. She was drenched in sweat like the others. Tommy walked over to her side and gave her comfort, their roles switched. In the distance to the west, they could see the sky lit up by the uncontrollable fire that was still ravaging the small hamlet of Gober.

Jake made sure his micro camera was powered on to record what he knew would soon be a once-in-a-lifetime discovery. After a brief rest, it wasn't long before they made it to the summit and found the seven white quartz cairns. They were all that remained of the barren landscape. The large old oak tree that once intersected the seven cairns was uprooted and toppled over like a slain king.

Jake showed Tommy the symbols around its trunk while Alex explored the exposed root side and the large crater left exposed.

"Get over here!" Alex shouted.

He had already jumped down into the crater directly underneath the wide, spidery base root system attached to the trunk. There were a set of hand-carved stone steps leading down about ten feet at an angle into the ground, ending in a tangle of branches and leaves. Had the large oak remained upright, the first step would have been just under a thick root at the surface level near the base of the trunk. On top of that first step he found a flat slab of rock that hid it. It was easily discernible from underneath, but if looking down to ground level, no one would ever have noticed it because a foot of clay was packed on top. It was the door in. It would have required substantial digging to get to it, but now the door was wide open.

Alex started clearing the branches at the bottom of the steps, handing them to Jake while the others lit up the crater with their flashlights. Once cleared, a tight-fitting, rock-lined shaft appeared with more stone steps leading down into darkness. The shaft was clearly constructed by man as evidenced by tool marks and the roundness of its circumference.

Excitement and adrenaline filled the air as everyone jumped down into the crater and walked down the steps, forming a queue behind the two Army men. Alex walked point. Jake ordered the others to stay back until he gave the all-clear.

Alex crept down into the shaft holding his newly acquired assault rifle in front of him and examined the walls and the steps with his flashlight. Jake did the same with a pistol in hand, both men cautious about more operators from The Gladii or even some kind of booby trap. But nothing happened and they reached the bottom landing where the tunnel opened up in height and width. Before them was a flat wall with a perfectly square, handleless stone door about six foot by six foot. Inset into the door's surface, about halfway up on its right side, was a rust-pockmarked iron plate. The door reminded them of something that dwarves used in the fantasy movie *The Lord of the Rings.*

Embedded within the iron plate, was a tarnished brass, seven-dial, rotating disc combination lock, and a thin, dark, vertical notch that looked like a keyhole. There were seven disc faces showing with the same numerical runes as on the custom-crafted Bowie knife blade. Directly above the disc faces were seven symbols etched deep within the iron plate—the same symbols they had found on the waybill and the tree trunk.

Jake gave the "all-clear" and the ladies and old man came down. They gathered on the landing and stared in awe at the large door. Jake had already unsheathed the long Bowie knife and had extracted the waybill map protected in plastic.

"Seven numbers, seven symbols," Tommy said. "And I bet the knife acts as the key for the slot."

"Exactly," Alex replied. "But what combination of numbers and symbols left to right? Do we go by what's on the waybill in that very same order or do we go by how they appear on the compass clockwise?"

"Right," agreed Jake. "I'm afraid if the combination is wrong then either we trigger a trap or the door malfunctions and we can't open it."

"That should be easy," Tommy said. "Let me see that waybill."

Tommy stared at the symbols. "John Ross customized this here lock so no one could get in without this drawing and without the knife key. There was only one original made of each and he controlled them both. I say the real challenge was that nobody would have ever found this dadgum tunnel if not for possessing these two items. That's how he really controlled the entrance—what you'd find on the surface of the earth, not below it down here. That's why he separated the two to make the test even harder. See what I'm saying?"

Rae jumped in, onto what Tommy was driving at. "So, getting to this point, at this door and with this type of lock, Ross wouldn't make it difficult or have someone guess at it. It's a matter of simply following what he originally wrote down on the waybill, right?"

Tommy nodded. "It's plain to see now why these two combinations of symbols and Cherokee numbers are so out of order on the waybill. We never knew why because that is the order of the lock. Trust me."

Tommy took charge. Starting left-to-right, he spun the brass discs until the Cherokee numerals lined up in combination with each symbol according to the waybill that Jake was holding up for him. It took him several minutes but everything fell into place.

When the far right dial was finally aligned, everyone heard a loud click from within the door.

"Jake, the knife," Tommy whispered, stepping back. "Stick it in that hole and give it a turn."

Jake gingerly slid the blade vertically into the slot. As he did so, he felt three distinct clicks as the blade's three notches connected with some internal mechanism. After the third click, the blade was buried to the hilt within the keyhole. And now he held his breath while turning the handle clockwise. At first it didn't budge, so he added a bit more pressure and the circular plate started grinding.

"It's rusted," he grunted, turning the handle harder. "I can feel it starting to give." A bit more strength, and he heard subtle snapping sounds as rust started popping off the internal gears. In an instant he had turned the plate 45 degrees. His sweaty palm slipped on the handle and he re-gripped it. A bit more groaning and he had spun the circular plate 90 degrees.

The door shook and a loud clunk from inside rattled the group. They stepped back as tiny fragments of rock shook loose from all around the door's perimeter. Jake moved back closer, took a hold the Bowie knife handle again, and this time pushed hard, even driving his shoulder into the stone face.

The door pivoted inward on the right side, the left being hinged from within. Alex slung his rifle and stepped up to help too, leaning a shoulder in. The door moved faster, nicely balanced by its superb construction. Finally, Becky added her extra weight next to Alex causing the door to open fast.

With rock grinding on rock, the entrance opened 90 degrees perpendicular from where it had started. A rush of cool air passed by their faces as Becky's momentum carried her forward off balance on tired legs. She stumbled into Alex and knocked him into the dark cavity beyond.

Alex tripped on a shard of rock jutting out from the floor just beyond the door and fell further forward until he landed flat on his chest. His flashlight rolled away and his shouldered rifle clocked him in the back of the head. Little did he know, he had triggered a booby trap.

From the ceiling, just inside the entrance, a metallic ping rang out and a large pile of rocks suddenly let loose. They came down all at once in a massive crushing heap. One sharp soccer ball-sized rock caught Alex's ankle and he yelled in pain. The prone Delta Force operative crawled forward as more rocks bounced off the smooth stone floor and around his body.

Jake firmly blocked Becky after he had heard the pinging noise. Just as the pile of rocks let loose, he yanked her back onto the entrance landing. They heard Alex howl.

When the dust settled they immediately aimed their flashlight beams inside. Beyond the three foot high pile of large rocks was a long rock-walled tunnel that appeared to have no end. They saw Alex writhing on the floor just beyond the rocks. Becky moved in first up to the pile now blocking the entrance.

"Mr. Alex, you okay in there?"

"Jeesh! Thanks for making me the guinea pig."

"I'm sorry, I'm sorry. Was an accident," Becky said as she heaved away large stones so she could get access to the downed man. Jake and Rae were right by her side clearing the passage while Tommy held a light on them.

"I'm just kidding," Alex shouted back, having retrieved his flashlight. "My ankle's a little screwed up. But I don't think anything's broken." His voice echoed down the tunnel behind him. He stood up to test his ankle. Seemed all right, the impact from the strike was lessened by his hard boots. He limped over to the pile and started inspecting the hole in the ceiling the rocks had dropped from. It was a three foot by six foot alcove cut into the stone with several, now retracted, support rods that had held up the deadfall boulders. "Boy, Ross went to great lengths to protect this vault."

"Yeah, be careful where you walk in there," Jake said, tossing a large rock aside, sweat dripping from his face. "There may be more traps."

While the others worked to clear a path, Alex used his flashlight and started scanning the tunnel, rifle back out. He first swung his beam down the length of the tunnel, but still couldn't see the end of it. He then inspected top and bottom, just inside the entrance foyer. It opened up to about ten feet wide and only like six feet tall, causing him to crouch somewhat. He especially kept an eye on the floor for more deadfall triggers, but nothing looked out of the ordinary. In fact, he was surprised at how relatively flat and clean it was. The stone walls, too, were carved pretty smooth.

And they glistened.

Stepping closer, as if hypnotized, he ran his hand across its bumpy surface and his eyes grew wide. There were gold veins the width of three fingers running all along its surface. "Holy shit," he whispered. Then he spoke louder. "This place is a gold mine. Literally. There's thick veins of gold running through the walls."

Several rocks tumbled away and the rest of the group spilled into the tunnel foyer, flashlight beams dancing about. When they looked at the shimmering walls they let out oohs and ahhs.

Rae was using a larger, heavy-duty flashlight with a wide, penetrating swivel-beam head that Alex had equipped her with from his vehicle. With a shoulder strap for easy carrying, she aimed the beam all around them, virtually lighting up their end of the tunnel like it was daylight. She then panned ahead and was able to see the very end. It ran almost perfectly horizontal about two hundred feet ending in what looked like a rock wall from her vantage point. "Guys, there's the end of the tunnel," she said. "Down there." Her voice echoed.

Tommy had the waybill in hand and was moving along the left or south wall searching for individual deposit doors. Alex joined him while Jake and Rae took the right side. Becky, eyes big and darting about, stayed in the rear closer to the entrance, spooked by the potential of another booby trap.

"According to the waybill there's a whole bunch of deposit vaults inside these walls," Tommy piped up so all could hear. "Small ones and bigguns. But I don't see nothing."

"There's nothing over here either. Just rock wall," Rae said. "No symbols or carvings or anything."

"I know. It looks solid," Alex said, on his side of the tunnel. "The vaults must be camouflaged somehow."

"Y'all said you're looking for more symbols, isn't that right?" Becky asked from behind them. Her head was pointed down looking at the floor with her little flashlight. "Well, y'all are stepping right over them."

"What?" asked Tommy, looking down, aiming his light on the stone floor near the base of the wall. The others did the same.

"Would you look at that," Jake announced. His and Rae's flashlight beams panned left and right all along the base of their stone wall. Barely noticeable on the rocky floor in equidistant intervals of about three feet apart were distinct characters or symbols. They walked quicker and deeper inside the tunnel, hugging the wall and announcing what they observed.

Alex and Tommy—limping and slowly shuffling along—did the same on their left side with similar results. They found a wide variety of unique marks; anything from single English and Cherokee alphabet characters to full words, from a smiley face to a stick figure, from an icon of a flying bird to a sitting dog, a pitchfork to a wheel.

Jake and Rae were soon in advance and the deeper they probed the more symbols they found. They were three quarters of the way down the tunnel when Alex told them to hold up. Looking back they saw Tommy facing and staring at the wall. Backtracking, they returned and regrouped. Becky was now near Tommy's side making sure he wasn't overexerting himself.

"Here's what I'm thinking y'all," Tommy said, looking down at his feet, a symbol of a mouse at the tip of his scuffed and muddy shoe. He extended his hand and drew an invisible line up from the symbol and onto the wall in front of him. "This mark must line up with a hidden vault somewhere inside this wall. Let's all just give this a test before we get too far in."

Tommy turned his flashlight around and started tapping the handle on the wall keeping aligned with the symbol on the floor. Everyone was quiet as the knocking echoed up and down the tunnel shaft. The sound remained the same solid tone from the floor all the way up about four feet. Then at around Tommy's eye level or about five feet is when it suddenly shifted to a different, deeper tone. But Tommy kept on tapping, not picking up the variation.

"Right there!" whispered Becky. "Go back. Go back."

Tommy tapped some more in his previous spot and still couldn't hear the change, but the others confirmed it. He stepped aside and Jake took his spot to repeat the inspection.

"Alex, the hammer you gave me. Get it out of my backpack." He turned his back on the operative who unzipped his pack and pulled out the tool, handing it to Jake.

It was a mason's hammer used for cutting and setting bricks or stones. One end had a square, flat head to be used like a hammer. The other end was sharp, like a small chisel, and used to create a cutting line around the stone block or brick masonry to be split. Jake felt with his hands first, pushing, prodding, looking for any indication of an indent or outline of a door or hole. Failing to find any kind of clue, he tapped with the square end in the deeper-toned spot and was able to detect an audio edge difference in about a twelve inch square area.

"Hit it harder, boy," Tommy urged. "Don't be shy."

Jake whacked at the rock surface and a poker-chip sized piece of flat rock chipped off. Underneath he noticed a white flaky substance. He hit that too and it crumbled away, but there was even more underneath in a lumpy texture. More swings in the square area and more thin layers of the rock veneer flew off, revealing a bumpy coating of this strange white material.

"I think it's some kind of mortar that the outer layer of rock was bonded to," Alex said, catching a piece of it in his hand.

Jake worked the square area for a minute, getting rid of the thin rock layer until it was all just mortar now.

"That's how they created the camouflage," added Rae. "This must be one of the cache doors. Jake, smack right into the mortar now and see what happens."

"Okay. Stand back." With an over-the-shoulder swing, Jake slammed the hammer dead center of the white mortar; and it blew a considerable chunk off, revealing a perfectly flat slate surface underneath. His thigh burned with pain but he willed it away. "There's another layer of rock behind it," he said, sweat rolling down the sides of his cheeks. He swung again and another large piece of mortar fell off. A tiny flake nicked him under the eye causing him to wince. Blood trickled out of the little cut. He paid no attention to it and tapped the slate. It rattled. It was loosening. Alex patted him on the shoulder.

"It's thinner. Use the chisel end now. Here's another hammer." He handed Jake a bit larger hammer—a two-pound, hand sledge he had already pulled from his own pack.

Jake flipped his mason's hammer around, laid the chisel end against the slate and tapped on the square head with the larger two-pounder. Tapping rang out up and down the tunnel, the walls haven't been worked like this in over 175 years. He chiseled an outline of a smaller square and then once complete he handed the sledge back to Alex and flipped back to the square end of the mason's hammer. With a single blow he punched right through the thin slate protective barrier making a neat six inch square hole.

"Tommy?" asked Jake, stepping aside. "You do the honors. Whaddya see in there?"

The bright-eyed old man placed his flashlight beam in the hole and standing on his tippie toes peered in. The hole went back about three feet and was square cut. Inside it was packed with ceramic jugs, small leather pouches, little wooden boxes, and clear glass bottles.

The bottles were filled with gold dust.

Tommy reached in and grabbed a wine bottle. He gave it to Becky. It was filled to the top with gold powder and corked. "Here you go honey, it's all yours. Have a little piece of this pie."

"Oh Mr. Tommy! Oh my God. I can't believe this." She was so excited she started weeping.

In his hand went, again, this time pulling out a box. It was made of fine cedar with a little gold latch on the front. Printed on top was the name "The Spanish King's Royal Cigar Company" and their cigar factory location of Mexico City. "Here Rae, see what's inside this one." He didn't even wait to find out himself. His arm went in deeper and wrapped around a leather pouch. Old Santa Claus was on a roll.

"Jake, check what's in that," Tommy said, tossing it to Jake who immediately pulled open the leather cord.

Rae gasped when she finally got her cigar box open. It was filled with gold nuggets.

Jake poured some of the contents of his pouch in his hand and his eyes grew large. Filling his palm were uncut diamonds, rubies, emeralds, and various other precious gemstones.

Tommy had already pulled out a small ceramic jug, the top stoppered. To Alex it went who placed it on the stone floor and jimmied the top off. He turned it over and spilled the contents. Out came small nuggets of silver. He shook the jug and the pile grew bigger. "Jee-sus."

"I can see a bunch more containers in there," Tommy said, flashlight still aimed inside the cache hole. He turned around and faced his friends. "Good Lord. If there's a cache like this for every single symbol on the floor of this tunnel I just, I—I don't know what to think."

"I say let's find a symbol of a horse first," said Alex, rising up off his knees. He left the pile of silver and jug where it was then limped down the left side of the tunnel and aimed his flashlight beam at the floor. Tommy was right behind him again, shuffling along.

Jake had already placed the gemstones back in its pouch and tucked it in his pants pocket. He then took the right wall and continued with the inspection.

Rae stuffed the box of gold nuggets in her backpack and helped Becky stow her bottle of gold dust in her own pack.

"Oh, hey ladies?" Alex shouted. "I almost forgot. Can you come here? I brought a bunch of candles with me." He had bent down and was unzipping his backpack. Out came a bag of forty small, tealight candles which he gave to Becky. Digging in his pockets he flipped them a couple of lighters. "Could you place these candles at intervals along the walls so we can have some extra light in here?

"Yeah, sure thing," said Rae. "Come on, Becky."

Continuing down the rest of the tunnel, noticing each new floor symbol as they went, Tommy, Alex, and Jake finally approached the end wall. Tommy had the waybill out again and remarked how there was supposed to be a large cache room presumably behind the wall. He kept his head down, staring at the floor.

"Watch it! Watch it, Tommy!" Jake shouted. "Duck down. Duck!"

Tommy flinched and crouched down not knowing what was coming. By inches his head narrowly missed a long rock finger jutting down from the low ceiling about five feet from the end wall.

"Freeze! Do not move, Tommy," said Alex.

Tommy was hunched over but looked up and saw the rock. His eyes wandered slowly to the ceiling, and he saw several holes with more of that white mortar exposed. Some of it had fallen to the floor in chunks. He could see behind the mortar, through the hole, a large suspended rock pile. He also noticed several iron support bars embedded in the mortar and jutting through the thin rock veneer.

It was another deadfall. This time triggered from above.

"Now slowly back away, Tommy," Alex ordered loudly.

Tommy complied until he was in the clear.

Alex pulled a piece of chalk from his pack. He then drew a rectangular box on the floor that mirrored the size of the deadfall directly above it. Inside the chalk box he wrote the words DO NOT ENTER—LOOK UP and even added some diagonal hazard lines.

"This will be fine for now but we need to create a real barrier later somehow."

"Or just trigger it and let it fall," suggested Jake. "That way it can't kill anyone."

"Yeah, fuck it. Let's do that." Alex unslung the assault rifle, told Tommy and Jake to move back, and then used it like a pole to touch the rock trigger. He pushed on it and instantly backed away, stumbling on his ankle. Nothing happened.

"Here, you do it," he said, handing Jake the weapon. "My ankle sucks."

Jake pushed a little harder with the tip of the barrel, felt the stone trigger give, jumped back and looked up at the same time something snapped loudly inside the ceiling. It then gave way in a massive dump of rock boulders.

The stones collided with the floor and bounced like basket balls in a crash of fragments and dust that echoed down the length of the tunnel. All three men were far enough away that no one was injured. They did however, hear both women's muffled screams at the other end.

Looking back some two hundred feet away they saw Rae and Becky's flashlights aim down toward them.

Jake pulled out his radio and keyed the microphone. He spoke slow and calm. "Rae, come in. We are okay. Over."

A beep and static came back, then Rae's harried voice. "My God you scared us. Was that another deadfall? Over."

"Copy that. Right at the end of the tunnel. We are inspecting the end wall now. Over and out."

Alex and Jake cleared some rocks around one side and made a narrow path through which to move to the end wall.

Jake found the symbol on the floor, directly aligned with the middle of the wall. Alex saw it next. Then Tommy.

It was a depiction of a horse on its hind legs.

Alex wasted no time. He smashed the wall first at a low level with his sledge hammer. The rock veneer easily chipped away. Jake joined in above him with the mason's hammer. As both men pounded away, they soon started seeing white mortar. Their adrenaline rushed and their hearts raced as they increased their mining.

Tommy stood shaking.

A full five minutes of pounding and they had gotten all of the mortar off a narrow rectangular section shaped like a regular door from the floor on up to about five feet. The slate protective plate had now been fully revealed. The men took turns cutting a perimeter guide line with the chisel end of the mason' hammer until they felt ready to bust through.

Becky and Rae had also come running down the tunnel and made it just in time for the final entry. Alex stood back and wound up to give the last blows. Jake double checked his micro camera to make sure it was still running.

The hammer swung.

The slate smashed inward. A black hole formed.

Another hammer blow and the hole widened.

One more swing and a large section of slate fell away. Flashlights pointed inside the opening.

There was a short, narrow hallway ending in a curtain of maroon cloth that hung from the ceiling and blocked what looked like a rear chamber. Holes were eaten away in the fabric. From behind, something bright glowed through the holes.

Tommy pushed forward and pulled the curtain aside. He stood there frozen, legs trembling.

On a pedestal off the floor about three feet high, his prize stood gleaming in a blinding reflection of solid gold, mounted on a thick rectangular base.

The fabled Golden Horse of the Cherokee.

Tommy stepped inside the tight chamber and circled around the beautiful trophy of an eighteen inch tall, Spanish Adalusian warhorse, rearing up on its back legs. The others crowded in, too, and gawked. Becky slid her hands up and down the horse's back.

Tommy's eyes went immediately down to the large rectangular base the trophy sat on. It was about four inches thick and had a handle on the short end. He pulled the handle, and a drawer smoothly slid out. The insides were made of cedar and lined with red velvet. Resting inside was a thick book covered in faded and scuffed brown leather, slightly moldy. The book measured about 12 inches by 18 inches and was definitely centuries old in its appearance. On the cover was a chipped, gold foil seal of a Spanish galleon.

"It's here," he whispered. The others squeezed next to him.

Tommy picked up the heavy book and rested it on the open drawer. He slowly opened the cover and on the right side, almost transparent fly leaf, was a beautiful illustration of the Spanish Habsburg Empire's coat of arms. Its shield was held by a winged angel floating in the clouds with cherubs flying around her.

Underneath were the elaborately ink scrolled words: *Casa de Contratación* and *Mapa de la Cherokees. La ciudad de Xualla y tierras de alrededores. 1540.*

"Spanish for House of Trade," whispered Alex, translating in Tommy's ear. "Map of the Cherokees. The city of Xualla and the surrounding lands. Year 1540."

"Where was Xualla?" Rae asked softly.

Alex cleared the lump in his throat. "Xualla was the mythical Indian village north of Mount Yonah and just south of present day Helen, Georgia."

"I know where Mount Yonah is," Jake said. "We did some Ranger school training there. Rapelled off the cliffs."

"Right," nodded Alex. "Xualla was like the capital of the region at that time. The city was said to have been located in the Nacoochee Valley where the Chattahoochee River runs through. Where present day Duke's Creek intersects it. Was fertile farming land, had a sizeable population, and was smack dab in the heart of gold country. All that's left there now is a small Indian mound thought to have been some type of fort or temple or burial chamber for the rulers."

Tommy spoke up. "Legend has it that the province was ruled by a beautiful Cherokee princess who had vast quantities of gold. It's where Hernando de Soto sent one of his lieutenants to woo her over, fixin' to steal her secrets. She killed the lieutenant and escaped into the mountains. Shortly after, de Soto enslaved her people, started torturing and executing them. She gave in and the mines were his for the taking."

"And what was the *Casa* or the House of Trade?" asked Jake, tapping the page.

Tommy answered him. "I read the documents of the *Casa* when I went to the Spanish Archives in Seville many years back. It was founded in 1503 by Queen Isabella I, just after the Americas were discovered. The *Casa* controlled everything with exploration and colonization throughout the Spanish Empire." Tommy ran his finger down the page, his thoughts drifting.

"Wasn't no Spanish captain could sail anywhere without the *Casa's* approval," he continued. "They kept all their trade routes secret, trained navigators, and employed the best mapmakers in the world."

Alex nodded. "Called *cosmographers* at the time."

"Exactly," said Tommy. "And look here." He pointed to more words on the sheet. "The name of the mapmaker himself. I'll be damned."

Alex squinted closer and read: *"Autor Juan Santos Gutiérrez, cosmógrafo.* He's the author."

"It's a match then," Tommy said gleefully. "Juan Santos Gutiérrez was the brother of the *Casa de Contratación* mapmaker Diego Gutiérrez, who drew the famous 1562 *Map of America*. I read that Juan Santos lived 20 years in Cherokee country drawing land maps for the *Casa*. First under de Soto as his chief cartographer and then under other Spanish explorers after de Soto died in 1542. After the Cherokee revolted in 1560 is when Gutiérrez disappeared. Along with this here legendary book."

Tommy couldn't turn the next page fast enough. It revealed the first of many 18 inch by 24 inch map spreads. The drawing seemed to jump out at them in 3D.

They gasped as a group at such an incredible, highly detailed, topographic map illustration. It literally was a work of ancient fine art.

"Oh my God," whispered Tommy. "It's unbelievable."

"Look at the terrain detail," Rae said, pressing against his shoulder to get a closer look. "There's even grass blades!"

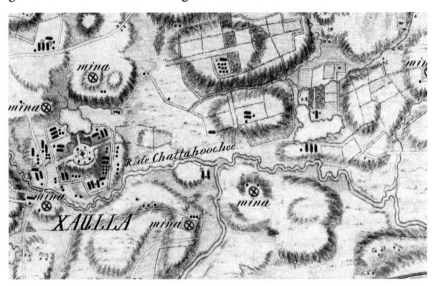

"We are looking at how the landscape was over 475 years ago," added an awestruck Jake. "I've never seen anything with this level of quality this old before. This is a masterpiece of cartography."

Alex nodded. "Look at these terraced farm fields, too, and that circular structure. That's gotta be the Indian mound that's left there at Nacoochee today. Oh man, and look there at the intersection of the Chattahoochee River with the creek. I bet that's modern day Duke's Creek. And the symbol of a circle with an X translates as 'mine'. They're mine locations! There's another. And another. Holy shit."

Tommy frowned, nose to the paper. "I can't see that close, dadgummit! Any y'all happen to have a magnifying glass?" He asked half joking.

"I've got the next best thing," Rae said, pulling out her cell phone. "A magnifier app on my phone." She tapped an icon on her iPhone screen then hovered the phone over an elaborate section of the map about two inches from the surface. She touched a small plus symbol to zoom the camera in even closer, and then told Tommy to look at the screen. It was like looking through a clear magnifying glass.

"Good Lord, would ya just look at that," he said in amazement.

Holding the phone steady, Rae tapped another tiny on-screen button which snapped a photograph of the same view. Now she had a static image and handed the phone to Tommy who could wield it in his hand and see it much better.

"Dadgum amazing!" Tired, he sat down, back against the Golden Horse rock pedestal with the atlas in his lap. He turned the next page.

And the next.

And so on.

Tommy was transported into another world as he immersed himself in pages and pages of maps. His lifelong dream had finally come true. After lighting several candles to provide illumination, the others left him alone inside the chamber to revel in the magic of personal discovery.

The others conversed about what to do next and it was agreed that Alex would post guard outside down the reverse slope and hide among the downed trees in case Black decided to pay them a visit. He slipped out with his weapons and thermal scope, concealed the tunnel entrance from the outside with branches, and left Jake, Rae, and Becky inside to start the long inventory process.

35

Steiner farmhouse

TOM BLACK'S LEGS WOBBLED. HIS FEET HURT. HIS clothes were soaked in sweat and he smelled like rotten fish. The mile and a half walk to the road entrance where his late adversaries had gone in had wiped him out physically. The obese man hadn't walked this much in twenty years. The tornado's devastation scattered debris directly in his path down East Cherokee Drive, and it being at night with only a flashlight to guide him, it took almost a half hour to get to the property entrance.

He had passed a flipped over tractor trailer trash truck and its residential garbage scattered all over. The driver was dead in a ditch. The rest of the main road was covered in downed trees and branches. But he did manage to find the still standing, rusty, old entrance gate where he took a breather.

Amid the forest devastation, he hiked in to the fork where he found Alex Vann's crushed Jeep and his father's beloved Chevy pick-up, also destroyed. By now he was heaving uncontrollably with ever-tightening chest pains and lightheadedness. To make matters worse, his flashlight batteries started giving way, dimming the intensity of the light beam as he searched for the farmhouse.

The time had come to find the bodies of those who'd dared to cross him. He needed to see for himself how the Raven Mocker ravaged them and to experience the profound satisfaction that his father had gone so violently.

Shining his small flashlight upon the front of the nearly collapsed farmhouse, covered in weeds and trees, he couldn't help but think of that evil Indian witch. His father's boogeyman stories really were true, he thought. In fact, the immortal demon might still be out and about seeking more victims. But then he remembered how Catherine had died. How he swore to God she was pushed from behind. *It had to be the Raven Mocker those many years ago.* And most importantly, the thing had spared *him.* Black thought the beast must have sensed his inner soul and knew he was special. That even now, in his sixties, he felt secure enough to approach its lands again without fear of attack. For Tom Black, his ego knew no bounds.

He tried entering through the front door but it was blocked, the ceiling imploded. He tried the exterior basement entrance and that, too, was inaccessible due to a tree sitting on the door. He checked for basement windows but couldn't see any.

Wheezing, he finally found a rear door and entered a dark kitchen filled with junk. A black hole marked the doorway down into the basement. But the old wooden set of stairs was destroyed, both stringers and treads were rotted to the core and lay strewn on the muddy stone floor below. There was however, a new rope leading down. It must have been how his enemy had all gotten down there to seek shelter from the tornado. Instead, they landed in the Raven Mocker's lair, he thought. Or maybe it was Smithson's rope left behind when he discovered their bodies, possibly doing a search of the house after finding their cars?

As he speculated on the rope, he tried to come up with excuses why he shouldn't enter the void below. A nervous tick started on Black's eyelid again. Hands on knees, bent over with a pounding head and shortness of breath, he felt like throwing up.

The bottom line, he was afraid.

Going into a pitch black, abandoned farmhouse basement with an evil witch possibly lurking about was what a stupid, incompetent motherfucker would do. But there was no one to delegate to anymore. He knew he had to do it, knew he must see the bodies with his own eyes, especially his father's.

Testing the rope to make sure it held his weight, he sat on his ass and dangled his feet over the eight-foot drop down. He held his breath and listened. Something was moving down there, around the corner in the next room. His heart raced even faster. Skirting over the edge, with the rope in hand, and his tiny flashlight clenched between his teeth, he lowered himself in. But his weak arm muscles couldn't hold his own weight and he slid down the rope, burning his hands. He landed on a dismantled piece of the stair and twisted his ankle, then cursed out loud.

Standing up, weight shifted to one foot, and leaning against the wall for extra balance, he limped around the corner and aimed his weakened flashlight beam. He heard movement again, something big, then a slow laugh, as if from an old man. A knot formed in Black's stomach and his heart squeezed. With a shaking hand and blurry vision, he pulled his pistol and aimed it in front of him, then entered the room.

Five ghastly bodies hanging from the ceiling stared back at him. Black screamed in sheer, gut-wrenching terror, the dim flashlight beam dancing all over the room, making it seem as if the bodies were moving in the dark.

Eyes darting wildly about, Black caught glimpses of each victim's skeletal remains in the flickering light. He screamed again in horror. He couldn't tell who was who because the bodies were so decomposed and stripped of all skin. Their rib cages were even spread apart, presumably their hearts all having being ripped out.

Tears of fear ran down his cheeks while searing pain filled his chest. Both eyelids fluttered with nervous twitching. He dare not go any farther. His rubbery legs wouldn't allow it. Suddenly, a loud cackling filled the room and a large black bird emerged from a pit in the corner. It bounded toward him, wings spread wide, casting a man-sized shadow on the far wall as his flashlight dimmed next to nothing.

The Raven Mocker!

Black moaned, then shakily fired his small caliber weapon toward the beast. Every shot missed. The defiant bird crept closer, beak opening and closing, cackling words of horror with every step.

Black limped backward, the empty click of a spent weapon echoing loudly. Back into the stairwell corridor he scrambled, and tossed his pistol as he fumbled to find the rope to escape.

His flashlight batteries then died and he was shrouded in pitch black. The billionaire Congressman now yelped like a little girl, one hand on the rope, trying desperately to pull himself up.

His heart felt like it was going to burst. Sweat flooded off of his skin. He tried with all of his strength, stretching the rope, and made it halfway up to grasp the edge of the kitchen floor with one hand. Just then the rope snapped. Little did he know that Alex Vann had sliced it in advance to weaken it.

Still holding onto the lip of the floor, Black discarded the cut rope and was able swing his free hand over to the wall to brace himself. With all of his might, in sheer darkness, he strained his arms to lift his big body up to the kitchen level. The effort proved fruitless. He was out of breath, dizzy, and had lost all energy.

Spent, he let go.

Slamming hard on the basement floor, he collapsed in breathless exhaustion, chest rising and falling uncontrollably.

Unable to move. Unable to speak. Unable to see.

But he was perfectly able to hear. And it horrified him to death. A slow cackling laugh, of what he perceived to be the approaching Raven Mocker, drew closer as the beast shuffled into the passageway to finish him off.

In that last moment before a massive heart attack snatched his miserable life away, Black thought he saw the glowing red eyes of the black bird demon piercing the darkness, searching for its next victim.

When his heart finally stopped beating, Black went black.

▼

Wednesday. 12:33 a.m.
Cherokee Tunnel

An hour later, an exhausted Alex returned. He showed Jake, Rae, and Becky several images he had taken with his phone of what he found at the end of the rope crumpled in the farmhouse basement. He explained how he heard terrifying screams and shots fired. When he inspected the farmhouse he found Tom Black's body and the wounded raven they had left behind.

Their trap had worked.

Too good.

Merely hoping to capture Black, their ruse killed him instead.

They would tell Tommy later, at the right time.

All throughout the early morning hours the team proceeded with the painstaking labor of finding each and every deposit vault's hidden door by mining the walls as before. After finding the map of the Blood Mountain mines in a later section of the book and showing a stunned Alex, Tommy had soon exhausted himself and had fallen asleep with the *Map of Thieves* still open in his lap. Nurse Holden stayed by his side to keep him warm.

During the re-mining of the Cherokee Tunnel, Jake had broken into a large vault with a cloth covered pile. On top of the pile was a billfold and inside was paperwork from the U.S. Department of Treasury dated January, 1838. Destination: the Dahlonega Mint. Inventory: seven gold bars—fifty pounds each. Jake had torn off the cover and marveled at the seven long gold bars, each one stamped with a "U.S." mark. After waking up and showing Tommy, the old man made sure to announce to Alex and Becky that this was Jake and Rae's finder's fee promised to them for risking their lives in helping finish his granddaddy's mission.

Rae had broken into a walk-in, closet-sized room that served as more of a utility or mining manager's chamber. It was stocked with larger mason and mining tools, crates, lanterns, and a table and chairs. On that table was the tunnel's ledger, compiled by Chief John Ross. The book's last entry was in May of 1838, days before the remaining hold-out Cherokees were rounded up into forts and held captive to await their long march west that upcoming winter. That journey would become the infamous Trail of Tears. That last entry made in the book was by Chief Red Fox and listed the deposit of his Golden Horse.

In Ross's ledger, they also found his family symbol; a dovetail pigeon. The group had then located the matching mark on the main tunnel floor and had smashed open his large deposit vault. Tommy immediately rifled through his family nemesis's valuables, promising various treasures to each of the team. Ross had stockpiled untold wealth in bottles, satchels, crates, and chests. Gold and silver ingots, powder, nuggets, copper, gemstones, even old coins. There were several paintings, silver dinner sets, several rare pistols, an elaborate sword, and even flamboyant high society clothing. It was a glimpse back into the wealthiest and longest serving dictator the Cherokee had ever known. And it looked to suit the greedy politician he was.

Tommy muttered over and over again, "Revenge, how sweet it is."

As dawn approached and light filtered from the east across a misty summit marked with shattered trees, Jake and Rae emerged from the tunnel for a breath of fresh air. Up the stone steps and out of the tree crater they climbed. A short walk over to the edge of the cliff and they were overlooking the Etowah River.

Below, it was shrouded in a heavy layer of fog, brightly lit from above as the sun's early morning rays cast the valley in its glow.

Jake put his arm around his woman's shoulders as they stared out on the horizon of the purple colored north Georgia mountains. "Well Rae, we freakin' did it."

"We sure as hell did," Rae said, exhausted. "Everything proved true. The vaults, the Golden Horse, the mining map, even the Dahlonega Mint gold, too. Now *that's* what I'm looking forward to."

"Yep, Tommy said that's our payment," Jake said. "Plus, all the other stuff he was doling out, too, from Ross's chamber. We came up *big!*"

"We sure did, my big Lollypopsicle," she said with a snort.

"Lollypopsicle?" Jake asked, pushing her away with a laugh.

Rae punched him in the shoulder, then hugged him around his waist. "That's for introducing me to Sergeant D'Arata as your *Sweetie Peaches Pie.* Payback's a bitch," she said with a grin, hugging him even tighter.

"That it is." Jake said. He grinned, then said it again, slower, smile gone, thinking of a young Confederate corporal setting out on a mission of revenge in 1864.

"That. It. Is."

EPILOGUE

Two weeks later
Cherokee Rose Manor

TOMMY'S MASONIC FUNERAL WAS ONE OF THE MOST honorable events Jake had ever taken part in. One of Tommy's last requests, before he had succumbed to another bout of pneumonia contracted on the night of the tunnel discovery, was to ask Jake to be one of his pallbearers. Dressed in his Army Blues—and with a white Masonic apron covering his waist—Jake was one of the handpicked men who had flanked Tommy's American flag-draped coffin. Another was Alex Vann, also dressed in Army Blues. The other pallbearers were members of Solomon's Lodge No. 1.

A private Masonic ceremony was held at the lodge location inside the Cotton Exchange building on River Street where the brothers placed Tommy's original Masonic apron and acacia sprig over his body, clothed in his original WWII Army dress uniform. Before the coffin was finally sealed, Jake also placed the Cherokee symbol book under Tommy's hands. The funeral procession shut down the heart of Savannah's Historic District as the coffin was transported by horse and carriage in a slow train south down Bull Street.

Through Savannah's beautiful squares, a parade of funeral participants walked along the city's main corridor. Masons from all across the U.S., veterans of WWII, and guests from all walks of life came to honor the passing of Thomas Black Watie IV. Even locals and tourists watched the spectacle from the sidewalks.

The procession ended at Forsyth Park where participants heard many a eulogy at the large park amphitheatre while Tommy's coffin rested nearby under the tall Confederate Monument. The day long event had finally ended with the pallbearers loading Tommy's coffin on a private plane bound for Atlanta where he would be interred inside the Watie Mausoleum.

Having returned from the airstrip, Jake and Alex were winding down back at Cherokee Rose Manor. Rae and Becky had arrived back at the house earlier with Sergeant Marco D'Arata. The house, and all possessions within, had been bequeathed to Jake after a reading of Tommy's will a few days back. The bulk of Tommy's vast fortune went to Alex, while Becky and Rae also received sizeable chunks enabling them financially independent the rest of their lives. D'Arata even received a bonus.

"Sad day," said Alex, his eyes bloodshot and glassy after taking off his sunglasses. He sat on a chair in the front parlor and rubbed the bridge of his nose while sniffling.

Jake sat across from him, Tommy's chess set between them on a table. He rubbed his thigh, the bullet graze healing nicely, but still itching. "Tommy was loved by many people all across this nation. I wish I had known him longer." Jake then twisted the large new ring on his finger. Tommy's Masonic ring was given to him by the old man himself before passing.

D'Arata entered the room bearing bottles of cold beer. He handed them to his Army colleagues. Rae and Becky shared the sofa behind Jake, wine glasses in hand, discussing how Becky would be moving into the manor, as the live-in caretaker until Jake and Rae figured things out. With Becky's share of Tommy's inheritance, she was also thinking on starting her own private nursing company.

In a parlor chair just behind Alex, sat another woman. She was short-haired, slim, and beautiful. Professor Marissa Morgan's left eye was slightly yellowed still and she had just gotten the stitches in her brow taken out.

After a surprise visit from Alex Vann two days after the tornado had struck her hometown of Waleska, Morgan was still in a state of total despair from the loss of her close university friend who had been killed during the storm. Alex's ghost-like appearance from the dead sent her over the edge in remorseful shock. She had an emotional break down in an admittance of guilt and desperately begged him for forgiveness and redemption. Alex wholeheartedly accepted her back and they were reunited as a couple once again. He also told her he put in a request to leave the Army. Alex also dropped the bombshell that the Cherokee Tunnel and the lost mining map had been discovered by their team and that he wanted her to be a part of its guardianship. The very next day at Reinhardt University, Morgan announced an immediate sabbatical leave. By nightfall the couple had hiked up into the Blood Mountain wilderness and had found the first of the rare earth mine locations marked on several pages in the map book.

Morgan stood up from her chair and placed a gentle hand on Alex's shoulder. "How's this for timing?" She asked softly, handing him an iPad with an app opened to the *Atlanta Journal Constitution* digital newspaper. "Look. They just found the rat's body."

Alex scanned the all-caps, breaking news headline, then read it out loud: "MISSING CONGRESSMAN LATEST TORNADO VICTIM."

Morgan ushered D'Arata out of the room. "What do you say we smell the roses out back?" D'Arata nodded and led the way down the hallway. He and Morgan both knew it would be best if they didn't hear anything from the conversation that was about to take place.

"Where was the body found?" whispered Becky.

"In the river," Alex said, reading the report. "Near Canton." He looked around and heard the rear door shut, then leaned forward in his chair in a lower tone of voice. "It's about ten miles downstream from where we dumped him and his bodyguards in."

After thinking back on how their group cleared the bodies from the land the morning after the tornado, Jake spoke up. "I've never been so worn out in all my life dragging all that dead weight down to the river."

"Tell me about it," said Alex. "It was dirty business."

"We had to do it," Rae said, reassuring them of their decision. "If the FBI found the bodies on the land, the tunnel would have been discovered. We had to cover our asses or we'd be implicated in their deaths somehow."

Jake nodded. "When the three Gladii were found in the river last week it was only a matter of time before Black surfaced, too."

"The article says Black and his ill-fated party are presumed to be drowning victims after being caught in the deadly tornado," Alex read.

"Phew. Hopefully, no one will ever know he had a heart attack in that basement." Becky said, keeping her voice down.

"And what about the Ranger—Wolf Four?" Jake asked quietly.

"My contacts in The Gladii gave me his identity," whispered Alex, still scanning the rest of the story. "He was compensated in gold for his assistance that night. Hush money. He knows what will happen if he speaks."

Jake nodded. "Good."

Alex looked over to Rae. "My lawyer said it will probably be a few more days until the Steiner property transaction is complete and put in my name, per Tommy's last wishes. Then you can go in and do your thing, okay Rae? Just a few more days and you can run with it."

"I'm good with that," Rae said, sipping her wine, itching to get started on the investigation of the victims in Jacob Steiner's basement. She had already started digging in north Georgia libraries for missing persons based on the names she had found, but didn't want to tip off any authorities until after the property was legally secure."

"I'm just glad all his land there was foreclosed on by the county years ago and no one ever purchased it," Alex replied. "Makes it easier for us to keep that tunnel secret once it's in my name."

"It still blows my mind Steiner's body was found exactly seven days later in that nursing home in Ball Ground," Jake said, shaking his head.

"What blows me away is there's no official government records of him ever existing," a dismayed Becky added. "No one even knows how old he really is. That is messed up—all that black magic and shit. I ain't never gonna look at a raven the same way again, that's for sure."

"Becky?" Jake asked nicely, "would you mind giving us three a little more private time? I need to go over a few more things." He winked.

"Sure thing, Sugar," Becky smiled, gathering herself up. "I think I'll go smell them roses, too."

With Nurse Holden gone, Jake quietly asked Alex if he had heard anything about the two dead gang members in Oakland Cemetery. Alex told him he had, that there was a tiny story buried on an Atlanta news website for just an afternoon saying it was an alleged drug deal gone bad.

"They were invisible in death as they were in life," Alex stated. "No one will miss them. But that Hispanic kid the cops found beaten and stabbed to death in the alleged West Point thief's car?" he said, raising his eyebrows. "Now that's making national news."

Jake shook his head. "D'Arata still maintains they gunned down the wrong man—that Angel Hernandez punk—but the FBI won't listen to him. They won't even compare the fingerprints they found at the museum. They said the pictures on the cell phone of Angel flaunting the McPherson hat and the Nazi artifacts was all they needed as proof he was the West Point thief. The even found the old man mask in his house. It's what the public believes, too, now that the media sold them the same bill of goods."

"The FBI always gets their man," said Rae, sarcastically. "They had their big SWAT raid, their speeches at the podium, and now they're the heroes. They won't change the narrative."

Jake shook his head. "They'll write Hitler's gun and Göering's baton off as a loss, happy they didn't have to implicate a corrupt U.S. congressman as the mastermind. The only lead we have is that Jaconious Johnson set up the theft, according to what Black told us in the limo."

"I paid Johnson a visit at his condo," stated Alex.

"You did?" asked a surprised Rae.

"Just a welfare check," he smiled. "I needed to return Black's Camaro, too. I warned him that if he ever decides to threaten you two again that my next visit would be me staging his suicide."

"Nice," said Jake. "Thanks for getting our back."

"When I accused him of hiring the thief," Alex replied, "he said it was all Black's doing, that he had no part in the crime. Blamed the dead guy."

"How convenient." Rae stood up and sauntered over next to her man, Jake. She placed an arm around his shoulders, thinking the remaining stolen WWII trophies were something she knew he would continue to pursue.

Jake wrapped an arm around her hips and spoke. "When D'Arata forced down that Cessna airplane with his main suspect missing—that Phoenix—that was all the reason the prick Colonel Perkins needed to close their end of the case, too. D'Arata was so disgusted he almost put in a request to go civilian like you did, Alex. But I talked him out of it."

"What about you, Jake?" Alex asked. "You've been cleared from the Army investigation board. Are you going back to MHI in Pennsylvania or going to move into this nice old manor in beautiful Savannah? I really need you two in my new mining company. Silent partners sound good? We've got an entire map book to decipher and lands to explore. You saw those nine rare earth mines marked at Blood Mountain on the map. Marissa and I found three of them so far. Come on. I know you guys want in."

Rae held her breath, not knowing of Jake's future career plans either.

Jake looked up at his love. "I've decided I want out of the Army. I've been in over twenty years and they've clipped my wings. These new black marks on my record will stop any future promotion. Yesterday, I sent my retirement request up the chain of command. They have to approve it still, but I think they'll be happy given all the unwanted publicity I tend to generate. I was going to wait until I got a final answer before I told you, but Alex here, just blew my cover."

"Since you wore a Masonic apron over your Army Blues today," added Alex, "they'll definitely grant your request. Any display of individual expression will surely make the politically correct commissars' heads explode. It's good to hear your decision. Congratulations, my friend."

Rae bent down and kissed Jake, long and full.

Catching his breath Jake said to Rae, "But I'm going to get those Nazi relics back somehow. And we've also got enough fodder for two new episodes on *Battlefield Investigators*. I think we've got our hands full. Plus, I say it's time to spend some of our finder's fee, courtesy of the U.S. Treasury. What do you think, Babe?"

"Cheers to that," Rae said happily, raising her glass.

"And cheers to you, Tommy Watie," Jake added, standing up. He tilted his bottle above him. Alex stood up, too, joining them.

Jake fought back tears. "May you rest in peace in that house not made with hands, old Brother."

THE END

FACT OR FICTION?

A breakdown of fact, fiction, and sources in order of the storyline.

Prologue: With the exception of Corporal Tommy Watie Jr., every character named in the opening was a real person. The re-enactment of the scene was also as accurate as my source material described from both sides of the incident. No one knows for sure which Confederate skirmisher actually shot Union General McPherson in the back, but there are two men who were given credit, Corporal Robert F. Coleman of the 5th Tennessee Infantry Regiment and Private Robert D. Compton of the 24th Texas Cavalry, according to letters written in the *Confederate Veteran* magazine, Volume 11, 1903 issue, pages 118-119. Captain Richard Beard of the 5th Tennessee claims Coleman was standing next to him and fired the shot when McPherson waved goodbye with his hat and fled on horseback. McPherson was knocked out cold upon hitting the ground face first and initially thought to be dead.

Beard also witnessed fellow regimental Captain William A. Brown pick up McPherson's hat, strip off the gilded hat cord, and claim it as a trophy since his own hat was so worn out. Others rifled the body of more possessions. Union Colonel R. K. Scott and orderly A. J. Thompson were taken prisoner. Captains Beard and Brown were soon captured along with most of the rebel skirmishers. All of McPherson's possessions were recovered with the exception of his hat. The hat remained with Brown all throughout his prison time in Ohio and upon heading home to Mississippi after the war. The hat never reappeared again.

The wounded Union Private George Reynolds of the 15th Iowa Infantry did happen upon the lone dying general and stayed with him until he passed. During that time, he stripped off the gold coat buttons and shoulder tabs to hide the fact McPherson was a fallen general. Reynolds also fought with a Union straggler who stole money out of McPherson's wallet. Union Lieutenant William H. Sherfy of McPherson's staff, who I did not include in the scene, also had his horse shot out from under him, too, but was not immediately near McPherson, nor taken prisoner. He was knocked senseless after falling from his horse and hitting a tree. His watch was crushed and stopped at 2:02 p.m., the time McPherson was shot. The general would die some twenty minutes later. Sherfy heard from Private Reynold's that McPherson's last words were a call for "water" and "My hat! Where's my hat?" Reynolds and Sherfy's testimonies were recorded in *Military Essays and Recollections* published in 1891 for the State of Illinois.

Tommy Watie IV: Tommy (WWII vet) is a fictional descendant of the real Thomas Black Watie, who was murdered by followers of John Ross in 1845. There is no Watie family in Savannah. Cherokee Rose Manor does not exist at that address.

Becky Holden is based on a real person who won a character name raffle for the Seneca Falls Historical Society in Seneca Falls, New York, where I lived for two years: the area where my first mystery book, *Crown of Serpents,* is set. We raised over $1,500 to have the winner's name in the book. The only connection between the real person and the fictional character was her nursing background and Girl Scouts. Savannah being the birthplace of the Girl Scouts, I had to have Nurse Holden eating some Thin Mints.

The Depot: The Seneca Army Depot and Jake Tununda's igloo bunker do exist. The Depot is located in the Finger Lakes Region of New York State. There are 519 igloos on the abandoned base along with the world's largest herd of white deer. This scene is a carryover from the first novel where Jake and Rae Hart are first introduced. Find out how he and Rae acquire their WWII-era Indian Scout motorcycles and become an "item" by reading *Crown of Serpents.* For more information on the Depot and to see a recent

3D commissioned map illustration I did for the preservation organization, please visit: www.senecawhitedeer.org

Ruloff's: Ruloff's Restaurant and Bar does exist in Ithaca, NY and they do have great burgers. Edward Ruloff really did murder his wife and daughter in 1845, hiding their bodies in a chest, and sinking them in Cayuga Lake to cover up his crime. His brain resides at Cornell University. This detail was a little shout out to my friends and former colleagues in Ithaca when I lived there for five years.

West Point theft: Background information on the multi-billion dollar industry of art crime was derived mostly from two books I read on the subject. The first is *Priceless* by retired FBI agent Robert K. Wittman, the founder of the FBI's Art Crime Team. *Priceless* takes you undercover into the black market of art thieves, scammers, con artists, and murderous thugs and what it takes to catch them. The other is *The Island of Lost Maps: A True Story of Cartographic Crime* by Miles Harvey. Harvey profiles the most prolific American map thief in history; Gilbert Joseph Bland, Jr., an antique dealer who stole countless valuable rare and antique maps all across the U.S. and Canada. The idea of a centuries-old Spanish/Cherokee mining map was borne from this book, hence the coveted *Map of Thieves*.

The master thief's silicone mask of an old man used at West Point does exist. I stole the idea from a real robbery that took place in December 2010 in Hamilton County, Ohio where Conrad Zdzierak, a white man, wore a black man mask. A black man fitting the description was mistakenly arrested. The mask looked so real the wrongly arrested suspect's own mother even thought it was him on surveillance tapes.

Those World War II replica smoke grenades do exist, too. I bought some on the border of Florida and Georgia and tried them out. They create a thick smoke screen for just a minute or two. I suppose if you did add some type of chemical they may last longer, but I didn't experiment *that* far.

There are Civil War general's uniforms at the West Point Museum, along with a display containing Nazi artifacts including Hitler's gold pistol and Göering's baton. However, in case any of y'all have sticky fingers, the displays are sealed with armored glass from what I've read. My only visit there was in 2004, well before I even conceptualized the thief character and how he would "case the joint" and pull off a daytime theft.

To read the incredible story of how Hitler's pistol came to end up at the West Point Museum, Google: "Hitler's Lost Treasure. Where Is It Now?" by Ron Laytner. Published in *Edit International* magazine.

Nathan Kull: My master thief character Nathan Kull came from a March 2010 *Wired* magazine article titled "Art of the Steal: On the Trail of World's Most Ingenious Thief" by Joshuah Bearman. It featured a young Canadian criminal named Gerald Blanchard. Google his name and check out the *Wired* article. You'll be blown away as much as I was.

I also pulled information to build his character from criminals profiled in *Priceless* and *The Island of Lost Maps.* And, of course, from my own experiences during my teen years when I was hardly an angel.

The Mason's grave and the town of Fitzgerald, GA where Kull hides his Nazi treasures in the end definitely does exist. And you'll be seeing this thief in an upcoming novel again for sure.

The villain and his district: Congressman Tom Black is a compilation of the worst of the worst from many local, state, and federal politicians all across this nation, courtesy of the Democrat and Republican parties. I wanted to create a villain that we can all agree to despise—a real political pig eating at the trough of power and self-gratification. His use of *stupid, incompetent motherfucker* comes from allegations of how Rep. Sheila Jackson Lee (D) of Texas treated one of her own staffers.

Black's new 15th district in Atlanta does not exist, but The Bluff most certainly does. I've taken a few rides through The Bluff and in places it is like a war zone. This truly is *Forgotten Atlanta*, as coined by Atlanta-based photographer/designer Dylan "ProphBundy" Scura in his photo series documenting the drug and crime-infested neighborhoods of the downtown. Look up his incredible imagery on Flickr or Facebook.

I planned on having a major scene inside The Bluff but it just didn't fit and I didn't want to force it. Instead, I had Sergeant D'Arata drive through making observations during his tail. To get a sense of the two gang members from the Bluff Boyz crew that appear later in the Historic Oakland Cemetery scene you'll want to watch the movie *Snow on tha Bluff*. It is a 2012 reality/drama film directed by Damon Russell depicting the lowest scum of our society: the wolves that prey on the hapless sheep.

Savannah: The guts of the storyline take place in Savannah then move up to Atlanta and the mountains. I wanted a reverse of Sherman's March-to-the-Sea. Plus, I simply love Savannah's Historic District. There's so much history and beauty. In fact, I had illustrated and published the *Savannah Historic District Illustrated Map*, which is an Amazon bestseller. This map also lands in the hands of Tununda, and yes, it was a shameless plug. Savannah was also a perfect place to tie in the Masonic connections between Tommy and Jake and a kick-off to the deadly action.

The ancestor room idea came from Dan Carlin's *Hardcore History* podcast in one of the Roman empire episodes. Carlin explained how family members revered their ancestors' military accomplishments by collecting memorabilia, and housing them in a certain room. It was considered a place of worship.

John Ross vs. Stand Watie: Both were legendary individuals of the Cherokee Nation, and both were involved in a lifelong murderous struggle for power that makes the Hatfields and McCoys look like child's play. Around forty murders are attributed to the internal Cherokee civil war that resulted from the state of Georgia and the U.S. government forcibly removing these Native Americans from their homeland, all because of the "discovery" of gold by the white man in 1828.

John Ross did serve for thirty-eight straight years as the Principal Chief of the nation even though it was split by factional fighting. His very close followers and family members did conspire and carry out the assassinations of Major Ridge, his son John Ridge, and Elias Boudinot (Stand Watie's brother) on June 22, 1839. Stand Watie was forewarned and escaped assassination. Five others were targeted for death but survived the night. Stand's younger brother, Thomas Black Watie, was attacked and survived, his hand nearly cut off by a hatchet. He was later executed in 1845 after being kidnapped, beaten, and stabbed by Ross's henchmen.

Family members of those slain vowed revenge against Ross, first for feigning knowledge of the murders, and secondly for knowing who carried out the murders and not bringing them to justice.

Ross and Watie did bury the hatchet in 1861, uniting under the Confederate flag at the outbreak of the Civil War. One year later, Ross became a traitor, as many predicted he would, stealing the nation's treasury as he fled to Washington and joined forces with the Federal government— the same government that caused the death of well over 4,000 Cherokee because of his own actions in the late 1830s. John Ross did die of a sickness in Washington in 1865 after trying to once again dominate Cherokee politics during a visit out West to the Cherokee Nation after the Civil War ended. He was a Freemason.

Brigadier General Stand Watie was the last Confederate officer to surrender to Union forces in 1865. He died in 1871. During the Civil War, Stand Watie was one of only two Native Americans to rise to a brigadier general's rank. The other was Ely S. Parker, a Seneca Indian who fought for the Union. Both generals were Freemasons.

Sureños-13 gang: They exist and they are most brutal. Their presence is felt from Duluth on south to Lindbergh inside the city of Atlanta, but mostly concentrated along the Buford Highway (Route 23) corridor. I received some real good information on them from one of my police officer/hockey buddies. And yes, they do recruit kids as young as 13 and 14 years-old and turn them into killers. I needed an obstacle for Nathan Kull to overcome and the carjacking and subsequent loss of his prized items provided an excellent parallel subplot by incorporating the gang.

The voice of the Waties: The 1949 cassette tape recording of the three Watie men was a trick used to bring voices from the past into the present day storyline. I especially wanted Corporal Watie's Civil War experience told and instead of boring the reader through another rehash of the past with Tommy, I thought why not hear it from Granddaddy himself. I came up with this idea from several real recordings of the "rebel yell" from aging Confederate veterans during the 1930s and 40s. The three Watie men heard in the tape also portrayed the tight family bond as well as the emotional side of war.

Masonic connections. There was indeed a well documented humanitarian ceasefire at the Dead Angle during the Battle of Kennesaw Mountain (northwest of Atlanta) on June 28, 1864. Confederate Lt. Colonel Martin did receive a brace (pair) of ivory-handled Navy Colt pistols from a Union officer. However, the Masonic connection to the ceasefire, to the best of my knowledge, is still an oral history passed down that remains speculative and one I'll keep digging into for concrete evidence. I included this in the story because of my own Masonic connections and how powerful our fraternal obligations can be, especially in times of war.

Le Maison Rouge: What more could a "hobbyist" politician want in throwing a birthday party for himself? This very popular events room does exist and it is everything as described, and more. From the first time I entered this red room, back in 2009, I knew it would be a great book scene.

Historic Oakland Cemetery: I just knew I had to get this cemetery in the book somehow. Not only is it filled with beautiful gardens and stately trees, but the mausoleums simply are unbelievable specimens of architecture, too. So much history resides here in her residents. In particular, the rows and rows of Civil War dead. The most touching monument for me is the Lion of Atlanta, guarding the unknown Confederate dead—several thousand nameless souls lost to war. There is no Watie Mausoleum, but it would fit right where I described its location.

Oakland Cemetery also introduced Alex James Vann in a most vicious way. This Delta Force operative and Cherokee "Witch Killer" is a crucial character to the rest of the story, giving Jake and Rae that extra added punch and historical insight into the legend behind the hidden *Map of Thieves*. Plus, my own son, Alex, wanted to be named after a good guy in this book. In *Crown of Serpents,* he was the bad guy Alex Nero.

The character Alex James Vann is a fictional descendant of James Vann whose treasure chest of $40,000 in gold powder is really said to be buried at the site of one of his farmhouses on the Federal Road in Hightower, GA. I've looked for it myself on several occasions, given the clues passed down in Cherokee treasure hunter Forest C. Wade's book *Cry of the Eagle*.

The Secret Cherokee Tunnel: According to *Cry of the Eagle*, this tunnel does exist. On pages 49-51 of his book, Wade explains how Chief Rising Fawn proposed the tunnel in 1835 to other heads of prominent Cherokee families after the signing of the Treaty of New Echota by the Watie/Ridge faction. Rising Fawn knew their nation's fate was sealed and all Cherokee would be removed out West by 1838. Over the next couple of years, the tunnel was dug as described, its location hidden somewhere along the bluffs of Settendown Creek, Hurricane Creek, or the Etowah River in the area between Canton and Hightower.

Wade made mention of the ambushed Dahlonega Mint gold shipment being the very first deposit in the tunnel. He also described how many wayfinding symbols were carved on rocks and trees, many of which he found and recorded in his book. There was also a treasure map drawing, too, which I borrowed some of the symbolism from.

John Ross was not mentioned as being the one responsible for the tunnel, nor was his own treasure deposited within. That was my addition.

The Bowie knife and waybill were also my creations—the waybill coming from real life waybills that the Cherokee did carry with them on the Trail of Tears to hopefully go back one day and claim their life savings.

The Raven Mocker: When I first heard and read about this evil witch I was pretty well mortified. What a way to die—having your heart ripped out and eaten. Adding that paranormal element into the Native American legend was a key ingredient for the story. But I honestly didn't plan on Tom Black having a heart attack and being killed by his perception of one of these Raven Mockers. In the end, I was going to have Jake take out Black up on the cliff overlooking the river where Catherine was killed, but I wrote myself into a corner with the tornado. And just by coincidence I had five basement victims of the Raven Mocker.

Things clicked and I thought, what an ironic and appropriate way for Tom Black to go; feeling triumphant that his adversaries were all killed and the treasure would soon be his. But then to have a heart attack as a result of the terror he experienced in that dark basement, and seeing what he thought was a Raven Mocker coming for him, was perfect in my opinion. It was exactly the fate that he intended for his father.

The lifelong father and son conflict between Tommy and his son Tom Black was adapted from a real life crime that took place in Fresno, California in 1992. Dan Ewell, the young, greedy, arrogant, lying son of a prominent wealthy businessman conspired with Joel Radovcich to kill Ewell's mother, sister, and father in a brutal slaying after his father Dale caught him in another damaging lie. His father cut him off from the family fortune and told him to make it on his own at age 21. Furious as to not being entitled to any family money, not being enabled any more, and forced to find a job on his own, he hatched a plan to access the fortune by virtue of killing those that had given him everything.

The Map of Thieves: As a professional map illustrator myself, I wanted to blend my own interest in military history with some kind of priceless historical artifact—the age-old standby being a treasure map. But I truly had to make it one-of-a-kind game changer with major ramifications if found. Gold was the answer, as it always is.

Gold was the Cherokee's manna from heaven as well as the reason for their ultimate demise. It was epitomized in this story by Cherokee James Vann, the second richest man in the U.S. in the early 1800s, before he was murdered. The Cherokee discovered gold well before Hernando de Soto and his Spanish expedition came to steal it for the crown in 1540. When the Spanish started mining it right here in north Georgia I figured a Spanish *cosmographer* or mapmaker surely must have recorded each and every mine location for the *Casa*.

From what I've heard, they also found many rare earth elements, too.

Around Blood Mountain.

Or so the legend goes.

ACKNOWLEDGEMENTS

With many thanks, first and foremost, to the scores of readers of my debut mystery thriller *Crown of Serpents* (2009). Y'all demanded a sequel and you got one. Your positive reviews, feedback, and persistence propelled me to write this second book in the Tununda Mysteries. Sorry it took so long.

Being a lover of military history and intrigued with Native American lore—especially those stories of lost or hidden treasure—I had a sense of direction on where the new story would go. But with a move to Atlanta, Georgia those choices narrowed down to the Civil War, and of course the rich Cherokee heritage in the north Georgia mountain region.

It was during my very first Masonic lodge presentation and book signing for *Crown of Serpents,* that the brothers of E.W. Hightower Lodge No. 679 of Nelson, GA turned me on to the secrets of the Cherokee that once lived in the area. Thank you to Brothers Bryan Lindner, Ralph Owen Dennis and especially to John Bohanan. John shared with me a personal experience along the Etowah River while metal detecting and hunting for Cherokee symbols. He also turned me on to the "Bible" of Cherokee treasure hunting called *Cry of the Eagle* (1969) written by the late Forest C. Wade, a native of the area. This book was the basis of the secret Cherokee Tunnel legend, learning of James Vann, and much of my early insight into "blood laws" and the political machinations of the opposing factions of Ross and Watie.

I was then encouraged to contact fellow Mason Charlie Lott, Commander of the Sons of Confederate Veterans—Georgia Division. Over a nice lunch and tour of his chapter's Civil War artifact collection in Villa Rica, he told me of the alleged Masonic humanitarian battlefield act that happened near the Dead Angle at the Battle of Kennesaw Mountain. I researched that story extensively through many sources—including Nicholas Eisele, the great-great-great grandson of Lt. Colonel William H. Martin. Although the Masonic connection is speculative through oral histories, I could never find to this day a "smoking gun" written record that proves it. I know it's out there, I just haven't dug deep enough. So I give thanks to Charlie and Nicholas for giving me an obsession to find the true source of that truce.

For their research assistance on Civil War and Masonic topics I'd like to thank: brother Jan Giddens of Kennesaw Lodge No. 33; Buck Dentmeyer, owner of Wildman's Civil War Surplus; Willie E. Johnson, Kennesaw Battlefield Park Historian; Clay Melvin of the Kennesaw Mountain Historical Association; Michael D. Hitt and Phillip Whiteman, Civil War historians; Amy Reed, curator at the Marietta Museum of History; Charles M. Brown, great grandson to Joseph M. Brown, former governor and senator of Georgia; and the Atlanta History Center.

Many thanks also to: Jeff T. Giambrone, historian and fellow Mason with Bolton Lodge No. 326 of Bolton, Mississippi; author Randy Golden; brother Danny Wofford of the Atlanta Masonic Temple library and archives; brothers Dwayne Morrison and Michael S. Downs of the Georgia Lodge of Research; Elaine S. DeNiro, CA, archivist for the Roswell Research Library and Archives; brothers Joseph P. Sutters and Lowell Hollums; the Arkansas Lodge of Research; brother Robert Herd's personal family treasure story; Mark K. Christ, Frank Johnson, and Civil War living historian John Chrobak; Ken Griffiths, Civil War author; and brother Savannah Dan.

For McPherson research, special thanks to: Jill McCullough, Clyde, Ohio Public Library and Brenda Stultz, curator of Clyde Historical Museum.

Additional thanks go to the following people for their help in crime-related, law enforcement, and military topics: Leslie Jensen, West Point Museum Curator of Arms and Armory; to brother Dwayne Gore, Jeff Lors, Eric C. Lindstrom, Eric Jed Abordo, officer Tim Shand, and fellow novelist Lee Gimenez.

For their Cherokee related contributions, thanks go to: Dan Morotini for turning me onto the Raven Mocker; Mike Anzinger and Jimmy Pendley of Conn's Creek area petroglyph legends; Billie Nix, author of *Jesus Wept*; Donna Byas, Paul Ridenour, and Dorothy McNeir Horner (Watie and Ridge family descendants).

For Atlanta related scenes thank you: to Dylan "ProphBundy" Scura for his *Forgotten Atlanta* (The Bluff) photoseries; to the volunteers at Oakland Cemetery; and to Dennis Baker of Le Maison Rouge.

Special thanks to Francis Barbieri and the Seneca Falls Historical

Society character name raffle winner, Becky Holden. We raised over $1,500 in fundraising money for the society. I surely had to give Becky some gold in the end.

I'd like to extend much appreciation to my critique circle for your valued opinions and proofing on the first reading. Thanks go to: Jean Galecki, Gene Conrad, Paula Howard, fellow Masonic brothers Tim Yarbrough and Jim Bard, and fellow novelist Alex Walker. A very special thanks to my meticulous editor Michael A. Halleran, a fellow brother Mason and author of *The Better Angels of Our Nature: Freemasonry in the American Civil War.* He gave me early encouragement on writing my first scholarly article on the research conducted from my first novel *Crown of Serpents.* That article is entitled "Betrayed by a Mason?" and available free on my website. For a new article I wrote on the lure of treasure hunting, visit **MapofThieves.com.**

Lastly, and most importantly, I give thanks to my lovely wife Laura and my boys Jake and Alex for all their support, patience, and awesome ideas.

T H E
T U N U N D A
M Y S T E R I E S

Book One (2009)
CrownofSerpents.com
 /crownofserpents

Book Two (2014)
MapofThieves.com
 /mapofthieves

If you love these two books in The Tununda Mysteries and wish to see a third, I can't urge you enough to share them with as many people as possible. Your passion for reading is my passion for writing. Word of mouth has the best credibility. Write a review for your local paper, magazine, or website. Talk about them in emails, on Facebook, and in book clubs. Give a book as a gift to friends, or a stranger. Any way you choose, just spread the word.

CPSIA information can be obtained at www.ICGtesting.com
Printed in the USA
LVOW10s0303060214

372439LV00005B/623/P

9 780985 653217